Ocean House

«Darou Al Bahr»

A novel

Part three of the Crooked Wings Trilogy

BY

RUDRA ALASTAIR SHARP

BlueInk
SCRIBBLE

They who have faith
and work in righteousness,
they are companions of the garden.
They will abide there forever.

Walla deena aamanoo wa ʿaminu
saalihaati walla aa'iku
Ashaabul Jannati
hum feeha khaalidoon

Verse 82
Surah 2
The Heifer
The Holy Koran

Contents

Foreword

Thank you for picking up «Ocean House, *Darou al Bahr*», the third instalment of the «Crooked Wings» trilogy. May the journey that unfolds herein take you joyfully with it.

Most likely you have come to it having read «Crooked Wings» and then «Spreading Wings», so you know who is who and who has done what, so far. Nonetheless, it may also be that you have come across this book unaware of its predecessors. With that in mind, the opening pages will hopefully bring you up to date, while perhaps jogging the memories of those for whom it has been a while since you encountered this universe.

Whether this is your first dive into the world of Pia and those who were drawn to her, or whether you have been with us from the inception, welcome.

At the conclusion of «Spreading Wings» I felt that the narrative had found its natural *denouement*. However, others were not convinced. I have bowed to the gentle pressure that has come from two sources. On the one hand there were the readers of the two «Wings» who have wanted to know what happens next, especially to Shaafia. On the other hand, the family who reside in the real «*Darou al Bahr*» in Casablanca, and it is a real house, the Laghrani family, have begged me to write a story about their house. I told them I could only do it in fictional form. «*Darou al Bahr*» in fact is much as I describe, somewhat boat-shaped on a large boat-shaped block on the Boulevard de Londres in Casablanca. It was designed and built by an Admiral in the French Navy early in the 20th century. I am told that

Winston Churchill himself visited the house at the beginning of the second World War. I have even had the personal privilege of sitting in the seat where he supposedly sat. Now all that being said, I hasten to add that the events in the story you are about to read are totally fictional. It is a novel after all. I have borrowed and adapted from many of the anecdotes the family have shared with me, which have formed the branches, but the totality is a tree of figments of my own imagination. Nonetheless, much of what takes place is very much a part of Moroccan life. I write this as a fascinated observer and cannot pretend to have the sensibility that a native writer would bring. Inaccuracies may well be detected and they are likely to come from naivety or misunderstanding what I have heard and observed.

Taking the narrative back to Casablanca where it all started, I find myself immersed in a myriad of new characters with names that may be unfamiliar to many readers. To help make sense of it all, and in case you get lost trying to remember who is who, I have added an addendum at the end with the list of characters and how they fit in.

I am deeply grateful to the Laghranis for all your stories and for your warm welcome, and thank you Jim W and the other enthusiastic readers of the earlier works for your promptings.

A salute to Susie L, whose indefatigable eyes have proofed so many of my endeavours.

And finally thank you (*du fond du cœur*) to my in-house Arabic expert, whose love and encouragement unceasingly spur me on. Shukriya.

Château des Mésanges

The delta-shaped land between the two great rivers that flow towards Bordeaux is called Entre Deux Mers, Between Two Seas in French. Its undulating green hills host endless waves of vineyards, monasteries, villages and châteaux. It has been that way in one form or another for two thousand years or more, grapevines and clusters of stone dwellings, both noble and humble.

Château des Mésanges was built some time in the fourteenth century as a defensive outpost during the Hundred Years War. Until the nineteenth century it remained in the hands of one family, the De Montrichards who skillfully changed sides politically over the centuries to ensure they survived and their château with them. Their long good fortune finally ran out when they incautiously invested in the company building the Panama Canal which went bankrupt, forcing the family to liquidate their assets.

The current occupants, the de Fortelle family, bought it in 1890. Like so many aristocratic dynasties, good fortune comes and goes in cycles. Although the earliest generations of the de Fortelle family were wealthy and prosperous, their descendants have been less fortunate and in recent years the building has begun to deteriorate, the extensive vineyard eventually being sub-leased to the *vigneron* next door and the châteaux occupants, as with so many old aristocratic French families, left to struggle in near penury.

The château has three wings, each built in a different century. The inner walls which date back to the original *défence*, were partially demolished to let in more light, some time in the early nineteenth century, when style surplanted defence, but in most respects the basic inner structure has remained much as it had been since each wing was built. The walls are more than a metre thick in places and still have slit openings for archers to defend the interior. The moats have long been drained and are now grassy ditches and flowerbeds, while the barbican defends nothing more than a handy storage place for firewood. The château dominates the highest knoll of rolling extensive grounds of woods and vines, famous in better times as a hunting ground for deer and wild boar. In its heyday, there were many hectares of red and white wine grapes, with *dépendances, chais,* barrel stores and cellars for wine production.

The family fortune precipitously plummeted in the unfortunate hands of Alphonse de Fortelle who had invested in a number of ventures, including several start-ups in Senegal which, one after the other, turned out to be fraudulent or quixotic. Whether a cause or outcome of his business failures, he had a serious drinking problem. He seemed to have placed certain moneys in locations where they could not be traced, and then he himself disappeared. Madame Thérèse de Fortelle, his wife, suffered in stolid silence and sought solace in the local Catholic convent. At the time, the local gossips were pretty certain that Alphonse had been spiriting money away in Lichtenstein or somewhere and had taken a mistress, a local girl who disappeared at the same time, to Argentina.

Their sons, Hugues and Théophile had witnessed this disintegration through their childhoods and then both had found a way to escape. Hugues, the older of the two, migrated to Australia, married an Australian girl in Sydney, had two children and started a financial business that became enormously successful. He would never set foot in France again. His younger brother took longer to leave and eventually found himself in Goa, India, where he was carried off on the back of a horse cart to an Ashram in which the Guru, an old woman, Swami Padmananda, told him to return to his «house of ghosts». She told him that the reincarnation of an ancient Indian sage, Ashtavakra, had been reborn and that he, Théophile, was destined to look after «her».

When Théophile returned to the Entre Deux Mers, there was nothing there but his Mother, who he found in deep distress. She had just heard that his older brother, Hugues, had drowned in the surf in Sydney along with his son Antoine. It was shortly after Théophile's return that the widow of Hugues, Claire and her daughter Pia, arrived to visit France for the first time.

From then on the fortunes of the de Fortelles took a rapid and miraculous up- swing and Château des Mésanges experienced a radical reincarnation of its own.

A Shrine

Twelve months since the arrival of Claire de Fortelle and her daughter Pia, who died in a pool of blood in Lourdes before the statue of the Virgin Mary, Château des Mésanges has been completely renovated and has also become a site of pilgrimage.

The château's total restoration, at enormous expense, was funded by the fortunes of Hugue's Australian enterprise. The rotten floors and crumbling beams have all been replaced. The high slate roof with its two towers is waterproof. The forty rooms are soundly floored, centrally heated, equipped with ensuites and furnished in style. Solar panels provide the château's energy while a much more potent spiritual energy infuses the residents.

While for the first seven years of her life, Pia de Fortelle had appeared to be severely handicapped with cerebral palsy, once she arrived in Entre deux Mers, she revealed her true ability and who she really was. Not only did she show herself to be the reincarnation of the ancient Indian sage Ashtavakra, as foretold by the Guru in India, but she also revealed an omniscience that utterly transformed those who met her.

Now the château serves as a shrine to the tiny but powerful, misshapen and ethereal child whose presence continued even after she had relinquished her damaged physical body. By her own request, revealed after her death, her body is buried in the resurrected cemetery behind the château chapel. Both grave and chapel now draw pilgrims from far and wide.

The confluence of souls drawn together in the presence of this gifted child has evolved into a community devoted to Pia and her mission of «*Amour*».

A shy and humble Moroccan girl, Shaafia Jilani, given a spiritual quest by a Sufi holy man when she was a child in Casablanca, becomes the means of communication for Pia, who she recognises as the goal of her quest. For Shaafia, Pia is the «Bird with Crooked Wings» she was told to search for. Although she could barely speak when she was alive, Pia used Shaafia to be her «voice» to communicate the kind of knowledge that transcends normal «knowing». That communication continued even after her body had been interred. There were others who could «hear» her from time to time, but Shaafia was the main vehicle of communication.

Just like Shaafia, the community in the château is drawn from those who have received a command. Although each has taken a different form, each command has been fulfilled by an encounter with Pia. Just as Théophile de Fortelle was sent home by the Guru in India to take care of the reincarnation of the saint, there were others.

Kate Dunlop only discovered her Australian aboriginal heritage as her grandmother was dying, but it prompted her to become a nurse and go out into the Australian desert to find it. There she joined a family group, deep in the desert and began to understand how they lived. Then the elders told her that her «spirit child» had been born in Sydney and she should return to find her. It was Pia.

The nuns of the convent near the château and the local priest quickly discovered what Pia could do. One after the other, she revealed to each that she knew who they were and what they had done. All of them came to be deeply devoted to her.

An American priest, who could not keep his vows, now serves as the host in the chapel. Prompted by Pia, he has been reunited with his child and the woman who gave birth to her. The child instantly recognised Pia, when she arrived, as they had known each other in a previous life.

Another American, Brad Purdue, a young postgraduate student of Indian Studies arrived too late to meet Pia in person, sent by the same Indian Guru, Swami Padmananda. Pia, through Shaafia, instructed him to write the book of Pia's life. He returned to Goa and the book is being edited ready to publish.

Now the château houses a community of like-minded souls, drawn together by the love of Pia, their love for Pia and the love she taught them to share, «*Amour*».

Although it is mysterious to them all, they sense that they have been given a mission and piece by piece it begins to unfold.

Epiphany

January the sixth is Epiphany, and in France it is considered one of the three most high holy days in the Catholic church calendar. It commemorates the showing of the baby Jesus to the three wise men.

The convent *«Le Nid des Oiseaux Serènes»* always holds a celebration mass on that day, complete with a nativity installation.

Everyone from Château des Mésanges was invited to attend.

For breakfast that morning they all came to the kitchen dressed in their best.

Marie-Louise, who had renounced her vows as a nun to become a fulltime servant of Pia, had prepared a special breakfast and Jourdan, who Pia had rescued from prison, had baked the most important traditional dish for the day, the *« Galette des Rois »*. As he brought two of them to the table, each one with a gold paper crown on the top, the redolent smell of warm pastry and orange flower filled the air.

«What is it?», squealed Berenice, Michael's daughter, with her eyes wide open.

Marie-Louise looked to Théophile to explain.

«Today is the day the Magi came to see the baby Jesus.» He looked over at Angela. «Do you know what is Magi in English?»

«The three wise men,» she said. Angela, a student from South Africa, had been brought to the château when she had nowhere else to stay, and as she was studying to be a translator had become a valuable asset.

«Ah yes of course.»

Zena, who was holding her daughter Berenice in her lap, leaned over her. «You know this story?»

The child nodded. «They came on a camel and they gave presents.»

«Well done,» said Michael, stroking his child's cheek. Then he looked up at Théophile.» So what does the cake represent?»

«The wise men had been told by an angel that a great king had been born. They followed the star to find the king. So, hidden in this brioche, it is not really a cake, there is what we call the «*feve*». It is a little statue. The word «*feve*» actually means a bean and in the original tradition that was what you found inside. I don't know why but somewhere along the way the bean turned into a little statue. These days it could be anything, even a character from Disney, but it represents the king. When we get a slice of this galette, one of us will find the symbol of the king, the «*feve*», and whoever finds the «*feve*» will get to wear the crown. That person will be the king or maybe the queen for today.

«I wanna be the king», yelled Berenice.

«You will be, if you find the «*feve*»,» smiled Théophile.

The two galettes sat in the middle of the table and Berenice could barely contain herself.

Thérèse had watched all this with a warm smile, now she leaned forward and looked at Michael.

«Grace?» she said. By now this was one of the French words he recognised and he smiled back and stood.

«Dear Friends,» he began, giving space for Théophile to translate. «Here we are in the house of love, ordained by our beloved Pia. On this day, in which God revealed his most precious son to the wise men, let us express our joy and our gratitude, that we too have received just as precious a gift from God.«

There was a murmured «Amen.»

«Dear God,» he continued. «Thank you for the bounty that you have bestowed upon all of us in this house. May each of us become as full a representative of your love as you would wish. As we enjoy this most excellent breakfast, may its meaning be clear to each of us. Amen.»

Once Théophile had translated for the French speakers, his Mother, Marie-Louise and Jourdan, Thérèse nodded and in her best attempt at English, said: «Is very nice grace.»

There was coffee and tea, juice and fruit, cereals and *pain grillé*, but Berenice was only interested in one thing and she kept begging that they get to the galettes.

In all this, Shaafia sat quietly watching and listening. And yet at the same time she seemed to be far off somewhere, barely present. After a moment Claire leaned across and put her hand on Shaafia's arm.

«Are you OK?», she asked gently.

It took some effort for Shaafia to respond, but she smiled and nodded. Then she seemed to gather herself up and focus.

«After breakfast we must go to the chapel,» she said.

Instantly Marie-Louise came round the table.

«*Qu'est-ce qui arrive?*», she demanded, what's happening? Whenever there was the slightest chance that Shaafia would reveal some kind of message from Pia, she was on the alert.

«After breakfast,» said Shaafia, and they could see she was making an extra effort to be present.

Finally they succumbed to the pleading of Berenice, and Jourdan began to cut the two galettes.

«What's in it?», asked Claire.

Angela translated as Jourdan described the round puff pastry filled with creamy almond paste, all flavoured with orange flower and sprinkled with sugar.

«And of course the «*feve*»», he said. He then bent to the task of cutting slices and handed them round. There being two galettes, there would be two royal winners. The outcome made everyone cheer with delight except for Berenice who did not win.

Théophile was the first, as he plucked a soggy statue of a little bird from his mouth.

«Just as Pia has said!», laughed his wife. «You are the king.»

He dutifully put the cardboard crown on his head.

And then it was Claire who got the other one, another bird.

«And just as Swami Padmananda said,» smiled her husband. «You are the queen.»

They sat side by side as the royal couple for the day.

To everyone round the table it seemed incredibly appropriate, except for one small person. Berenice did her best to smile, but everyone could see how disappointed she was. Claire took off her crown and bent over to the child. «Would you like to be my princess?»

Through barely concealed tears she nodded, and Claire crowned the new princess who was instantly all smiles.

When breakfast was complete and everyone had congratulated Jourdan on his fine mastery of the galettes, they all headed for the chapel.

The candles had already been lit, as many of them had begun the day in the early morning with meditation, each in their own way.

Everyone filed in, Jourdan and Marie-Louise having taken off their aprons. Berenice settled onto her Mother's lap, while her Father trimmed the candles. Shaafia sat very still in a corner, indrawn, as if she had almost left her body.

They all settled quietly.

Then very subtly the atmosphere in the room began to change. The electricity in the air became palpable. A ray of winter sun beamed across from the eastern window and bringing to life the mural of the birds on the opposite wall.

Shaafia looked up at the ray.

«Revelation,» she said quietly, in both languages.

The others waited.

«The Lady in Blue and White has come,» she said in French, and Angela took up the English translation.

«The Magi, the wise men journeyed so far, following a sign. So have all of you.»

There was a long silence which even Berenice had no desire to interrupt.

«They came looking for that which is true. Most everything in the world is an illusion, but only that which is true is eternal and unchanging. The wise ones have always looked for that.»

A stillness descended on the chapel, a suspension of time.

«Only love is true, nothing else. Amour.»

Marie-Louise softly chanted it to herself as she had begun to do very often. «Amour. Amour. Amour.»

Her soft voice lifted into the silent space and the others bathed in it.

«You, you are now wise.» Shaafia's voice, speaking in French, was soft but very clear. « You have come to know that love. It has been revealed to you. This is why I came. Now you are wise enough to know what is true and that truth will radiate out from each of you. Little by little, heart by heart, you can bring great light to this world.»

«Does Pia say this?», whispered Marie-Louise.

Shaafia shook her head.

«The Lady in Blue and White.»

«The Holy Mother?»

«It is she.»

A deeper silence engulfed the chapel.

Finally a gust of wind brushed the trees outside the chapel windows and Shaafia looked up.

«That is the message.» she said.

Michael came forward and bowed deeply in front of the altar.

When he stood up, turning to face the room, he had tears in his eyes.

«We are incredibly blessed,» he said. «In all my life, I have wanted to have a direct interaction with the divine. Pia did that for me. Now that her work is complete, she has opened the door to a remarkable source of God's love. The Holy Mother herself. In this little chapel, how fortunate we are. It is so rare, so rare.»

Thérèse nodded as Michael's words were translated by Angela.

«We shall carry them to the convent today.» She looked lovingly at Shaafia.

«You will remember what she has told us?»

Shaafia smiled gently and shook her head.

«I cannot say.» she said. «The message may not be the same next time.»

Théophile said: «Brad needs to know what was said. I mean, maybe he could still put it in the book. It could be at the very end.»

Brad Purdue was the American student who Théophile had met when he first went to the Ashram of Padmananda in India. After the guru had sent Théophile back to his «house of ghosts» to take care of the reincarnation of Ashtavakra, a little later she had sent Brad there too. He had missed meeting Pia in person but she had made it clear that he was to be the scribe, the writer of the book about Pia and what she communicated and how it changed the lives of those who met her. Brad was now back in India working on preparing the book for publication.

With Angela as the note-taker, they all tried to remember, using both languages, as exactly as they could, what Shaafia had communicated. Shaafia herself said nothing, allowing the others to do the work. As it turned out the best memory was held by Marie-Louise. To her every word was treasure.

When they all agreed that the essence of the message had been captured, each of them bowed in reverence at the altar and then went off to get ready for Mass.

Théophile called India and found Brad hard at work in Chennai. «Listen to Love», the book about Pia, was in the final stages of editing. The editor was Indira Shetty the girl they had met in the Ashram of Padmananda.

«I tell you, man,» Brad said, «this girl is brilliant. It's going to be a hell of a good book. She is sharp.»

When Théophile read the notes that had been made in the morning, Brad was ecstatic. «Oh, man. That was exactly what we were missing. It brings it all together. Like a final message about the way forward. She is telling us to get wise and go out and help others to get wise. I love it. Indira's going to love it, too.»

Something about the way Brad said the name Indira gave Théophile a twinge of intuition.

«So you and Indira work well together?»

«Oh sure. She's right on. Bossy as hell but smart.»

«You like her?»

«You betcha.»

Théophile smiled to himself.

«I am happy to hear that.»

The convent chapel had followed the tradition of removing all decorations before Epiphany except for the nativity. The small wooden manger held statuettes of the usual animals and shepherds, but where the crib would normally be in the centre, the nuns had placed a photo of Pia with her Mother.

It was a risky thing to do for a Catholic convent but the nuns were unanimous in their love for Pia. Every single one of them had been touched by her and for all of them, their vocations had been deeply transformed. It was not that any of them had renounced anything of their previous calling, except Marie-Louise, but instead that calling had been powerfully nurtured and reinforced.

As the congregation assembled, Marie-Louise whispered to Sister Geneviève, the Mother Superior, that the Holy Mother herself had come that morning and had given them a most wonderful message in honour of Epiphany.

«We must talk of this after Mass.» said Geneviève.

Father Lefait, who had weathered so much turmoil as he came to recognise who Pia was, now conducted the traditional Epiphany service. Angela provided a quiet translation for the English speakers. At the conclusion when it was time for Communion, Father Lefait smiled at the non-Catholics.

«We have come to that part of our ceremony that Pia has completely transformed for us. I would wish to continue in the practice that she inspired.» This meant that instead of the usual ingredients for communion, there was bread and wine. Father Lefait knew that every time he did this, he ran the very real risk of being discovered by the church but he was becoming more courageous as he went along. He was fairly certain that there was no-one in the chapel who would betray him.

As each one came forward to receive the bread and the wine, the organ played quietly in the background and the thinnest of winter suns shone a fine ray across the wall behind the altar highlighting the suspended body of the Christ on his cross.

As she came forward, taking only the bread, the very last to come, Shaafia gazed up at the figure. As she did, a small tear ran down her cheek. The priest noticed but said nothing. Then she turned and went back to her seat.

After the Mass, they all assembled in the big lounge of the convent for morning tea. Marie-Louise was on the edge of her chair itching to repeat the message from the early morning.

Sister Geneviève smiled at her as the tea was served. «We hear that on this holy day there has been a very holy communication.»

«Thanks to Shaafia.» said Marie-Louise.

Shaafia shyly smiled but said nothing.

Marie-Louise gave a breathless but accurate rendition of the message which was absorbed in devoted silence by all the nuns and Father Lefait.

Finally ending the long silence, «What is remarkable is that this is not from Pia,» said Sister Geneviève. She looked down at Shaafia sitting quietly as if she had no part to play. «Pia was not present?»

Shaafia shook her head. «Just the Lady in Blue and White.»

«It is a very powerful message.» said Father Lefait. «It is one to contemplate deeply. To make the comparison with the Magi is most powerful to me. It makes each of us aware that we too are like those wise men. Each of us searches to find what is the truth.»

Angela was doing her best to keep the anglophones up-to-date.

Michael then said: «To me there is an enormous challenge here. That if we are to begin to see ourselves as wise and that we have come to know that kind of love that Pia has taught us, then what do we do with that wisdom and that knowledge? That is our challenge.»

The whole room seemed to nod in acknowledgement.

At the end of the morning, as they were preparing to return to the château, Father Lefait came over to Shaafia.

«You have brought us an extraordinary gift for Epiphany.» he said.

She smiled shyly and nodded.

«Can I ask you something?» he said quietly.

She looked up into his face, perhaps guessing what he was about to ask.

«I couldn't help but notice, in the chapel, that communion was very moving for you.»

She nodded.

«But communion is not part of Islam, is it?» Shaafia had taken the bread but not the wine.

«No.» she said quietly.

«Can I ask what moved you?»

«I looked up at the statue and I thought of the Mother who gave birth. Her son. He suffered so much.»

«Ah.» he said softly. «I see.»

Guests

In the cold January days that followed Epiphany, the château and the convent dropped back into their regular routines. The nuns, all rugged up against the wind and occasional wafts of snow, took it in turns to be on hand when visitors came to the château. Visitors came almost every day. Many had become regulars from the district, but others came from much further afield. Some came back in gratitude for what they had experienced in previous visits, and almost inevitably brought new people with them. Letters were often brought and accepted in the chapel and donations flowed freely.

At the same time the château had begun to turn itself into a proper *auberge*, with a website with photos and a structure of prices for overnight stays. Before any paying guests could be welcomed, there were endless bureaucratic steps in this process and it took the patience of Théophile and Claire to see it all through. For Thérèse it was beyond her understanding but she loved the activity and endlessly counted her blessings as she saw her totally restored château fill with joyful activity.

Marie-Louise and Jourdan made meals that nurtured everyone, every single time. Meal times were dynamic familial affairs as everyone shared what they were working on and what they were experiencing inside themselves.

Even though the vines lie dormant and still in the winter months, Vito Zagni, one of the senior partners in Hugue's financial firm in Australia and Jacques the neighboring *vigneron*, had been in constant communication with Théophile as they created the new joint entity for the combined vineyards. Very often Théophile felt like he was a new trainee in an unfamiliar world, while the other two spoke with such authority, but in decision-making, they ensured he was included. While Vito was the authority on money matters and marketing, Jacques brought his family knowledge of the vines. Théophile was gradually getting used to accepting the large amounts of money involved, watching Vito investing in the new structure with gusto. So much of Théophile's early life had seen an abject lack of money. Now he seemed to be operating in a world where money was not an issue, and it flowed easily.

In all this Shaafia remained quiet. She participated in the daily routines of the château and was often called upon to meet with visitors who had heard about who she was and the rôle that she had played for Pia. She would be attentive to their questions, open their letters and often felt herself able to recall something that Pia had said that seemed to be appropriate. More and more her own intuition seemed to lead her to the right answer for each one.

She was treated with great respect, sometimes bordering on adoration, which made her more than a little embarrassed. The nuns embraced her with a warm combination of sisterly love and deep admiration. They felt that she was one of them, precious and deserving of protection. However if a visitor became too insistent, the nuns would turn into firm gatekeepers.

Several weeks into January, Shaafia was delighted to receive a note from her previous teacher Madame Clae. It was Madame Clae who had encouraged Shaafia to come to Bordeaux from Morocco to study to become a translator. Madame Clae had returned to her native Bordeaux having had to retire from her Casablanca teaching job. She was now living with a cousin in the Bordeaux suburbs. Her little note hoped that Shaafia was doing well and gently asked if they could meet.

Once they had spoken on the phone, they arranged a day for Madame Clae to come for a visit.

On a crisp but sunny morning in late January, a tiny pale blue Renault Twingo roared its way up the drive and a very large lady of advanced years squeezed herself out of the driver's seat. And there was Madame Clae. Shaafia ran to her and they hugged each other for a long moment.

«It is so good to see you!» exclaimed Madame Clae with tears in her eyes as she pulled back. Then she turned. «May I introduce my cousin Clara?»

Shaafia shook hands with the lady and gazed up into her face. A slight frown darkened Shaafia's face as she looked at her, before she turned and invited them inside. As they walked across the forecourt past the barbican, Madame Clae gazed up at the highstone walls and the twin slated towers.

«It is a wonderful château. How lucky you are to live here.»

«Oh yes, Madame Clae, you cannot imagine how grateful I am to be here.» said Shaafia.

Her teacher laughed. «I think it is time that you *tutoyer.*» she said, inviting her ex-student to use the familar *tu* rather than the formal *vous* that Shaafia had always used out of respect. «Please call me Hélène.»

Shaafia smiled shyly and dipped her head. «Thank you Hélène.»

As they walked close to the chapel entrance, Sister Catherine emerged to welcome them.

Once Shaafia had introduced her guests, the nun invited them into the chapel. Hélène smiled and said: «When I married my husband in Morocco, I became a Muslim. I have not set foot inside a Christian church since then.»

«Even after that husband of yours walked out on you?», sneered her cousin.

It was clear that Madame Clae was used to her cousin's way and she let it pass. Shaafia and the nun exchanged glances.

«But, I have to say», said Sister Catherine gently, «this is not really a Christian chapel. It is something much more interesting, in a way.»

«It is not?» asked Clara looking puzzled. «But you are a nun.»

«I am.» the sister smiled again. «I have also had the wonderful good fortune to have met Pia and she has changed my life and reinforced my vocation.»

«But you are still a nun, a Catholic nun.» Clara had stopped in her tracks, feeling uneasy.

«Because of Pia, I am more of a nun than I ever was.»

Very quietly Shaafia took Hélène's arm. «Come and see this chapel. It is very peaceful.»

Hélène gratefully took the opportunity, holding on to Shaafia, and she let herself be led. Clara did not want to be left behind and hurried to catch up. Sister Catherine held the door open for her as she scuttled to catch up to her cousin.

When Shaafia and her teacher entered the chapel, Michael was there and he rose to meet them. Once again Shaafia did the introductions and then let Sister Catherine tell the story of the chapel, why it had been left in ruins for years, after the accidental death of a baby girl about to be baptised and how at Pia's command, it had been resurrected.

Madame Clae had heard all about this from Shaafia, but it was new for Clara.

«Hélène has told me something of what has happened here.» she said. «But I find it hard to believe that some young handicapped child could do all these things that you say she did. It is not believable.»

Sister Catherine nodded. «I can imagine how strange it is to hear what has happened here, but trust me, I swear by the vows I took as a nun, what we tell you is the truth.»

«But you still live in a convent?» asked Clara.

«Of course. Our sisters take it in turns to be here to greet people. At all other times we are like regular nuns.»

«What does the church think of all this?»

Sister Catherine took a long look at her questioner before she replied.

«A nun follows her vocation. We live by faith.»

«Would you like to sit for a while?» asked Michael, deciding that he needed to move things along. Although he had not followed the conversation, he had felt the tone was not so friendly. He was doing his best to acquire some French, but he was not yet very confident.

Sister Catherine left them there and after a moment Michael followed her out. The three women took seats side by side at the back of the chapel. As soon as Shaafia closed her eyes, Hélène saw her and she did the same. Clara however stared around her, with something of a dark look in her eye. What kind of chapel was this that has a wheelchair in front of the altar? Why was there a statue of an Indian woman with four arms sitting on a tiger placed on the altar beside a scruffy-looking stuffed kangaroo? Clara stole a look at Shaafia, this small dark-skinned Moroccan girl who was supposed to be the medium for the handicapped child. Was she really? Or was this is all some kind of fake cult?

As if reading the thoughts, Shaafia opened her eyes and looked directly into Clara's. The look was unblinking, penetrating and Clara could not hold it. Instead she stood up, ready to leave.

She looked down at her cousin and saw tears running down her cheeks.

«Hélène?» she said.

Madame Clae slowly opened her eyes and gazed up at her cousin.

«This is such a peaceful place.»

«You are crying.»

«It is true. I have not felt such peace in a very long time.» Then she smiled at Shaafia. «How lucky you are to live here.»

Shaafia smiled and then as she stood up, she invited them to come into the main lounge for morning coffee.

Clara ran her eyes round the chapel one more time as if she were taking inventory, to commit it to memory, then she followed the others out.

Théophile and Claire had gone off to Bordeaux on business errands, and Angela had gone back to the university to continue her studies as a translator. Berenice had come down with a cold so she and Zena were not there either. Michael smiled as Shaafia brought in her guests. A warm fire was blazing in the giant fireplace under the portraits of the De Fortelle ancestors and Thérèse stood in front of it, almost like an added symbol of the dynasty.

As Shaafia introduced her guests, Marie-Louise brought in a brand new and wonderfully silent tea trolley with fresh *madeleines* made by Jourdan. The old rickety trolley that had served limply for years had finally been replaced.

Once everyone had been served, Marie-Louise retired to the kitchen and they sat round the fire. Clara turned to Thérèse and asked about the history of the château. In the past, Thérese would have been reluctant to talk much about that because of the shameful deterioration that had taken place. Now however, sitting in the cosy warmth of a fully renovated and centrally heated château, she had no hesitation at all.

She proudly detailed the significant events that the château had seen over the centuries until she arrived at the great good fortune that had so recently descended.

Clara had let her talk uninterrupted for some time, but now she intervened.

«So your son, the one who I am sorry to hear had died in Australia, he was the one who made all the money for this renovation?»

«That is the case.» nodded Thérèse.

«And he was the father of this girl, the girl with the handicap that everyone seems to think is some kind of gifted medium?»

Thérèse studied her guest carefully before answering.

«Hugues was Pia's father, yes.» and she said no more.

There was a strained silence in the air until Michael excused himself to go upstairs to take some *madeleines* to his daughter. He wasn't able to follow the French conversation anyway. Once he had gone, Hélène felt she needed to make up for the intrusive questioning of her cousin.

«Madame de Fortelle,» she said, using the formal «*vous*» in addressing the doyenne of Château des Mésanges, «it is a most wonderful history that you have shared with us. And Shaafia has shared her own experience of being here which I find so enchanting. I have lived a very simple life as a teacher in Casablanca, teaching French and English. To see that one of my students has done so well and been made so welcome warms my heart.»

Shaafia smiled at her teacher.

«I am very grateful for everything that has happened here,» she said.

«But is it true?» asked Clara, who had been itching to redirect the conversation, «that somehow this child could communicate things and that you could interpret what she said?»

«It is true.» said Shaafia and felt no need to say anything more. She was very aware of what was churning away inside her guest.

« I find it hard to believe. Hélène has told me that you hear her thoughts in your head and you say them. Even after she died.»

«I was as surprised as anyone.» said Shaafia looking steadily at the lady. »I had never heard of such a thing before. But then it happened.»

Thérèse had watched this and decided she should say something. «This young girl has an amazing gift. I was the most sceptical of people, as a good Catholic would be, of such things, but she has proved beyond all doubts that what she says is the truth.»

«Do you hear her thoughts now?» asked Clara.

Shaafia shook her head.

«Would you be willing,» said Hélène suddenly standing up, «to show us through the château?»

Thérèse smiled warmly, most grateful for the tactful change of direction. «With pleasure.» she said.

As they climbed the newly secure and silent staircase, Thérèse proudly showed off the new ensuite bathrooms and the tasteful furniture that Claire had selected. The fact that Claire was an accomplished interior designer was a great pride for Thérèse, as she referred lovingly to her daughter-in-law's obvious skills.

As they walked up to the next level, Hélène asked Shaafia if she was intending to go back to the university to finish her degree.

Shaafia shook her head.

«I don't think so.» she said at last.

«But you have a scholarship, do you not?»

«Yes.»

«So,» said Clara, homing in on this new piece of information, «You are taking money from the French government but not studying any more?»

Hélène cut across her with a tone of exasperation. She was beginning to feel very uncomfortable about her cousin's attitude. She put a protective arm round Shaafia's shoulders. «If you have decided not to continue, then you should tell them.»

«Yes. I will. I had not thought of that.» said Shaafia.

By the time they had visited many of the rooms and taken a quick and chilly walk outside, it was time for lunch.

Claire and Théophile made it back and they joined Shaafia's guests in the big kitchen.

Hélène, although she taught English in Casablanca, was not as fluent in English as Shaafia expected. She had trouble catching Claire's Australian accent so Shaafia had to gently help out. Clara had no English, so she looked to be included by way of translation. She wanted to know how Hugue had made his money and just how much had been spent on renovating the château. Most French people are reticent to talk about money but she was not. Hélène, writhing in the discomfort of her cousin's unpleasant intrusions, tried to divert the conversation as best she could.

She tried to start different conversations in English with Théophile and with Claire, but every time she did, her cousin would cut across it in French.

There was a growing air of tension throughout the lunch, despite the wonderful *gigot d'agneau* prepared by Marie-Louise.

This all came to a head as coffee was being served.

Hélène could stand it no longer and she burst out in rapid-fire angry French that neither Shaafia nor Théophile wanted to translate for Claire. The result was that Clara got up and stormed out to her car leaving her cousin behind.

Hélène sat in her chair at the long kitchen table with her head down, as the roar of the tiny Twingo receded down the château driveway.

Shaafia came over to her and put her arms around her teacher's shaking shoulders.

«It is for the best.» she said softly.

«Do you think she will come back?» Hélène lifted her head and gazed at her student.

«No.» said Shaafia. «She is so filled with anger and torment, she cannot think properly. She is very sick. It is not good for you to be near her.»

«But what will I do?» Hélène had tears running down her cheeks and Shaafia kept her small arms around her.

«God will take care of you. *Inche Allah.*» she said. Then she looked up at the rest of the group, who had been watching with empathetic silence.

«I would like to ask that Hélène be able to live here with us. She has been brought to us for her protection.»

«I do not wish to intrude.» said Hélène miserably.

Thérèse carefully put down her coffee cup and looked around the table. «I have experienced much sadness and discomfort in my life. In the last year, so much has happened and so much good has come back into my life. Now I have the chance to extend that goodness to others. So yes, of course I would be very content to welcome you to Château des Mésanges.»

Hélène lifted her eyes and looked around the table. As she did, the others, one after the other, smiled and nodded. Théophile had quietly let Claire know what was being said.

«I have a small pension,» said Hélène. «So I can of course pay for staying with you.»

Théophile felt called upon, as the man of the house and newly acquainted with plenty of money. «There would be no need of that. We would be honoured to have you. Without you, Shaafia would not have come to Bordeaux.»

Then Shaafia said: «It is your destiny to be here. You have served so honourably as a teacher for all these years, now you can offer yourself in a new kind of service.»

Hélène frowned. «What do you mean?»

«I do not know yet, but it will become apparent.» Shaafia looked around the table. «None of us comes here by accident. We are brought. It is our destiny. *Bismillah*.»

Thérèse gave a little chuckle, which surprised everyone. «I do believe I know which service you can offer. I wish to learn to speak English, and Claire wishes to learn to speak French. You are exactly what we need.»

The entire table smiled, almost with relief.

Once Michael caught up with the translation, he added: «Us too. My whole family needs to be able to speak French.»

«It would be my honour.» said Hélène, clearly moved by the suggestion.

«We will help you to retrieve your things from your cousin's house.» said Théophile.

At this moment Marie-Louise, who had watched all this in silence, now banged her hand on the table. «I shall be the one to do that. I know how to deal with such people.»

Shaafia smiled, remembering how Marie-Louise had helped her when she first went to the University.

«Perfect,» she said. «Marie-Louise is formidable.»

An hour later Hélène left with Marie-Louise in the big Mercedes van.

At the end of the afternoon, the van came back up the driveway.

As Marie-Louise unloaded the two somewhat battered suitcases, Shaafia came out to meet them.

«It was not easy.» she said, as a statement not a question.

Marie-Louise nodded. «That woman is as you rightly said. She is sick in her head.»

Hélène climbed out of the van, barely able to stand. She was shaking and obviously had been crying the whole way back.

Shaafia put her arms around her.

«You will find peace here.» she said.

They installed Hélène in a room on the third floor. As she gazed around her at the newly painted room, the very stylish ensuite bathroom and the quality furniture and bed coverings, she shook her head.

«I have never lived in such a beautiful room.»

«It is what you deserve.» said Marie-Louise.

Leaving Hélène to unpack, Shaafia walked down the stairs with Marie-Louise.

«That woman is going to give us trouble.» said Marie-Louise. «She has read that article in the paper. She threatened to tell the police and I don't know who else.»

Shaafia nodded. «I could see that from the moment she arrived. She has so much anger in her. She needs a lot of love from us.»

«Love?» snorted Marie-Louise. «I think she needs a good beating.»

«No.» smiled Shaafia. «Imagine what Pia would say to her.»

«Does she say something?» Marie-Louise stopped on the stairs, but Shaafia shook her head. «There is no need.»

They went on down the stairs until Marie-Louise suddenly stopped.

«But I see that you are right. After all the Lady in Blue and White, Our Lady, she said it is all about love.»

«Exactly.» smiled Shaafia, and they descended together.

Trouble

At first, Héléne was very shy and diffident with the household, not sure how she could fit in. Everyone else had the bond of having known Pia, so she felt like an intruder.

Shaafia became her guide and companion. She explained the rhythms of the château.

«Most of us start the morning in the chapel.»

«But it is for Christians, is it not?»

«Not at all. It is a holy place for anyone who wishes to be with God. For me I can pray there as well as I would in a Mosque. And Théophile, he prays to the statue of the goddess on the tiger. Marie-Louise prays to Pia.»

«It is a most peaceful place,» said Hélène. «I will join you.»

Little by little she became more comfortable and the others could see her slowly begin to soften and relax. She felt a certain urgency to begin to pay back in some way the generosity that had been shown to her.

«If you wish,» she said shyly to Thérèse, «we could begin to have classes in English.»

«I wish it very much.» Thérèse smiled at her new guest. «And I would ask that you *tutoyer* from now on.» In this, she was asking that Hélène treat her as an equal and use the more intimate pronouns.

«It shall be as you say.» said Hélène. «You are most gracious.»

They sat together in the warmth of the parlour by the fire and very gently began.

When the family came together for lunch, Thérèsa very proudly said, with her newly-acquired linguistic knowledge: «Welcome to lunch. I wish you a very nice lunch.» Everyone was very impressed.

«Très bien, Maman.» said Théophile, before adding in English, «You are a good student.» This made his Mother blush with pleasure.

In the afternoon the would-be French speakers had their turn, including Berenice who had recovered from her cold. She had already begun to pick up quite a bit of French, especially from Marie-Louise who she had come to adore. She would hang out in the kitchen, and Marie-Louise would talk to her as if she already spoke French and bit by bit the child soon picked up quite a few phrases. Her favourite expression was: «*Oooh la vache*» which she heard Marie-Louise use all the time with different intonations depending on whether she was pleased or displeased. The expression can go either way.

The adult students were slower, Claire, Michael and Zena.

The fire in the parlour blazed away as a cold wind howled around the château.

To begin, Hélène asked each one to say, in English, what they would like to say in French. Then she coached each one in their chosen sentence. Berenice was by far the quickest to pick up her sentence.

«Je suis une très belle fille.» she said with a flourish of her skirt for emphasis.

A daily routine settled into the château, and by the end of January there was a happy sense of camaraderie. The weather was less conducive to visitors but still the nuns took it in turns to be present. Most of the January visitors were regulars, while there was still a trickle of new people coming to see the grave of Pia and sit in the chapel, mostly inspired by the stories they had heard from their friends.

Nothing more was heard from Hélène's cousin, so she began to relax and feel at home.

The peace, however, did not last.

When Théophile answered the phone one morning and heard it was the University looking for Shaafia, he knew it was the work of Clara. When he told Shaafia, she simply nodded.

She was asked if she planned to continue her studies, and when she said that she would not they then told her that her scholarship would be suspended.

She finished the call and went quietly into the chapel. She sat for a long time making sure that she was calm inside. As she sat there, the winter sun shone across the wall with the mural of the birds and she gazed at it. She imagined the birds in flight, free to rise and take the wind. Somehow, as she looked at the birds, she began to feel that she too should rise and take to the wind.

Later when Théophile gently raised the question of the call, she smiled at him and said: «I knew it would come.»

«You are not worried?»

«No.» she said. «There will be more. There will come a time very soon, I think, when I will have to leave France.»

«Why? We will pay you as we do already, so you do not need the scholarship.»

«I know and I am so grateful for that. But I know that there is something more I have to do.»

«You can do it here.» Théophile leaned forward looking intensely into her eyes.

«You are so important to us. You were and you still are the voice of Pia.»

She smiled. «Not the only one.» Théophile had been able to hear her too, but not always.

«Ah yes but you were her first voice, her most powerful voice and now even more than Pia, you have become the voice of the Virgin. Truly you have an amazing gift.»

«It is true. Thanks be to God. I am eternally grateful that I was granted that gift. But I must tell you. I am beginning to feel that they are asking me to go.»

«Pia is asking?»

«It is more than Pia. It is as if there are voices letting me know that it is time to move. I do not know who they are, but they are full of love and I feel that they will go with me.»

Théophile sat back and gazed at her.

«Then that is how it should be. Where will you go?»

«I am not sure, but most likely I will go home to Casablanca. They will tell me so I will wait.»

He nodded. «Wherever you are supposed to go, please know that we will support you, always.» And he leant forward and gave her a hug.

She melted into his arms and stayed there for a long time.

Finally she pulled back. «We will see each other again. It is our destiny.»

«We will. After all we have done it many times.»

The next phone call was from an official from the department that oversees visas. Someone had reported to them that she was living in France on a student visa but was no longer a student. It was clear who that «someone» would have been.

When Shaafia shared that with Hélène she was horrified.

«I always sensed that my cousin was a very unhappy person but I never expected that she would be so, what can I say, vindictive.»

«Clara is filled with darkness.» said Shaafia. «She is suffering. We must pray for her and we must send our love in her direction. If we do not, the darkness will consume her.»

Her teacher smiled sadly at her student. «I have so much to learn from you.»

There were no more phone calls for a few days and everyone began to relax. They had all been told of the calls and what they were about. Shaafia had also said that she felt it would be time to leave soon, and although they were all very upset to hear that, there was an acceptance that it would happen.

The nuns were aware of the calls and when Sister Geneviève came to visit, she took Shaafia aside for a quiet chat.

«This woman who is making trouble for you, do you wish to do something about it?»

Shaafia shook her head. «No. There is nothing to be done.»

The sister nodded. «We can pray for her.»

«Yes. She needs our love.»

Sister Geneviève smiled. «Amour.»

Then Shaafia frowned. «She is not just someone who is unhappy about what she has seen, she is also a test for us to be strong. So far we have all been protected, but now we are being forced to take care of ourselves.»

«As it has always been in every path of faith,» nodded the nun. «We will be strong.»

The next phone call was not to Shaafia but to the convent.

The head of the Catholic Church in Bordeaux had been alerted to the presence of the nuns at Château des Mésanges and wanted to know if there was any truth to it.

Sister Geneviève had been evasive if even a little untruthful, and she hoped that it was enough. It was not. Several days later she and Father Lefait were summoned to Bordeaux.

When they returned, they went straight together to the convent chapel for a long time before summoning the nuns for a house meeting.

«We have both been reassigned.» announced Sister Geneviéve.

«We are forbidden to have anything to do with the Château.» added Father Lefait.

There was a stunned silence.

«Shaafia has told me that something like this would happen.» said Sister Geneviève. «We must all be strong. We must take the gifts that we have received from Pia and from Shaafia and put them to good use.»

The nuns nodded silently taking in the news.

Sister Catherine said finally. «We can take great solace from the message of Epiphany. We were told by the Virgin Mother herself that we were all wise and that we should share our love. We can do that, even if we cannot serve at the chapel of Lucia any more.»

There was a general agreement with that and the room resonated with a warmth that they all felt.

Father Lefait led a final prayer in which he invoked both the grace of the Virgin and the love of Pia. In this setting at least he could do that without fear of recrimination.

As it turned out neither Sister Geneviève nor Father Lefait were immediately reassigned, so for the next few weeks, other than no longer going to the Château, life in the convent went on as usual.

And then at last Shaafia received the call she had been expecting.

One morning she emerged from the chapel, her face radiant.

As the others trooped in for breakfast, they could see something had taken place. Berenice climbed into her lap immediately and snuggled up against her chest.

«I love you,» she said. «Je t'aime.».

Marie-Louise watched from across the room as she brought in the aromatic cafetière. «Something is happening?» she said.

Shaafia nodded.

«A message?» asked Michael. He had sat with her in the chapel and had experienced a different atmosphere that had taken him into a deep meditation.

«It is time to go.» she said to the whole room.

By now they were all expecting it.

«We will miss you,» said Claire. «But you will always be a part of this family, wherever you go.»

«We will buy you a first class ticket.» said Théophile as he cut the fresh homemade baguette brought in by Jourdan.

«No, no.» said Shaafia.

«We insist.» said Claire. She had nodded approvingly when her husband had made the offer. She was pleased that at last he was beginning to accept that he had money and he could be generous.

«It is a very short journey,» said Shaafia, «just two hours.»

«Nonetheless,» added Thérèse, who had watched all this calmly. »You have brought us so much joy, it is right that you should enjoy a good journey.»

«And you must buy a new suitcase,» said Claire. «You can't go first class with your old one.» The battered suitcase that Shaafia had brought with her had been her treasured companion, but it was beginning to fall apart.

The rest of breakfast was accompanied by lots of speculation as to what Shaafia might do when she went home.

This began with Michael asking if she had received any specific instructions.

«No,» said Shaafia. «They tell me they will be with me and I will know what to do when the time is right.»

«It seems to me,» said Michael, «that the words we heard on Epiphany are taking form.»

«What do you mean?» asked Zena. Of everyone round the table, other than Hélène, Zena was perhaps the one person who had the least obvious relationship with Pia and there was a part of her still questioning. She had been a good Catholic, religious and observant, but having committed the sin, in her own eyes, of having given birth to a priest's child, she struggled to understand what Pia represented. There was nothing in her upbringing to prepare her. The nuns had helped her to feel more accepting of her destiny and she was happy that she had been able to marry Michael. Nonetheless, who Pia was and what Pia had been able to do was a deep mystery for her.

Michael put his hand gently over hers, his white hand contrasting with her dark skin.

«Do you remember what the last part of the message from that morning was?» When she looked puzzled he said: «You can bring great light to this world.»

She nodded cautiously.

«I believe this is what Shaafia will do in her home country.»

«Pia goes to Africa,» said Théophile.

Journey

The following day Claire and Théophile took Shaafia shopping. Berenice insisted on coming too. Although Shaafia found it endlessly embarrassing to have things bought for her, she was beginning to accept that it was inevitable.

Claire had gently reminded her of her first argument with Pia when Pia insisted that Shaafia be paid.

«There is no way we can repay what you have brought us.» said Claire, sensing Shaafia's reluctance.

They parked the big Mercedes van in an undergound parking lot and took her to the cavernous luxuries of Galerie Lafayette. It was the kind of department store Shaafia had never set foot in. The entire ground floor had endless arrays of perfumes and Hermés scarves, and the prices were astronomical.

Above, there were several floors of women's clothes and it was all too mind boggling for a simple Moroccan girl to comprehend. When Claire asked her what she would like, she had no idea. So Claire took charge. Knowing that Shaafia was going back into traditional Muslim life she selected conservative clothes, but all from famous brands and of superb quality. In the end it was mostly Berenice who was the decider. Claire would choose something and hold it up for Shaafia. Shaafia would simply nod at everything, but Berenice had opinions.

«Black is not a nice colour.» she said forcefully at one point when Claire chose a dark pure wool sweater. Berenice was very keen on pale blue.

Some of the best items actually came from the girls' section because Shaafia was so petite.

She ended up with an armload of wonderfully soft dresses and blouses. She could only imagine what it all cost.

Then they bought a Samsonite hardshell suitcase to pack it all in. To finish the morning, Théophile noticed a Moroccan restaurant in the same street and they went in for lunch.

Here Shaafia felt more at ease as she described what was on the menu. The waitress spoke to her in Arabic which fascinated Berenice. It was the first time she had heard it.

« I want to talk like that! » she said.

The tajines that came to the table were full and steaming, and both Théophile and Claire were thrilled with the aromas and the flavours as the lids came off. However, Shaafia quietly said that her Mother made much better tajines.

«Then we will have to come and visit you! » laughed Théophile.

«I want to go too! » shouted Berenice, in such a loud voice that the whole restaurant heard.

«I will be happy to show you my country. » said Shaafia shyly.

After lunch they went to the Royal Air Maroc agency and booked the flight. There was no first class, only business class on such a short journey.

«Well at least you will be able to enjoy the business lounge before you go. » said Claire.

Shaafia did not even know what that was, so Claire had to explain.

They were about to head back to the car when Shaafia suddenly stopped.

«I must buy gifts for my family. » she said. «When I went home to see my father, I went so fast I did not bring any gifts. »

«Then you definitely must do that. » said Théophile.

«It is a very important tradition in our culture to bring gifts. But I must buy these gifts with my own money. »

Claire was about to protest but she caught a look from Théophile and she let it go. Instead she asked: «How many in your family? »

«We are many. I must have something for each one. »

«Luckily, » said Claire, «when you travel Business Class you get to take two suitcases. At least let us buy you another one. Please. »

It was mostly to please Claire that Shaafia accepted.

They put all her morning purchases in the Mercedes and then went back to the shops.

For her five sisters she chose clothes, agonising over each one as she thought of them. Her older sisters with their young families were more traditional but the two young ones were much more modern. She hesitated as she thought of her sister Nayla. She had been nasty to Shaafia almost all her life. Now as she held that sister in her awareness she began to understand more deeply what was behind it. She chose a very plain and simple blouse, much less beautiful and expensive than for her other sisters. It would not matter what she gave to Nayla, Nayla would hate it.

For her little brother Habib, knowing his passion for football, she bought a whole bag of goods mostly featuring his hero Messi.

She chose soft stuffed animals for her three young nieces, and she bought many small boxes of chocolates for her neighbors.

She left her other brothers till last, feeling very unsure how to deal with them. She thought about clothes but felt no energy for it. She closed her eyes for a moment, standing in the middle of Rue Saint Catherine, the longest pedestrian street in Europe. People moved past her chattering and window shopping.

«I don't know what to buy for my brothers. What will help them?» It was somewhere between a thought and an inner prayer.

«Go to Mollat. We will show you.» She could not tell who the voice was or where it came from. Was it someone in the street or did she imagine it?

When she opened her eyes, Claire smiled at her. «So what do you think? Do you like the idea of books?»

Shaafia stared at her. How did she know?

Mollat is the biggest bookstore in the city.

«Yes,» she said. «Books would be good,» although she knew that some of her brothers would probably never read them.

Mollat is a collection of many small shops each with a shopfront to the street, in the very centre of Bordeaux. Inside however, the interior walls have been removed so it has become a rabbit warren of books on every conceivable subject, novels, text books, different languages, books for children, comics, photography books, and on and on. Where to start?

And then another piece of magic happened. «Say the name and we will show you.» she heard.

In each case, following her inner guides, she walked to a shelf and pulled off a book, almost without looking.

Théophile and Claire followed on, fascinated by how fast she was and how she went from one end of the store to the other, several times.

As she stood in the queue to pay Théophile whispered. «Who chose the books?»

She whispered back: «I don't know but it wasn't me.»

The purchasing of all the presents was costing her a lot and Claire itched to help out. As they carried all the purchases back to the car, she mentioned it to her husband. Théophile whispered: «No, this is her thing. We will support her in a different way. This is important to her.»

They loaded everything into the Mercedes and then she had one more set of gifts to get. The most important gifts were for her Mother and for Rachi, her lifelong friend who was not able to come with her to Bordeaux because her family had forbidden it.

She bought beautiful shawls and bathroom things that she knew her Mother would never buy for herself, and for Rachi she bought a modern outfit by a French designer that she knew Rachi would never be able to buy for herself.

As they drove back to the château, Shaafia allowed herself to swim in an inner pool of gratitude. How fortunate she felt. She was guided, protected and inspired by beings who poured love and wisdom into her. She had the money to pay for all her gifts. She had two suitcases full of what she would take with her to go back to the place of her birth.

Beyond all that, however, what she carried inside was of so much greater worth.

In the late afternoon, Shaafia went with Marie-Louise to the convent. First she found Sister Geneviéve to share what she had been told.

The big nun enfolded the small girl in her arms.

«And so it is just as you said. Each of us is being sent out to do the work that God asks of us.»

When she heard what day Shaafia would be leaving she nodded.

«It is perfect,« she said. «Father Lefait will be leaving for his new position in Martinique very soon and I will be going to a retreat in Lourdes. We will have a special Mass and a great lunch to send us all on our new journeys.»

The final act of the day was to call Casablanca. She called her neighbor Brahim, because her family did not have a phone. She told him that she would be coming back to live there, and he was very pleased. He was very fond of her and proud that she had done so well. He promised to tell her family, and he was sure someone would be there to greet her. Based on her previous experience she was not so sure, but she thanked him for being her messenger. She asked what he would like her to bring him and very sweetly he said that to see her shining face would be all he needed. She had already bought his family a box of very good Bordeaux chocolates.

In the evening, Shaafia took all her purchases upstairs and lovingly wrapped and labelled each one. They would occupy one of her Samsonite suitcases entirely.

In the final days of her stay, Shaafia spent time with each of her adopted family.

She wanted to thank each one for what they had brought, to acknowledge that each one was a part of a wonderful adventure that had brought them together. She found herself eloquent with gratitude.

When she sat with Hélène there were tears. Hélène was feeling more than a little terrified that her most important contact was going to leave, but Shaafia assured her that Pia would look after her, and so would the Lady in Blue and White.

«Even though I became a Muslim?» she whispered.

«Those labels mean nothing,» said Shaafia, «It's what is in our hearts that counts.»

Théophile set up a phone call so Shaafia could say goodbye to Brad. Théophile had to smile when Shaafia suddenly said: «So you will soon be married.»

Obviously there was a strong reaction on the other end, and she smiled at Théophile. Then she said into the phone: «Sometimes in meditation I do receive messages.»

When Brad had recovered his composure, he told her that he would write an afterword to describe how the followers of Pia were beginning to be sent out to the world. She reminded him that he was one of them.

When she had a quiet time with Claire, walking in the cold leafless forest, well rugged up, Shaafia told her that she knew that she would have very important work to do in Morocco.

«Pia's work,» nodded Claire. «I think it will take all your time and effort. Théophile and I have talked about this and we will continue to support you financially.»

«No, no. You do not need to do that.» Shaafia tried to be as firm as she could, but she knew resistance was unlikely to succeed. «In Morocco it does not cost much to live.»

Claire gave a her a long warm hug. «But we both know this is what my daughter would expect of me. How can I resist?»

The following day Claire brought her a large Galerie Lafayette shopping bag. When Shaafia opened the bag, in between the carefully placed layers of tissue, she found a set of superb travelling clothes, exactly her style and size. Claire knew how to design an outfit. Claire insisted she try it on to be sure, and when Shaafia stared at herself in a full length mirror she felt she was looking at a completely new person.

«I want you to feel comfortable as you travel,» said Claire.

«They are so beautiful.» Shaafia was fingering the fabrics. «I could never imagine I would ever have such wonderful clothes.»

«They are what you deserve.»

Then she produced one last gift. She noticed that Shaafia had a simple cloth shoulder bag that was obviously well-used. She had slipped away to a boutique that had all manner of beautifully made handbags and had chosen one that was elegant but not ostentatious.

When Shaafia unwrapped this last gift she could not hold back her tears.

She held the crafted leather to her chest and inhaled its aroma.

They hugged each other with great love.

«Open the bag.»

Inside was a thick envelope. When she opened it she was horrified at how much was there.

Claire put her hands to Shaafia's lips and shook her head.

The day before her flight, Mass took place. Although the head nun and the priest would also be leaving soon, this Mass would be in honour of Shaafia and to ask blessings for her journey. It would also be a time for the nuns to express how much they loved Shaafia and how they sensed that she was going on what they would recognise as missionary work. Every one of them had been deeply affected by their contact with Shaafia from the first moment she had been brought, homeless and lost, to their convent. To them she had been the means by which Pia had reached each one of them and had enriched their vocations immeasurably.

The whole château family was invited of course.

As the Mass began, with Shaafia sitting in the front row, surrounded by so much love, she closed her eyes and allowed herself to drop deep inside. The organ played in the background and in her inner vision she could see the Sharif, the holy man who had first sent her in quest of the bird with crooked wings. It was as if he were standing on the Casablanca railway bridge where he had blessed her as a child. Now with a gentle hand gesture he was beckoning to her. Inwardly she said to him: «I am coming.»

Father Lefait led the Mass and gave an eloquent address to Shaafia, thanking her with all his heart for what she had given them all.

She smiled shyly as he spoke, remembering that it was not so long ago when she was unsure that she would be welcome in a Christian church.

When it was time for the nuns to chant they all looked at her so fondly, it made her cry.

At the conclusion, they had what they had come to think of as Pia's communion.

Accepting the bread from Father Lefait, Shaafia gazed up at the crucifix for the last time. As she stood there, the twisted statue seemed to dissolve into light. She put her hands up to her heart and bowed.

She felt incredibly blessed.

A full and sumptuous lunch had been prepared with all the ingredients coming from the convent itself: fresh vegetable soup without the usual *lardon*, in honour of Shaafia, home-made pain de campagne, roast chicken, and then a grand tarte au pommes with chantilly cream.

Around the huge convent table the nuns wanted to share their stories of Pia and remembrances of how they had first met Shaafia. They laughed endlessly as each told their story and the lunch was filled with joyful animation.

Long into the afternoon, the lunch went on until Berenice had fallen asleep and it was time to leave. The farewell hugs went on for a long time and many of the nuns wanted to give her a little something to remember them by. She ended up with a collection of little scarves, several small statues of the Virgin, and quite a few jars of jam.

On the day of her flight, Shaafia went very early and sat quietly in the peace of the château chapel. One by one the others came. Zena carried in a drowzy Berenice who snuggled up into Shaafia's lap.

A single candle flame rose, still and erect on the altar until suddenly there was a breeze, as if someone had opened a window. Those who had their eyes closed instantly opened them. An electricity filled the room. It was something they had all come to recognise. The door flew open and Marie-Louise rushed in, closely followed by Jourdan.

«She is here,» whispered Marie-Louise and dropped to her knees in front of Pia's wheelchair.

They all turned to look at Shaafia, still with Berenice in her lap.

«Know that I am with you.» said Shaafia, and her body seemed to swell out and become fuller. Angela quietly translated.

«Wherever you go. I am with you. As you have been told. You are wise. The wise know how to listen inside. The wise learn to tell only what is true. You go with all my love. Amour. Amour. Amour.»

There was a long and full silence as each of them absorbed what they had heard.

Berenice broke it by scrambling off Shaafia's lap and coming to the front of the room looking up into the vaulted ceiling of the chapel.

«Bye!» she called, as if she were watching a bird ascending on the breeze.

At breakfast, the table filled with pastries from Jourdan for Shaafia's sendoff, they all talked animatedly about what had been communicated.

«That was Pia, wasn't it?» asked Michael, wanting to be certain.

«In a certain way, yes,» said Shaafia as she avoided Berenice trying to put a big piece of *pain au chocolat* into Shaafia's mouth.

«What does it mean?» asked Zena.

«Pia is not Pia any more.»

«But she spoke, this morning?»

Marie-Louise smiled at Shaafia. «She is with God. She is not handicapped in her body. She is a different Pia.»

Shaafia nodded. «It is like that.»

«She is the voice of the eternal,» said Marie-Louise settling back in her chair with her cup of coffee. «I am her servant.»

Claire leaned over and stroked Shaafia's hand. «When she spoke to you before, your body would change. It would become a bit like hers. But this morning it was different. You were beautiful and, I don't know, kind of glowing.»

Thérèse agreed. «*Tu est si belle.*» Then, in her best newly-acquired English, she said: «So beautiful.»

«So now you go to Morocco, « said Théophile, «not just with our blessings and the blessings of all the nuns, but also from Pia herself.»

Shaafia nodded.

«Just like the wise men,» said Michael. «They went back to their homes and they spoke about what they had seen.»

«Where did they come from?» asked Claire. It was not something she ever thought about.

«Well, mostly it is academic speculation, but most branches of Christianity believe they came from Eastern empires. Some say Arabia, some think Persia, some even think that Gaspar the third King was from India.»

«Maybe he knew King Janaka.» smiled Claire, patting her husband on his arm. The reader of past lives in the ashram in India had confirmed that Théophile had been a king in India, King Janaka.

«So now we have a very wise person from Africa who goes home to tell of the wisdom she has gained.»

«I wanna go.» said Berenice and snuggled closer against Shaafia.

«Maybe you will come and visit me.» whispered Shaafia into her ear.

Her new suitcases, filled with her fancy wardrobe of clothes, her presents from the nuns and many gifts from everyone in the château, as well as all her own gifts for her family and neighbors, sat at the door as she emerged from the chapel for the last time.

Dressed in her new travel outfit, she hugged them all, one after the other, telling each that she loved them, and that they would see each other again and again.

Although the Mercedes van was big, it wasn't big enough for all of them. Marie-Louise had begged to be the driver, and Théophile conceded. Berenice was adamant that she would be going, and while her parents tried valiantly to talk her out of it, they totally failed.

So Thérèse, Michael, Zena, Hélène and Jourdan stood together as the van moved off. Dressed in her new outfit, she had hugged each one long and warmly yet again.

Théophile had called the convent to say they were on their way, and so when Marie-Louise drove up the long drive and circled the fountain with the statues of the little birds, there were the nuns and Father Lefait, all warmly dressed against the cold, waving and blowing kisses. Shaafia asked that the van not stop as she knew she would melt into their arms and not be able to go on.

She looked back as they drove away.

How she loved these nuns.

The Rocade, the circular freeway round Bordeaux, was quiet, and before she knew it, they were driving into the airport. Leaving Marie-Louise to park the van, they found a trolley for the suitcases and escorted Shaafia into the terminal.

She found herself very cordially welcomed at the business class departure desk. The woman was suitably taken with Shaafia's outfit and handbag as well as her expensive suitcases.

At last it was time to say goodbye.

She hugged each one and made them promise that they would come to visit her.

As she hugged the small girl she loved so much, Marie-Louise gave her a tiny medallion of the Virgin. «Protection,» she whispered as she stroked Shaafia's cheek.

Shaafia dropped it into her new handbag.

Berenice clung on as if she would never let go, but eventually Shaafia whispered something into her ear and she pulled back to stare into Shaafia's eyes, and let her go.

As she passed through the security check, she turned and waved one more time.

And then they were gone.

She was on her own.

And yet inside herself she felt not alone at all. It was as if she carried them all with her, their love, their goodwill, their blessings. And beyond that, she now carried inside her the company of others, some formless entirely, others with ethereal forms, but all made for a loving and powerful force to carry her forward.

Claire had insisted that she go straight to the business lounge and when she found it, it was almost a disappointment. She had expected it to be luxurious but it was not much more than an airport waiting room with comfortable chairs, a warm buffet of food and a large array of complimentary Bordeaux wines. The business lounge was shared by different airlines but on this day it was nearly empty. In one corner, a gray-haired man in a suit bent over his laptop but other than the staff of the lounge, no-one else was there.

She was greeted by a young woman in a uniform who offered her a glass of champagne and asked if she needed any help. Shaafia smiled and shook her head. She helped herself to a cup of tea and some cookies and sat by a window over-looking the aircraft outside, several planes with different coloured tails, all nosed into the terminal, lined up ready to carry passengers to other parts of the world. She thought they looked like giant birds, but their wings were certainly not crooked.

There was some quiet piano music in the background, and she found herself becoming very still on the inside.

Then she began to feel a presence. She closed her eyes to concentrate.

There was an inner vibration that was calling her.

Then she heard the voice.

«She will need your help.»

This came to her in Arabic.

Then she heard another voice, not on the inside, but someone yelling in French. A girl with a headscarf was hurrying into the lounge looking behind her and talking loudly into her cell phone.

«They will take my phone as soon as they see I have it. Listen to me. They kidnapped me. I mean really. They came to the apartment. They had a key. They hit me. They held me. This woman guards me all the time. She is really tough. They threw my things into a suitcase and dragged me here.»

Then another woman came into the lounge, fast. She was solid and business-like. The minute she saw the girl with the phone, she grabbed her, hit her across the head and lunged to take the phone. As she did, the girl was screaming into the phone as it disappeared: «I love you! I love you! I love you.»

The woman snatched the phone easily, pushed the girl onto a couch and held her with one arm while stowing the phone into a handbag with the other.

Growling at her in Arabic, the woman told her to be quiet and not to move.

The staff of the business lounge had watched all this with horror, although the man with the laptop seemed oblivious as he had headphones on.

One of the staff, a young man in uniform, came over to the couch.

Speaking in French he asked: «Is everything OK?»

«Yes, yes,» said the woman in Arabic-accented French. «I am very sorry for the disturbance. She is a bit upset. She will be fine in a minute.»

«Can I bring you something?» he asked.

«No thank you. We are fine.»

Shaafia watched them, using the reflection in the window, so she appeared to be looking out at the planes. As she looked at the girl in the reflection she saw how the woman was applying some kind of pressure to the girl's arm, making her writhe in pain. The girl collapsed back against the couch and lay still with her eyes closed. Tears ran down her face. The other woman looked around to see if anyone was watching and seemed to relax a little when she thought there was no-one. The staff were still very aware of them but did nothing more.

As she watched them in the reflection, Shaafia also went inside to sense if there was anything being communicated.

«Wait,» she heard. «She will turn to you.»

Then she closed her eyes and began to repeat her Koranic prayer. She had repeated it almost constantly since she had been given it as a child. Now it was part of her, as close as her heartbeat.

Images began to form in her mind. She could see the girl struggling against swirls of force coming against her. She was reaching out and calling. Far off she could see a young man, but as Shaafia watched, he seemed to fade and the girl became overwhelmed by the forces she faced.

After some time, Shaafia opened her eyes and looked across the room. The girl was staring at her. Very subtly Shaafia dropped her head in acknowledgement before the big woman looked over and scowled.

Shaafia got up to take her empty cup back to the food counter. She was not used to the way things are done in the business lounge and the woman behind the counter smiled very sweetly and thanked her.

Then Shaafia turned and walked towards the two women sitting on the couch.

The big woman watched her warily.

« *As-Salaam-Alaikum.* »

The woman responded but had the dark look of not wanting to be approached.

Shaafia looked down at the girl who was watching her through lowered eyelids.

«Are you flying to Casablanca today?»

The big woman nodded with the merest grunt in response.

Then Shaafia dropped down next to the girl on the couch.

«Are you from there?»

The big woman cut across her with a sharp voice. «She is not well. Please do not disturb her.»

«Oh I am sorry to hear that.» Then she took the girl's one free hand. The woman had a strong grip on the other.

Gently stroking the free hand, Shaafia said: «I am going back to be with my family. I have been studying to be a translator in Bordeaux.»

The girl shyly looked up out of her lowered tear-filled eyes.

«Did you study here in Bordeaux?» Shaafia kept her voice soft and comforting. The woman was scowling, but obviously she did not want to make too big a fuss and draw more attention from the staff.

The girl nodded very slightly but with her free hand she very subtly responded to Shaafia's touch.

Then their flight was called.

The young man in the uniform came over to them and invited them to follow him to the boarding gate.

They were the only three business class passengers on the flight to Casablanca, and were ushered on board before any of the other travellers.

As the Royal Air Maroc stewardess showed her to her seat, Shaafia had to smile to herself, remembering her first journey to Bordeaux, terrified and alone. Now she was returning in a fancy outfit with a wonderful handbag, being treated like a princess.

She was offered a fruit cocktail and aperitif snacks even before the other passengers were allowed to board.

Across from her, the other two women refused any refreshments and the older woman used her size to hem in the girl against the window, even though there was nowhere she could go.

Shaafia settled back into her capacious business class seat and closed her eyes, returning to her Koranic verse. There was a part of her that wanted to dive into a deep pool of gratitude, gratitude for everything that had taken place in the city she was leaving, gratitude for the people she had come to know and love, and beyond all that gratitude for the love that coursed through her. Amour, Pia's love, the love that had no object or subject.

At the same time she was aware of the girl across the aisle. As she repeated her verse she felt more and more that she had a task in front of her with this girl. As she thought of her, she sensed the same presence she had sensed in the business lounge.

«Be ready» said the voice. «We will give her a chance to talk to you.»

She opened her eyes and looked across at the girl, but she was hunched over staring out of the window.

Once the plane had filled, with no other passengers seated in the business class seats, the doors were closed and the plane began to taxi. As she listened to the flight instructions in Arabic, Shaafia began to feel the first sense of going home.

She was pushed back into her soft seat like a welcoming caress, as the plane gathered speed. A ripple of happiness ran through her body and she found herself smiling as she watched the land of Bordeaux drop away.

She was leaving France and she was happy.

Once the plane had climbed to its flight path, the stewardess brought the lunch menu. Shaafia declined the wine for aperitif, surprised that it was even offered but she reasoned that it was an international flight so even a Muslim airline would have to offer wine. The menu did include a Moroccan wine. She accepted an apple juice punch instead.

As the lunch was laid out before her, with a linen table cloth, china plates and silver cutlery, she remembered how the rest of the passengers would be eating with plastic spoons on plastic trays. How lucky she was.

The two women across from her had been given their lunch too, but the girl seemed to be far away and didn't touch hers. The other woman however had begun eating with gusto.

Suddenly she lurched forward and threw up into her tray. Instantly the stewardess was beside her, helping her out of her seat to go to the toilet. The girl had turned in shock and revulsion at the mess, but as soon as the woman had been escorted to the toilet, she looked at Shaafia, who beckoned to her.

The girl jumped from her seat, ignoring the mess.

«I will help you,» said Shaafia.

«Please, please,» the girl begged.

«Quickly, what is your name?»

«Houda Bin Salah.»

«Are you going to stay in Casa?»

«Yes. My family sent this woman and the others to bring me back.»

«Give me your address. I will find you.»

«They are forcing me to marry a man I do not like. A terrible man. Please please help me.»

Quickly Shaafia wrote the girl's address in a little note book that she had in her new handbag.

«Now go back.» said Shaafia. «Have no fear. I will help you.»

Looking fearfully in the direction of the toilet, Houda went back to her seat while the stewardess, along with other crew members, were doing their best to clean up.

Shaafia had no interest in continuing her lunch and she put it aside. Then she sat back and closed her eyes again.

The voice was soft inside. «She has destiny. I gave her that name. She will do what I could not finish.»

«Who are you?»

«I am her grandfather.»

The woman who had been guarding Houda came back from the toilet white- faced and furious.

She began screaming at the stewardess about being poisoned.

Houda shrank back against the window. Shaafia watched carefully from across the aisle.

After fruitlessly trying to placate the angry woman, the stewardess turned to take Shaafia's meal away. She saw it was mostly untouched and she apologised profusely.

«It is not your fault,» said Shaafia. «The food is excellent. I think that woman probably has a stomach bug.»

«You are probably right.» said the stewardess very quietly. «May I at least bring you a cup of mint tea?»

The rest of the flight was uneventful.

The minute the door was opened, Houda's bodyguard hurried her out, hurling one last insult at the stewardess standing at the door. Houda glanced quickly at Shaafia, who gave her a subtle little wave before she was gone.

As Shaafia passed the open door, the stewardess thanked her for her understanding and apologised for the disruption.

«This has never happened to me before.» she admitted.

Shaafia smiled. «You were very professional.» she said.

As a business class passenger she was guided straight to the head of the immigration counter and was through and out to the baggage claim in minutes. Houda and her guardian were already there and the woman had a strong grip on the girl's hand.

Shaafia's two new suitcases and the others' all came at once with their yellow priority tags. By the time Shaafia had pulled her two Samsonites off the conveyer and put them on a trolley, Houda had already been hustled towards the exit.

There was the usual crowd of men with name placards waiting outside the exit doors, but she ignored them, not expecting to be met by anyone, so it was a shock when suddenly she saw her brother-in-law Ahmed, her sister Zarifa's husband.

He greeted her very warmly which made her a little suspicious, as previously he seemed to be resentful that he was being asked to do anything for Shaafia. When she had left in December, she hadn't even bothered to ask him to take her, simply booking herself a taxi.

Now as he eyed her new suitcases and her fancy handbag, he smiled. «You have done well in France.»

She nodded. «It is very good of you to come for me. I was not expecting it.»

«No, no,» he said, «you are family. Of course I would come.»

Then she knew he was going to be trouble.

She had intended to change money at the airport but she did not want him to see that she had so much in her handbag. He took charge of her trolley as they left the terminal building.

As they crossed the kerb, she saw a very large black BMW with two men in sunglasses standing beside it. Just as she passed, they opened the back door as Houda and her bodyguard approached and they bundled her into the back seat.

Inwardly Shaafia sent a prayer. «I will find you Houda. Do not be afraid.»

She stopped to watch the car take off into the press of taxis.

«Do you know them?» asked Ahmed.

Shaafia shook her head.

«Big money.» said Ahmed.

When they reached his Renault, he put her bags in the back but she held tight to her handbag.

Once they had cleared the airport, he began to ply her with questions. How was life in Bordeaux? Why was she coming back? What was she planning to do? Shaafia gave simple non-committal answers. In reality she had no idea yet what she was going to do. She had great faith that it would be revealed to her at the right time, but there was no way she would say that to her brother-in-law. Then he began to ask her about the people she had worked for in Bordeaux. Maybe Shaafia could put in a good word for him with them. They obviously had lots of money and they had certainly appeared to pay Shaafia very well, judging by her luggage and clothes. He was planning to start a new business and he was looking for investors. What did she think?

She took the easy way out and claimed to be very tired. She promised they could discuss this when she had rested.

The evening was setting in, when he drove up the narrow alley to the family house. The minute she heard the car, her Mother rushed out to greet her, quickly followed by her two younger sisters, Hawa and Yamina.

«My dearest Shaafia,» cooed her Mother, holding her daughter in her arms. «I am so happy you have come back.»

She hugged the two girls, both at once.

«I have gifts for you both.» she whispered.

Ahmed excused himself and Shaafia thanked him for coming. «Let's talk soon.» he said, and left, while the two girls having oohed and aahed over the beautiful suitcases, wheeled them into the courtyard. Holding her Mother's hand Shaafia followed them.

She paused at the fig tree, old and gnarled but still surviving.

«Mui,» she said to her Mother. «Whenever I see this tree, I think of Dada».

Her Mother nodded. «Dear Dada, she was so good to you when you were little.» Dada, a homeless runaway sub-Saharan slave had been Shaafia's nanny when she was young. Dada was with her when the Sharif had given her the quest to find the bird with crooked wings. Shaafia always remembered Dada in her prayers.

The two girls put the suitcases in the girls' sleeping area while her Mother ushered her into the kitchen. She had prepared dates and sweetened goat's milk to welcome her daughter home.

The girls joined her and they sat together as she described something of her life in Bordeaux. She kept it very general, the university, and what the city looked like, but they wanted to know more about the château.

This was cut short by her youngest brother Habib who came flying into the house.

«Is she here yet?» he called.

When he saw her in the kitchen, he jumped into her arms. He was almost as tall as her and nearly sent her flying to the floor. She managed to save herself and held him to look at him.

«You are growing fast.»

He proudly showed what he was wearing. His best Barcelona Football shirt with the number 10 on the back. She had bought it for him on her last visit.

She laughed. «So you haven't torn this one yet?»

He grinned. «No, but I gave the other one to my friend because he doesn't have one.»

«Good boy.»

«Did you bring presents?» he asked.

«Maybe.»

«Can I have mine now?»

«Why don't we wait till everyone is here, then you can all open your presents together.»

«Some of our brothers aren't exactly regular in coming home on time, or even coming home at all.» said Hawa.

«If they know Shaafia is here they might make the effort. You could get lucky.» said Yamina, equally scathing of her older male siblings.

«Sadik will come,» said Habib. «I just saw him.» Sadik was the second youngest boy and was Habib's buddy.

However as the time for the evening meal approached, one after the other all the brothers put in an appearance.

Sadik was the shyest of all the boys and he diffidently said *Salaam* to his newly arrived sister. She gave him a hug and he blushed.

Next was Toufik, who came in smelling of cigarettes and covered in engine grease. His Mother yelled at him to get cleaned up, the minute she saw him, and he gave Shaafia a nod on his way to wash.

On his way out he passed their neighbor Brahim who walked in with Loqman. Loqman had a scowl on his face which did not shift when he saw his sister. He was only slightly older than Shaafia but they had never been close.

Brahim was very pleased to see Shaafia, and again she found herself having to front so many questions. Out of the corner of her eye she noticed Loqman watching her with his dark look. She could see that something was troubling him and she sensed it was to do with Brahim. Brahim taught at the college where Loqman went and on several occasions had to step in to make sure Loqman was not expelled for bad behaviour.

«Nothing has changed with Loqman.» she thought.

When Samit arrived, he stood in the doorway with his hands on his hips. «So the star of the family decides to pay us a visit.»

Samit had been the main communicator for the family while Shaafia was in France. He fancied himself as an intellectual and he certainly wrote well. However, he also seemed to have no interest in being employed, spending most of his time in a corner café not far from the house debating world affairs.

He was not unfriendly and he gave his sister a hug. He studied her clothes. «Well, Madame, it looks like you have become very stylish.» He fingered the cloth of her sleeve and nodded. «Very nice.»

She smiled at him. «This time, my brother, I do not come empty-handed.»

«Books?»

«Could be.»

«Give.» he demanded, but with a twinkle in his eye.

She shook her head. «Not yet. First we eat.»

The two oldest girls, now married with small children, arrived with their husbands. Zarifa and Afifa had both brought steaming pots of food to add to the evening meal.

There was greeting and hugs for the little ones and endless questions.

Shaafia never got to finish a complete sentence.

Ahmed tried several times to get Shaafia to talk, but every time she was interrupted and so he soon gave up.

They were about to serve the meal when the other two boys came in together. Ayman and Ihab had both grown moustaches, wore dark glasses and walked with a kind of arrogant swagger which Shaafia noticed right away. They carried darkness with them and it made her shudder. She greeted them courteously and they were civil towards her, but there was an air of distrust in the air.

Brahim excused himself to go back to his family, even though Shaafia's Mother invited him to stay and eat with them.

Now the only family member missing was Nayla. In a quiet aside to her Mother, Shaafia asked about Nayla.

«She has her own life.» sighed her Mother. «When she decides to come she tends to bring disharmony so in one way, although I am ashamed to say this, it is better that she is not here.»

Shaafia nodded. There would have to come a time when she would be forced to confront her sister and she was not looking forward to it. At least on this night she would not be required to start that battle.

The big tajines were brought to the communal table and the lids were lifted to reveal a tantalising aroma of spicy vegetables and chicken. A big bowl of Harissa sauce was on hand to add the last spicy touch.

Now that her husband had passed, Shaafia's Mother would have liked to see the oldest of her sons take his place as head of the family. Ayman was not at all interested in doing that. So she took it upon herself to play that rôle. Now she stood at the head of the table and called them all to be silent. It took a moment to quiet them all, especially the two little granddaughters. One was crying and the other was running and needed to be caught.

«It is so good that I see you all here.» she said. «Our family has had more than its share of trouble, but on this day, we are happy. Our dear Shaafia has returned. We thank God for that. *Ham de Lila.*»

«*Ham de Lila*» was repeated around the room but not by everyone. For some of Shaafia's brothers, her return did not bring them any happiness and they let it show. A larger than usual evening meal was what brought them.

Her Mother repeated the prayer that her husband had recited all his life and then they settled down to eat. The questions kept flowing in Shaafia's direction and she had trouble getting to eat anything.

Finally as the meal was completed and mint tea was served, the two older sisters both said they would have to take their children home.

Shaafia wanted to distribute the presents before they went. She went into the girls' sleeping room and returned with one of her two Samsonites which all by itself caused a stir. Everyone knew what one of those cost.

She quickly turned the codes for the lock so that none of her brothers, who she did not trust, could see the combination.

She had wrapped everyone's present and had affixed their names to it.

She started with the babies first. Zarifa's daughter Khadija had just turned three and was a wild and happy child. She tore at the paper of her gift and when she found the soft white stuffed monkey inside, she let out an excited shriek which made everyone laugh. Afifa's baby and Zarifa's younger one were too little to unwrap their own so their mothers did and were all smiles as two more stuffed animals emerged.

As they needed to leave, Shaafia gave her gifts to her two older sisters, sensible dresses made of fine embroidered cotton that they both loved. Their husbands accepted large boxes of fine Bordeaux chocolates with pleasure and there were hugs and kisses all round before the two families left.

As he passed her, Ahmed said: «Let's talk.»

Now Shaafia turned to her Mother, although she could see that Habib was itching to be next.

As her Mother unwrapped her gifts, she had tears in her eyes. She would never have bought a cashmere sweater for herself, nor a silk shawl with fine tassles. She had never in her life been able to afford the fine bath soaps and perfumes in their pretty boxes. She held up all her gifts and then being made to model the clothes, the two younger girls made the shrill high-pitched joyful calls that are so common in Morocco when people are happy.

The two younger sisters got their gifts together and they rushed off to the girls' sleeping area to put them on immediately. When they emerged they sashayed from side to side, showing off their new fancy jeans and colourful t-shirts. Ihab started to whistle at them and Shaafia's Mother frowned but it was not too dark, as she said: «They are not very modest, my daughters.»

«*Mui*,» smiled Shaafia, «They are modern girls.»

For Habib, Shaafia had chosen various memorabilia celebrating his idol, Lionel Messi, and he was thrilled. He threw his arms around his sister and kissed both her cheeks.

For each of her other brothers there were the books that she had been guided to buy. She was interested to see how they would react.

She went up in age. Sadik's book was written in French for young adults which told the story of a young man who went to explore in Equatorial Guinea and discovered treasure. She knew Sadik was not a great reader, but she hoped this book would inspire him to read more. He shyly thanked her and gave her a little quick hug.

Then Loqman opened his gift. His dark look had faded and he opened his gift with interest. Also in French, his book was an historical account of the life of the great-grandfather of the Prophet Abraham. His name was Luqman and it was said he lived for five hundred years. In the Koran he is referred to as «The man to whom God endowed wisdom». When Shaafia had been guided to choose this book, buried way in the back of Mollat, she felt a great thrill of excitement. Maybe this would inspire her brother.

His reaction was carefully neutral. He turned the book over and read the back cover. «Hmm,» he said, «trying to get me to behave, are you?»

She smiled.

«I thought you might like it, even if it doesn't do that.»

He gave her the required hug.

With Toufik she scored. When he tore off the paper and saw the glossy photo book on the history of Harley Davidsons he was ecstatic. He had no hesitation in giving his generous sister a huge smelly hug.

«Well somebody got lucky.» sneered Samet, and he leaned forward for his gift.

It wasn't his turn.

Ihab had his back against a far wall watching all this through his dark glasses even though it was now dark outside.

«Ihab?» said Shaafia turning to him. «You were not expecting a gift from me?»

«Why should I? What did I ever do for you?»

She studied him for a long moment and the room seemed to be still, held in suspense.

Something arose inside her, that made her smile. «It is not what you have done for me, it is what you will do for me very soon.»

«Like what?»

«We shall see.» and she passed him a wrapped gift.

It was Victor Hugo's «Les Miserables».

«You have not read this book?» she asked.

«Nah. Too classical for me.»

«When you read it, you will find the main character is just like you.»

«Jean Valjean,» said Samet, proud of his literary prowess. «Good pick, sister.»

Ihab had spent some time in prison as had the main character in the novel.

«Now,» said Samet. «Surprise me.»

His gift was heavy and he weighed it in his hands. When he took off the wrapping, there were two books.

«One for last time, one for now,» said Shaafia. She had promised to bring him a book on her previous visit but had no time.

The first was a thin plain little book with the title «The Science of Non- Philosophy» by François Laruelle. Samet frowned. «What is this?»

Shaafia smiled. «I thought you were an expert on philosophy.»

«Yeah and maybe sometimes I fool even myself.» He quickly read the back cover and he nodded. Then he turned to the second one and laughed as he read the title. «The Cultural Heritage of Arabic Cafés.».

«You know where I spend my days.» he said.

«You are part of a long tradition.»

He was pleased as he flipped through the pages and saw famous cafés where intellectuals and poets throughout the Arabic world had met over the years. Many of them were the most famous writers and artists in Egypt, Algeria, Tunisia and even Morocco.

He gave her a genuine hug.

Only Ayman was left.

Shaafia had always felt intimidated by her oldest brother, who had never said a generous word to her in her life. Nonetheless, when she had held him in her awareness in the Bordeaux bookstore she was guided to a shelf that surprised her. Who would have guessed it would be an Arabic novel?

Like his brother, he had not removed his dark glasses and had stayed with his back to the wall. Shaafia held up his wrapped gift. She had no fear of him now. She could look directly at him, challenging him almost.

He pushed himself off the wall and took the two steps needed to reach her.

«Thanks.» he said gruffly.

It was a novel, written in Arabic. «For Bread Alone», by Mohamed Choukri.

«Have you read this book?» she asked.

He shook his head.

«It's a great book.» said Samet. «I wrote an essay on that and got a really good report.»

Ayman shrugged. «Better read it then.»

As a last gift, Shaafia brought out a big box of artisan chocolates from one of the best Bordeaux chocolatiers which was passed from hand to hand.

The quality of the chocolates was expressed in the silence as they each bit into one.

The other presents in the suitcase were for Nayla, Rachi and the neighbors. Shaafia closed the suitcase and spun the lock.

«My daughter,» said her Mother. «You have been most generous to us all.»

There were murmurs of agreement even from her most reticent brothers.

When at last she unrolled her sleeping mat next to her two younger sisters, and lay back for the first time in the house where she was born, Shaafia turned to her Koranic verse.

The repetitions of the verse took her deep inside herself, where she felt deeply at peace.

«And now the work can begin».

Was that her thought or was it some inner voice?

She could not tell.

The First Day

It brought a sweet inner smile when Shaafia heard the Muezzin call in the early morning. She was home, sleeping as she had done all her childhood on a simple mat on the floor next to her sisters.

Hawa and Yamina quietly got up, not to disturb their sister, dressed for school and went out to breakfast. Once they had gone Shaafia sat up and began to repeat her treasured Koranic verse. After a while the repetitions became more and more subtle and she found herself floating in a soft airy place where diaphanous beings floated by. She felt at peace, without any need to think. As she floated in this space she began to recognise some of the forms. To her delight, her sister Adila, who had died when they were both so young, appeared and waved to her. Dada was there. Her Father was there giving her his blessing. It was as if they were welcoming her home not just to the physical house but also to their world, whatever that was.

She finally emerged, feeling deeply moved by where her soul had been.

Her Mother was cleaning up from breakfast and Habib was on his way to school, proudly carrying some of his Messi gifts to show his friends. He gave her an impulsive hug and ran off.

«So my daughter,» said her Mother, bringing her a cup of mint tea and a warm piece of freshly baked flat bread. «What are your plans?»

«I am not sure yet.»

«God will show you. *Inche Allah.*»

They sat quietly together sipping tea.

«My brothers?» asked Shaafia, «How are they doing?»

Her Mother shook her head. «It is hard for me to say this but I fear for them.»

«There is something about Ayman and Ihab that is different.»

«It is true.» sighed her Mother. «You see the way they walk, how they look?»

«They wear dark glasses even inside.»

«They have found some work at least.»

«So that is a good thing, isn't it?»

«To work is good, of course. I only wish it was a different kind of work.»

«What do they do?»

«They work for a man who is in business, but I fear he is not such a good person. They are maybe what you would call security. I worry that they will get into trouble, or get hurt.»

«They are like bodyguards?»

«I am not sure. But they seem to have money suddenly. And they live in an apartment that their boss owns.»

«That at least is a good change. Do they give you money for the house?»

Her Mother shook her head. «I have not been brave enough to ask.»

«I will speak to them.»

Her Mother had to smile. «You are the smallest of all my children,» she said, «and yet you have become so strong.»

Shaafia accepted her Mother's invitation to join her in the *hamam*. Their house had basic running water and a toilet, but the *hamam* was where they went for bathing.

As they walked the short distance, Shaafia reminded her Mother of when she went with her Mother and sisters to the *hamam*, after the Sharif had given her his blessing, and how she had developed all those strange lumps. Her Mother nodded.

There were very few women there, as they each gave the coin to the attendant at the entrance and received their black liquid soap and the wooden bucket. After they had soaped and scrubbed each other's backs with the rough gloves that take off the dead skin, they sat in the hottest part of the *hamam* to sweat.

It was as they sat together, by themselves, that Shaafia decided to tell her Mother about Pia. She reminded her Mother of what the Sharif had told her and how she never forgot. She looked and looked for that bird, not really knowing what she was looking for. Her Mother was a little shocked when Shaafia described being taken in by the nuns in Bordeaux when she had nowhere else to live, but as Shaafia described their generosity she began to smile. Clearly they were good people and Shaafia obviously loved them.

The room filled with steam as they sat side by side. Shaafia described her early difficult relationship with Madame de Fortelle which changed after her son died. Then when the son's wife arrived in France from Australia, Shaafia met Pia and heard her voice inside. She peered at her Mother through the fog to see what her Mother's reaction was. She had her eyes closed, so it was hard to tell, but as Shaafia went on describing how Pia knew things that no-one else knew and the effect she had on the people around her, she saw her Mother nodding.

«In our tradition, although it is not spoken of openly, there are such people,» her Mother said. «That you should be the one to convey her wisdom is a great blessing.»

And so, just as her Father had understood, so Shaafia could see that her Mother did too. It filled her with joy.

«So now you are here,» said her Mother. «It must be God's will. *Ham delilah.*»

Sweaty as they both were, Shaafia gave her Mother a long loving hug.

After the *hamam,* Shaafia caught the bus to go to the commercial centre of the city to her bank. It made her smile to think of herself, just a simple young Moroccan girl, with her own bank account.

She had carefully locked her new handbag in her suitcase in case any of her brothers had thought to explore her belongings. Sadly she could not trust any of them, at least the older ones.

Now she sat jammed in with commuters of all shapes and sizes holding her precious cargo against her chest.

The impressive facade of the Attijariwafa Bank on Boulevard Moulay Youssef greeted her as it had the first time she ventured there. Now dressed as a fashionable young woman, she caught sight of herself in the glass as she approached. There was a flash of deep gratitude as she saw her reflection, a sense of confidence that filled her with strength of purpose.

The young woman who ushered her into an inner office was clearly rather impressed with her outfit and her handbag. They reviewed her account together, Shaafia handed over her euros, got herself a good supply of dirhams and organised getting herself her first ever credit card. When all her transactions were complete, the young woman gave her her business card and invited her to make contact any time she had need. They shook hands, and the young woman walked with Shaafia to the entrance.

Returning to her Mother's house Shaafia gave her a large wad of dirhams, and her Mother kissed her on both cheeks.

«You must also take care of yourself, my daughter.» she said.

«I do *Mui*,» and she told her Mother about getting a new credit card. «I have a bank account, so my money is safe. I will give you money each week.»

Her Mother had never had a credit card and was not even sure how it worked. Her life had been always cash in hand.

Shaafia's next outing was to see her friend Rachi. She had carefully locked her remaining gifts in her Samsonite which by now was almost empty. She took out the gifts for Rachi, relocked the suitcase and walked the few blocks to her house.

Rachi's Mother came to the door and was delighted to see Shaafia.

«You have finished all your studies?»

So Shaafia had to explain that she was not going to complete her Degree, that she was in fact back in Casablanca to stay.

«So it was not a good thing to go to France?»

«It was a wonderful experience to go to France,» said Shaafia being careful what she said, knowing how against the whole idea Rachi's parents had been. «But I have decided to come home and support my Mother.»

«You are a good daughter, we must find you a very suitable husband.»

She ushered Shaafia inside, where she found Rachi cooking. Rachi threw down her big wooden spoon when she saw her friend and threw herself into her arms.

«I am so happy to see you.» she moaned into Shaafia's hair.

«You must stay for lunch.» said Rachi's Mother.

Shaafia helped with the last preparations for lunch, wanting to be alone with Rachi before she gave her the gifts.

Rachi's older sisters and her brother had all married, and now lived in their own houses so she was the only child left at home. Her Father came to join them for lunch.

He worked in the post office round the corner and always came home for lunch, except during Ramadan.

The conversation was all about Bordeaux and once again Shaafia very carefully chose what to say. Like his wife, Rachi's Father was very gratified to hear that Shaafia had decided to come home to help her Mother.

He nodded at Rachi. «You see? We made the right decision for you.»

He believed this was absolutely the right thing for a good Muslim girl to do, look after their parents. He spoke about how happy he was that his last daughter would soon be married and bring him more grandchilden. Once she was married then he could think about retiring.

After lunch, Rachi's parents both went for a nap, and the two girls went up onto the flat roof to talk. They whispered quietly, not just to avoid disturbing the sleeping couple, but because Shaafia wanted to tell Rachi exactly what had happened since last they spoke.

Rachi opened her gifts and cried tears of pleasure. Right then and there she put the new clothes on. They were soft luxurious fabrics and she fingered them with delight.

«I will never be allowed to wear these outside in the street but they are so beautiful. How could you afford to buy such things?»

Rachi already knew about Pia and the château and that Shaafia was being paid to be a translator. Now Shaafia shared what had happened since her last visit home and how she knew that she was being sent back because there was work to do.

«Do you know what is this work?»

«Not yet. They will tell me.»

«You can still hear Pia?»

«Not so much. I hear others. Sometimes I know who they are, sometimes I do not.»

«You are not frightened by this?»

When Shaafia shook her head, Rachi added: «You are sure they are good voices? I mean it could be dark magic.»

«No. I am certain that all of them are virtuous. The light is in them and I feel so good when I am in their company. I know they are good.»

Rachi stared off into the distant grey haze of the afternoon warmth of the city. They stood together and watched as a pair of crows rose and circled above them. Several blocks away Shaafia could see the minaret of the Mosque. She felt a strong pull to go there, as if the minaret was calling to her, like the Muezzin's call for prayers.

Rachi broke into her thoughts.

«How lucky you are.» she said. «You have had such good fortune.» Then she turned to Shaafia. «Do you think they would help me?»

«I think so. I also think you are being asked to be patient.»

Rachi sighed. «I am not very good at that.»

They went downstairs and as Rachi still had her new clothes on, her Mother, who had just emerged from her siesta, was amazed.

«Such beautiful clothes. This is what they wear in France?»

Shaafia smiled. «Not all the time. This is for special days.»

«Yasser will be very impressed to see you in these.» said her Mother running her fingers over the soft fabric.

At the mention of her future husband, Rachi glanced at Shaafia. She was not looking forward to that event at all.

As they parted, Shaafia promised to come and visit often and Rachi gave her a long, almost desperate hug.

She was drawn to go to the Mosque, but decided to see her Mother first. When she arrived home her Mother was in the courtyard hanging clothes.

«Ah,» she said, «Haj Kabir is looking for you.»

«He was here?»

Haj Kabir was a sufi, the head of the Mosque to which the Jilani family had gone all Shaafia's life. He was greatly revered, and she was surprised that he would come to see her.

«No, he sent one of his boys. He asks that you go to see him before evening prayers.»

Shaafia smiled to herself. She had already heard the call to come. «Then I must go right away.»

She ran into the girls' sleeping area, changed her clothes to look less French, and took a box of chocolates from her suitcase to take as a gift.

Walking the few blocks to the Mosque, she found herself repeating her Koranic verse in time with her steps. Her heart felt light.

When she arrived, she washed her hands and feet and went into the women's section of the Mosque. She sat for a long time, her verse repeating itself as naturally as her heartbeat. Then she felt a presence behind her and there he was.

She bent to kiss his hands and he put his hand on her head.

«I was aware that you were coming. I saw you in my mind.»

She smiled and offered him the chocolates, and he chuckled as he unwrapped the gift. «Oh you are tempting me to indulgence with such luxuries.»

He invited her to follow him and took her to his residence next to the Mosque. Here Myriam, his wife, made mint tea and they sat together in a small courtyard as his young son ran and played around their feet.

He opened the box of chocolates and watched as his little son agonised over which one to choose.

He handed the box of chocolates to his wife after she had poured the tea.

«Please remove this terrible temptation.» he joked to his wife.

«You wanted to see me?» asked Shaafia shyly, once his wife had taken the child and the chocolates back to her kitchen.

«Yes,» he nodded. «I have received a request. Do you know of Haj Hussein?»

She frowned. The name seemed vaguely familiar.

«Your Father knew him well. He was a great man, a learned sufi. Many people benefitted from his compassion and his wisdom.»

«He is here in Casablanca?»

He smiled. «In a way I could say yes, but in truth he passed away quite some years ago. He is still however very present to me.»

«The request is to do with Haj Hussein?»

«He gave it himself. In my dreams he came and he told me that the girl who can hear the divine is coming home.»

A shiver ran along Shaafia's spine, an electricity that she had become accustomed to associating with Pia. There was a presence in the courtyard as the Sufi was speaking.

«I believe he was referring to you, my child.»

She nodded, not able to speak.

«He told me that she, which means you, have already promised to take care of his granddaughter.»

She stared at him.

«Houda.» she whispered.

He nodded, surprised. «Yes, that is her name.»

«He gave her that name.» smiled Shaafia.

«I believe he did. So you know this girl?»

Shaafia described her encounter at the Bordeaux airport and what had happened on the journey.

He nodded as she spoke. When she got to the point where the grandfather had spoken to her, he nodded and put his hand up to his heart.

«Such a gift as you have been given is rare and is indeed divine. It is my honour to know you.»

A small tear ran down her cheek and she bowed her head.

«*Sidi,*» she said, using the honourific of respect. «I do not feel worthy of what you say and yet I know this is my destiny.»

«To feel worthy or not, that is not a useful activity. For whatever reason, you have been chosen, *Ham delilah,* and I see that you are willing. To be willing is the right activity.»

She nodded and dried her eyes.

«So what am I to do? What does he ask of me?»

He stroked his beard frowning.

«I must be honest with you, I am not sure.» he said. «So far, he has said that you will take care of Houda. How that is to be done, I cannot say.»

«Can you tell me what you know about her? I know that she lives here. She gave me her address.»

«So this is what I know. It is something of a long story.»

He leaned forward and poured more tea.

« Haj Hussein, although he was a greatly respected sufi and a wonderful scholar and teacher, was not such a successful man in the material world. Through his wife, his family owned a wonderful house near Murdoch Park and many sufis and scholars would meet there, chanting the Koran and holding scholarly debates. I went there many times, as did your Father. Sadly however, Haj Hussein did not have the means to keep the house in good condition. In addition, and this is a very sad thing to have to say, he had two daughters and no sons. One of his daughters, Daad, engaged with the darkness.»

«What does this mean?»

«Why and how she began to practise black magic, I do not know, but she became enslaved. Once you enter that dark tunnel it is very difficult to emerge again. They say it is like being caught in the teeth of a crocodile. The teeth of the crocodile point back into the rear of his mouth. The more you struggle, the further into his mouth you go.»

He paused, watching Shaafia's reaction. Her face was calm, and yet he could see that she was sensing the significance of what he was telling her.

«She is still doing this?» asked Shaafia. It was as if she already knew this.

«She is. She has become very powerful and she has an entourage of other women who are the same. Some are very clever at disguising themselves and appear like normal women. They might work in a bank for example.»

Shaafia jumped as if someone had prodded her with a sharp stick.

He leaned forward looking closely into her eyes.

«What do you see?»

«She works in a bank.»

«Who does?»

«It is my sister Nayla.»

«Ah yes. This has just been shown to you?»

«Your words were like a sword cutting through a curtain that I did not know was there. Always I have been wary of her but I never knew why. When you gave that example, suddenly I could see it.»

He nodded. «Your Father knew that she was like this.»

«He never spoke of it.»

«No. He knew that it would only make things worse.»

Shaafia nodded, feeling a lot of love for her Father who had such discipline.

«It is strange,» she mused, «that such darkness can thrive in this world.»

«In truth,» said Haj Kabir, «in this world, there are what you might call the never ending opposing forces. For all the good there is in the world, there is the opposite. That such a good man as Jamil Jilani should have such a daughter, that such a holy man as Haj Hussein should have such a daughter, this is the mystery of the universe.»

«I have always felt that my sister was not a nice person, but I had never thought that she was, perhaps, a witch, one who practises evil against others.»

«I suspect that your Father knew you would discover this for yourself at some point.»

She nodded and then she smiled. «My two younger sisters said to me that they thought she was a witch and I had an intuition that there might be some truth to that. Now I know.»

They sipped their tea in a long silence. Shaafia was coming to terms with this knowledge of her sister's intent, while beginning to understand that she herself had been protected from Nayla's malevolence. She was also feeling a new and powerful force inside her, a warrior-like determination. «I will fight,» she felt herself vowing. «I will fight.»

Then she looked up. «This woman is the Mother of Houda?»

«No she is not.»

«Oh yes. You said Haj Hussein had two daughters.»

«The younger daughter is Rana. She was very beautiful when she was young.»

«But not evil?»

«Not at all. She is a most wonderful person, loving and generous.»

«She is the Mother of Houda.»

«That is so.»

«And yet something terrible is happening to Houda. Is it because of the other daughter, Daad?»

«It is hard to say. I will tell you what I know.»

He leaned forward and poured more tea. As he did, his wife came out to see if the pot needed reheating. His little son came running out behind her and ran up to his Father. Haj Kabir opened the folds of his robe to catch his son and scooped him up into his arms. He tickled the boy who squealed and wriggled away.

«We speak of Rana, the wife of Bin Salah.» Haj Kabir said to his wife and she nodded.

«Myriam knows her well.» he said to Shaafia, «They are the same age and grew up together.»

«Rana is a very dear person,» said his wife, «but she has a very difficult life.» She poured the last of the tea for them both, took the pot, called to the boy and led him back into the house.

Haj Kabir sipped his tea, then put it down.

«I will speak of Haj Hussein.» he said. «In this way perhaps you will know what it is that you are supposed to do.»

Shaafia sipped her tea and felt a calmness come over her. It was as if she had now arrived at a new place in her journey. On the one hand was the knowledge, the certainty of what her sister was and had been for so long. On the other, she felt the excitement of what was being revealed to her about the work that she would do. The reason for her return to Morocco was becoming, bit by bit, clearer and clearer.

«Haj Hussein was born into a family of Sufis, as you and I have been. His family was poor, and they lived in a small house just a few blocks from this

Mosque. The house is still there. His Father was devout but not so fortunate in business. He had a small shop where he made and repaired chairs. He was very good at carving wood, but somehow his family always seemed to struggle. He had three sons. His oldest son Omar went into the military and served in the French Navy.»

He paused to sip his tea. As he did, his wife returned with a fresh pot. Once she had gone back inside, he went on.

«This son is part of the story of the house but we shall come back to him in a moment. Hussein was the second son, and from an early age it was clear that he had some kind of gift. My Father told me that he had a light around him, even as a child. He would spend days in the Mosque sometimes sitting by himself and often in tears. People would ask him why he was crying and he would say that everywhere he looked it was so beautiful that it made him cry. My Father believed, even as a child, he could see things. He was a very special child. Some people thought he was perhaps not right in his head, but my Father could see that he had something. I first met him as a young man, when my Father became the head of this Mosque. I could see he was already something of a sharif. He had God's benevolence in his eyes.»

«You could see he was a sharif?» asked Shaafia.

«Most surely. And as his life went on it became more and more clear to me. My Father, he was very sure of this. So his Father passed away when he was quite young and the third son who was a very simple young man, took over the shop with the woodwork. Hussein had no ability with his hands at all. He was considered by some people to be a burden on his family because he did not work. Mostly he prayed.»

«He was a Haji?»

«He was. When my Father decided that I should take the Haj, he invited Hussein to go. My Father paid for him. We went to Mecca, the three of us. Much happened to me there that I will not speak of now to disrupt this story, but one day I will tell you. What I will say is that Hussein became even more of a sharif there. He became a great sharif. He became Haj Hussein.»

«*Ham delilah.*» said Shaafia.

«So now I go back to his brother, Omar. In the French Navy he had served under Admiral Bousquet. He had impressed that Admiral so much that when the Admiral retired, he invited Omar to come and work for him in his house. It was Admiral Bousquet who built that house. Perhaps you have seen it on Boulevard de Londres. It is shaped like a boat, and even the land on which it sits is shaped a bit like a boat.»

Shaafia shook her head. «I do not know it. I have never been to that part of the city.»

«I will take you there. It is very close to the Royal Palace.» He looked at her and saw that she had a slight frown. «I am not tiring you with this long story?»

«No. Not at all. It is just that as you speak, I see images, fleeting images of people and places. I do not know what it means. They are not people that I recognise.»

He nodded. «Perhaps I am invoking them. Does it frighten you?»

«No. I think it is important. Please go on.»

«So Omar went to work for the Admiral in his house. By now Omar was married and had two children. There is a row of small buildings behind the big house and Omar and his family lived there. The Admiral's wife had died of the Spanish flu, but he had a daughter, whose name was Florence. She lived with him in the house, it is called «*Darou Al Bahr*», Ocean House. I do not remember now how it came about, but somehow Omar took his brother Hussein to the house. Something very mystical happened there, because Florence became completely attached to Hussein. She told him, I think almost as soon as she met him, that she was to marry him.»

«She was Muslim?»

«Not then. She converted very soon after she met him.»

«She is Houda's grandmother?»

«Exactly.»

«She is still alive?»

He shook his head. «When Haj Hussein passed, she died the following day. Some people believe it was black magic practised by her older daughter.»

«Daad.»

«I do not believe that. I believe that Florence had the capacity to choose when to go. When he went, it was a day full of the most powerful energy. He warned us that it was his time, and we gathered in the house and we chanted and prayed with him. Many sufis gathered there. He was by then very frail, but he looked radiant, and then at a certain moment he gazed at us all, one after the other, and took his final breath. It was a blessed passing. The following day Florence died too.»

«And Houda's Mother?»

«Ah yes, I got a bit lost in the story. As I said, Rana, the younger daughter, was very beautiful and many men wanted to marry her. However, Haj Hussein was in financial difficulties, so he looked for a suitor who had money to take care of her and hopefully provide support for the house.

«But the Admiral owned the house, didn't he?»

«Yes. He designed it and had it built.»

«But you said that Haj Hussein wanted someone to support the house.»

«Ah, please forgive me, I have left out one important step. Yes. Soon after Florence married Haj Hussein, her Father became very ill and he was taken back to France to the military hospital in Marseille, where he died. And so Florence inherited the house and whatever other assets her Father had.

For many years they lived happily in that house, Florence gave birth to the two girls, Daad and Rana, and the house became a centre of spiritual learning and fellowship. Great sufis would come there. My Father would take me very often and I would hear wonderful discourses and the most elevating chanting.

However, the money that Florence inherited from her Father did not last long. I am afraid as great a sufi as Haj Hussein was, he was not gifted when it came to money.

Various men persuaded him to invest Florence's inheritance in property or business assuring him that he would profit. Somehow he did not recognise that these projects were almost all unwise. And at the same time, he was open-hearted in his generosity. While he had money, he would give it away. He would take care of poor families, or women who had lost their husbands.»

«Florence could not stop him?»

He smiled. «She was very devoted to him. Whatever he did, she supported.»

Shaafia nodded. «Devotion is important, but also important is to take care of your family.»

«That is true. In this case devotion to her husband was the dominant force. Eventually there was very little left.»

«Do you think that was why Daad took to black magic?»

He shrugged. «Perhaps. It could have been a factor. Maybe as she saw her Father lose all his money, she felt powerless.»

«So the daughters were both married?»

«Daad, as the older daughter, married and moved with her husband to Fez where he worked. I do not know if she was already in the grip of the dark practices or not. However, I would say that in the beginning, there was peace in the house, once she had gone. I did hear that her husband refused to help support Haj Hussein, but of that I am not sure.»

«She had children?»

«One son. I do not know what became of him.»

«And Rana?»

«As time went on, the money situation became more and more pressing. There were many men who admired her. Eventually it was that man Hamza Bin Salah. He was a big businessman. He had been introduced to Rana by one of his friends. I am told the minute he saw her, he was certain he must marry her. When he approached Haj Hussein, it was at a time when the money situation was very serious. Hamza Bin Salah promised to take care of Rana and provide financial support for Haj Hussein and Florence. Haj Hussein was sure it was a gift from God and he agreed.»

«And Rana accepted to marry him.»

«She had no choice. This was still the time when girls were expected to marry the man their parents choose for them.»

«Haj Hussein thought this was the right man to marry his daughter?»

«He was persuaded. It is one of the few actions in his life that I think he regretted.»

«He knew what kind of man he was?»

«He most likely did, but he was persuaded it would protect his daughter.»

«So this Hamza Bin Salah is Houda's Father.»

«That is so.»

«And now he is forcing Houda to marry someone that she does not want to marry.»

«It could be. This I did not know.»

«It must not happen,» Shaafia said with quite some force.

The Sufi gazed at her for a long moment, then he said: «We will see.»

His wife came out to remind him that it was almost time for prayers and he got up. «I am so happy to see you and to share with you what I know about our beloved Haj Hussein. I think we have much to think about. We must speak again soon and I will take you to see the house.»

Haj Kabir went into his house to prepare for evening prayers and Shaafia went to the Mosque. She washed her hands and feet before she entered and then sat in the women's area and closed her eyes. It was the first time she had been to the Mosque since her Father had died. She thought of him as she sat there and sent a deeply felt prayer of gratitude for his life.

«This is the work.» she heard. Unsure of whose voice this might be, visions passed before her closed eyes. Some she knew, the Lady in Blue and White, but others were new to her. Perhaps one of them was Haj Hussein but she was not certain. At the same time there was the presence of her sister Nayla and other women, all with dark auras around them. Drawing her consciousness into focus, she banished the dark visions from her mind, and as she did she heard the voice of Haj Kabir over the loudspeakers beginning the prayers.

She felt a warmth fill her heart and she went through the ritual movements as the prayer was called, and at their conclusion she sat quietly bathing in the afterglow of the devotions.

She walked the few blocks home, and as she passed her neighbor's house, she saw Brahim and suddenly remembered that she had a gift for him. She ran back to her house, unlocked the suitcase and returned.

He had waited for her sitting on the small wall in front of his house, and he smiled as she presented her gift.

«You are most generous.» he said, impressed with the fancy box the chocolates came in.

«I am very grateful to you for being such a good neighbor.»

«We should always take care of each other.» he responded.

«I appreciate that you take care of my brother.»

He nodded. «I rather wish he would take care of himself. He is not a bad person, but he seems not to be able to stay focused on his studies.»

«Something has happened again? Yesterday he did not look happy.»

«He did not do the assignments his class was given. I had to negotiate a settlement. He must finish the work by the end of the week.»

«I am sorry that he gives you such trouble.»

«I try to help as best I can.»

She thanked him again and went home.

She helped her Mother with the evening meal and greeted her sisters as they came home. They had homework so they were excused from helping.

When Loqman came in, Shaafia looked him right in the eye and told him about what Brahim had said.

«You will do the assignment?» she asked.

«If I have to,» he muttered. «It's such boring stuff.»

«Brahim is good to you. You owe it to him.»

«I know.» and he wandered off into the boys' sleeping area.

When she finally went to bed, Shaafia lay in the dark, listening to the easy breathing of her two sisters. She had a lot to think about. Her mind was full of thoughts and questions, and she was restless.

At last she got up and went outside.

There was a bright moon, almost full, and she sat under the gnarled branches of the fig tree and gazed up at it.

She recalled how her Australian friend Kate had shared that she could silence her thoughts by leaning her head against a tree. Kate had learned this from the Australian aborigines in the desert.

Now Shaafia leaned back and tilted her head so that it rested against the old trunk of the fig.

It was as if her thoughts were sucked out of her mind, like dust blown away in the wind.

A deep peace descended and she stayed a long time, still and quiet.

First Steps

Once again in the early morning Shaafia feigned sleep till the house became quiet, and then she emerged. She sat with her Mother in the morning sun in the courtyard, over mint tea and flatbread dipped in olive oil.

«Why did Haj Kabir want to see you?» her Mother asked.

Shaafia had to be a little evasive in her response, not sure how her Mother would respond.

She said that Haj Kabir had a feeling that she was back in Casablanca and he wanted to see her.

Her Mother smiled.

«He thinks very highly of you.»

Shaafia nodded.

Then she made a decision and said: «He told me something that was very surprising. It is to do with Nayla.»

A dark look came over her Mother's face. She nodded grimly. «I suppose you would have to know about that at some point. Your Father and I did not want to scare you children.»

«You have known what she is, all along?»

Her Mother nodded.

«How did you find out?»

«Your Father knew. He could see it and there was a sufi whose daughter had been the one to turn her.»

«The daughter of Haj Hussein.»

«Yes.»

«Do you know how that happened? Why Nayla became like that?»

«Your Father used to say that all his children came into the world with a little bundle of mysterious objects. Each child had to discover what they carried and make use of them as best they can. He always felt you did very well with what you brought. Nayla chose a different path.»

«My brothers are still trying to find theirs.»

«It is so.»

«Hawa and Yamina think she is a witch.»

«They are as clever as you. They will do well.»

They sipped their tea in silence.

At last Shaafia said: «Do you worry about what Nayla is doing?»

«Of course. She is a curse on our family.»

«But you continue to welcome her.»

«She is also still my daughter.» Then she added: «And if I were to banish her from the house, she would be even worse. Better the devil you can see than the one you cannot.»

«Have you ever told her that you know what she is?»

«She knows. She is not stupid. She could see that her Father knew and did not approve, but she did not care.»

«There must be some way to deal with her.»

«Be careful my child. What she does is not something easily dealt with. It is better not to confront her.»

She accompanied her Mother for shopping and Shaafia paid for everything. Her Mother proudly introduced her newly returned daughter to all her friends and the shopkeepers. They visited the little shop where her Father had worked with his brother, her uncle Samad, selling all different kinds of tea. He seemed happy to see Shaafia. She kissed his hand and gave him a small box of chocolates from her diminishing store of gifts.

She stood still in the middle of the shop and sensed how it was.

Then she turned to face her uncle and very sweetly asked him: «How much do you give each week for my family?»

Her Mother was shocked that she had asked such a direct question, and Samad frowned.

«It varies according to how business is going.» he said with more than a little edge to his voice.

«To whom do you give it?»

«Usually to one of your brothers.»

«This must change.» said Shaafia, and there was a note of determination that made him take a step back.

«In what way?»

«You will keep a book of the sales you have made, every day. Do you already do this?»

He shook his head. «Not exactly.»

«Then I shall buy such a book and bring it to you. You will write what you have to spend and you will write exactly what money you receive, and then you will give exactly half of what is left after your expenses to my Mother. Every Friday before you close before prayer time, my Mother and I will come, or she will come with one of my younger sisters, Hawa or Yamina. You will show the book to me or my sister to show what expenses you have had and how much money you have made in the week. You will give the money to no other person.»

He was stunned.

Her Mother stared at her and several times opened her mouth as if to speak, but thought better of it.

Finally Samad said: «Your Father and I worked together for many years. We did our best. It was not always easy. I hope you do not think I have been anything but honest.»

«I do not make any suggestion like that, but I sense that it is time to change. I fear that if you do not, then this business will not prosper. We will return this Friday.»

Then she kissed his hand again and smiled at him.

«With this change I think we will do well.»

Shaafia then told her Mother to take whatever tea she needed.

As they left the shop her Mother was breathless. «I would never have dared to speak to Samad like that. You have become so strong.»

Then she frowned. «You do not trust your brothers?»

Shaafia stopped in the middle of the busy street and looked into her Mother's eyes. «Do you?»

Her Mother shrugged. «It is difficult,» she said, almost in pain.

«It is important to understand what is going on around us.» said Shaafia, putting her arms around her Mother. «I have learned that if I do that, then I know exactly what to say and what to do.»

Her Mother kissed her cheek.

«You are a blessing to me.»

They stopped at a small shop further up the street that sold all kinds of paper and writing materials. Shaafia bought a large ledger book and a very nice pen and walked back to Samad's shop.

«So each week you should start a new page and then conclude that page each Friday.»

«I sense that you do not trust me, my child.» he said with just a slight edge to his voice.

Her Mother had hovered nervously close to the door but now she came forward.

«No, no Samad, I am sure that is not what Shaafia intends.»

«Uncle,» said Shaafia looking directly at him. «I am doing this to help you. With this book, you will know exactly how your business is doing. It will help you to be a better shopkeeper. I am sure that if you use this book well, God will be pleased with you.»

What she said struck him.

He nodded.

«*Inche Allah*, may it be so.» Then he smiled at his sister-in-law. «The next generation has some new ways of doing things.»

Shaafia invited her Mother to go with her to the Mosque for the midday prayers.

They put away their shopping in a small storage area outside the women's prayer room and went in. There were no other women there that day. As the prayers began, and they went through the movements, Shaafia felt a great wave of powerful energy surge through her body. When the prayers were finished, she sat silently with her eyes closed for a long time till her Mother gently coughed as a sign she wanted to go.

As they left the Mosque, they saw Myriam the wife of Haj Kabir.

«He asks if you will walk with him this afternoon.» she said.

Shaafia nodded and they agreed on a time.

As they walked back to the house with their shopping, her Mother asked. «You have powerful prayers my daughter. I feel them.»

Shaafia nodded. «It is prayer that makes me strong.»

At the appointed time, Shaafia arrived at the home of Haj Kabir.

His little son wanted to come too, but his Father firmly told him it was too far. The boy was left yelling with annoyance, held by his Mother as they left.

As they walked, he picked up the story of the house they were heading towards.

«As I told you yesterday, this is a big house, made of stone and very solid. The admiral designed it himself.»

«*Darou Al Bahr.*» she said, relishing the sound of the words.

He nodded. «It was his choice of name.»

«He spoke Arabic?»

«Just a little I think, but his daughter Florence certainly did. She could recite poetry.»

«I would like to have met her.»

«I think she would have liked to meet you.»

It was several kilometers up a long hill, and she could see that he was not walking easily. His breath was shortening and she made sure she kept to his pace. They no longer talked.

As she walked she began to hear her Koranic verse begin to repeat itself. Her verse spoke of the «Companions of the Garden». It seemed to match the steps she was taking and she felt deeply that Haj Kabir and she were companions like that.

Then she heard a voice. It seemed to come in rhythm with her verse. She recognised it, having heard it before.

«My house will be your house. My garden will be your garden. Many companions will come there.»

It was Haj Hussein.

Suddenly Haj Kabir stopped and she thought maybe he needed to rest. He sat on a low stone wall and smiled at her.

«He is happy to see you.»

She nodded and smiled back. To be in the company of someone who was able to hear what she could hear was an enormous comfort.

He got to his feet and they walked on.

At the end of a long incline, they turned the corner and there it was.

Arriving at the sharp corner of Boulevard de Londre and Rue de Rome, the first sign of the house is the white bridge-like front of the first floor overlooking the long pointed garden.

They stopped to wait for several cars before they crossed Boulevard de Londre. The long high whitewashed stone wall that flanked the garden on both sides had a gate some one hundred meters along the Boulevard.

With some difficulty Haj Kabir pushed it open.

As she stepped into the garden she breathed in. There were flowers somewhere and their scent was strong. There were birds in the big trees and she could hear them twittering. She looked around. It was really nothing more than a jungle. Obviously no work had been done for years. Broad stone steps, cracked here and there, led up to a wide wooden front door with a portico. Lying in the sun on the steps were maybe a dozen scrawny cats who took off as soon at the gate was opened.

As she stood gazing up at the house a great sadness came over her. There was beauty but an enormous heaviness as well. She turned to Haj Kabir who was watching her.

«What happened?» she asked.

He sat on one of the lower steps to catch his breath and gestured that she join him.

«As soon as Haj Hussein and Florence passed, the decay began. By tradition and by law of course the house should have passed to both daughters, but Haj Hussein had made a Will that left the house only to Rana. There was some other moneys which he left to Daad. Strangely enough Daad did not seem to mind. She took the money, what little there was, and went back to Fez with her husband.»

«But she did mind.» said Shaafia, sensing something in the air.

«Oh yes,» nodded Haj Kabir. «She set about destroying it.»

«She cursed it.»

«She did.»

«But Rana did not fight back.»

«She could not. Her husband hated this house and wanted nothing to do with it. He is a fancy man who likes modern things and fast cars and gold. He forebade her to come to the house and refused to give any money to look after it. I heard that he wanted her to sell it to a developer to build something new and modern, but she refused.»

«So no-one cares for this house?»

«Omar is the caretaker. You will remember I told you that he is the older brother of Haj Hussein.»

«But it does not look like he takes much care of it.»

«He cannot do much. He is very old now and a sick man. He has had a very bad time since his brother died.»

«It is the work of Daad also?»

He nodded. «He still lives in the house at the back, but you will not like to see what state it is in.»

«He had a wife, you said, and some children.»

«They died, all three. It was a terrible sickness that took them, as if something ate them from inside, they got thinner and thinner and weaker and weaker. It was a terrible thing and there was nothing anyone could do. Somehow Omar survived but only just.»

«Why didn't Rana's husband just sell this house?»

«He cannot. It is in her name. It is Rana's house. And she will not sell it. He has been very cruel to her trying to make her sell it but she will not. She wants to make sure it is there for her daughter.»

«Houda.»

«Haj Hussein made Rana promise just before he died.»

Shaafia nodded. «Houda has a destiny.»

«Perhaps. And somehow it is to do with this house.»

They sat side by side for a long moment as Haj Kabir got his breath back. At last he stood up.

«The door is not locked, we can go in.»

Inside was much the same as outside. The high elegant ceilings had paint peeling away, and the chandeliers were coated in cobwebs. Many low benches covered in fading red rugs lined the walls and under the bay windows of the two large reception rooms, one either side of the entrance. The cats had made good use of them.

There were layers of dust, dry leaves and dead insects everywhere and signs of old leaks running down some of the walls. He took her through to the kitchen and it was in much the same state. What had once been a large working kitchen with a big gas fired stove obviously had not been used for a long time. Several of the windows had broken glass.

«Omar does not do anything about this?» she asked at last.

«He does almost nothing to tell the truth. He lives here and that is all he does.»

As they walked through what were once large elegant rooms Shaafia felt the weight of the curse that had been laid on the house. It was almost as if she was wading through it, like dark murky water.

Towards the back of the house there was one other reception area, perhaps a kind of parlour. On one wall was a large framed sepia photo of a couple standing at the entrance of the house. The glass of the frame was very dirty. She stood on a bench and wiped it with the sleeve of her dress.

The man was tall and bearded with shining eyes. Next to him stood a woman much shorter than him, but staring into the camera with a fierce intensity.

«Haj Hussein.» she said.

«And Florence.» he added.

As they looked at it, the sun came out from behind a cloud, and a ray of sunlight came across the room from a far window through the tree branches beyond and illuminated the photo.

Shaafia gave a little gasp of delighted surprise.

«You see?» said Haj Kabir with a big smile.

She nodded. «It is a good sign.»

As they stood looking at the sun-dappled photo, there was a noise behind them and an old man shuffled into the room.

«*Sidi.*» he said softly, bowing to Haj Kabir.

«Omar, this is the daughter of Jamil Jilani. She wished to see the house of your brother.»

«To her I say welcome, though what you see is not something I am proud to show.»

He had a very formal soft way of speaking and he bowed to her as he spoke.

She gazed at him for a long moment and he dropped his eyes.

«You are not to blame for what has happened to this house.» she said gently. «I pray that you will live to see it come back to its former state.»

«*Inche Allah,*» he whispered.

He opened a rear door for them and escorted them out into the garden. The sun shone through the overgrown bushes and large trees and birds sang in the branches. Although the garden was totally untended there was peacefulness there.

They stood on the edge of a raised stone platform that looked out over the lower garden sloping down towards the point. There had once been a long archway of curved wooden beams with sculpted epaulettes running down the centre, but many of them had fallen under the weight of overgrown vines and brambles.

«It will come back.» she whispered.

As they turned to leave, Shaafia reached into her handbag and took out some dirhams.

Omar bowed deeply as he received them.

«*Ham delilah,*» he whispered.

As they walked back towards Haj Kabir's house, it was mostly downhill and he could walk more easily.

«So you see what state it is in.» he said. «What can be done about it is the question.»

«And Houda,» she added. «We must be patient. I believe it will be shown to us.»

«You are very wise.» he said.

She went into the Mosque for evening prayers and sank deeply inside as Haj Kabir called them. Images of the ravaged house and the thin feeble man who lived there floated through her mind. She dedicated her prayers to their wellbeing. After the prayer had concluded and all the other women had left, she sat with her eyes closed repeating her Koranic verse.

«The time will come. The time will come.» she heard, and felt a deepening peace inside.

When she got home she was surprised to see Ihab sitting under the fig tree smoking. He stubbed out his cigarette when he saw her and blew the last whiffs of smoke away from her.

«I have been waiting for you.» he said.

She came up to him and looked into his face. He was much taller than her and he had not shaved. Her direct look unsettled him and he looked away.

«Here I am.»

«Well, you said I would do something for you, when you gave me that book.»

«Have you begun to read it?»

He shook his head.

«So what will you do for me?» she asked.

«I did it already. You know I work security now.»

«Yes. I am glad you have found a job. I am happy for you.» She held back from suggesting that maybe now he was working he could contribute to the family's finances. This was not the moment.

«What exactly do you do?» she asked instead.

«Whatever my boss needs. Ayman and me, we have the same boss.»

«It is good that your brother is working too. Is it hard work?» She had no idea what doing security might mean, but she remembered seeing the men who hustled Houda into the black BMW at the airport and she feared that maybe this is what her brothers did.

He shrugged. «Sometimes.»

Then he turned away from her, hawked deep into his throat and spat beyond the tree. Then he turned back.

«Anyway I found you a job. If you want it.»

She gazed at him and something inside shifted. There was a ripple of energy, a warmth that arose, and she sensed that whatever he was offering was beneficial.

«What is it?»

«You are a translator right ? You can translate into English?»

«That's what I did in France.» That had been her story to all her brothers.

«So my boss needs a translator for English. He's a big business man but he doesn't speak English, well not much. He has these important guys coming from London to talk business. I heard him say he'd need a translator and I told him about you.»

«Is this a permanent job?»

He shook his head. «I don't think so, just while these guys are here. A couple of days. What do you think?»

«I did not finish my Degree, so I am not really qualified.»

«He won't care. I told him you worked for millionaires from Australia in a château and he was impressed with that.»

«Well,» she said. «If that is the case, why not.»

«Good.» he said. «He wants to see you tomorrow. I will call him and let him know.»

He pulled out a cell phone and walked away down the alley to talk. She sat with her head against the tree and watched him. It fascinated her that he even had a cell phone. That was a good sign she thought.

He was back in a few minutes, grinning.

«Ayman and me will pick you up in one of his cars tomorrow morning.»

Connections

It wasn't a BMW but it was black, with darkened windows and leather seats.

Shaafia had put on her best outfit chosen for her by Claire, and her brothers were impressed when she approached them, waiting down the alley from the house.

«Nice clothes, sister,» said Ihab.

Ayman drove the Renault through the morning traffic with Ihab in the other front seat. They were heading out towards the airport.

As they drove, Ayman had the radio on really loud with Arabic rap blaring from big speakers, but later Ihab turned to tell his sister about their boss and Ayman turned it off.

«He's a young guy, not much older than us. His Dad is really wealthy. He runs a chain of five-star hotels, Marrakesh, Fez, Tangier. His Dad had a stroke a few years back and he can't do much. He is still the brains of everything, but now him and his brother run everything.»

«What is his name?»

«The Dad?»

«The family.»

«Rami Razak is the Dad and our boss is the older of his two sons, Walid.»

«So how did you two get to work with him?»

«A friend of mine. I met him when I was in prison.» She noticed that he seemed to have no embarrassment about his prison stay, in fact almost sounding proud of it.

He went on: «He worked for Walid before, then after the Dad had the stroke Walid needed more people.»

«And what do you both do exactly?»

Ayman laughed. «Lots of stuff. Better that you don't know too much about some of it.»

«Just security mostly.» said Ihab, not wanting to scare his sister.

They arrived at a big estate with high walls that had shards of broken glass along the top. There was a big iron gate with a guard house just inside. When the Renault pulled in, a guard in uniform came out, recognised the car, gave them a wave and opened the gate.

The estate had expansive grounds with rows of palms along the curving driveway, a tennis court and a swimming pool with cabanas round it.

There was one large white house with colonnades and several smaller houses on either side.

Ayman pulled up in front of the colonnades.

«Welcome to our version of your château.» grinned Ayman.

With one brother on either side, Shaafia was ushered into a large formal reception area with huge potted plants and a water fountain running down a stone wall in the centre. Ihab sat with her in a circle of wide cane chairs with red silk cushions, while Ayman disappeared deeper into the house.

He came back a moment or two later with a young man in a white linen suit with a carefully trimmed black beard and piercing black eyes.

Shaafia stood up as he walked in and he ran his eyes over her as if appraising her worth.

Inside herself she sensed a surge of power and she felt strong. She looked at him directly and smiled.

«My brothers tell me you are looking for an English translator.» she said, her voice strong and clear.

He returned her direct gaze and their eyes locked.

His eyes narrowed, then he said. «How good are you?»

She did not shift her gaze as she said: «How will you tell?»

He grunted and turned to a low table which had a pile of brochures on it. He took one up and handed it to her.

«Can you translate this?»

«Into French or Arabic?»

«Arabic.»

It was a glossy three-page fold-out brochure describing a luxury resort on the Canary Islands in English. He reached down and took up another sheet as she began to read from the one he had handed her. She could see that the one he held was in Arabic. She read the one in English aloud, then translated it clearly without hesitation.

He nodded.

«Try this.» He gave her another sheet with mostly financial statements and columns of numbers.

She read it more slowly being careful to get the right amounts of the figures.

«OK,» he said. «Lucky for your brothers you turned out to be what they said.»

Ayman and Ihab both smiled and nodded. She sensed they were actually a bit afraid of their boss.

«Who did you work for in France?» he asked.

She gave him a business-like description of Claire and Théophile, describing what she knew of Hugue's financial company in Sydney, and then the project of renovating the château and re-establishing the vineyard.

«Big money. Do you have a reference?»

«I did not ask for one. You could talk to them if you wish.»

He looked at her for a long moment, then he said: «Sit.» Then he turned and yelled into the back of the house. «Tea!»

A moment later an older woman in a maid's uniform pushed in a trolley with a big silver teapot and small glasses with gold rims. She laid down several plates of crescent shaped pastries, arranged the glasses, and poured the tea from high up to cool it.

As everyone took up their glasses and sipped the scalding hot tea, he leaned over to her and asked: «What do you charge?»

She returned his look and smiled. «It will depend how much work you have, how many hours or how many days.»

«Let's say one week, mornings only.»

Inside she realised she had no idea what she would charge. But instead of feeling panic, she waited and the amount came spontaneously as an inner prompting.

She repeated it aloud with quiet confidence.

Her two brothers' eyes widened. She had asked a lot.

The young man held her gaze and then grinned: «You are confident.»

«I know my worth,» she said, and bent forward to pick up of one of the pastries. She took a delicate bite without dropping her look and she saw him smile.

«OK,» he said. «Monday next week a group of Englishmen will arrive. You will be their translator for five mornings. If I need you for more than that, then we can renegotiate. Your brothers will drive you.»

«Thank you.» she said, while inside herself she felt a great thrill of powerful achievement. What inner support she had.

There was a movement behind them and they turned to see an old man being wheeled into the room by an equally old man in a white uniform.

They all stood as he was wheeled into the circle of chairs.

«Ba,» said the young man, «this is the girl who will translate when the English come.»

Shaafia gave the old man a little bow and he smiled at her.

«You don't look old enough to be a professional translator.» he said. His voice was severely muffled and she could see that one side of his face did not move.

«I trained in Bordeaux.» she said.

«Are you married?» he asked.

«No sir.»

He grunted. «Pity. Young girl like you. Surely there must be a young man who would marry you.»

She shrugged a little shyly, «Not yet.»

«Walid is getting married soon. The girl he is marrying is from a very good family, her Father is a great businessman.»

It was as if a bomb had gone off inside Shaafia's heart. She knew instantly who was being described. Walid was to marry Houda. She knew it.

She turned to Walid, the son, and she smiled: «Congratulations. I wish you a long and happy marriage.», while inside she had the opposite intentions.

Walid described to his Father what Shaafia had told him and the Father nodded.

«Not only a pretty girl but very smart as well.» Then he gestured to the attendant and was wheeled away.

«Good,» said Walid. «That's all settled. Your brothers will bring you on Monday.»

Then he stood up, gathered up his brochures and walked away. Ayman and Ihab helped themselves to several of the pastries and then they all went out to the car.

As they drove back, Ihab said: «Wow. You're good.»

Ayman nodded. «He didn't scare you?»

«Not at all.» she said.

They drove in silence. Shaafia closed her eyes sitting in the back seat. She could see Houda, as she had been at the Bordeaux Airport. «I will take care of you. Do not worry.» she said inwardly.

They dropped her off at the corner of the alley. As she was about to get out of the car, she said: »Now you are working, I think it would be right that you give our Mother some money each week to help with the family.»

Ihab shrugged. «Yeah, I was thinking we should.»

«I think our Father would be very happy if you both did that.»

«We don't earn all that much.» muttered Ayman. «Not like you.»

«Even so, a little bit would be good. Imagine how pleased our Mother would be.»

«Yeah. Maybe.»

«Please do it. Every Friday, whatever you can manage.»

Shaafia left it at that, but she was determined not to let it go.

As she walked back to the house, she paused at the fig tree. «Dada», she thought to herself, «Your little Shaafia has come a long way.»

Then she went inside and told her Mother what had happened.

Her Mother was a bit concerned as Shaafia described what she thought her brothers actually did. «At least they are doing something,» she sighed.

«And I told Ayman and Ihab that they should give you something to help with the family.» Her Mother smiled and gave her a hug.

When Shaafia recounted how the question of what she should charge for being a translator came up, and what she asked for, her Mother was wide-eyed.

«Ah my daughter, your Father would be so proud of you.»

She walked to the Mosque for the midday prayers. As she entered the women's section she saw the wife of Haj Kabir.

«This afternoon,» she said, «Rana Bin Salah will come to see me for tea. I would like you to meet her.»

Shaafia nodded. Little by little all the pieces of the puzzle were being assembled. She said she would be delighted to meet the daughter of Haj Hussein.

Once the prayers had been concluded, again she sat quietly allowing herself to be drawn deeply inside.

«If you have faith in our support for you, you will always succeed.» This came to her like a chorus, or a chant of different voices from some subtle form of temple somewhere. It was deeply comforting, and she arose from her meditation with a joyful smile on her face. As she walked out into the sun, the wife of Haj Kabir was there.

«You look like your prayers have been answered,» she smiled.

«*Ham delilah.*» smiled Shaafia.

As she walked the few blocks home to lunch with her Mother, she began to consider how best to approach her meeting with Houda's Mother.

The big white Mercedes was just turning away from the Mosque when Shaafia approached. She saw the back of a woman walking into the house of Haj Kabir and she knew it must be Rana. She wore heels, and her long dress was most likely silk as it shone as she walked. She wore a head scarf.

Shaafia held back to allow Rana to be greeted before she herself walked in. When she did, the wife of Haj Kabir turned to greet her.

Myriam introduced Shaafia as the daughter of Jamil Jilani.

«Ah. Blessings upon him,» nodded Rana. «I remember your Father very well.»

They kissed each other on the cheek and then Myriam invited them to sit. A young girl came out from deeper into the house to bring tea and pastries.

Shaafia smiled to herself, seeing how she was moving from one tea and pastry scene to the next.

She sat quietly sipping her tea as Rana told her hostess about what had happened to her daughter. Houda had run away when her Father had announced that she was to marry the son of Rami Razak. She had been in Bordeaux for her studies and had just come back for the vacation.

Shaafia leaned forward and asked: «What was her study?»

«It was not something useful, I am afraid. Her Father wanted her to study business so she could appreciate what he was doing. As we have no son, he had thought maybe she might be able to run some of his business when he became old. However my daughter is very headstrong. She insisted that she wanted to study fine arts, literature and film. What good does that do?»

Myriam said: «Shaafia has just come back from Bordeaux, too.»

«What did you study?» asked Rana.

«Translation.»

«That is much more useful. Maybe you met my Houda at the University.»

«At the University?» said Shaafia and not telling a lie, she said: «No I don't think I met your daughter at the University.»

Rana nodded and then she leaned forward and spoke in a conspiratorial voice so the young girl who was hovering in the background would not hear. «She secretly took a boyfriend.»

«A French boyfriend?» Myriam had raised her eyebrows in appropriate shock. Shaafia matched her look as best she could.

«Exactly.»

«Not Muslim?»

«Probably not. I don't know.»

«Did she, I mean was it a serious relationship?» It seemed clear to Shaafia that Haj Kabir's wife rather liked a bit of scandal and couldn't quite keep her excitement hidden.

«How did you find out?»

«My husband has business associates in Bordeaux, and he had someone hire a detective to check up on what Houda was doing.»

«He suspected something?»

«Accidentally she had sent something on her email that we saw, and which suggested that she was having this affair.»

«So what did you do?».

«We brought her home, straight away.»

«She was willing?»

«Not at all. We had to send someone to make her come back.»

«You had to kidnap her?»

«No, no. Just strong persuasion.»

Shaafia asked. «So she is back now?»

Rana nodded. «She is here. She is not happy about it, but that is what has to happen.»

«And she is to be married soon?»

«As soon as possible.»

«You are happy with the match?»

Rana pursed her lips. «I cannot say happy exactly. My husband has been very firm that he will choose the husband for our daughter, just as I was told to marry him. It is tradition. Her husband to be is from a very good family. Rami Razak is a good man and has done very well. He has trained his sons well. My husband believes this marriage will unite the two families and help to merge the businesses in the future, especially as we have no son to do that.»

«What does your daughter say?» asked Shaafia.

«You are not married, are you?» asked Rana, clearly not wanting to answer the question.

Shaafia shook her head. It was the day for that question.

«It is not good for a young girl not to be married. Who will take care of her?»

Shaafia smiled. «So far, in my life, I have felt that I have been very well taken care of. *Ham delilah.*»

«Of course, God in his infinite mercy takes care of us all, but still, in life, women need the protection of a husband.»

Myriam motioned to the young girl hovering in the backgrund to pour more tea, and then sent her away to the kitchen.

«I am looking forward to the wedding.» she said, once the tea had been served.

«You and your husband are of course invited.» said Rana, then she turned to Shaafia. «I would like to invite you and your family to join us.»

«That would be an honour.» said Shaafia dutifully. «I am sure my Father must have met your daughter when she was little.»

«Perhaps he did. I remember your Father used to come to my Father's house, but once I was married we did not go to the house so much. But maybe he did.»

Then the conversation turned as Myriam told Rana about Shaafia doing so well in Bordeaux, and finding such well paid work with the wealthy Australians. She told Rana about how, the previous year, Shaafia had come back with enough money to offer *zakat* for a big feast at the Mosque.

«If only my daughter could have done something like that, we would have a lot less to worry about.» said Rana. «Your family must be so proud of you. Will you be looking for work here in Casablanca?»

«Yes, of course. I want to support my family.»

«And you can translate into English?» When Shaafia nodded, she went on. «Well if I hear of anyone who needs an English translator I will let you know.»

«That is very kind of you.» smiled Shaafia.

The rest of the afternoon was filled with more local gossip as the two older women talked about mutual friends and what was happening in and around the Mosque. It seemed that they both liked a bit of scandal as long as it wasn't about them.

Shaafia said little, but smiled when it was appropriate. Inside herself she was sensing how there was a slow and potent gathering of energy. This meeting was a step in a process that was unfolding. One way or another she would fulfill her promise to Rana's Father and to Rana's daughter.

When the white Mercedes returned to pick up Rana, Shaafia declined to accept a lift. She wanted to go into the Mosque for evening prayers.

Once prayers had finished, she walked the few blocks home as the evening settled in. The smell of cooking was in the air, and women were rounding up their children to take them inside. All these women had married, as is the tradition, she thought. Will I have to do that?

As this thought floated through her head, she heard the voices. «You have a destiny. Follow it.» And she laughed out loud. Why would she even bother to think about such things as marriage.

An old man who was sitting and smoking at the entrance of his tiny ramshackle house saw her laugh.

«Heh, heh, what's so funny?» he sneered.

She stopped and looked at him.

«If you could see what I can see you would laugh too,» she said.

«You must have better eyes than me, I don't laugh,» he responded.

She went over to him and sat down beside him. «Look around us,» she said. «What do you see?»

He gazed off down the alley. Then he said: «I see what I always see. This dirty street, these miserable houses, these ratty kids.»

«I see light. I see that God has put each of us here for a reason. If we see the world the way He does, then it is a very beautiful world. Look at the sky. Look at that crow up there on top of the building. How clever he is.»

He followed her pointing finger and looked up.

«I don't notice the sky much.»

«If you did, you would be happy.»

Then she got to her feet.

«Be happy,» she said «and you will laugh.»

As she walked away he called after her.

«You are a good girl. God be with you.»

She smiled to herself as she went on. «I do have a destiny.»

When she got home the first person she saw was Nayla.

Her sister smiled when she saw Shaafia. «There you are little sister.» She gave Shaafia the double-cheek kiss that felt like nettle stings to Shaafia. She herself made a distant moue to avoid contact with her lips.

«I have seen the beautiful clothes that you have given to our Mother and sisters,» said Nayla. «I hear you have something for me too.»

«I have brought something for everyone in the family.» said Shaafia evenly. Then she added: «I thought about each one and I chose what I thought would be appropriate.»

«Let's see it.» said Nayla, putting an arm round her sister and guiding her inside.

As they passed into the kitchen the two younger sisters, Hawa and Yamina, were helping their Mother prepare the evening meal.

When they saw Shaafia they both squealed in delight.

«We heard about your job. How brave you are!» said Hawa.

«What job?» asked Nayla.

«Shaafia's going to work for the boss of Ayman and Ihab, and she asked for a big salary and he said yes.»

Nayla turned her narrowed eyes on her sister. «Is that true?»

Shaafia nodded.

«So going to Bordeaux has turned you into an important person.»

«It taught me to know my own worth.»

Their Mother had said nothing in all this, but now she put down her spoon from stirring a large pot and came over to put her arm around Shaafia.

«I am happy to hear you say that. I hope all my children learn that from you.»

«You think I don't know my own worth?» sneered Nayla.

Her Mother smiled. «That, my child, is for you to know.» then she turned to Shaafia.

«Did you have a nice tea with Myriam?»

Shaafia smiled and then turned to face Nayla, with a penetrating look, knowing that what she was about to say would strike her sister.

«I met with the daughter of Haj Hussein.»

Nayla caught the look exactly and she frowned. «Which daughter?»

«Oh,» smiled Shaafia, «Not your friend, the other one, Rana.»

«What do you mean «my friend?»

Shaafia looked at her other two sisters and her Mother. «I heard that Nayla was good friends with Daad, the older sister. Isn't that true?»

Nayla still had a narrow-eyed look, as she said: «I have met her.» Then she seemed to shake herself, and said: «Anyway let's see the gift you brought.»

«Wait here. I'll bring it.»

When Shaafia went into the girls' sleeping area to open her suitcase, she stopped for a moment to take a breath. She was a bit amazed at her own courage to goad her sister like that. Inside, however, she felt strong. She had been guided to say what she did and there was no turning back.

It was the last gift so now one of her Samsonites was empty.

She took her gift out to the kitchen.

The two girls and their Mother watched as the wrapping paper came off. It was a very simple, obviously quite cheap white blouse. It was pure cotton but nothing fancy.

Nayla held it up. «This is it?»

«Do you like it?»

«I saw what you gave them,» Nayla said, gesturing at the two younger girls, «and our Mother.»

«And?»

«You want to insult me.» Suddenly her face was infused with anger. She threw the blouse down and attacked Shaafia with her hands going for her throat.

As the other three women screamed, Shaafia found herself diving deeply inside.

The voices inside were calm but insistent. «You must tell her that you love her and you must say that she cannot harm you. Your breath is your weapon.»

Instantly Shaafia was back in the room and felt the intense pressure of the hands on her neck and her sister spitting vitriol in her face.

She blew out her breath into her sister's face, despite the pressure on her throat.

It was as if she had struck her sister with a hammer. Nayla fell back, crashed into a chair and fell to the floor. Shaafia stood over her, and in a calm but powerful voice she repeated what she had been told:

«Nayla, I love you. And I tell you that you cannot harm me. Not now, not ever.»

There was a charge of electricity in the kitchen that seemed to freeze them all. Her two sisters were staring at Shaafia, who put her hands up to her throat to gently massage it.

Suddenly Nayla came back to life, she leaped to her feet, took a step towards Shaafia and flung the blouse at her.

«You are going to be so sorry!» she snarled. «So sorry.» And she was gone.

The electricity in the room subsided.

«We told you she was a witch.» said Hawa, now laughing in relief.

Their Mother put her arm around Shaafia. «I think Nayla has met her match. But I am sorry to say that she will now do whatever she can to take revenge.»

«I have no fear of her.» said Shaafia quietly. «I know what she is and she knows that I know. Now she has seen what I am. I am not afraid.»

«Do you think she really is a witch?» asked Yamina.

«I think she has been trapped into something that is very dark. I don't know what you would call it, but is very sad. We must give her our love. That is the strongest antidote.»

«How can you love someone like that? We hate her.» said Hawa.

«She is still your sister.» said their Mother, and she turned back to her pot which was in danger of burning.

Soon several of their brothers turned up for the evening meal. As they served it up, the two girls told the story of what had happened.

Samet sneered: «You don't believe all that rubbish about witches do you? That is so ignorant.»

«She attacked Shaafia.» said Hawa.

«It's called anger, that's all. She has been angry since she was born.»

Before she went to sleep that night, Shaafia took the white blouse and walked down along the laneway. In one of the small houses she saw a woman feeding her children. The woman wore a threadbare dress and so Shaafia left the blouse by their door and went home.

As she lay down ready for sleep, with her Koranic verse reverberating softly deep inside, Shaafia went back over her day. So much had taken place and each event seemed to be connected to all the others.

She had fearlessly named her price, she had found the connection to Houda, and she had confronted the darkness of her sister and triumphed.

It felt like she had been invited to explore a new house, one that revealed different rooms, each with its own style, but all of them part of the house itself.

What this house was, she could not tell, but it was hers.

Getting down to Business

Friday is a big day in Casablanca. The markets throng with shoppers getting ready for the end of the working week. Businesses look towards closing their books for the week and making one last sale before everything closes in time for evening prayers.

Shaafia's Mother had insisted that all her children come for the evening meal after prayers, not that most of her sons were interested in going to the Mosque but the invite for a big meal always seemed to work.

In the morning Shaafia went to the bank in the commercial centre of Bordeaux to withdraw money to give to her Mother to buy what was needed. Her credit card was ready and she gazed down at it as the girl handed it to her. It was a symbol of her independence and her newfound power.

As she left the bank, she passed the agency of Maroc Telecom, the biggest phone provider. She looked at the displays in the window, then she went inside.

When she returned home, she told her Mother that there would be a telephone installed in the house the following week, and she showed her Mother her new cell phone.

«How amazing. Is it expensive?» asked her Mother.

Shaafia smiled. «It will be worth every dirham.»

«You will have to teach me how to use the new phone when it comes. But who will call us? We have never had such a thing and most of our friends don't have them either.»

«The boys have cell phones, Ayman and Ihab. You can be sure Nayla has one. Now you can call Zarifa and Afifa and you can talk to your grandchildren on the phone.»

«Do you think so?»

«Why not? These days most people have phones.»

«You will call me, won't you?»

«Of course I will.»

As they went together to buy the ingredients for the evening meal, her Mother told everyone she met that she was getting a telephone. Shaafia had to smile.

Her Mother came with her for the midday prayers at the Mosque, and could not resist telling several of the women that she would be getting a phone at home. They asked her for her number, until Shaafia told her that they did not have one yet.

In the afternoon Shaafia went back to see Rachi. When she got there, her Mother answered the door.

«Oh Shaafia, I am sorry to say that Rachi is not in a good mood. It would be best if you did not see her today.»

«She is not well?»

«She's not sick. I didn't mean that. She is,well, not happy right now.»

«Maybe I could come tomorrow?»

«Yes. Of course. Perhaps you would join us for lunch. We have invited the family of Yasser to come. You can meet them.»

Then she stepped out of the house and took Shaafia by the arm. A little way from the house she stopped and turned to face Shaafia.

«Maybe if you are there it will help. Rachi is so unhappy that we want her to marry Yasser. He is a good young man. Maybe you can help her to see his good qualities.»

«Then I will come for sure.» said Shaafia.

In the late afternoon, as the time came for businesses to close, Shaafia and her Mother went to Uncle Samad's shop.

He smiled as they came in.

«You just missed Samet. He came asking for the week's money for the family, and I had to tell him that there was a new arrangement. He was not happy.»

Shaafia studied the new ledger book. Her uncle had been diligent, listing his expenses in one column and then the daily sales in the other.

The biggest item sold was the green tea.

«You only sell one brand of green tea?» she asked.

«Yes, it has been our brand for many years. Your Father preferred that one.»

«But other people might like something else.» said Shaafia. «I would recommend you have at least three types of green tea. You will make more money, I am certain.»

«You think so?»

«I am certain. Please try it and we will see next week how it works.»

Her uncle looked at his sister-in-law and shook his head. «The new generation.»

«I have to say,» said Shaafia's Mother, «that I have tried some other green teas and I like them very much.»

«Very well. I will give it a try.»

Shaafia had noted the total for the week, and now she asked for the family's payment.

He handed her an envelope with dirhams in it, and she opened it and did a quick count.

He watched her with a frown. «You do not trust me?»

«It is always good to check.» smiled Shaafia, carefully making sure there was no malice in her voice. «This is a business and we can help you to make it an even better business.»

Her Mother had to smile. «The new generation.»

Shaafia closed the envelope and gave it to her Mother.

They wished Samad a happy weekend, and left him with a few things to think about.

Going back to the shop where she bought the ledger for her uncle, Shaafia bought herself a hardbound notebook and some good pens so she was ready for her translation assignment.

In the late afternoon, the older sisters came with their husbands, and, whenever he could, Ahmed kept trying to make eye contact with Shaafia. She smiled at him, but made sure she was too busy to talk.

There was no sign of Nayla.

There was endless hugging and catching up, especially for the two older girls who had their own families to take care of. Shaafia hugged the little ones, telling them that they had all gotten so big while she was away. They all brought the stuffed animals that Shaafia had given them, although the white monkey that Khadija had received was not nearly as white any more. Zarifa told Shaafia that the monkey was inseparable from the child and had been fed and bathed many times.

The sisters heard about Shaafia's new job and were very excited for her. Both were amazed when their Mother recounted how Shaafia had asked for a big fee and got it. They were full of questions, who was the man she was working for, what did their brothers do for him, where did he live, and on it went. Shaafia felt like she was being interviewed, but her sisters were full of admiration and love so she didn't mind too much.

Ahmed nodded, and said: «You are so sophisticated now. You and I should work together.»

Before she could reply, Hawa excitedly told them about Shaafia's fight with Nayla, and they were fascinated about how Shaafia had handled it. It was perhaps the first time the family had talked openly about Nayla and what they thought she had become. Zarifa and Afifa were more inclined to see her like Samet did, rather than someone who was indulging in black magic, but still they were shocked at the story.

«Shaafia has bruises on her neck.» said Yamina, who was enjoying the drama perhaps more than she should.

To change the subject, their Mother announced the news of getting a phone in the house, and everyone was excited. Shaafia was forced to show them her new cell phone which impressed them all.

They went on talking animatedly as they worked on preparing the evening meal, and one by one the brothers began to turn up.

Samet came in fuming about no-one trusting him any more. He had gone to his uncle's shop to collect the money for his Mother and had been told there was a new arrangement.

Shaafia turned to face him and asked him why this made him so angry.

«Oh you, Miss Ever-so-smart from Bordeaux, you think you're running this family now?».

«Perhaps if any one of you boys was man enough to do it then I wouldn't have to.» she said, without a trace of enmity in her voice.

Then she said: «When our Father was dying, he asked me to give each of you boys some money and I did. Why do you think he did not tell me to give anything to the girls?»

Samet thought for a moment. «Because he was old-fashioned and thought men should be the inheritors?»

«No. It wasn't inheritance anyway. It was my money. One of his daughters had earned that money. Maybe it was his way of trying to spur all of you boys, or maybe even just one or two of you, to get your lives together and behave like real men, responsible members of the family.»

«Well it's not my fault that no-one seems to recognise my talents. You were lucky.»

«I have been very lucky, you are right. But it wasn't just luck. I took a risk, I went for it.»

Then she came close to her brother and put her hand up to his face. She was much shorter than him and younger, but in that movement she was more like his big sister. «You could be someone special if you only learned how to stop being so afraid.»

He stared at her. He was about to say something and she could see the play of emotions in his face. Then he turned and went outside. Everyone else had heard all this and were struck by it. The sisters could not stop hiding their smiles.

When Toufik came in, as always smelling of exhaust fumes and cigarette smoke, he gave Shaafia a big hug. «I showed all the guys the book you gave me. They'd never seen a book like that.»

«I am glad they liked it. Do you work with them?»

«How do you mean?»

«What you do with motor bikes. Is it a business?»

«No, just some guys. We fix bikes, that's all.»

«But not for money? It's not a paid job?»

He shook his head and realised the whole room was looking at him. He was a shy boy and was not comfortable being the centre of attention.

«But you are good at that? Fixing bikes?»

He shrugged. «I suppose so.»

«How did you learn?»

He shrugged again. «I don't know, I just like bikes.»

Shaafia studied him for a minute, then she said: «If you went to a mechanics school, you could do really well. You could get a well-paid job, maybe even start your own business.»

He shuffled his feet. «I suppose so.»

«I could help you,» she said. «Think about it.»

«Listen to your sister,» said his Mother. «She is very wise.»

Afifa put an arm around Shaafia. «You have changed so much since you went to France. I like the way you say things.»

Next to arrive was Habib, who came flying in with great excitement.

«I'm in the team!» he yelled to the whole room.

His Mother turned to him and said: «Well that's good news. When will you play?»

«It's tomorrow afternoon. Actually I'm not in the first eleven, I'm a sub. But I am in the team.»

«Well that's a great start.» said Shaafia, giving him a hug. Then she pulled back, making a face. «But you have to go wash, you smell awful.»

«OK!» he said, and ran off.

«At least one of my sons is achieving something.» said their Mother, which made her daughters smile.

Loqman had obviously been home for a while but now emerged from the boys' room. When he saw Shaafia, he came up beside her and said quietly: «I did the homework.»

She nodded and put her hand up to her chest.

The meal was ready to serve when Ihab and Ayman walked in. They had made an effort to wear nice clothes, had clearly been to the *hamam* and shaved. Neither was wearing dark glasses. Ihab went up to his Mother and gave her an envelope.

«It's from us both. It's not a lot but it's what we can manage.»

Their Mother held the envelope to her chest, and there were tears in her eyes.

«I thank you both.» she said, and then turned back to her pot to hide her emotion.

Shaafia grinned at Ayman and gave him a thumbs up and he reddened with embarrassment.

The meal was served with lots of talking and jostling to reach pots and pass dishes. Shaafia watched all this and felt a deep sense of gratitude. Whoever was guiding her and prompting her to speak was bringing such good changes to this family who had endured so much.

«This is why I came back.» she thought.

«This is just the beginning.» came back an inner voice as if they were in conversation.

The following day Shaafia went with her two younger sisters and their Mother to the *hamam*, and Shaafia paid for them all to have extra massages. As they lay there being pummeled by the strong women who ran the *hamam*, they talked animatedly to each other. There was an air of good feeling between the four of them.

Walking home, their Mother suddenly said: «I have not felt so happy for such a long time.»

For the lunch with Rachi's family Shaafia dressed in conservative local style, knowing that Rachi's parents prefer girls to be traditional.

She found one last small box of chocolates that had somehow gotten buried in her other suitcase which she took as a gift.

When she got there, she gave the chocolates to Rachi's Mother, and Rachi was overjoyed to see her. The other family had not yet arrived, so there was a moment where the girls could be alone. Shaafia told Rachi that she had come the day before, but her Mother had said she was not doing well.

«Oh I just threw a big fit, that's all.» said Rachi. «My Mother didn't want you to see me in a rage.»

«So today I get to meet Yasser and his family.»

«I am so glad you will be here. I need someone on my side. I feel so alone.»

«Is the wedding soon?»

«That's why they are coming, to discuss all that. It's like I have no say in anything. Like I am just a cow on a farm or something, milk me or send me to market, but don't ask me what I think.»

«I still have a feeling something will happen. I don't know what it is, but I think you just have to be patient. I would suggest you don't do any more rages. Just look like you are going along with it and we will see what happens.»

«I suppose I can do that. Anyway throwing a fit doesn't do me any good. It doesn't change anything.»

Shaafia nodded. Then she leaned forward and gave her friend a hug. «Something good is going to come out of all this, I am certain.»

Then Yasser's family arrived and the girls were called to come and greet them.

Yasser himself was quite tall, more than a little shy, with dimples when he smiled which he did a lot out of nervousness.

Shaafia was introduced. They had obviously heard a little about her before. Yasser's parents were both quietly spoken people who seemed to be very polite and careful in what they said.

They sat for lunch round a large low table, and most of the talking was done by Rachi's parents. Her father was a great talker who had opinions about everything. Yasser's Father seemed to be the sort of man who goes along with whatever is being said without argument. He nodded a lot and said «*Wacha*» in agreement.

The two ladies got down to marriage discussions and the potential couple said nothing at all. Now and then Shaafia would make eye contact with Rachi and they would smile at each other. She tried it with Yasser, but he dropped his head and was unable to hold her look.

When lunch finished Shaafia had an inspiration.

Looking to Rachi's Mother, she said: «Do you think maybe it is time for the future married couple to get to know each other a little? If I were their chaperone they could go for a walk. In fact my little brother Habib is playing soccer this afternoon and I promised I would go. Could they come with me?»

There was a worried look between Rachi's parents, but suddenly Yasser's Mother came to life.

«I think that is an excellent idea. They hardly know each other.»

«Come on then.» said Shaafia, standing up and beckoning to Yasser and Rachi. She wanted to be quick before Rachi's parents could step in.

They were out the front door before any more could be said.

The football ground was part of the school and only a couple of blocks away. Yasser walked carefully so that Shaafia was between Rachi and him.

«Is Habib really playing football today, or did you make that up?» asked Rachi, but she was obviously very pleased to have escaped.

«Well, a bit of both,» admitted Shaafia. «He is a sub so he might play.»

«He is your brother?» This was the first word Shaafia had heard from Yasser. He had a quiet but pleasant voice, and she smiled at him.

«He is the youngest of all my brothers. He's just a kid but he loves football.»

«Is he good?»

«I have no idea. I have never seen him play. Do you play?»

«I do.»

«In a team?»

He nodded.

The game had not started when they got there, so kids were running all over the place with various adults trying to marshal them. There was a small pavilion on one side where several of the parents had already set themselves up.

«Let's sit up the back.» suggested Shaafia.

With Shaafia between them, they sat on the top-most tier looking down over the heads of various family groups.

After a few minutes a man in a uniform stood in the middle of the field and blew a whistle, and the kids all stopped running. He yelled instructions, and somehow two teams of kids lined up on either side of him.

Shaafia strained to see whether Habib was in the group, but from where she sat they all looked much the same.

One group of kids put on orange-coloured sashes so they could tell who was on which team. Then the game began.

They watched for a while and nothing much happened. Shaafia turned to Yasser and said: « How do you feel about getting married?»

Rachi leaned in to hear what he said.

«It's what my parents want,» he said.

«That doesn't answer my question. How do you feel?»

He shrugged. «I don't know. I suppose I have to get married sometime to someone.»

«How do you think Rachi feels?»

He dared to look at Rachi for a quick moment, then he looked down.

«She doesn't want to get married to me.»

«How can you tell?»

A little fire came into his eyes and he looked directly at Shaafia. «I'm not stupid. It's obvious.»

Suddenly there was a roar from the parents on the tiers below them. Some kid had scored a goal.

There was a pause, and several kids came off the field and others ran on. Shaafia jumped to her feet. «There he is!» She pointed out Habib and they followed him as best they could. Not much happened, and as far as they could tell Habib didn't get to touch the ball.

The game ended, and the parents poured out of the pavilion to greet their players. Shaafia took Rachi and Yasser down to find Habib. When he saw his sister he ran over and gave her a big hug.

«Did you see?» he yelled, «I got to play.»

Shaafia introduced Yasser to her little brother. «Yasser plays football, too.»

«Who do you play for?»

When Yasser told him his eyes widened.

«Really?» then he asked: «What is your family name?»

When Yasser told him, his eyes got wider. «I have heard of you. You scored some goals this year.»

Yasser nodded modestly, and Rachi looked at her future husband with a new respect.

Just then a soccer ball flew past them and Yasser effortlessly caught it with his foot, flicked it up in the air, bounced it off his chest and then juggled it with one foot for a few bounces, then he passsed it to Habib, who managed to keep it in the air and passed it back.

Just then Rachi's Father appeared. He had obviously needed to check that his daughter and her prospective husband were behaving. However, when he saw Yasser's skill with the ball, he smiled.

«You see how good your husband is?» he said.

Rachi nodded.

«We want to come and see you play.» she said to Yasser, and he blushed.

«I want to come too.» yelled Habib.

Shaafia sent her little brother home to get cleaned up, and she turned to walk with Rachi and Yasser.

As they walked back to Rachi's house with her Father, Shaafia noticed how Rachi now walked next to Yasser and at one point gently and surreptitiously took his hand, just for a second.

As they entered the house, both Mothers could see that a subtle change had taken place.

There were smiles all round as Yasser and his parents prepared to leave.

Yasser shook hands with Shaafia and whispered: «Thank you.»

Once they had left, Shaafia and Rachi went up to the roof to talk.

«So?» said Shaafia with a smile.

«I don't know.»

«I think there is something between you. I think this is what is supposed to happen. I think you will be happy. And I see something else. I think you will not stay in Morocco very long.»

«Really? Where would we go?»

«For some reason, I see you in Bordeaux, but this time with your parents' blessing.»

«*Inche Allah*,» said Rachi, and gave her a long and loving hug.

As Shaafia left the house, Rachi's Mother took her hand. «You are a blessing. Thank you so much for what you did. I think you have helped our daughter so much.»

Once again, as she walked home, Shaafia bathed in the feeling of being guided to say and do things that really benefitted others.

«Oh my Pia,» she thought inwardly. «How grateful I am to you.»

Translation

The following Monday Shaafia lay quietly repeating her Koranic prayer as her sisters went off to school, then she dressed ready for her first day as a translator. She chose an outfit that made her look as professional as possible, not too much like a local Moroccan girl, but more like a girl who has been trained in Bordeaux.

Her Mother was suitably impressed, and when Ihab came to collect her he was too. She had her solid notebook and pens, and her new cell phone, so her new handbag would be put to good use.

Once again Ayman drove, and as they went Ihab filled her in on the three Englishmen who had come the previous day. Walid had entertained them at home with dancing girls and lots of alcohol.

«I hope you are not too shocked by this.» said Ihab, with just a hint of sarcasm in his voice.

«In Bordeaux,» she said in response, «alcohol is part of the culture. Our château is in the middle of a vineyard. I have helped with the *vendange*, the harvest.»

«So you drink wine now?» asked Ayman.

«No, I chose not to, but it doesn't offend me.»

«Anyway, Walid is a very international man, so he knows what Englishmen like.»

«You were there yesterday?» she asked.

«We acted as driver for the girls. They were very sexy.»

«It sounds like you are both very happy in your new work.»

She saw Ayman grinning in the rear vision mirror.

Not far from the Razak compound, Ihab pointed to a large apartment building.

«The Razaks own that. We get to stay in one of them.»

«By yourselves?»

«With a few other men who do security.»

«Do you have to pay rent?»

«It gets taken off our pay.»

As the car made its way up the curved driveway, she saw Walid standing with a group of men looking at an enclosure off to one side of the big house. When he heard the car, Walid turned and walked across and opened the door for Shaafia.

«Come and see my peacocks.» he said.

As she got out of the car, Walid said: «You boys can put the car round the back. I won't need you till the end of the morning when you can drive your sister home.»

When they reached the enclosure it became clear that in fact Walid did speak just a little English, enough to communicate on a basic level with his guests.

«Zis is Shaafia who will translate for our meeting.»

«Good morning.» she said in English.

The three men all looked at her with interest. One was much older than the other two and she wondered if he was their father.

«Nice to meet you,» said the older man. «My name is Graham and these are my associates, Ben and Alex.«

They all shook hands.

Now that Shaafia was there, Walid launched into Arabic to tell the story of how he and his father had imported their peacocks from India. Shaafia followed easily, and when the Englishmen asked questions she could work back equally fluently.

After a while Walid invited them all inside to begin their formal meeting.

As they walked, Ben, one of the young men, walked beside Shaafia. «You are very good,» he said, «where did you train?»

«Bordeaux University.»

«Ah, Bordeaux. I love Bordeaux.»

«You have been there?»

«Often.» Then he grinned. «I had a very cute French girlfriend for a while.»

«But not any more?»

He shook his head. «I think I was too English for her.»

Shaafia told him where she had worked, that it was a château in the Entre Deux Mers. He was impressed. He told her that he loved their wine.

Then he said: «You have a bit of an Australian accent.»

«Really?» And she laughed. «My employer was an Australian woman so maybe that is why.»

In the main reception area of the house a large morning tea had been set up with different pots of tea and many pastries.

Several computers had already been set up.

A young woman in a uniform was ready to serve as they came in, and Walid told them in his awkward English that in their honour there were three different kinds of tea. «Unless it is coffee that you would prefer.»

They settled into the comfortable couches, and the girl served the tea or coffee of their choice.

Shaafia chose English Breakfast tea.

Walid said: «You like that?»

«In our château we drank it every day. Australians like English tea. They call it a «cuppa».»

This made the Englishmen laugh.

«We do too.» said Graham.

Once the tea had been completed, the girl took the trays away and they got down to business.

It turned out that Graham was the owner of a large business that built and ran resorts mostly in the Caribbean. He was interested in exploring new options in Africa. He had visited several of the Razak hotels and he was impressed. He was looking for a local partner. He outlined what he had in mind and Shaafia had no trouble translating. Walid listened to him with great focus, asking questions now and then, but mostly nodding. The other two men were experts in their own fields. Ben was the chief financial officer of the company, while Alex was head of operations. When Ben spoke, it was trickier for Shaafia because he began talking numbers, but she did well.

By the time for lunch approached, Shaafia had been translating for several hours nonstop.

Walid turned to her as they stood up. «You are not too tired?»

«No.» she said.

«You did well. Your brothers will take you home.»

«Thank you.» she said, and she turned to the Englishmen.

«I will see you tomorrow.»

«You are not staying for lunch?» asked Graham. «Hey Walid, we need some female company, don't you think?»

The slightest frown crossed Walid's forehead, so fast that probably only Shaafia noticed.

«OK.» he said, then in Arabic he said: «Can you stay? I don't want to displease them.»

She smiled and turned to Graham: «It would be a pleasure.»

Ihab appeared and Walid told him his sister was staying for lunch. He and Ayman should wait in the kitchen. Ihab shot Shaafia a look that was hard to read. Was he jealous or was he worried for her safety?

Walid escorted them into a large marble-tiled dining room with a huge round table, only half a metre off the floor. Around it were many cushions.

«I hope it zis not too difficult for you.» said Walid in his English, pointing at the cushions.

For Ben and Alex it was not hard, and they plopped themselves down with ease. Graham, however, was not so flexible so Shaafia helped him to arrange some cushions so he could sit sideways with his legs sticking out.

«Should've done more yoga when I was young.» he muttered. «Thank you, my dear.»

Shaafia sat next to him, while Walid sat between the other two Englishmen. Walid gave a loud command and three women came in carrying huge steaming tajines. When they placed them in the centre of the table and lifted the lids, the aroma was intoxicating. The Englishmen were delighted and wanted to know what was in them. Shaafia realised it was good that she had stayed for lunch so she could help.

As the lunch progressed, Graham was very interested to hear all about Shaafia's life. She skipped over her early life, describing it simply as a regular child growing up in a big Moroccan family. She was more forthcoming about going to Bordeaux to study, but careful about what she included. Nonetheless, he seemed to be very interested in everything she said. In fact it seemed like she was doing most of the talking and not eating so much. Walid smiled at her. He was very happy with her entertainment skills.

The lunch concluded with many plates of sweets to choose from and some mint tea. The plan was that Walid was taking them in the afternoon to see his Father's hotel in Rabat.

«We must let you get some rest.» said Graham to Shaafia as they got up from the table. One of his legs had gone to sleep so she had helped him to get up. «You have worked hard today.»

Walid called loudly for Ihab, who came immediately.

«Your sister is ready to go,» he said. «Bring the car round.»

Then speaking to Shaafia in Arabic, he said: «I know I said mornings only but I see that he really likes you. I want you to stay for lunch every day. Can you do that?»

«Are you offering me an increase in my fee?» she smiled sweetly.

«Oh, you are good!» he grinned. «You got it.»

She said goodbye to Graham and the young men and they shook hands and thanked her for her great work.

As she sat back in the car returning home, she felt a release of tension that she hadn't realised was there. But she had done well. She knew it, and she could see that they were all pleased. Now she could rest.

The next two days were much the same, except that plans and drawings had been pulled out and they began to talk in earnest about how they might work together.

On the Thursday, the routine changed. The Razak family were in the process of acquiring a large plot of land outside Essaouira on the Atlantic coast. Walid was hoping that he could create a joint venture with the English group.

They set off very early in a massive brand new black Mercedes Benz with Walid at the wheel. They took the freeway for most of the way, and Walid seemed to ignore totally the speed limit.

Graham sat in the front seat with Walid while Shaafia sat between the two younger Englishmen in the back. They were both very interested in asking Shaafia about life in Morocco, where she grew up, what she thought of the government and the king. At first she was cautious about what she said, but as the conversation went on, she saw that they were genuinely interested in trying to understand the country and the society they might be investing in.

When they reached the site, there was a high wire fence all round it with barbed wire curled across the top. The site had been bulldozed and had no trees or buildings on it. Outside the wire, however, there was a kind of shanty town of huts made out of cardboard and plastic sheeting. There were many placards attached to the wire fence protesting in French and Arabic against what had happened.

Walid swore when he saw that there were quite a few people standing with placards in front of the gate where several security guards were standing just inside. One of them had a very large German Shepherd on a leash.

«Someone tipped them off that we were coming.»

Ben asked Shaafia to describe what the signs said. They were about the taking of people's land.

Walid heard her description and he said: «It wasn't their land. They were squatters. We are negotiating with the legal owners. It's a consortium of local businessmen. We will meet one of them today.»

«If they were squatters, why are they protesting?» asked Graham.

«They are just looking for a handout,» sneered Walid.

As soon as the Mercedes approached the site, the guards opened the gates to let it come in. Shaafia was surprised to see that the guards actually had guns.

Inside the gate there were several other cars parked, and as they pulled up, two men came out of one of the cars to greet them.

Walid introduced the Englishmen to the two local representatives, and Shaafia found herself rapidly crossing from English to Arabic and back.

With sounds of the protest in the background, they walked towards the waterfront. One of the local men, a heavy-set man with a thick beard, apologised for the protests. He said he had called the police and asked for help, but the police had said, as the protesters were not actually on the property, there was nothing they could do. Shaafia caught Walid quietly suggesting that he should pay the police, then they would act.

They approached the edge of the water where there were remnants of several rickety piers and some abandoned fishing boats. The man with the beard promised that they would be cleared away as soon as possible. The coastline was rocky, and gentle waves rose and fell across them, drowning out the sounds of the protests.

As they stood looking out over the gently undulating water, there was a very complicated conversation about groundwater, subsoil, rock stratas and tide levels, all of which tested Shaafia well beyond her usual vocabulary. Alex, who was asking most of the questions, as a construction person, was apologetic, but as he told her, he needed to know what were the local conditions.

In truth, the two local representatives were no more used to such discussions than Shaafia, so most of the questions went unanswered. Walid promised that he would engage an expert to flesh out all the questions. Shaafia was relieved when they moved onto more easily translatable subjects like what kinds of structures could be built, what the local laws were about building structures out into the water, and what the local taxes were. The question of finding sand to make beaches was brought up. The Englishmen were assured that bringing in sand would not be a problem. Morocco has plenty of sand, said the man with the beard, chuckling at his own joke.

As the conversation continued, they walked the boundaries of the property which was some five hectares in size. There was discussion of parking lots and swimming pools, palm groves and camel rides.

As they neared the entrance to the property, coming closer to the protesters, Shaafia noticed that most of them were women and not such young women at that. She felt a wave of compassion for them. She could imagine that they had probably lived on this property for years, their families scraping out a living from the sea. Inwardly she sent up a prayer, asking: «What can I do for these women?»

As she gazed at them, she had a vision in her head. She could see the resort being built, long white buildings opening to the sea, the palm trees that had been discussed were the main vegetation and then to her surprise, off to one side, she saw a village of neat little white and blue houses, a small jetty, and fishing boats bobbing gently in the sea. There was a sense of harmony. She wondered at it and inwardly asked to understand what it meant.

«They belong here.» she heard. «There will be no harmony until they become contributors to the wellbeing of whoever lives here.»

At that moment Graham asked her what the crowd was actually yelling.

«They say they have always lived here. They were born here. They have been thrown out and no-one cares about them.»

«But they were not the owners?»

«No. People like this could never be the legal owners because they would not have the money.»

«What will they do?»

She shook her head. «They will suffer.»

He nodded. «I have seen this before. Some of our resorts in the Caribbean had that problem, and even now some of them have uncomfortable relations with the locals.»

Then it came to her. «This resort will be a great success if you do one thing.»

He looked at her. She had said this with such a tone of certainty that it struck him.

«What would that be?»

«I can see the resort.» she said. «The road does not start here,» pointing to the existing entrance. «But instead it comes in beside the sea over there, so the arrivals have a glimpse of the Atlantic when they come. There will be a long sandy beach with cabanas. The resort buildings are all low and one storey, set in a semicircle, all looking out over the water, but here is the one thing that will make this resort remarkable and ensure its harmony.»

He was looking at where she was pointing.

«Over there is a traditional fishing village where all these people can live. They will work for the resort, but also they will show visitors what traditional Moroccan life is like. There will be little shops that sell local crafts and clothes. The men will take the guests out fishing. It will be prosperous and happy. It will be famous for its innovation and good relations with the locals.»

He turned back to look at her with a broad smile.

«You are not just a good translator,» he said, «you are a visionary.»

She smiled back. «I can see things.»

Graham called to the other two and he conveyed what Shaafia had just said. Walid was in deep conversation with the two local men and did not join them.

Alex smiled. «You are probably pretty close to what we would build. I am impressed. But the idea of the village. That is new. I really love that idea.»

«And one more thing,» added Shaafia, hoping to say this before Walid rejoined them. «When you sign the contracts with the Razaks, you must insist that all this is in writing. You must insist.»

«You think he might agree but then not do it?»

«He is a Moroccan businessman.» she said with an enigmatic smile.

Graham said very quietly as Walid began walking towards him: «I like it. I like it a hell of a lot.»

Suddenly a shot of electricity shot through Shaafia's body, and she knew what it was and where it came from.

She looked up into Graham's face and gazed steadily at him. «I believe you.» she said. «I will speak to those women.»

Then she left the men and walked out to the front gate.

«I will speak to them.» she said to the guard, who stood with a gun slung across one shoulder. The big dog had turned to face her but the guard held the leash tightly.

«You need me to come with you?» he asked. «They are wild, these people.»

«No thank you.» she smiled at him and he opened the gate.

As she walked towards them, she heard a voice in her head. «The woman with the white head scarf is a healer. She is the one.»

She saw immediately which one it was. She was in the centre of the group and obviously their leader. Shaafia went straight up to her and addressed her in the Berber language that her parents spoke.

«Greetings to you. I can see the pain that you are suffering as you have lost your homes and a way to make a living.»

The woman had a wizened dark brown face suffused with wrinkles, but her eyes were very clear. She peered at Shaafia, moving in very close to her.

«Are you with them?» Her voice was smoky and rough.

«I am their translator.» Shaafia replied, holding the woman's scrutiny. «I come with a message from them. They are good people and they understand why you are here. They wish to make a commitment to you.»

They all crowded round her as she spoke. She described the idea of building a village in which they could all live, and they could work and be paid by the resort.

One younger woman who had no teeth shouted from the back of the group. «Yeah, that's all fine but what about now? It will take years to build, won't it. How do we live before that?»

«What you say is important,» replied Shaafia. «I will take this point back to them.»

There seemed to be a wave of an outbreath from the group as if somehow they collectively felt that there was truth in what Shaafia had told them.

She looked around the group, making eye contact with each one. As she did, she knew they were with her. She could feel it.

«Please put down the placards,» she said quietly. «Go sit under the tree over there and I will come back.»

The woman in the white head scarf told them all that she believed what Shaafia was saying and that they should do as she asked.

She watched as they retreated to the shade of a eucalyptus tree which sheltered some of the ramshackle dwellings.

She had a passing thought. «Oh tree, please take all their negative thoughts. Let them sit in peace.»

Then she turned back to the gate. Suddenly she realised that all the men were looking at her: Walid, the local representatives, the Englishmen, and all the security guards.

As she was let in the gate, Walid demanded: «What did you just do?»

She glanced at Graham and gave a subtle nod, before she looked directly at Walid.

«I speak Berber like they do,» she said. «I have persuaded them to stop their protest.»

«How did you do that?» he asked suspiciously.

«They are just frightened because of what has happened, but I have told them that they will be taken care of.»

«You had no right to say that,» he growled.

«I told them that if they were cooperative then they could be part of the resort.»

«We don't employ people like that. They have no training.»

«They have something more valuable. They live here, they love this place.»

«What would they do?»

So she described her vision, the idea of the traditional village, shops selling artefacts, and fishing expeditions in traditional boats. Although this was all in Arabic, Graham knew what she was telling Walid and chipped in that he loved the idea. Alex added his support as well, and Walid pursed his lips in thought.

For him the most important thing so early in the negotiations was to keep the Englishmen happy. Maybe the idea would fade away once they all signed the contracts.

«Well, that's something to think about.» he said.

« I believe,» said Shaafia, «if you were to give each of them some money, to live by for a while, then they would not protest any more.»

«No,» said Walid, «you pay them, they'll come back tomorrow for more.»

«I don't think so.» Shaafia looked up at him with serious eyes. «The woman who leads them is a good woman. She can be trusted. And what is more, if we do this, she will be an advocate for the project.»

Graham said: «This is very smart. If we can get good relations with the locals, it makes everything so much easier. I think we should do it.»

Walid's face went through several different visible expressions, but then he smiled. «Oh well, what's a few thousand dirhams in the bigger picture. I will put it down as part of the first phase expenses.»

Then he turned to Shaafia. «I hope you don't expect to get an even bigger fee after this. Community relations officer or something?» but he was smiling as he said it.

She looked steadily at him. «In a few years from now you will remember this, and your gratitude will prompt you to do something good. That will be my fee.»

«What are you, some kind of mystic?»

She smiled. «I am what you see.»

«OK,» he said. «Go tell them that this afternoon we will return here and give them a reward for their goodwill. Take their names so that they don't go and round up a thousand others to get in on it.»

Shaafia went back to the group and opened her handbag to take out her notebook and a pen. The woman in the white head scarf looked at Shaafia's bag and gently stroked it with her right hand.

«Very beautiful.» she said.

Shaafia took her hand and held it. As she did, she recognised that the woman had healing hands. She smiled and gently ran her fingers across the woman's hand.

They smiled at each other. The woman knew that Shaafia could see who she was. Then on an impulse Shaafia put her hand into her bag and found the small medallion of the Virgin that Marie-Louise had given her. She gave it to the woman and closed her hand over it.

«Protection.» she whispered.

The woman did not look at her gift, but simply nodded.

Shaafia wrote down the name of each of the women present and the few men who were with them, most of them elderly. She told them that she would return that afternoon with one thousand dirhams each. They were shocked. A thousand dirhams would be a fortune for them. She said that only those whose names she had would receive the money.

The woman in the white head scarf stood next to Shaafia, and she looked at her group. «We are poor people but we are not thieves. We look after our families and we work hard. We pray to God that what is happening today is his will. We thank God for sending this sweet girl to help us.»

There was a heartfelt murmur of concurrence from the group.

When Shaafia walked back to the gate she told Walid: «I have promised them one thousand dirhams each.»

His eyebrows shot up but he grinned. «You are a very expensive part of my team,» but she could see that he was content. Graham was very happy and that was even more important.

As they walked back to the car to head for lunch, Graham said to Walid: «I have such a good feeling about this project, I have to say.» which Shaafia translated with a broad smile.

As the big car swept out of the gate and the guard closed it behind them, Shaafia leaned over to wave to the group under the tree and they waved back.

Walid had booked a lunch in the best restaurant that Essaouira had to offer. As he drove, he told the Englishmen that the fish from this town was the best in all of Morocco and the restaurant he had booked had been awarded generous mentions in the tourist guidebooks.

He pulled into a carpark near the fishing port and immediately a young boy rushed up to help him with the parking, not that he needed it. However, the boy was of course looking for money. Walid gave him a coin and told him if he guarded the car really well he would pay him double when they came back. Shaafia explained all this to the Englishmen, and said you could find boys like this in every town in Morocco.

As they walked towards the centre of the town and passed under the arch in the high stone walls of the old city, Walid described some of the history of the town, it had a long Jewish history and many old synagogues..

Across an inner square he pointed out the restaurant where he had booked lunch.

Instantly an electric shock ran through Shaafia and she almost shouted.

«No! It's not good! Don't go there!»

Walid stopped in horror. «What are you saying?»

«Don't go in there. There is something dangerous.»

His eyes narrowed. «Are you mad?»

This was all in Arabic, and Graham wanted to know what had happened.

«I have a feeling there is something not good about this restaurant.» she said in English.

Suddenly across the square there was yelling, and people came running out of the restaurant.

Walid ran over to one of them and asked what was happening. «Kitchen fire,» the man said. Then as he looked across, Walid saw smoke coming from the entrance.

Then he started to laugh. He came back to Shaafia and he said: «You are a mystic. How did you know that?»

She shrugged. «I see what I see.»

«OK,» he said. «How about you use your mystic powers to find us another place for lunch?»

She grinned right back. «I will.»

She had never been to Essaouira before, but she began to walk and the others followed. She was drawn to a small narrow alleyway off to one side and turned into it.

It was a dead-end, but at the far end was a small building with a hand-written sign in Arabic saying «*Hout*», Arabic for fish.

«Here.» she said.

«Are you sure?» asked Walid.

Instead of answering, she went inside. The aroma of fish cooking and herbs was exquisite. The place was crowded, mostly men and locals by the look of them. The man who greeted them had a massive belly and a wide black moustache. When he saw them, he said: «Five! I only have one table left so you have to squeeze.»

The last table was right at the back and they did indeed have to squeeze in. Shaafia found herself wedged between the two younger Englishmen.

Walid caught the man's eye. «Menu?»

«No,» the man said: «today it is,» and he named some kind of fish that neither Walid or Shaafia had heard of.

«Only one kind of fish?»

«On Thursday yes. If you want tuna come back tomorrow.»

«Is it good?» asked Walid, feeling uneasy for his guests.

The man patted his belly. «Would this belly lie to you?» Then he gestured round his little restaurant. «Happy customers.» Sure enough everyone there seemed to be enjoying the lunch.

At the next table a man overheard what was being said and turned to Walid. «Asad is the lion of fish cooking. We come every day.»

«OK.» said Walid.

A small boy brought a big silver teapot to the table with little glass cups, and poured mint tea.

Within minutes their dishes arrived, a big oval metal plate with a long white fish flanked with potatoes and green vegetables. They could each serve themselves from the plate in the middle of the table. The aroma was mouth watering.

As they began to eat, they smiled at each other. It was superb.

Asad came back and looked down. «Did I lie?»

Walid had to smile. «That belly of yours tells the truth.»

It turned out that the restaurant did not even offer dessert. All they did was one fish dish and mint tea.

When it came time to pay, Walid had to smile. He leaned over to Graham, and he said. «What I just paid here for everything would have bought just one dish at the restaurant I booked.»

Graham grinned. «I think this is the best fish dish I have ever had, and we have some fabulous fish chefs in our Caribbean resorts. I know a good fish when I taste it.»

As they left the restaurant, very well satisfied, Walid walked beside Shaafia. «There is no end to your talents,» he said.

«Be careful,» she responded, «I might put my fee up.»

«It might be worth it.»

They detoured via a bank to get the cash for the women out at the resort site, and then headed back to the car. The boy who had helped with the parking jumped to his feet and gave the windshield a quick rub with a filthy cloth.

Walid gave him a ten dirham note and the boy's eyes widened.

«Thank you. Thank you. Thank you.» he said, nodding his head many times. «You come back and I will take care of your car every day.»

Walid smiled at him.

«We'll look out for you for sure next time we come.»

As the car approached the group waiting under the tree, they leapt to their collective feet. They had probably stayed there all day.

The guards came out of the gate, but Walid waved them back.

He gave Shaafia the big wad of notes.

»This was your idea,» he said. «so you can have the pleasure. But make sure they keep their promise. No more protests.»

«You can trust them.» she said, and approached the group.

The woman in the white head scarf lined them up and one by one they received their one thousand dirhams, ten one hundred dirham notes to each one. It was obviously a lot of money to them and they each put their hands up to their hearts as they accepted it.

The woman with the white head scarf was the last one. Somehow Walid had miscalculated and Shaafia found she had two thousand dirhams left.

«This is for the love you show your people,» said Shaafia. «If they stay peaceful and make sure no-one else protests, then you will all thrive.»

«It will be as you say,» said the woman, «and may God bless you every day of your long life.» She put her dirhams carefully inside her robe, and then gently put her hand up to Shaafia's cheek and stroked it.

«God sent you.» she murmured.

On the drive back to Casablanca, Shaafia fell asleep and to her embarrassed horror, when she woke up, as the car stopped at Walid's house, she was lying against the shoulder of Alex.

«Oh, I am so sorry,» she said, but he patted her on the head. «That's OK little sister, you earned it.»

Ihab and Ayman had obviously had a very lazy day with nothing to do. As they drove Shaafia home they wanted to hear about her trip, but she was so tired she could barely function.

Her Mother had prepared the evening meal, but Shaafia had a few mouthfuls of soup and nearly fell asleep at the table.

That night she slept deeply and dreamlessly.

The last day of the Englishmen's visit was the Friday.

It was clear by the time Shaafia arrived that some kind of agreement had already been made.

They sat for the final meeting and began signing documents. If the sale of the property in Essaouira went through, then they would form a joint venture to develop the resort. Graham's company would design it, the Razaks would find the contractors to build it, Alex would be the overall supervisor, and they would own the resort in equal shares. The issue of the traditional village was not even a question. It would be a feature of the development. Walid had been won over by the English enthusiasm.

Nonetheless it was included in the documents, just as Shaafia had suggested.

As all this was concluded, champagne was brought out. Shaafia gently refused a glass, and was given grape juice instead.

The celebration lunch was sumptuous. There were many different dishes of lamb, chicken and local vegetables redolent with *Harissa* and other traditional spices, bottles of Moroccan wine, and then plates of local *patisserie* of all kinds.

Graham heaped praise on Shaafia for all that she brought to their meeting.

«My dear,» he said, stretching his legs out alongside the low round table. «I have to say that your contributions to this endeavour have been priceless. You are much more than just a good translator, you have other qualities that I find quite remarkable.»

She dipped her head shyly as he said all this, still having to translate for Walid at the same time.

He agreed.

«Any time you need a translator for this project we know who to ask.»

«Can I have your business card?» asked Graham. «I would like to stay in contact.»

Shaafia had to smile. She had never in her life thought of having her own business card.

«As I have only just come back from Bordeaux, I do not have one yet, but as soon as I do, I will send it to you.»

He gave her his, gold lettering on a textured white cardstock.

They got up from lunch, and Walid asked Shaafia to follow him to his office so he could pay her for the week.

He had a splendid dark wood desk with a luxurious upholstered leather chair. On the walls were pictures of his Father's hotels.

He took her on a quick tour of their assets.

«You must come and see them,» he said, «you would be impressed.»

Finally he dropped into his chair and gestured for her to sit opposite.

«So we agreed on a price for mornings only, but you have done more or less a full day. So we double it. Is that suitable?»

She smiled at him. «What would you say if I said no?»

«It wouldn't surprise me.» he smiled back. «You are not like the women I am used to working with. I don't know how they trained you in Bordeaux, but it is impressive.»

She nodded. «I was trained by the best.» In her mind she was thinking about the kind of training she had in fact received from Pia.

«You will accept a cheque?»

«Of course.»

«You have a bank account here?»

« Attijariwafa.»

He was impressed. He wrote her the cheque, signed with a flourish, and passed it across the desk. She glanced at it and smiled. «You have the honour of giving me my first pay cheque since my return. May it bring you good fortune.»

«I think you have brought me good fortune already.» Then he leaned back in chair, and he said: «Would you consider coming to work for me full-time?»

«You need a translator all the time?»

«Not as a translator but, maybe, a personal assistant?»

She gazed at him for a long moment, and what she could see told her exactly what her response would be.

«I am very flattered that you should ask, but I am afraid I could not accept your offer.»

He frowned. «You didn't even ask what I would pay you before you say no?»

«It is not about money,» she said, looking very directly at him. «I have things that I must do. I cannot work full-time for anyone. If you need translation from time to time, then of course I would be happy to come.»

He nodded.

«If you worked for me, I think you would be very successful.»

«Maybe, but it is not for me.»

«When you get your business card, I would like one.»

She put her cheque in her handbag and stood up. «I wish to thank you for this cheque, and I wish to thank you for inviting me to do this work. It has been very enjoyable.»

«And I wish to thank you,» he said back. «You did a lot more than just translate.» Then he grinned. «Anytime I need someone to find me a good restaurant I will call you.»

She smiled.

When they returned to the front of the house, Ihab was there with the car. The three Englishmen escorted her out.

«Without you, I am not sure we would have gone ahead,» said Graham. «You are a wonderful ambassador for your country.»

Shaafia bowed her head and put her hand up to her heart.

«I wish you all success with this project,» she said. «I will look forward to coming to Essaouira to see it all finished.»

«You will be our honoured guest, I promise you.»

They all shook hands, and she got into the back seat and asked Ihab to lower the window.

As the car pulled away, Graham called: «Don't forget your business card.»

All the way back her two brothers grilled her on what had happened. She was discreet, as she could not be sure how much to say. When they asked how much Walid paid her, she smiled and said: «I was happy with what he gave», but that was all.

She asked them to take her to the Attijariwafa bank so she could bank the cheque. They were impressed. They were paid in cash, and neither of them had ever had a bank account.

Finally they dropped her off at the end of the alley, and she began to walk the last block home. She felt a deep satisfaction. She had found work, she had done well, and she had been guided all the way.

She passed the small grubby cafe at the end of the lane that led to her house, and inside she saw Samet with a group of young men sitting round a table with empty coffee cups in a haze of cigarette smoke.

On an impulse she went in.

The owner, who she had known since she was a child, smiled at her. «Your brother comes in every day. I think soon he will put down roots like a tree and start to grow here.»

She smiled. «It is time he grew something.»

When she approached the table Samet, who was in the middle of a heated argument, looked up.

He scowled at her. «Now what?»

She looked around the group of young men who were scrutinising her with interest. She knew most of them at least by sight.

«Nothing,» she said. «I saw you all here and I decided to find out what you were fighting about.»

«We weren't fighting,» said one of the boys. «Just arguing about the state of the world and what political system is the best. Your brother is pitifully anticapitalist.»

«As opposed to the braindead socialists over here.» retorted Samet.

«Not to mention this diehard capitalist.» said another boy, pointing to a young man in what looked like a kind of western suit.

«So you couldn't come to a conclusion?» asked Shaafia.

One of the other boys laughed. «What would be the good of that? Then we'd have nothing to argue about.»

Shaafia smiled. Then she remembered something from one of her classes at University. Although she had mostly studied languages, still she was required to take a range of other courses.

«I suppose,» she said, «if you took Samet's perspective and mixed it with this businessman here and then added the socialists, you would have capitalist socialism. Then everyone would be happy.»

«Not me,» yelled Samet. «It's a fraud.»

«It seems to work OK in Sweden.» smiled Shaafia. She was amazed at herself being able to remember that. The boys were a bit amazed, too.

«Hey Samet! Your sister is smarter than you.» smirked one of the socialists.

«Kid goes to Bordeaux,» Samet sneered « and comes back thinking she's an intellectual giant.»

Shaafia went over to him and kissed him on the cheek. «You should try it one day.» Then she waved to the other boys and left.

The owner gave her a friendly wave as she went out. Then she turned and came back. «Have they paid for their coffee?» she asked.

He wagged his head from side to side, «Well these are not exactly my best customers from that point of view.» he said.

She dug in her handbag and pulled out a one hundred dirham note. «This should help.» she said, and was gone before he could protest.

When she reached home, only her Mother was there, beginning to get the evening meal ready. Shaafia gave her a wad of dirhams to which her Mother protested.

Shaafia stroked her Mother's cheek. «I banked a very large cheque today. I want to share my good fortune.»

Then she reached up and wiped the small tear that touched the corner of her Mother's eye.

As they walked together to her Uncle Samad's shop to collect the moneys for the week, Shaafia described what had taken place in Essaouria. Her Mother nodded now and then, her eyes widening as Shaafia described what she had done.

«You learned to do this kind if work in Bordeaux?» she asked.

«In a way.» smiled Shaafia, «It was part of the training.»

In the shop, they were pleased to see that he had created a stand different green teas, and he was beaming.

«I sold twice as many boxes of tea as last week. You were right.»

Shaafia studied the ledger and nodded.

«You did well this week.»

«I think you brought me good fortune.»

«*Ham delilah.* sighed her Mother.

This time Shaafia accepted the envelope without opening it. She simply passed it to her Mother.

They took samples of the new teas to try, and added whatever else her Mother needed for the coming week.

They stopped at the Mosque for evening prayers.

As the prayers were broadcast, Shaafia revelled in a deep inner peaceful-ness. How perfect seemed to be the unfoldment of events. It was as if there had been a plan made by some invisible ethereal force, which was being enacted in just the right way at just the right time. Her sense of gratitude was deep and heartfelt.

They sat quietly together at the end of the prayers until her Mother whispered that they should go to prepare the evening meal.

Shaafia opened her eyes and smiled at her Mother.

Her Mother said: «To pray with you has been a new pleasure for me. You bring so much hope into my life.»

They gave each other a loving hug and got up to leave.

As they were putting on their shoes Myriam, Haj Kabir's wife, approached them with a message from Rana Bin Salah. Rana wished to invite Shaafia to have tea with her to meet her daughter Houda. Myriam said that Rana felt that maybe Shaafia would be a good influence on her daughter. She had told Myriam that her daughter was deeply depressed, wouldn't eat and wouldn't communicate, and she hoped that maybe Shaafia might inspire her.

Shaafia smiled inwardly. How perfect. Here was the next step in the divine plan.

Myriam gave her Rana's phone number so she could call to accept the invitation.

As they walked, Shaafia called.

Rana was extremely pleased to hear from Shaafia, and thanked her so much for accepting the invitation. They agreed to meet on the following Sunday. Rana would send the car to pick her up, and they agreed that Shaafia would be at the Mosque as the big car would have trouble coming up their narrow lane.

There was another evening meal with most of the family turning up. Once again Ihab and Ayman brought their contribution. Nayla did not appear. Ahmed tried several times to corner Shaafia, but each time she found a distraction.

Everyone wanted to know about Shaafia's first week at work. She down-played most of it, just saying who she was translating for and what their project was. However, Ihab had heard the story about the fire in the restaurant and he told it with great dramatic flare.

«Now our boss thinks that Shaafia is a mystic.» he chortled.

Ayman added that the Englishmen seemed to have fallen in love with his little sister, and wanted her to be available whenever they needed a translator.

Then Samat told them about Shaafia impressing his friends at the café. «Now some of my friends think she is an intellectual giant.»

Shaafia let all this wash over her, although she was not so happy being the centre of attention all the time.

At the end of the meal, Shaafia noticed Sadik, the second youngest, shyly looking at her, so she went over to him. «What's up little brother?»

«I started to read the book you gave me but there's lots of words I don't know. Can you help me?» Although Moroccan schools teach in both Arabic and French, obviously Sadik's French was not so competent.

Shaafia took him outside and they sat under the fig tree and she asked him to read some of the book aloud. It was not very complicated language, but still he struggled. She gently helped him out as he went along.

«Do you have a dictionary?» she asked. He shook his head, so she said: «Tomorrow we will go and buy you one.»

«Samet has one,» he said shyly. «Maybe he would let me borrow it.»

«You should have your own. I insist.»

That night as she heard the late call of the *Muezzin* from the Mosque, she dropped deep inside where her Koranic verse was already pulsing.

More waves of gratitude washed over her, and she dropped into deeply happy sleep.

Small Steps

The following morning brought an animated breakfast, with fresh baked flatbread, samples of the new teas, and plans for the weekend.

The girls would all go to the *hamam* first, and then Shaafia would take Sadik to buy his dictionary. She also planned to find a printer who could make business cards.

Habib wanted to remind Shaafia that she had promised to take him to see Yasser play football with Rachi in the afternoon. She assured him she had not forgotten.

Sitting together in the heady steam of the *hamam*, the younger girls talked animatedly with their friends. Shaafia's Mother sat with some of the older ladies and boasted mostly about what great things were happening now that Shaafia had come back.

Shaafia sat quietly, allowing her body to absorb the heat, feeling her pores opening and her mind at rest. Into this stillness came a presence, a very sweet and comforting presence. «We are with you. We will show you the way. You have great faith in us and we have great faith in you. You are one of us now.»

She was bathing in a new kind of cleansing, on the outside in the steam of the *hamam*, and on the inside any doubts that she ever had, any sense of her own limitations, these were being washed away.

At last it was time to move on and her Mother came over to her.

«You look very peaceful,» she said.

«Mmm.»

Shaafia could barely speak.

The girls all dressed and headed for home.

As they passed the cafe at the corner of their lane, Shaafia glanced in and saw the huddle of Samet's friends. She told the girls to go on and she would catch up in a moment.

Hawa looked at her with scorn. «You're going in there? It's a den of smokers and dropouts, dumb arguments and empty theories. Why would you want to hang out with them?»

Shaafia smiled. «Maybe I can be their lifesaver.»

«Ha!» snorted her younger sister, «Good luck with that!» and ran to catch up with her other sister.

As Shaafia walked in, she slipped another one hundred dirham note to the owner, who beamed.

She walked up to the group and, without being invited, pulled up a chair next to Samet.

One of the boys said: «Hey you paid for our coffee yesterday, you can come any day!»

«I paid today as well but maybe that's the last time.»

Samet cocked his head on one side and said: «What are you up to?»

«I have a challenge for you.»

The boy in the suit leaned forward. «Money involved?»

«Could be.» she said.

«Go on. Challenge us.» said one of the other boys, blowing cigarette smoke up into the air away from Shaafia.

«I have a feeling you all fancy yourselves as writers, thinkers and judges of the state of the world.» she said looking round the group. There were six of them and they all looked at her with interest, even Samet. «How about you begin to show the world what you can do?»

«Oh yeah? Who would listen to us?» said one of the boys.

She turned to Samet. «Did you show them the book I gave you about cafés?»

He had a grubby cane basket at his feet, and he bent down and pulled the book out. He laid it on the table.

Shaafia went on. «In almost all of those cafés, in Egypt, in Algeria, in Marrakesh, people like you have met and argued. But they also wrote poetry, made art, wrote articles, published books, and a lot of them became the best minds in the Arabic world.»

They looked at her, wondering what she was getting at.

«Maybe one day, this little café, humble though it is, will be recorded in a future book, like this.»

«How?» asked the boy in the suit.

«Samet writes great letters. I have received them. He has a good way with words. What about the rest of you? Tell me what your talents are.»

She looked round the group. They were moving their heads uncomfortably, and she could see it was a challenging question. No-one wanted to say anything. She looked at the boy in the suit, he seemed to be the most open.

«That boy next to you,» she said, »what is he good at?»

«Yusuf?» The boy clapped his neighbour on the shoulder. «He paints. He does clever satirical paintings.»

«Yusuf,» she said, pointing to the boy next to him. «What about him? What does he do?»

Yusuf put his hand on the shoulder of the boy in question. «I hope you don't mind, brother.» he asked. «Nabil is a poet. He's a bit embarrassed about it.»

And so it was all round the table.

«So here is my challenge,» said Shaafia. «Next Saturday you all come here with something to show. It must be something that you think the world needs to see or the world needs to hear.»

«Then what?»

«Then you critique it, the whole group does. Suggest improvements or edits.»

«We are good at that,» grinned Samet. «Almost too good. OK, then what?

«Do you know what a podcast is?»

They nodded. The boy with the suit dived under the table and brought out a very battered laptop.

She nodded at him. «Do you know how to make one?»

«My brother does. he said. «He works for Telecom.»

«So then you put all the best pieces together on the podcast. You choose a good name for it and you begin to promote it. Get followers on Instagram, Facebook and Google, and all those ways of getting noticed.»

They stared at her. She had so much certainty about her. She saw them nodding, trying to imagine that what she was challenging them to do might actually happen.

Then she got to her feet, looked around the group.

«Next Saturday.» she said, and walked out.

«Come back soon!» called the owner.

As she walked the short distance to home, Shaafia marvelled at herself. She didn't know anything about podcasts or Instagram or anything. It just came out of her mouth.

But she knew a fire had been lit back in that café.

When she got back to the house, Sadik was nervously waiting.

She gave him a hug and they set off.

As they passed the café on the corner, she glanced in. The owner gave her a cheerful wave, but the boys at the back had their heads together in serious conversation.

The bookstore closest to their house was a bit of a walk. As they went along, Shaafia asked Sadik about school. He shyly admitted he didn't like going to school much and he found most of the classes difficult.

«What do you like to do?»

He shrugged. «I don't know.»

«Well, don't worry,» she said. «One day you will find out. Maybe school is not so important for you.» As she said that, an image of her Uncle Samad's shop came into her mind. Was there something for Sadik there?

When they finally reached a more upmarket shopping area, she took him into a small but well-stocked bookshop. Just the smell of the shop filled her with pleasure. When she was a small child and the family was poor, they could not afford books. Sometimes, she and Rachi would come to this bookshop and browse. They could never afford to buy anything, but the owner was always welcoming.

He was an older man with a long white beard, dressed in a long white robe with a little round hat. She knew him well, as he was a regular at the Mosque.

When he saw her, he asked where she had been, as he had not seen her for a long time. So she had to give a short version of her last several years.

Meanwhile, Sadik wandered around in the bookstore looking at all the different shelves.

When she finally joined him, she said: «Do you see anything you would like?»

He shook his head. «It's very scary.»

«What do you mean?»

«All these books. People wrote all these books and no-one is reading them. They just sit there. Look how many there are.»

«You find that scary?»

«Mmm. I don't think I like books.»

«I didn't know that. If I had known I would have brought you something else.»

«That's OK. You didn't know.»

«So you really don't want a dictionary then?»

He looked at her and bit his lip, then he shook his head.

«Why didn't you tell me?»

«Because you gave me a gift. I didn't want you to feel sad.»

She gave him an impulsive hug.

«So if you had been my gift advisor, when I was choosing a gift for my brother Sadik, what would it have been?»

«I don't know.»

«Well if you get an idea, you have to tell me, and I will get you the kind of gift that would make you happy.»

«OK.» he said.

They were about to leave the shop, when Shaafia saw a book on display. It was a glossy coffee table book about Bordeaux. Although she had not spent any time really exploring the city, she recognised some of the photos, the big fountain at Quinconces, Le Grand Théatre and the Pont de Pierre crossing the river. As she leafed through it, she showed Sadik the photos and told him what they were. Then she had an inspiration. She would give this book to Rachi.

She had the book gift-wrapped, and they walked out into the street. As she waited to cross the busy road, trucks and taxis jousting with each other in the hazy air, she noticed a printery off to one side. She remembered her desire to get a business card.

The proprietor showed her many samples. She asked Sadik what he thought and he touched them, felt their texture and looked at the colours.

Then he held one up. It had a finely textured finish and solid dark blue lettering.

«This one.» he said. «It should have a white background with blue writing.»

She took it from him and felt the texture. He was right. It felt good to touch. And his choice of colours? The Lady in Blue and White floated gently behind her eyes and she smiled.

«Perfect.» she said. «You are good at this.»

He shuffled his feet in embarrassment.

She ordered a box of one hundred cards to be printed in Arabic on one side and French on the other. She used her credit card for the first time. The cards would be ready in a week.

As they left the shop, she said: «That was great. Let me say thank you with an icecream.»

He glowed under her praise and was very happy to sit with her on a bench in a little park with a double cone.

By the time they made it home, Habib was beside himself with anxiety because it was getting time to go to see the football. He wanted to get a good seat so he could see Yasser play.

Shaafia had a quick lunch, then with Habib almost running, they went to Rachi's house.

Rachi's Mother was very happy to see them, and again she wanted to thank Shaafia for what she was doing.

«You are such a good girl.» she murmured as she kissed Shaafia's cheeks. Then Habib had to suffer being kissed as well.

Rachi came out and she had obviously made quite an effort to get ready. She had applied some make-up and she looked very pretty.

Shaafia smiled but decided not say anything.

They caught the bus to go across town to the stadium where Yasser's team played. Shaafia quietly asked Rachi how she felt, and in response Rachi squeezed her hand.

«I have something for you.» said Shaafia.

As the bus rattled along, stopping often, to Habib's annoyance, Rachi opened her gift.

She gave Shaafia the biggest hug, even as the bus began to get more and more crowded.

«I can see where you were.» she said.

«And where you will be, very soon.» said Shaafia.

There were long lines to get into the stadium and Habib could barely stand still with excitement.

Once they had bought their tickets, Habib insisted they find a seat as close to the goal as possible. They found a spot, several rows back, where he could see well, so he was content.

The teams came running out onto the ground amid roars of approval from the spectators. Somehow Habib had been lucky enough to choose the end of the ground where the supporters of Yasser's team were in the majority, wearing the team colours and shouting the team song as their players ran out.

Shaafia glanced at her two companions. Habib was ecstatic and Rachi was glowing. She felt deeply happy herself, although football was not one of her favourite things.

The game proceeded and Habib soon saw that Yasser played very well. He passed superbly to his team mates and then, in one exciting moment, he shot for goal. The goalie managed to deflect it and the crowd groaned in disappointment. However, Habib was amazed.

«Did you see?» he yelled, »That was our Yasser who did that. He's brilliant.»

Rachi gave him a big hug.

At half time they went and got some drinks and snacks. Habib saw one of his friends from school and boasted that Yasser was his good friend.

The second half produced no scores at all but the crowd didn't seem to mind. There was lots of shouting and encouragement from all around them.

With the scores level, it was time for a shoot out.

The opposing team scored and the crowd around Habib groaned.

Then it was Yasser who was shooting for his team. He angled the ball in a wide curve that looked like it was going too far left but somehow it swung back, too high for the goalie to stop it. Habib leaped to his feet with every other fan around him yelling with excitement.

There were five scoring shots altogether and it was four each at the final round. The opposing team set up for the last shot, and to their horror, the shot went high and over the net. Now if only the home team could score, they would win.

Yasser took the ball. He paced back from it and eyed the goalie, who was dancing on the spot and waving his arms. The crowd was silent in expectation. Yasser took a wide turn before approaching the ball, lifted his leg high behind him then dropped his foot lightly onto the ball, so it ran low along the ground. The goalie had been fooled by the wide approach and leaped out wide, only to see the ball run behind him low and into the goal.

The crowd went berserk. The players all raced in to embrace Yasser, and he disappeared under a mound of sweaty bodies. Shaafia looked around to see what Habib thought of that, but he was gone. He had rushed down to the fence, jumped over it and joined the crush around Yasser.

Rachi stood there with an enormous smile on her face.

They went down to the fence to look for Habib, who finally emerged as the team made its way through a throng of admirers back to the changing rooms.

Yasser had agreed to meet them after the match so they went round to the players' entrance.

They waited a good half hour before he finally came out carrying his tote bag. Rachi could not hold back, she lunged at him and held him. He looked over her shoulder at Shaafia and she could see the effect of her assault.

He saw Habib jumping with impatience and disentangled himself to say hello.

«Close game, eh?» he said to Habib.

«You were so good.» said Habib.

Yasser invited them to go a café not far away for some tea. The café was full of fans of his team, so it wasn't very peaceful as people came up to their table constantly to clap him on the back or ask for an autograph.

After a while, they left the café and the crowd began to thin out. Yasser told them that his parents had watched the match, but he had asked them not to see him afterwards so he could talk to Rachi. They had no problem with that.

They found a park bench to sit on and Yasser said that he had some very special news. A scout had been to the club and had watched them train and play. He wanted to meet with Yasser to discuss the possibility of getting a contract to play with a professional club in Europe.

«Which club?» asked Habib, with his eyes wide in amazement.

«Les Girondins,» said Yasser.

«Bordeaux!» yelled Habib. «They are really good.»

Shaafia had to smile and she saw Rachi was doing the same. Rachi reached down into her bag and pulled out Shaafia's gift.

«Shaafia gave this to me today.» she said, and passed him the book.

Yasser looked at Shaafia for a long moment as if he were studying her. «How did you know?» he said at last, his voice perhaps a little shaky.

She shrugged, but Rachi said: «Shaafia knows a lot of things.»

On the bus ride home Habib could not stop talking. He relived the whole match, kick by kick till he got to the shoot out. The two girls let him go and sat there. Rachi took Shaafia's hand and held it, squeezing tightly.

When they got back to Rachi's house, Habib gave a breathless rendition of how his hero had triumphed and Rachi's parents were enthralled. They could also see how happy their daughter looked.

By the time Shaafia and Habib got home, they were both exhausted. Habib was still wanting to tell what happened but he was becoming incoherent. His Mother made him wash up, gave him some soup and sent him to bed.

Shaafia followed soon after.

Houda

Shaafia spent Sunday morning helping her Mother clean the house with the two younger girls. Sadik was around and helped a little bit. Habib went off to football practice, dying to tell all his friends about his friend Yasser who might be going to play for Bordeaux.

After a quick early lunch, Shaafia began to walk to the Mosque for the midday prayers. She would stay there until she was picked up by Rana's driver.

At the far end of the lane, she saw Tawfik with several of his friends revving up a small bike that was making a cloud of blue smoke.

When he saw her, he came over.

«Sorry,» he said, «it's a bit loud.»

«Can you fix it?»

He nodded. «The man who owns it gave it to one my friends, because he thought it was finished, but it's not. It's a good bike, if you know what to do with it.»

«And you do?»

He nodded.

«Have you thought any more about what I suggested?»

He watched the boys revving the engine then he nodded. «Yeah.» he said.

«So?»

«Maybe.»

«How about we ask Brahim what he thinks. He would know the right school.»

«OK.» he said, then he turned and ran back to the bike, which had just died.

She watched him for a minute and she could see that he was in charge of the group and the other boys deferred to him. Going to Mechanics School would be the right thing for him.

She revelled in the atmosphere of the midday prayers with the resonant voice of Haj Kabir over the loudspeakers taking her deep inside herself.

Somewhere in there she found herself addressing Haj Hussein. «Now I can begin to fulfill my promise to you.» she said.

In response, she felt waves of love ripple through her body. She knew that he had heard her.

She waited with Myriam in the shade of the courtyard next to the Mosque. The little boy ran around their feet with a small ball.

As she watched him, Shaafia thought about Yasser. Not so long ago he was a little boy like this and now he was a great soccer player. How quickly life changes, she thought, as each one's destiny becomes clear.

When the big white Mercedes arrived, it was only the driver. Shaafia kissed Myriam on the cheek, tried unsuccessfully to do the same to the little boy and headed for the car. Without thinking, she went to the front door on the passengers side to get in. When she opened it, he looked at her with puzzlement.

«You want to sit in the front?»

«Why not?» she smiled, closing the door behind her. «I'd be lonely back there all by myself.»

He smiled in return and the car silently slid away from the Mosque.

She had a reason to be sitting in the front. She asked him whether he liked working for the Bin Salah family.

He shrugged non-committally.

«It's OK.» he said. «It's regular work and I have a family to support.»

«They treat you well?»

His face and hand gesture told him that it was a question he would prefer not to answer.

«Have you been with them a long time?»

He nodded. «Maybe ten years.»

«My Father used to know Madame Bin Salah's Father very well. Did you know him?»

He shook his head.

She let it go. She had wondered if he might be an ally.

They left the inner suburbs of Casablanca and headed out towards the coast. Finally several small side roads led to a big white-walled compound that reminded Shaafia immediately of the Razak compound. Like would be marrying like, compounding.

At the security gate, the driver pressed a button on his dashboard and the gate automatically opened. Inside were wide manicured lawns and Shaafia marvelled at the amount of water it must take to keep it like that. At the end of a long gravel driveway, lined with red flowering plants, stood a wide-veran-dahed two-storey white building with a flat roof. The house was U-shaped and the car rolled into the centre where a large portico served as a landing place.

When the car pulled up, Rana came out to greet it.

She kissed Shaafia on both cheeks and thanked her profusely for accepting her invitation.

Shaafia smiled. «I am very happy to come.» she said.

Rana ushered her into a wide open foyer with a central fountain filled with lush ferns. The sound of the tumbling water gave a very soothing atmosphere to the area.

«It is very beautiful.» said Shaafia.

«My husband designed it. He likes using a lot of water.»

«It must be very expensive.»

«No.» replied Rana. «Our land is big enough to have many solar panels and we have big bores that pull water from underground. We don't have any electricity or water bills at all.»

They moved into an adjacent room that had a circle of wicker chairs and couches, adorned with red silk cushions. Rana took out a small device from her pocket and pressed a button. A moment later a young girl in a uniform appeared.

«Please ask Houda to join us.» said Rana, and the girl dropped her head in a sort of short bow and left.

«Please sit.» Rana gestured to the circle of chairs and couches.

Shaafia looked at the circle and tried to judge from where Houda would appear. She wanted to alert Houda not to let her Mother know that they already knew each other. She chose a chair facing the door the servant had used and happily her hostess chose a chair opposite, so having her back to the door.

When she heard footsteps however, Rana stood up to meet her daughter and Shaafia did the same.

As Houda walked into the room with a deep scowl on her face, Shaafia held up her fingers to her lips. Houda's eyes narrowed and then widened.

«This is Shaafia.» said Rana, turning to face Shaafia.

Shaafia smiled. «I am very happy to meet you.» she said. «I understand we were both studying in Bordeaux at the same time but somehow our paths did not cross at the University.»

Houda dropped into a chair beside her Mother so they were both facing Shaafia.

«What did you study?» asked Houda. She was wearing designer jeans and a loose open blouse. Her hair was tied casually at the back. She looked like any modern, wealthy young lady at ease in her wealthy environment. Round her eyes, however, were dark rings and her face was tight with tension.

«Translation, but I didn't finish the course.»

«Nor did I.» said Houda, with no attempt to hide her bitterness.

«Well,» said Rana, «let's have some refreshments.» and she pressed the button on her device.

Within seconds the girl in the uniform returned with another girl carrying trays with teapots, ornate little cups and covered dishes with patisseries. They laid everything out on a low coffee table and nodded before leaving. Neither of them said a word.

As Rana poured the tea, she talked glowingly about what she had heard about Shaafia's time in Bordeaux, working for the Australians, making enough money to offer *Zakat*, but finally coming home to support her family. Houda sat back in her chair, accepting a cup of tea and listening with half closed eyes. Shaafia was sure she had heard all this before.

Rana said, when she sat back with her own cup: «I do hope you two could be friends. I think it would help Houda to feel not so upset about being back.»

«You know why I am «upset»» sneered Houda accentuating the word.

Shaafia said: «You are to be married.»

«Not by choice.»

Rana said: «Just as I had no choice when I married your Father. It is something a woman has to get used to and make the most of.»

Shaafia nodded, not agreeing, but making sure she was not impeding whatever progress they were going to make. Inside herself she was acutely conscious, listening to other levels of communication. She felt deeply calm and content to allow the situation to unfold. Although she knew the answer to her next question, she felt an impulse to ask it.

«Who are you going to marry?»

Houda simply scowled and let her Mother, who had forgotten that she had already told Shaafia, do the talking.

«Maybe you have heard of the Razak family?»

Shaafia let herself smile broadly. «Rami Razak?»

«Yes, exactly. You know them?»

«Until last week I would have said no. But I spent the whole of last week working as a translator for his son Walid. He told me he was getting married. What a coincidence.»

«Really?» Rana had to laugh. «That is so strange. How did that happen?»

Shaafia looked at Houda, who was eyeing her with great interest. There was no scowling now. She sensed something.

«Two of my brothers work for Walid. Ihab, one of them, heard that Walid was looking for an English translator, so he recommended me.»

«Walid's English is pathetic.» sneered Houda.

Her Mother ignored that and asked: «So what do you think of him?»

«He is very business-like. He appreciated what I could do and he paid well.»

«The Razaks are a very good family. They have done so well and they have so many connections. I heard they are beginning to work with international partnerships.»

«Yes. English,» said Shaafia.

«Well, well.» said Rana.

Shaafia could tell that Rana was actually very nervous. She sat on the edge of her chair and her teacup tended to rattle in the saucer.

Shaafia put down her cup and sat forward.

«Can I make a suggestion?» she asked. Rana looked at her expectantly, so Shaafia went on: «Perhaps it might be good if we girls had a walk in your lovely gardens and just talked, girl to girl.»

«Oh.» said Rana. Then she turned to her daughter. «Would you like that?»

«Sure, why not?» and Houda stood up. « Anything to break the boredom of being a prisoner in this house.»

«Good.» Rana's smile was pathetically weak. She pressed her button and the two serving girls appeared almost instantly.

«We are done.» said Rana, and the tea things disappeared.

«Why don't you show Shaafia our solar panels and the water works out the back. I was just telling her about that.»

«OK.» said Houda, already heading out through wide double glass doors.

Shaafia smiled at Rana and put her hand on the older woman's elbow. «I think this will work out. Just give her some time.»

«Thank you so much.» whispered Rana.

Taking her handbag with her, Shaafia walked out after Houda.

Houda was waiting for her under a wide shady tree with pink blossoms. «What is this?» she demanded. «Who are you?»

«Let's walk.» said Shaafia quietly.

Beyond the house was a grove of trees with a small open gazebo in the centre. Houda led her in there. In the gazebo was a circle of benches.

Houda dropped onto one of the benches and looked fixedly at Shaafia. «So now for God's sake, tell me what the hell is going on. Who are you?»

Shaafia smiled and settled on a bench opposite Houda. «I have a lot to tell you. And I think the reason I am here is so that you can find out who you are.»

«What does that mean?» Houda snapped back. She wanted facts.

«So listen. Listen very carefully.»

«OK. I'm sorry. I'm stressed out. I'm a prisoner in my own house, I am being made to marry some horrible businessman who I don't like and I have no say in anything.»

«If you listen very carefully, you will find out that you are none of those things.»

There was such a calmness in Shaafia's voice, an assuredness, a confidence, that finally made Houda take a breath, sit back and listen.

«Alright.» she said.

Glancing back at the house to make sure they were alone, Shaafia leaned forward and spoke softly. «I have many different things to tell you about.»

«Please.» said Houda quietly.

Shaafia gave a description of meeting the Sharif when she was a young girl, the long search for the «Bird with Crooked Wings», going to Bordeaux to study, ending up in a convent with nuns, and then finally meeting Pia.

Up to that point Houda had listened and said nothing but when Shaafia began to describe being able to hear Pia's voice, she stopped her. «Wait. You could hear her voice? But she couldn't speak.»

«She chose to speak through me. Why she chose me, I cannot say, other than for some reason it was my destiny to be her voice.»

«What did she say?»

«Many things. Amazing things.» And Shaafia went on to give examples of what Pia knew about the people who came to see her, how she could give people remedies that would help them in so many different ways.

«How come she could do this?»

«It was a gift she was born with. The nuns now consider that she is a saint. And in India there are people who know who she was in a past life, a crippled saint. They say she has come back to do that work.»

«And you believe that?»

«Without a doubt. She has proved it over and over again. Everything I do now is because I know who she is and what she wants us, those who have met her, what she wants us to do to help other people.»

«People like me?»

Shaafia nodded. «People like you.»

«Do you think I will ever be able to meet her, so she can fix my horrible life?»

Shaafia shook her head. «She has left us, at least in her physical form.».

«She's dead?»

«She died when we went to Lourdes.» And then Shaafia described how although Pia had died, she could still communicate. Houda's eyes got wider and wider.

«Even though she was dead, she could still speak?»

Shaafia nodded. «Not just to me, to several others.»

Then Shaafia added the last elements of the story. «But as Pia began to finish her communications, there were other voices.»

«Who were they?»

«The first one was the Virgin Mary.»

«*Maryam Al Adra?*» asked Houda using the Arabic name.

«Yes.»

«She talks to you?»

«When she wishes.»

«How do you know it's her?»

«I have no doubt.»

«Does she talk to you now?»

«Not so much. Now there are others.»

«Others? Like who?»

«There is one who spoke to me and that is why I approached you in the airport.»

«Who was it?»

«Haj Hussein.»

Houda jumped up and almost screamed: «*Ba Jedi?*»

Shaafia gestured for her to sit. She nodded. »Yes, your grandfather.»

Tears ran down Houda's cheeks. «I miss him so much.»

Shaafia waited as Houda sniffed, blew her nose and then leaned forward.

«What did he say?»

«Before you even walked into the Business Lounge I heard a voice who said: «She will need your help.». I didn't know who it was or who needed my help. But then you walked in.»

«I needed help alright.»

«And then in the plane, voices told me that they would find a way for you to speak to me.»

«That bitch threw up!»

«Exactly.»

«Oh my God!» and she started to cry again. «*Ba Jedi*. You are looking after me. Please, please help me.»

«He has asked me to take care of you. He says you have a destiny.»

Houda stared at her.

«What does it mean?»

«I don't know yet. Except that it has to do with *Darou Al Bahr.*»

«Our house?»

«He told me: «My house will be your house. My garden will be your garden. Many companions will come there.»

«What does that mean?» then she smiled through her tears. «I keep asking the same question.»

«That's OK. I am the same, except that I have learnt how to accept that things seem to unfold the way they should, even if I am not comfortable along the way.»

«Do I still have to marry Walid Razak?»

Shaafia became very still, as if checking inside her self. Then she shook her head.

«I don't think so.»

«Oh, thank God. Thank God.»

Then Shaafia made a decision.

«They don't let you have a phone, do they?»

«That bitch took it at the airport and they won't give it back.»

Shaafia took out her own cell phone.

«Be quick. Call the boy in Bordeaux.»

Houda jumped. This was such a shock but she grabbed the phone and dialed. Her whole body shook as she waited.

Then he was there.

«Benjy Benjy, it's me.»

Then her eyes widened. «Oh no.»

Shaafia watched Houda's face as so many emotions raced across it.

«Did they hurt you? Are you OK?»

Then a great sadness took the place of all other emotions.

«Not ever. Benjy? Benjy?», and he was gone.

She sank back onto the bench and Shaafia reached to retrieve her phone. She slipped it into her handbag then sat next to Houda cradling her in her arms.

Houda cried and cried, her whole body shaking with it.

After a long time, she pulled out her handkerchief and blew her nose.

She looked at Shaafia with utter misery lining her face. «My Father's hired thugs trashed his apartment. They were the ones who kidnapped me. They smashed his computer, they took his phone and his camera. They said if he ever tried to talk to me they would come back. He is terrified. He does not want to ever see me again.»

«He is not part of your destiny.»

Houda looked at Shaafia for a long moment, then something shifted inside her. «You are right,» she said. «May he go to Hell!»

«No.» said Shaafia gently. «You should remember him with love. You should thank him for being just one small part of your destiny. That part of your life is finished now. Pray that he has a happy life.»

Houda bit her lip.

Shaafia could see her mind churning.

«You will need time to get used to this.»

Houda jumped up and began to walk away from the gazebo. Shaafia followed.

There were endless rows of solar panels angled to catch the sun, and at the far end of the property a row of wind turbines.

«So your Father pays no electricity bills or water bills?» asked Shaafia.

«Ironic, isn't it,» sneered Houda, getting some of her old spirit back. «He makes his money from petroleum, but he lives in an energy-neutral house.»

«He works with petroleum?»

«Bin Salah Transport has the biggest fleet of road tankers in Morocco. He owns more than a hundred gas stations from Tangier to Agadir.»

Shaafia had to smile.

Suddenly Houda stopped and looked deeply into Shaafia's eyes.

«Tell me what to do.»

Shaafia looked right back and their eyes locked. There was a flow of energy between them. For Shaafia it was as if she could see that the outer Houda was like a mask that the inner Houda had worn for so long that she did not realise that it was just a mask.

«They will guide us.»

«But right now? What can I do?»

Shaafia took Houda's hand and they turned, walking back through the solar panels towards the house.

«First you smile. You thank your Mother for everything she has done for you. You tell her you understand how hard it must be for her to see her daughter having to suffer the same fate as she did. You give her a big hug and you tell her that you love her.»

«I do love her. Thank God for my Mum.»

«Your Mother has suffered so much, but it will soon begin to change. It will change for you both.»

«And maybe we can go back to *Darou Al Bahr.*»

«You will.»

«OK,» said Houda, drawing herself up. «My grandfather was such a great person. If he is telling you what to do, then I will do whatever he says.»

«The greatness that he had, that he still has, he sees in you. You have to begin to see that too.»

«You have it, don't you.» said Houda stopping on the path to look at Shaafia.

«We all have it.» said Shaafia. «And one more thing. For now at least you must look like you are willing to go ahead with the wedding. Don't pretend too much enthusiasm, just be quietly accepting. I suppose that was how your Mother managed when she married your Father.»

«OK.» Then she stopped. «Does my Mother know anything about this, I mean the voices, my grandfather talking to you?»

«Not yet,» said Shaafia, «but there will be a time when she will know. She too has a destiny. She is like you, she does not know who she truly is.»

Houda frowned. «You know, I never thought about this, but she is as much a prisoner as I am.»

Shaafia nodded. «She has had to face many challenges, and everything she has done has been to protect you.»

As they walked towards the house, they saw Rana waiting for them.

«You must be thirsty.» she called. «Come and have some juice.»

Houda ran to her and threw her arms around her Mother's neck. «I am so sorry for being such a bitch. I am so sorry.»

Rana looked over the shoulder of her daughter to Shaafia, with her eyes wide, then gently she pulled back to look at her daughter.

«I am sorry, too,» she said, «but what can we do?».

«We will do what God wants us to do. *Inche Allah.*» said Houda.

«We will.» whispered her Mother with tears in her eyes. Then with her arms round her daughter, she guided her inside, and Shaafia followed with her heart full of gratitude.

Fruit drinks were on the table in the front room, with plates of little cookies.

Once they had sat, Shaafia said: «We have been speaking about your Father, Haj Hussein.»

Rana put her hand up to her heart and smiled. She looked at Houda, and she said: «I knew that you and Shaafia would get on. I am so happy that you have met her.»

«So am I.» said Houda.

Shaafia asked about the wedding plans, which were still in the very early planning stages. No date had been chosen, but the plan was to have a large pavilion erected in the grounds of the house, both for the wedding ceremony and the huge celebration feast to follow. Evidently Hamza Bin Salah was currently down in Agadir negotiating for more land to build new gas stations on the freeway that ran south.

«When he comes back, I hope that we can invite you for a meal and you can meet him.»

«Thank you. That would be a pleasure.»

«And then maybe, closer to the wedding, when we have the Razaks come, we will invite you too, seeing that you know them.»

Shaafia had to smile. That would be a very interesting meeting.

At the end of the afternoon, the big white Mercedes stood at the front door to take her back to the Mosque.

Houda and her Mother gave Shaafia the warmest of hugs and wanted to stay in touch. Shaafia shared her phone number with Rana.

As the car negotiated the narrow roads away from the compound, Shaafia was quiet, allowing her mind to be still, her Koranic verse pulsing subtly inside.

Now and then the driver would look across to see if she wanted to speak, but he seemed to accept that she did not.

When they reached the Mosque, she thanked him for driving, and went inside for evening prayers.

She was early and the women's section was empty. As she sat quietly she sensed the presence.

«We will advance slowly. Destiny will reveal itself, one step at a time. We are always with you.»

With her eyes closed she rested in the deep sense of being protected.

After evening prayers, as she walked back home, she passed the house of her neighbor Brahim and saw him at his desk by the front window. He looked up when he saw her and beckoned.

She approached and he opened the window.

«Your brother Toufik came to see me.»

She was very pleased. «About going to school?»

«He said you had persuaded him to study mechanics. I think it is a brilliant idea. I see him with the other boys working on bikes. It is obviously his passion.»

«Do you know which school would be the best?»

«My brother teaches mathematics like I do. He's at the Automotive College. I have offered to take Toufik there tomorrow.»

«Oh, thank you so much.»

«It is the least I could do. Now your Father has gone, I feel a lot of responsibility towards your family.»

Shaafia put her hand on her heart. «May God bless you for that.»

«May God bless you too.»

That night, as with every night since her return, Shaafia allowed the waves of gratitude to wash over her in time with the cadences of her Koranic verse, until she dropped into deep sleep.

Momentum

The following week was quiet, as if Shaafia needed time to integrate all that had happened so quickly since her return.

Each morning she would wait till her younger sisters left for school, lying on her sleeping mat awake but repeating her Koranic verse, then she would get up and join her Mother for breakfast. Sometimes one or other of the brothers would be around, Habib and Sadik going off to school, sometimes a sleepy Samet would stagger out.

She and her Mother would go to the *hamam*, and then shopping when it was needed. She felt a deep connection to her Mother and in turn she could see that her Mother deeply appreciated the company of this daughter who she never really understood well when she was young, but now treasured as a remarkable companion.

Sitting in a quiet corner of the *hamam*, sitting in the steamy mist, Shaafia had shared with her Mother her encounter with Houda and how she had changed Houda's state. Her Mother said little, nodding as she listened.

Finally she said: «As you tell me the effect that you are having on so many people, I have only one regret. Your Father was not blessed to stay on this earth long enough to see what you can do.»

«And yet,» smiled Shaafia, «Perhaps he can see what is taking place on this earth.»

Her Mother nodded. «Perhaps.»

At midday each day, she would go to the Mosque for the prayers. Sometimes she spent time with Myriam. With Haj Kabir she shared her meeting with Houda, and he listened in silence nodding now and then. Finally he said: «*Ham delilah.* Truly you are doing a divine work. I shall look forward to seeing how this work will unfold. I see that surely you bathe in the light of the mission you have been given. You glow with it. I salute your destiny.»

All this moved Shaafia deeply.

Some afternoons she would spend time with Rachi who was a changed person. Now she was intent on planning her wedding. She and her Mother had now become a formidable team. Shaafia watched it all but felt she had no need to get involved. Again and again Rachi would get excited about the prospect of going to Bordeaux, even though Yasser had not yet made any formal arrangements. The football agent was looking into getting Yasser to visit Bordeaux to meet the players and see how the system worked, but there was nothing in writing.

Shaafia told Yasser when they spoke on the phone that she had good friends in Bordeaux, so if he needed any help, he only had to ask.

On the Monday, Toufik had returned from his visit to the Automotive College. He proudly announced that with Brahim's help he had enrolled and was beginning classes right away. The term had been running for some weeks already, but Toufik told Shaafia that he had an interview with the mechanics teachers who could see that Toufik knew a lot already.

He was filled with enthusiasm and he gave his sister a big hug by way of a thank you. He was not a demonstrative person by nature, so this was a bit of a surprise.

On the Wednesday Shaafia went back to the commercial centre to collect her business cards. When she held the first one in her hand the texture and the colour pleased her very much. The young man who had made the card said he would keep the template because she had only ordered a hundred, and he was sure she would need more very soon. She thanked him for his optimism. She then crossed the road to the bookstore and she left one of her cards there, just in case someone needed an English translator.

In the evening when Sadik came home from school she gave him one, too. After all, it was his design, she told him. He was very proud of it and showed everyone who would listen.

Early on Thursday morning a small van inched its way up the alley to the house. Two young men in overalls had come to install the phone. Wires had to be run from Brahim's house to make the connection, but by the end of the morning there was a brand new shiny black phone sitting in the kitchen.

Once the technicians had made sure it worked, Shaafia helped her Mother to make the first phone call to Zarifa. Her Mother tended to shout as if she were reaching her daughter without the help of the device. After a while, Shaafia suggested that she hang up and that Zarifa call her to show her what the sound of an incoming call was. The minute it sounded, her Mother grabbed the phone, and was delighted to find that it was not Zarifa but Afifa. Zarifa had called her sister to give her the new phone number. Shaafia could see that her Mother was going to be a great user of this new toy and she was happy for her.

That afternoon, Shaafia decided to go through her suitcase to decide what to keep and what to give to her sisters. She came across a little notebook she had forgotten about. In it were phone numbers that she had used in Bordeaux, the château, the convent, and a few others. As she looked at it she felt a strong desire to talk to her «French family.»

She sat outside under the fig tree, and once she had worked out how to make an international call, she dialled the château. The phone rang several times and then there was Marie-Louise, who promptly screamed in delight into the phone when she heard who was calling.

«*Ah ma Belle*, how happy I am to hear your voice. *Comment ça va?*»

There was so much to say. Above all to this ex-nun who had now devoted her life to serving Pia, Shaafia wanted to tell her about the voices, not just the Virgin but other voices now, voices that connected her with the land she was born in.

Marie-Louise was in the middle of telling Shaafia how delighted she was to hear all this, when her voice disappeared and another voice was yelling into the phone. It was Berenice who had heard Marie-Louise say Shaafia's name and grabbed the phone. Now she spoke to Shaafia in her quickly growing French. She wanted to tell Shaafia that sometimes, when she sat in the chapel, Pia would come and sit with her.

Meanwhile Marie-Louise had run to find Théophile, and he too was delighted to hear her voice. He told her of the developments in the château and the vineyard, and the great news that the book that Brad had written about the life of Pia, «Listen to Love», had been edited by Indira and it was about to go off to the publishers. Théophile had sent some photos that would be included in the book.

«We will all be a little bit famous very soon.» he said.

Shaafia had to smile when Théophile told her that Brad was getting married to Indira. She knew that already. Théophile and Claire would be going to the wedding and he asked her if she would like to come. The temptation was great, but she sensed within herself the imminence of what was coming in Casablanca and she knew she had to stay.

When she told Théophile, he understood. «Pia's work must go on.» he said.

He promised to give her love to Claire and to Thérèse who had gone shopping. Shaafia sent her love to Michael and Zena, too.

When she closed the phone, she sat back against the fig tree and closed her eyes.

How happy she felt, cocooned in the warmth of those who knew what she knew, who understood what she understood, and who shared the love that she bathed in.

On the Friday, after lunch, as Shaafia and her Mother set out for Samad's shop, Sadik appeared and she invited him to come with them. As they walked, she asked him about school. He was non-committal, and she could see that school had not improved and was not much better than torture for the poor boy.

When they reached the shop, there were several ladies buying their supplies for the weekend. As they waited, Sadik looked around the shop and began rearranging some of the items on shelves that had been left untidy. Shaafia watched him and remembered her intuition.

When there were no more customers, Samad pulled out the big ledger. As Shaafia opened it, Sadik came over and peered over her shoulder. She explained to him what it was. She showed him the income and the outgoing columns and how they balanced.

Suddenly Sadik turned to his uncle, and he said: «How do you know what to put in the shop?»

His uncle smiled. «My customers tell me what they want.»

Sadik nodded. «There's nothing that I would buy in this shop.» he said thoughtfully looking at the shelves and boxes.

Shaafia felt an inner warmth that was deeply pleasing. She asked him: «What would you suggest?»

He shrugged, feeling a little intimidated, suddenly being the centre of attention.

«Maybe some good cookies, like American chocolate bars, maybe things from other countries. Things that kids like.»

«You think young people would like that?» asked his Mother, fascinated that he seemed to come to life in this shop.

«I don't know, maybe.»

«Then I will try it out.» said Samad. «The last time someone made a suggestion like that, I did very well.»

Then Shaafia broached the subject that was burning inside her. «I know you have been thinking of getting someone to help in the shop. Have you done anything about that?»

He shook his head. «I had been hoping that Abd might be interested, but sadly his electric guitar is all he seems to care about.» Abd was his youngest son. His three older sons had careers already, two were married and the other was about to be.

«Maybe another member of the family might be interested.» said Shaafia.

He frowned. «Who?»

She put her hand on her younger brother's shoulder.

His uncle looked at his nephew with raised eyebrows. «Sadik?» he asked.

Sadik looked at his sister and then at his Mother. «You mean I could leave school and work here all the time?»

«Would you like that?» asked his Mother.

He looked around the shop then he nodded. «I would like it very much. I like this shop. And I would be doing the work my Father did.» It was probably the longest sentence he had ever delivered in public.

They talked about it, and the more they did, the more it seemed like the perfect fit. In the end, as the envelope went into her Mother's handbag, unopened, it was decided that Sadik would start work the following week. His Mother would go to the school on Monday and inform them that he would not be coming back.

As they left, with Sadik smiling broadly, Samad stood in the door. «I look forward to welcoming my new assistant. This has been a very good day.»

For the traditonal family Friday dinner, the two older sisters came with babies and husbands. The two men sat outside in the courtyard while the sisters and babies had a joyful, chaotic reunion and cooking session. Ahmed had decided that Shaafia was never going to talk to him, and he now simply scowled when they made eye contact.

As they cooked, their Mother talked happily about how her family seemed to be doing so well, the boys were more occupied than they had ever been, and Sadik was about to start work in Samad's shop. She was in the middle of all this good news when Nayla walked in. An icy silence hit the kitchen and they all eyed her warily.

«You all sounded very happy as I came in,» she said. «What did I miss?»

Zarifa looked coolly at her younger sister. «We were sharing good news.»

«Oh yes? Like what?»

Her Mother said: «I have a phone. That is good news, don't you think?» and she showed Nayla her new shiny device.

«How modern you are.» said Nayla with undisguised sarcasm.

As they were looking at the new phone, Ayman and Ihab came in and both kissed their Mother before handing her their joint envelope.

«And my sons are now contributing to the family which is a wonderful thing.»

Nayla looked at Ayman. «You getting religious or something?»

Ayman was quick to anger and she knew it. She wanted to provoke him, but Shaafia was close to him and she took his arm.

«My brothers know their duty. They are loyal to this family and we appreciate it very much.»

He felt the gentle pressure of her arm as if it were caressing his skin and he softened.

«Do you contribute anything?» he asked Nayla with a quiet menace in his voice.

«Of course,» she said. «I brought pastries.» And she produced a ribboned box with the name of a famous bakery on it. However as Shaafia looked at it, she could see the box was not new.

«That's very sweet of you.» she said, and took the box before Nayla realised what was happening. «We can have these tomorrow.»

Nayla frowned and lunged to take the box back. «No, they are for tonight. They'll be stale tomorrow.»

Sensing something was not right, their Mother said: «We already have pastries. Shaafia is right. Thank you, Nayla. »

«So all you contribute is a few cookies?» said Ayman, not wanting to lose the track of what was just said.

«If I made as much as you guys seem to then I would.»

«So you don't?» he persisted.

«Who cares what you think.» she snorted.

«Enough!» said their Mother. «It is Friday and the family is here and we will be civil to each other.»

The meal was served but there was palpable tension in the air.

This boiled over when Nayla heard Yamina tell Ihab that Nayla had attacked Shaafia.

Ihab turned on his older sister. «Is that true?»

«We had a slight disagreement.» sneered Nayla.

But then Hawa crowed: «But Shaafia won! We saw it. Nayla is no match for Shaafia!»

Nayla leapt to her feet, threw her plate down and faced the family.

«I see how it is. You are all against me. Well you will be sorry. You don't know what I can do.»

Then she was gone.

The silence in the room lasted several seconds, and then Samet began to laugh. «Well that gets rid of a bad smell.»

The boys smiled, but Shaafia held up her hand. «She said we don't know what she can do. I think we do.»

«Empty angry words, that's all.» said Samet.

«No.» said Shaafia, and there was something about the way she spoke that made everyone look at her.

«You think she is into black magic, don't you.» said Zarifa with her two daughters in her lap. They had both become scared by what was happening and she was sheltering them.

«We think she's a witch.» said Hawa.

Their Mother sighed. «Your Father and I have never wanted this to be spoken of. We did not want to alarm you and we hoped it was a passing phase, just as she was growing up, but there is something about your sister which, I am sorry to say, is dangerous.»

«Oh, come on.» said Samet. «She's just got anger management challenges, nothing else.»

«Let's test that.» said Shaafia. She went to where she had hidden the box that Nayla brought. «If you think she is not dangerous, take one of her cookies.»

She opened it in front of Samet. They were the regular crescent-shaped pastries found all over Casablanca.

«You think she put a curse on them?» he sneered.

«Find out.» she said, so he took one and made a great show of putting the whole thing into his mouth at one go. Then with his mouth full, he said: «Not exactly fresh.»

The rest of the family watched nervously but in fact nothing happened and they started to relax. Those who had not heard about Nayla's attack on Shaafia were told, and then other topics of conversation took over and Nayla was forgotten.

When the meal was over, the two older girls and their husbands went home. The husbands had stayed carefully in the background during Nayla's tirade, but neither of them had enjoyed being there much. They mostly came out of loyalty to their wives.

It was late into the night when Samet began screaming. The whole house woke, and everyone rushed to the boys' sleeping area.

He was bathed in sweat. He looked at them all staring at him and tried to get calm. «What's the matter with all of you? I just had a nightmare, that's all.»

Their Mother brought some water and he drank it. Then he went outside and threw up.

The box of pastries went into the refuse bin and everyone went back to bed.

In the morning when Samet finally emerged, he took a cup of mint tea and sat outside. Shaafia joined him.

After a moment he said: « So you really think she was trying to poison us?»

She nodded.

«Why would she want to do that? I mean I know she is angry. She's always been like that.»

«Some people are born with the gift of goodwill and a desire to help people. Others have the opposite.»

«Why?»

«I could try to explain it, but it might test your beliefs too much.»

«Try me.»

So Shaafia told him about her history, the Sharif, Pia and her ability to hear voices. She told him about the Guru in India who had shown them who Pia had been in a previous life. Pia had proved to them again and again that she knew so much about them all. She knew things that none of them had shared with each other.

As she spoke she saw that he was actually willing to listen.

Finally he said: «I have always thought I had a good mind and that I knew a lot of things. I felt, I suppose, a bit superior to most people.»

«You do have a great mind,» she said, «but you are not using much of it.»

He looked at her in silence.

«OK.» he said at last, draining his cup. «If what you are telling me is true, then I have a lot to learn.»

«You do. And when you do, you will be amazed.» she said. «I am amazed at what I have been given, every single day.»

«Would you be willing to tell my friends what you told me? They already think you are something of a genius. I think they might be more open to your way of seeing things than I am.»

She smiled. «Maybe. Then your podcast would be famous.»

They walked together to the corner café. The owner smiled broadly when he saw Shaafia, and she gave him the usual one hundred dirhams.

«She is my best customer.» he said to Samet.

He looked at his sister. «Are you turning into a saint?»

«Would you recognise a saint if you met one?»

«Probably not.»

The rest of the group was all there and they stood up when she came in.

«Coffee is on her again.» said Samet.

«Gentlemen, please sit.» she said in English.

They smiled and sat.

The boy in the suit pulled out his laptop.

«We did what you said.» and he opened it.

It was in Arabic and was called «Out of Dark Corners.» On the face page was a cartoon of them all huddled round the table in the back of the café. It captured them very well.

Shaafia looked at Yusuf. «Your work?»

He nodded.

Then other pages were revealed, one after the other. Each boy had his own page.

Shaafia asked each one to explain the rationale for his piece and then read it aloud.

Mostly they wrote about themselves, young articulate men, unable to fit into the regular roles that society expected of them.

Nabil's was poetic, poignant in its imagery. He was indeed a poet. He spoke about looking for the right path.

Samet's piece was an essay on the uselessness of the standard education curriculum, charging that it only trained children to pass exams, not how to live a worthwhile life. It was passionate and logical.

The boy in the suit, whose name was Dari, had written about his Father who he described as having so much potential, but who could not read or write and who worked joylessly in a menial job. The piece had a bitter edge of victimhood and he read it with anger in his voice.

When all the pages had been shown and read, they looked at Shaafia. She looked around the circle, from one boy to the next.

«Do you think it is ready?» she asked.

No-one seemed brave enough to respond.

«What do you think?» asked Dari, closing the laptop.

Shaafia waited a short second to check inside herself, and then she smiled. «The way to find out if this is any good, is to launch it.»

They nodded as a group.

«So put it out there.» she said, «You do know how to do that?»

«We have been looking at podcasts and websites all week.» said Nabil. «There are so many.»

Dari said: «My brother helped with the layout and he knows all about how to do it.»

«OK,» she said. «Now you know what to do, you had better start work on the next issue.»

Then she got up and left the table.

She walked quietly to the Mosque, very pleased with what had happened. The boys were good, clever, and now motivated.

She was deep into the midday prayers when Haj Hussein came flashing into her inner screen. She couldn't see him, but there was a blaze of light and she could hear his voice.

«They need you. Events are about to happen and you must be with them before it begins. Go now.»

She knew he meant Rana and Houda. As soon as prayers were done, she went outside, put on her shoes and found a quiet corner to call. It took a while for Rana to answer.

She was delighted to hear Shaafia's voice.

Shaafia hoped that she was not disturbing Rana, but Rana assured her that she was not. The house was quiet with her husband being away down south. She told Shaafia that she and Houda had been talking by themselves outside in the gazebo. Rana again and again thanked Shaafia for the miraculous change in her daughter.

As Shaafia had not said anything to Rana yet about her connection to Haj Hussein, she told Rana that there was something else that she had to say to Houda and she would like to do it in person. She asked if it was possible to come that afternoon.

Rana did not hesitate. Of course, she said, and insisted that Shaafia come for tea. She would send the car immediately and Houda would come to greet her. Shaafia told her that she was outside the Mosque and she would be happy to wait there.

As she waited for the car, she called her Mother. The phone rang for a long time till Hawa answered it. Shaafia asked if their Mother was there. Hawa said she was but she was too nervous to answer the phone.

Shaafia had to laugh.

«We will have to train her.» she said. Then she told Hawa that she was going to have tea with a friend and would be home later in the day.

When the big white Mercedes pulled up, there was Houda. She jumped out and gave Shaafia a huge hug before they both got into the back seat. As the car set off Houda leaned into Shaafia so they could talk in whispers.

«Is something happening?»

Shaafia shared what had just happened in the Mosque. «I don't know what it means yet,» she said, «but we must be ready.»

For the rest of the journey Houda described how everything seemed to have changed. She said that inside herself she felt strong and ready to face whatever was meant to happen. She and her Mother were close now, like allies. She had trouble not starting to cry as she tried to thank Shaafia.

Very gently Shaafia insisted that it was not her. She was simply the messenger.

«So thank you for being the messenger.» said Houda through her tears.

«I think it is time that I told your Mother what has happened to me and that her Father talks to me.»

«She will understand.»

Rana was on the front portico to greet them when the car pulled in.

She gave Shaafia a warm hug and escorted her inside with an arm round her shoulder.

The tea was brought in and when the serving girls had retired, after their little bows, Rana poured the tea.

Then they sat back and Rana looked at Shaafia expectantly. «Have you told Houda already?»

«Yes, but I have something to tell you, too. This is quite long but you need to know about it.»

So once again Shaafia recited her narrative. She was getting very good at it. She watched for Rana's reaction, but she could see that Rana was entranced and not at all upset by anything in the story.

At one point, once Shaafia had got to the part in the story where she was able to communicate whatever Pia had to say, Rana turned to Houda. «You know about all this?» and Houda nodded.

«You believe it?»

«Totally.» said Houda with a smile.

Once Shaafia had reached the point where she was being told to go back to Casablanca, Rana said: «You know in my Father's time there were sufis who could do what you can do. Sometimes in our house, in *Darou Al Bahr*, there would be people, mostly men I have to say, who seemed to have all sorts of gifts. They would come and go. My Father was discreet but I knew that he had gifts too.»

«And he still does.» said Shaafia, and went on to talk about what had happened at the Bordeaux Airport and in the plane.

Then Rana began to laugh. «Oh I love that. They made her throw up. I really did not like that woman at all. My husband hired her and he trusted her, so I had to go along with it.»

Then Houda said: «I forgot to ask you this: did the voices tell you to go to work for Walid?»

Shaafia smiled. «No, but maybe they prompted my brother.»

Rana asked: «You did not know that he was going to marry Houda?»

«Not until he said he was getting married, and then I got it.»

«What a wonderful gift you have been given.» said Rana. «I would have loved to have met your Pia. And the community in the château, all drawn together by their search. It is truly a wonderful story. Someone should write a book about it.»

Again Shaafia had to smile. «They have. It is coming out very soon, at least in English.»

Rana sat quietly for a moment, thinking about what Shaafia had told her. «I am so happy that you told me all this, and I am even more happy that you have been guided to help us. You have been sent to help my Houda when I felt so helpless myself.»

«I think perhaps now you will not be helpless anymore. You both have abilities that have been hidden from you, and now is the time when you will be shown who you are and what you can do.»

Rana sat back in her chair as if suddenly she needed time to absorb all that she had heard.

Then Houda said: «But there is one more thing.» Then she turned to Shaafia. «Tell her what happened today.»

And so Shaafia did. «I was in the Mosque. All they said was: «They need you. Events are about to happen and you must be with them before it begins. Go now.» So I called you right away.»

«But you don't know what it means?» asked Rana. «Nothing has happened. It has been a very quiet day.»

The phone rang.

Shaafia knew instantly that this was the beginning of whatever it was. She and Houda watched Rana's face as it turned ashen, and then a look of horror came over her.

She said a few strangled words of thanks for the call and put the phone down and dropped into her chair.

«*Mui?*» asked Houda softly, going over to her Mother and crouching down in front of her chair.

«He's dead.» whispered Rana.

«Who is?»

«Your Father. Hamza.»

«He's dead?»

Rana took a breath and said: «There has been a big explosion south of Agadir. They said it was a suicide bomber, probably from Polisario. There was a big gathering of people at the new rest stop and gas station being opened on the freeway. Many people were killed.»

Houda jumped up and pressed a button. A panel on the wall slid back to reveal a large flat-screen television. When she turned it on, the Government channel was showing the destruction at the rest stop and describing the death toll. There were hysterical witnesses shouting about what they had seen, some of them still covered in blood. There were ambulances and police cars everywhere and the whole scene was panic-stricken chaos.

Then the phone went again. Rana picked it up and mostly listened, saying «W*ahaa*» very often and nodding.

Shaafia and Houda watched closely, ready to help.

Rana put down the phone. «It was Taj. He is going down there right away.»

Houda said: «Taj is my Father's brother. They are the co-owners of Bin Salah Transport.»

Rana dropped back into her chair and closed her eyes, and then the phone rang again.

«Please, no more.» cried Rana, and began to weep.

Houda picked it up. «Yes, yes we know.» she said, and quickly hung up. Then she reached for her Mother's small device and pressed the button.

The girl came running looking terrified. «We heard on the radio. Isn't it terrible what has happened in Agadir?»

«Yes. Terrible.» said Houda. «My Mother cannot take any more phone calls. Please answer the phone, keep a list of who called and say that we are not available.»

«Yes, yes. Of course.» The girl gave her little bow and was gone.

Houda unplugged the phone. «There is another phone in the kitchen. She will answer it there.» she said.

Through all this, Shaafia sat quietly. While she was alert to what was happening in the room, she was also attentive inside herself. She saw a shifting set of images and she began to sense that there was a scenario for her to follow. She couldn't tell if Haj Hussein was present, but she felt that she was part of a conference of invisible but subtle participants who were all contributing to the scenario.

As the dramatic story was breathlessly told and retold on the television, they began to detail the people who had been killed. There were no names mentioned, but some were government officials and some were representatives of the companies involved in the rest stop and the gas station.

Houda used the remote and turned it off. The panel slid closed and the television disappeared.

She turned to Shaafia. «This is it, isn't it.»

Shaafia nodded.

«He knew. My grandfather knew it was going to happen.»

Then she came over to Shaafia and knelt in front of her chair.

«Did he do it? I mean did he deliberately....»

Shaafia shook her head. «No. They are witnesses, not actors.»

«But he wanted to protect us, my Mother and me, by sending you.»

«Yes. But it is more than that. Now that this has happened, it will lead to many important things. You and your Mother will have to be very strong and very clear. I will help.»

Rana seemed to rise out of herself, having heard this.

«You are right.» she said, standing up. «There will be so much to do. We have to have a funeral and bury his body. We will have to make many decisions. At least Taj will be there. He can organise most of the details.»

Then she blew her nose and pressed the device.

«We will start right away.»

The girl came running.

«You must know that the terrible event south of Agadir has struck this family.»

The girl looked stricken but stood to attention as Rana went on. «You will hear sooner or later, so you might as well hear it from me. You must tell all the staff that my husband was killed in the explosion.»

The girl screamed and Rana overrode her with a harsh voice.

«Stop that. We have to work. All the staff will remain in the house at all times. I need everyone. No-one is to leave till I say so. You will begin to plan for large gatherings of people. Call our regular caterers and order for at least three days, at least two hundred people. Have the pavilions erected immediately. Tomorrow morning everything must be in place.»

The girl bowed and ran.

Shaafia pulled out her phone. «I will call my Mother. I think I should stay here with you, if you don't mind.»

«Yes, yes. Please do stay.» said Rana. «We will prepare a room for you.»

She pressed the device again.

The girl came running back.

«Prepare a room for Shaafia.» The girl bowed and was gone again.

Shaafia felt a strong desire to pray.

«Do you have a prayer room?»

Rana shook her head. «My husband is not, was not, at all religious, so he would not allow for such a thing. But there is one room where I have kept some of my Father's most precious things and sometimes I go there and I pray. Would you like to go there?»

A long central corridor with many rooms on both sides led to a small room that faced out to the back of the house. The walls had several large posters with calligraphy of Koranic verses. There was one large lounge chair with faded upholstery and bookshelves with many old books, some bound in leather.

Shaafia breathed in, then she nodded. «This is perfect. If you wish to join me, you are welcome. I have a silent prayer that I do every day. You may sit with me if you would like.»

There were several prayer mats folded in one corner and they each took one and sat in a semicircle in front of the big chair. As she closed her eyes, Shaafia had a vision of the chapel in the château, with its altar, the simple crucifix, the white statue of Durga on her tiger and the ragged stuffed kangaroo. It made her smile.

Her Koranic verse pulsed steadily inside.

Then she was drawn deep inside herself where the swirl of images that had come earlier now became clearer and she could see what they referred to, now as two spheres suspended opposing each other. In one there was bright light and she could see Rana and Houda, and others, men with beards, women in simple robes, surrounded by light. In the other was a woman she did not know, dressed in black, who had a dark aura around her. Next to her stood Nayla, whose eyes shone like red coals in a fire. There were other women around them, all shrouded in the same dark glow.

At last she ascended slowly from her inner focus and found the other two women staring at her.

«You have light round you.» whispered Rana.

Shaafia waited until she felt ready and then she said: «What has taken place will bring many changes. We must acknowledge the goodness that lies in each one.»

«What should we do?» asked Houda.

«Have a funeral.» said her Mother.

«There will be help.» said Shaafia. Before she stood up, she bowed to the chair, much as she used to do to the altar in the chapel.

As they walked back to the centre of the house, Rana said: «I should be feeling very upset, I should be feeling the grief of losing my husband, I should be angry at the people who did this to him, but I do not. I think it is because you are here. I think something happened in my little secret room.»

Shaafia nodded. «You are your Father's daughter.»

Rana shook her head. «It is no guarantee. You have not met my sister.»

Suddenly Shaafia stopped. «I think maybe I just did. What does she look like?»

Back in the lounge, Rana pulled out the album of her wedding day. There standing next to her was her unsmiling sister, unlike everyone else in the photo.

Shaafia nodded. «I saw her, just now, in my meditation.»

«She is not a good person. I feel sad that I have to say this, but it is the truth. We have had to protect ourselves from her.»

«In every family it seems there is someone like that.» said Shaafia. «In my family also we have a sister who is the same. In my meditation I saw them together.»

«My «lovely» aunt will be delighted at what has happened.» sneered Houda.

«She may try to take advantage of it. We must be vigilant.» said Shaafia. Then she asked: «You say you have had to protect yourselves from her. What do you mean?»

«My husband refuses, well he refused, to believe in any of this, what he called fake black magic, but my Father saw it clearly before he died. He asked one of his mystic friends, a strange man who comes here now and then to put a ring of protection round this house and its compound. I am convinced that it works. She has never come here and I believe he has prevented her from penetrating in any other way.»

«Is that man here now?»

«I don't know. He just appears sometimes.»

When Rana used her device and the girl appeared, Rana asked her for a report on what was being organised. The girl had been diligent and had begun to set up what would be needed for the funeral and the endless arrivals of wellwishers and mourners.

Rana nodded as the girl went through her list.

«You did well. Have you kept a list of callers?»

The girl handed her a paper.

Rana scanned the list, nodding.

«Walid called.» she said to Houda.

Something struck Shaafia and she sat up.

«Walid.» she said. «Call him back. He can help. I feel it.»

Houda looked at her in surprise. «Really?»

«It will be very good to have a man here. He is almost part of the family, so I think it will be very helpful.»

Rana nodded. «An excellent idea.» She went over to the phone, reconnected it and made the call.

Shaafia leaned in close to Houda. «You will not have to marry him, this I promise, but right now he is very useful. You must greet him well, treat him with respect, as if you are now quite ready to be his wife. Can you do that?»

Houda gazed at her new friend.

«I believe in you. I have faith in you. If you think that is what I will do, I will do it. You watch. I can be very charming if I want to.»

Rana put the down the phone.

«He is coming right now. He is bringing some of his people. He has been most generous.»

Shaafia smiled. «I thought he would.» Then she added: «Did you happen to mention that I was here?»

Rana thought for a moment. «I don't think I did. It was all a bit rushed.»

«Then it will be fun to see his face when he gets here.»

It took no more than twenty minutes before several cars in convoy rolled up the drive.

As Walid walked into the house there was Shaafia. He stared at her for a moment and then he laughed. «Why am I not surprised to see you here, mystic girl?»

Houda had held back a little shyly, but now she came and stood with her new friend. «Why do you call her mystic girl?»

«Oh this girl has some interesting abilities. I learned that last week. And if she is your friend, you are lucky.»

«I am.» she said.

Then he turned to Rana and put his hand to his heart. «We came as soon as we could. Tell us what you need to do and my team will jump in to help.» He gestured behind him and there stood about ten people, including both Ayman and Ihab.

When Shaafia saw them, she waved and they were both wide-eyed seeing their sister. Walid introduced his team. Shaafia's brothers were there to help with security, some of the women were for the kitchen and one woman was his personal secretary who he said could organise anything Rana needed.

Rana sent for her own security man and they spoke about what would be needed with hundreds of guests coming, parking their cars, keeping track of who was coming, keeping out those who were not acceptable, coordinating walkie-talkies. Walid told Ihab and Ayman to do whatever Rana's man needed and they nodded. The girls went off to the kitchen to join Rana's kitchen staff. The secretary took out her laptop and settled on a couch to catch the to-do list.

As they were speaking, the phone went, and it was Taj.

He reported that he was negotiating to receive the body of his brother, but he would not get back with the body till late at night. He asked whether he should arrange the funeral, but Rana said she would do all that. She thanked him for taking care of her husband.

Then there was discussion about the funeral. A special pavilion was already being erected near the gazebo. A second one would be reserved for greeting and feeding the guests.

«I will call Haj Kabir.» said Shaafia, «If you think it would be appropriate.»

«Yes, perfect.» said Rana.

Shaafia took her cell phone into a quiet corner. She knew it was close to evening prayer time but she hoped she could catch him before they started.

Myriam answered and was horrified when Shaafia told her what had happened.

«Yes, of course he will come,» she said. « and I will come with him.» He had already gone into the Mosque.

Tea was brought and there was a break in the organising. Houda sat next to her supposedly future husband and told him how grateful she was that he was willing to help.

«That's what families should do,» he said. «Our families are part of one unit now.»

Houda smiled dutifully.

Walid turned to Shaafia. «So have you two known each other long?»

Shaafia smiled. «Not so long, but we have a wonderful connection. My Father and her grandfather knew each other very well.»

«So when you came to translate for me last week, did you know I was going to marry Houda?»

«Before I went to your house, I knew that she was getting married but I didn't know who was the lucky man. When your Father told me you were getting married, then I got it.»

«But he didn't say who I was getting married to, did he?»

Again she smiled. «I got it.»

«Mystic girl.» he said with a grin. Then he added: «By the way, you will be pleased to know that we are all signed up with the English. Thanks to you, they are super keen on the project. We have finished signing the documents to purchase the property and we will start design right away.»

«I am available whenever you need me.» she said, and gave him one of her new business cards.

He held it in his hand and felt the texture. «Very nice.» Then he slipped it into his wallet.

«Can I have one?» asked Houda, «Not that I need a translator.»

«You speak English?» Walid asked.

«Of course.»

«I have to say,» he acknowledged, «That my English is very basic.»

«Next time you have English guests I can help to entertain them.» she said.

He smiled and Shaafia nodded.

Houda was doing well.

Once the tea things had been taken away, they went back to the business of planning, until finally Walid called all his people together and they left.

They would all return in the early morning ready for the funeral.

«It's funny,» said Houda quietly to Shaafia, as they stood under the portico waving as the cars left, «Now that I know how things might go from here, I rather like him.»

Rana went inside to take another phone call, and Shaafia grinned at Houda. «Have you changed your mind about marrying him?»

Houda laughed. «Not at all. Now I feel free from the dread of getting married to him, I can see him just as a person. He's not so bad.»

«I think he will be incredibly useful to you and to your family, if you can keep up the appearance.»

«I was charming, wasn't I?»

«You were perfect.» said Shaafia, and gave her a hug.

At the very end of the day, the driver took Shaafia home to get some clothes and whatever she might need for her stay. He dropped her at the end of the alley, too narrow for the Mercedes, and waited for her.

When she got to the house, her Mother, two younger sisters and Habib were watching on the little old TV they had had for years. As she walked in, her Mother said: «Did you hear what happened in Agadir?»

Shaafia told her that the family she was visiting had lost a member of their family and she would be staying with them to help. They instantly wanted to know all about it but she didn't want to get into details. She promised to tell them all about it when she got back. She did add one detail, that Ihab and Ayman were there helping.

Her Mother was pleased.

«They are becoming good boys at last,» she said. «*Ham delilah.*»

Shaafia only had the two big Samsonite suitcases, so she took one with the few things she thought she would need. She promised herself to buy a smaller suitcase for events like this.

«Do you need any help?» asked Hawa, as she wheeled it out.

«No thank you.» smiled Shaafia and kissed her Mother, her sisters, and a slightly protesting Habib, before heading off down the alley.

When she returned to the compound, she found Rana still organising things and endlessly answering the telephone. She gave Shaafia a distracted wave when she saw her.

The serving girls brought in some trays with different dishes on them but no-one seemed too keen to sit and eat. Houda too was answering calls, mostly detailing the funeral times.

Shaafia sat with them for a while but saw that she had no obvious role to play.

Instead she walked around the house and out into the extensive and quite exotic garden where small fountains played and there were fish ponds. All of it spoke of immense wealth, but as she looked at it all, she felt the transience of it. One man had spent a lot of money and energy on creating this, and then suddenly in one explosive moment, he no longer existed.

Now he was gone, perhaps all that she saw would soon no longer be relevant to his surviving family. She sensed that maybe they would be free of all this. They were not companions of this garden.

When Shaafia finally retired to the guest room they had prepared for her, indulging in the hot shower in the ensuite bathroom, she sat on the luxurious double bed and repeated her Koranic verse.

As her inner focus deepened, she felt the presence of Haj Hussein, and there was another presence which became a vision. She could see a tall man with thin white hair, dressed in a long white robe with bare feet. She wondered if this was her Sharif, but she could not be sure. Then it became clearer who he was.

«The circle of protection for this house will soon no longer be required.» he said. He was speaking in the Berber of the south as her parents had done when she was young. «The spiritual house will take back the protection it had before. We will be there, you and I.»

When she ascended from her inner focus, she knew what it meant.

Very soon, *Darou Al Bahr,* the house built by the Admiral, Haj Hussein's house, would become the home of Rana and Houda, just as Haj Hussein had suggested. The spiritual protection for the daughter and granddaughter of Haj Hussein would go with them.

And Shaafia would be there too.

Transition

The day of the funeral was intense from its very beginning.

As Shaafia awoke, there was shouting outside her window. She looked out and she saw Rana's security man running and shouting towards the gazebo. In the gazebo sat the man in the long white robe who Shaafia had seen in her meditation.

Her room had a french window that could be opened from the inside. She pulled on the handle, and as the door swung outward, she stepped through, calling the security man. He stopped when he heard her voice.

She came over to him and said: «Please don't disturb him. I know who he is.»

«How did he get in?» he asked. «All the gates are secured and the security cameras are all on. If anyone tries to get in, the alarm goes off.»

«Ah,» she smiled. «He is a bit special. In a way he was in here all the time but you couldn't see him.»

He looked at her suspiciously. «You are sure about that?»

«Let me go and talk to him.» she said.

He shrugged and stood still, watching as she walked towards the gazebo. «*Sidi.*» she said softly.

He turned to face her and she put her hand on her heart in greeting. He raised his own hand, palm outward, in a form of blessing, and she dropped down in front of him to kiss his hand. His hand was soft as tissue, almost translucent.

«Thank you.» she said, speaking Berber.

«We are taking good care of you.» he said softly.

«We are blessed. *Ham delilah.*»

She gazed up at him for a long time, and it seemed to her that they were in some kind of silent but deep conversation until he raised his hand again and closed his eyes.

«Be at peace.» he said, «A *salaam alaikum*».

«*Shukriya.*»

She walked back to the security man. «He is here to make sure everything goes well for the funeral.»

«Is he on the list of expected guests?»

«No. It is like he is part of the house, if you can understand that.»

«No I can't, but if you know who he is then that's OK.»

They began to walk back towards her open french window.

As she went in, he said: «Thanks for your help.»

She showered and dressed, then went to find Houda.

«How are you?» she asked. Houda had made a great effort to look good for the occasion. She wore the appropriate clothes as a bereaved daughter, but she had put on make-up as well. Her future husband would see her behave well and look charming.

«I didn't sleep much.» she said. «I kept seeing what it must have been like for my Father to be in that explosion. I felt sad of course, but also, this is a bit awful to say, but I felt a relief that the pressure that he was putting on me has now gone.»

«It is an honest reaction.» said Shaafia, and gave her a hug. Then she told Houda about the Sharif who appeared in the gazebo. She described how she explained it to the security guard.

Houda was amazed.

«He just appeared?»

«I saw him last night in my meditation. There are beings who can do that. He is the one your grandfather asked to protect this house and you and your Mother.»

When she saw Rana she told her too, and Rana nodded.

«I see him, now and then. He certainly doesn't need the security gate.»

There was a lot of activity already happening in different parts of the house. The kitchen was a hive of cooks and preparers yelling at each other.

Attendants were out watering the garden and raking the driveway. Two small white vans from the caterer had already arrived and were backed up to the kitchen.

Walid arrived with Ihab and Ayman and the other members of the team. As they were offered tea and fruit, Shaafia stood with her two brothers.

«So how come you are here?» asked Ayman.

Shaafia smiled. «I met Rana at Myriam's house. Did you know her Father and our Father knew each other?»

«Who was her Father?» asked Ihab.

When Shaafia said the name Haj Hussein, Ayman frowned.

«He lived in a big house shaped like a boat, was that him?»

«Yes. It's called *Darou Al Bahr.*»

«I've been there,» he said, «when I was just a kid. There used to be lots of chanting and sufi ceremonies. It was a great house with a big garden.»

«It's in ruins now.» said Shaafia. «Haj Kabir took me to see it.»

Then Walid called his team together with lots of orders being given, and people began running. Her brothers went out to help with the arrivals and their vehicles.

Houda and Rana went to make preparations for the funeral which included washing the body. As she thought of them performing that task she found her Koranic verse surging up inside her, and she sent them her deepest blessings. Washing a body that had been in an explosion was probably not an easy task

Wondering how she could best help, she sat in a corner with her tea. Inside herself she was quiet. She was alert to see if there were any messages, but there was nothing. Instead she sensed that for now she had no outward rôle to play and she could wait.

Haj Kabir arrived with Myriam and several men in white robes. He also brought Omar, Rana's Uncle, who walked with his head down not wanting to make eye contact with anyone. She went over to greet them.

Omar stood still as she approached him and he shyly looked up at her. She took his hand and led him to the refreshments table. She poured him a tea, as the others helped themselves to fruit and pastries.

They spoke in hushed words about the terrible events of the day before until Taj, the brother of the dead man, came out and greeted Haj Kabir and the men he had brought to assist with the funeral prayers. He led them out to the pavilion where the funeral would take place, while Myriam stayed with Shaafia.

«You know,» said Myriam in a whisper, «Even though it is a terrible thing to say on such a day, I wonder if perhaps this is going to lead to better days for both of these women.»

Shaafia nodded and whispered back. «I believe you are right.»

As guests began to arrive, Houda and Rana both appeared, and from then on there was an endless bustle of greetings, condolences, kisses and handshakes, introductions, gifts, and food plates.

The funeral itself took place in the pavilion. The body was wrapped in white cloth and the prayers were sung by Haj Kabir and his group sitting round it in a circle.

The big white hearse that was ready to take the body to the family cemetery stood waiting by the front portico until the appointed moment.

Taj and several other men carried the coffin into which the shrouded body had been gently lowered.

A long cavalcade of cars followed the hearse.

Shaafia rode with Rana and Houda. They were both holding themselves very carefully together sitting in the big Mercedes, holding hands. Shaafia sensed that the best support she could give them was to be there, knowing that they both drew strength from her presence.

In herself she felt powerfully calm, alert and attentive. She was very aware of the presence around her, not of the people offering condolences or playing roles in the funeral, but of beings who were also there, equally supportive but unseen.

The burial entailed more prayers while the coffin was lowered into the grave and the gravediggers began to shovel the earth to cover it..

Neither Rana nor Houda showed any outward emotion, their faces still, carefully expressionless. They seemed to have both donned identical masks to see themselves through the motions required of the grieving family.

The ceremony was short, the prayers rose into the warmth of the morning, crows circled overhead, and then the mourners began to walk back to the cavalcade.

As she walked, Haj Kabir came up beside her.

«Haj Hussein is with us.» he said quietly.

She told him of her encounter in the early morning and he nodded.

When she told him what she had heard about *Darou Al Bahr,* he stood still for a moment as if he had suddenly seen something.

«As we have thought it would happen.» he said.

The cavalcade wound its way back to the house, where tables of food had been laid out in the other pavilion, and waiters in trim white uniforms began to circulate with silver trays.

As the day wore on, some mourners left while still others arrived, coming from other cities, bringing an endless line of people to speak to Rana and Houda, family members, business associates and neighbors.They held themselves stoically side by side, against the onslaught of wellwishers and condolences. Shaafia was often introduced as a friend of the family, and on several occasions someone asked for her business card, having heard from Walid how good she was.

Every now and then he would come over to her and they would talk. He gave her some more updates on the Essaouira project. He told her that Alex would be returning in a few weeks to begin work on the planning. Shaafia promised she would be available.

In the late afternoon, Rami Razak, Walid's Father, came in, piloting a motorised wheelchair escorted by his other son, Khalil. After he had spent some time with Rana and Houda, he looked for Shaafia.

«Walid tells me you are a good friend of the Bin Salah family.» he said, after they had greeted each other. «He also tells me that you were very useful in his negotiations with the English. He is very impressed with your talents.»

Shaafia smiled. «I am glad to hear that the arrangements have gone very well.»

«He even went so far as to offer you a position and, he tells me, you said no. May I ask why?»

«As I told Walid,» she said, still smiling, «I have things that I must do, so I could not commit to work for anyone full-time. I told him I would be happy to translate whenever he needs it.»

«May I ask you what you mean by «things to do»?

She took a moment to sense what she could say to this man. Then she said: «It is not clear to me yet, but I sense that I have things to do here in Casablanca. I believe I was sent back here for a reason.»

«Really?» he nodded. «May I ask who sent you back?»

Now she laughed. «Oh,» she said, «it was not a person exactly, it was more like an inner call. Does that make sense?»

He nodded.

«I think it does.» Then he leaned forward and took her hand, which surprised her a little. «Walid has told me a little about what happened in Essaouira.»

As the day drew to a close and the guests began to leave, Walid rounded up his team and got ready to take them back. They would not be needed for the next day, but traditionally the third day is a really big day of feasting and condolences where even more people were expected. His team would be back.

Houda gave him her best bereaved daughter but friendly fiancé smile, and thanked him for being such a wonderful representative of the family.

He kissed her on both cheeks which she didn't seem to mind at all. Then he did the same to Rana, telling her that if she needed anything she should call.

He gave Shaafia a friendly wave as they went.

In the late evening when the last of the guests had left, Rana sat with Houda and Shaafia out in the gazebo. The evening was warm and a light breeze moved the vanes of the wind turbines so that they hummed gently in the background.

«Now I am a widow.» said Rana softly.

Shaafia said: «It is the beginning of a new life in a way.»

«I am sure you are right,» sighed Rana, «but at this moment it feels like the end.»

«When something ends, then something else begins. It is the cycle of life.»

«I cannot imagine yet what that could be.»

Then Shaafia repeated what the Sharif had told her about the shifting of protection, and both Rana and Houda stared at her.

«He is taking our protection away?» asked Houda.

«No, no. He said it would not be needed for this house but it would move to what he called «the spiritual house»

«*Darou Al Bahr.*» whispered Rana.

Shaafia nodded.

«I see what he means. We do not need to live in this great big compound any more.» said Rana, and a gentle ripple of soft laughter came up. «It was never really my home. I did my duty but it was always his domain. Now I feel that this is a moment when all this can change. *Ham delilah.*»

«I think you are right, » said Shaafia. «It is time to fulfil your Father's wishes.»

They sat in silence for a long time, each of them absorbing what they had just said to each other.

The two following days were filled with endless arrivals, greetings, condolences, news of distant events, and social connections. In all this Rana played her new widow rôle with poise and stamina. Houda did the same.

Very often Shaafia found herself being introduced to distant members of the family, second cousins, and uncles by marriage. As she met each one, she was aware of them, not just as they appeared on the outside, but she was also aware of their inner state. In some she could feel their spiritual attainment, in others the potential for darkness. Some she sensed that she would meet again and that they would be meaningful in some way, most were not like that. Although her face grew tired from smiling all day, her heart was light. She knew she was in the right place.

She stood with them at the front of the house, on the final night, watching as the last guests were waved away. The caterers had loaded their little trucks and left. Walid's team got ready to go.

Rana thanked him again and again, kissing him on both cheeks. Houda did the same and he seemed to be very happy with that.

«I am sure we will see you again soon, mystic girl.» he said. He did not kiss her on the cheeks, but instead put his hand to his heart.

«You know,» said Shaafia, with a little smile playing round her lips, «Our paths are destined to cross many times. I can see it.»

«You are scary what you can see.» he said.

Once again in the quietness of the late evening the three women sat out in the gazebo.

There was nothing more to be said, as if they had arrived at a point of completion. Tradition had been followed, decorum honoured, social obligations fulfilled.

There was peace.

Darou Al Bahr, the beginning

The following morning Shaafia rose early, repeated her Koranic verse, and went out to see if the others were up.

Rana and Houda were both there, having breakfast.

They greeted each other with warmth and Rana poured tea for Shaafia.

«So now we begin the rest of our lives.» said Rana. «I am sad that Hamza will not get to see his daughter marry the man that he chose for her, but that is God's will.»

Houda nodded. She agreed with what her Mother had said but not for the same reason. She held firmly to Shaafia's promise.

Shaafia watched all this, but began to feel that there was a new wave of tension coming. At first she could not tell what it was, then she began to feel it had to do with the Bin Salah business. It seemed to thrum in her head.

Something was not right.

The phone rang.

Rana took the call.

Houda did not seem to sense anything, and when her Mother was gone, she wanted to talk to Shaafia about how she felt released, how she could go out now, how she could have a life, she could see friends and go to restaurants and all the good things she used to do. She had already asked her Mother if she could now have a cell phone and her Mother had agreed. Shaafia let her chatter on, but held an awareness of Rana.

When Rana came back from the call she looked very upset.

«Taj is going to be very difficult.» she said.

Houda asked what she meant.

«He says he has to take over the company entirely, so it will be his. He says that he is the only person who can do that now his brother is gone. He says that we will have to give him all the rights to the company. He said he would take care of us, of course, but I felt a deep dread as he talked. It is an awful thing to say, but I fear he will cheat us. I don't know what to do.»

Shaafia felt a great surge of energy pass through her body. «No!» she said, «Do not think of yourself as weak. There is nothing to fear.»

The two Bin Salah women looked at her.

«There is work to be done.»

«What work?» asked Rana.

«There must be legal documents of ownership, aren't there?»

Rana frowned. «I think so.» she said. «Honestly I know nothing about any of it. Hamza did everything. He told me very little about what he did. That was his life.»

«Now that must change.» said Shaafia. «As the widow, you will be required by law to sign many legal documents before he can take control.»

Rana shook her head. «I suppose so. I am not sure. You know about this?»

«No,» said Shaafia, «but I sense something.»

Then her eyes widened, as if she had been shown something new and surprising.

«It is Walid.» she said.

The two women stared at her.

«What does this mean?» asked Houda.

«You will of course have company lawyers, but your husband must have had his own personal lawyer.»

«Yes of course. We know him well, he is also our family lawyer, he has been with us for many years.»

«He will know what to tell you. He will say that because your husband held the controlling rights of the company, you now have them.»

«Are you sure?»

Shaafia shrugged and took Rana's hand. «I am saying what comes to me. You must talk to this lawyer and you will find out, I am sure. He will say that you can appoint your own person to represent you.»

«Taj will say he should be the one.»

«It does not matter what he says. That person is Walid. I am sure of this.»

Rana took a long moment to try to take in what Shaafia had said. At last she said: «You surprise me that you can speak about such things, the world of business. And yet in a strange way my husband spoke about this. This was his idea behind the marriage to Houda. He saw Walid as his successor, once he and Rami Razak had agreed on the terms of the marriage. Some time in the future it was his plan to hand over to Walid. He had watched the way Walid worked and he was very impressed. So much so that he had already done something about this with the lawyer, in case anything happened to him. I do know that.»

The talk of marriage made Houda go white, but Shaafia subtly raised her hand in a comforting gesture.

«Call your lawyer first,» she told Rana, « and find out for certain. Do not mention Walid yet. Just ask your lawyer what happens now that your husband has gone.»

Rana came over to Shaafia and held her cheeks in her two hands. «Truly God has sent you to us.» she whispered, then left to make the call.

Houda immediately came over to Shaafia. «You said I wouldn't have to marry him.»

«You don't.»

«But if he is not marrried to me, can he still be the head of the company?».

«You will have to play the rôle of future wife, as you have so well these last three days, but hold faith. Step by step. All will go well.»

«Please God. Please God. Please God.»

Although she was bigger than Shaafia, still she melted into the smaller girl's arms for comfort, and Shaafia gently rubbed her back.

«Have no fear,» she whispered. «We are protected.»

Finally Houda pulled back.

She had tears in her eyes and she wiped them away with a sleeve. «I will be strong,» she said with determination. «I will be like you.»

Rana came back with a grim smile. «You are amazing, Shaafia. What you have said is true but it will not be easy to do. The lawyer will study all the papers that he has and he will get back to me. He believes that the controlling interest in the company is legally now with me.»

She dropped into a chair as if she had just been running. Then she sat forward. «He did say one strange thing. Just last month Hamza had told him that he wanted to be sure all the papers were in order so that his brother could not ever take control of the company. Just one month ago.»

Shaafia nodded. It was the kind of twist to a story that she had become very used to.

«So now we wait.» she said. «Your lawyer will do his work. I am sure that your brother-in-law will have his lawyer do his work too and there will be a battle. You must be like a warrior. You will have to be strong and resilient.»

«I will.» said Rana. «I invoke the spirit of my Father who is surely looking after us.»

«This is certain, and he is not alone.»

Rana nodded. «*Ham delilah.*»

»So should we call Walid?» asked Houda.

»No. Don't say anything to Walid yet, but I am certain he is the right person.»

«I believe you.» said Rana.

«And I do, too,» added her daughter.

Later in the morning the driver was called to take her home.

Rana and Houda gave her long and heartfelt hugs, and she promised to stay very much in touch with them in the coming days.

«You will tell us if you «hear» anything?» asked Rana.

Her Mother was delighted to see her and demanded to know everything that had happened. They went to the *hamam*, and while they sat in the steam, Shaafia shared as much as she felt was necessary.

In her turn, her Mother shared what was happening in the family. For so long she had felt a sense of hopelessness about all of her sons, and now she saw Ayman and Ihab with good employment. The other sons were all showing signs of progress, too.

Samet had shown her the first podcast and she was cautiously impressed. While she did not really understand what it was, at least it showed that this group of boys, who looked so useless, were producing something.

Toufik was very happy in his college and talked enthusiastically in a way he had never done before. Sadik, too, was as happy as she had ever seen him now he didn't have to go to school. But more than that, she said, he seemed to love going to the shop. Of all the boys the only one who still seemed lost was Loqman.

Shaafia said: «He will find a way.»

There had been no further visits from Nayla, and her Mother began to wonder if in fact she was cutting herself off from the family altogether.

Shaafia knew this was not so, but she did not want to add anything negative to her Mother's new outlook.

«And then there is Habib.» smiled her Mother, «My last born is now the number one fan of Yasser. Yasser just gave him a shirt with his number on it and Habib is over the moon.»

After the *hamam,* they walked the short distance to the midday prayers in the Mosque.

Once the prayers were concluded, they sat quietly. Her Mother was becoming very used to Shaafia going deep inside herself after prayers and she loved to sit in that atmosphere.

As they walked home, her Mother said: «When I sit with you in the Mosque, I feel as if your Father is back with us. You are becoming more and more like him.»

In the afternoon, Shaafia went to visit Rachi, who greeted her with great excitement.

«Did you hear?» she asked, «Yasser has been invited to go and train with Les Girondins. He has been offered a one year contract.»

«Will you go too?»

«We are talking about it. He asked the agent if he was married could he bring his wife and he was told it might be possible.»

«Then you had better get married as soon as possible.»

Rachi held Shaafia in her arms. «Isn't it strange, I was so upset about getting married and not being able to go with you to Bordeaux, and now I am happy to be married and I may be going to Bordeaux after all.»

«We must insist that Yasser let you go to the University and study.»

«We already talked about it,» said Rachi. «He doesn't need to be persuaded.»

«He will be a very good husband to you.» nodded Shaafia.

«And what about you?» asked Rachi, «Do you want to get married?»

Shaafia shrugged. «People keep asking me that, but I don't see it at the moment. If it's meant to happen, then at some point it will.»

«You have other work to do.»

«I do.» and she told Rachi a little of what had happened over the last three days.

When she saw Rachi's Mother, Shaafia asked about the wedding and her Mother smiled.

«As soon as possible.» she said.

The next few days were quiet and Shaafia began to enjoy a period of deep peace. She went with her Mother to the *hamam* and to go shopping. She bought herself a small carry-on suitcase for future use and she went every day to the Mosque.

One afternoon after prayers she sat with Haj Kabir in his courtyard and they talked about the events of the previous week.

She told him about Hamza's brother and he shook his head.

«Always in families, you see competition. It is a sad fact of life.»

Then she mentioned the Sharif who protected the house, and he smiled. «He is a very interesting being. He has gifts that he doesn't show to everyone. That you have seen him is a sign that he trusts you.»

Then she reminded him about the protection moving to *Darou Al Bahr* at some point. He did not respond immediately, but sat quietly rocking gently in his chair.

Then he nodded.

«It will happen.»

On the Friday, Shaafia spoke to her Mother about Sadik. She felt it was right that he should be the one to bring home the family share of the shop each week. Her Mother agreed, but said that Shaafia should train him first.

She went to the shop in the afternoon, she introduced the idea to her Uncle. He nodded.

«He is a trustworthy boy.» he said, «I agree with your idea.»

As she looked around the shop she could see that it looked a little neater, more organised, and somehow seemed to have more light. There were displays of new products which she recognised as being the sort of things Sadik had mentioned. She had to smile as she saw famous American brand names that had never appeared in the shop before. She wondered who would buy Hershey bars.

When she approached Sadik about being responsible for the weekly payment for the family, he smiled shyly. «And I will add my share from my salary.» he said proudly.

Once again on the Saturday, Shaafia took Habib when she and Rachi went to watch Yasser play. The team lost and Yasser did not have much to show for the afternoon, but Habib was ecstatic.

What he loved most was when Yasser took the time after the match to coach him on how to better control the ball with his feet.

Rachi and Shaafia watched as they played.

«We are planning to get married in two weeks.» whispered Rachi.

Shaafia smiled. «You look very happy about that. And Bordeaux, any news?»

«Not yet, but the agent said he thought it was looking good.»

«But you will get married, even if there is no going to Bordeaux?»

Rachi nodded. «Yes.»

The café podcast had received a few hits, but not much, and the boys were disappointed. When Shaafia dropped in to see them, they showed her the results.

«The question is,» she said, «How can you make people aware of what you have made? How do you stand out when there are so many podcasts like yours?»

«That's not true,» said Samet. «Ours is unique, brilliant.»

«Maybe, but yet to be noticed.»

«So how then?»

«You have to be authentic. You have to stand out.»

They shook their heads.

«You will find it.» she said. «You will find a true voice and then people will want to listen to what you have to say.»

As she left, the café owner gave her a warm salute.

Rana called the following morning. She described what had been taking place the previous week. Her lawyer had done his research, and he had assured her that she was legally in control of all Hamza's assets. At the same time Taj had been pestering the lawyer constantly. He wanted to buy Rana's share if he could not control it any other way. She had told the lawyer she was not selling.

«You have not mentioned Walid yet?» asked Shaafia.

«No. I thought about what you said and I agree. Right now Taj thinks he will be able to persuade me eventually, so he keeps calling. Some days he is very polite and kind, being gentle with a newly widowed woman, but on other days he forgets about that and he becomes insistent.»

Shaafia let all this sink in and then she felt an inner settling.

«You have done well.» she said to Rana. «Let him think that he is only dealing with you for now, it will make him careless.»

Then Rana told her that they had decided to visit *Darou Al Bahr* that afternoon. Would she like to join them?

After the midday prayers, Shaafia stood with Myriam waiting to be picked up. She shared something of the challenge that Rana faced with her brother-in-law.

«It is so strange,» said Myriam, «that a family with so much wealth, so much good fortune, will still fight amongst themselves to get even more.»

It was not the big white Mercedes that appeared but a bright red Porsche Cayenne with Houda at the wheel. She came fast and braked hard. Her Mother sat a little white-faced next to her.

«You like my new wheels?» called Houda, as she jumped out and ran to give Shaafia a hug.

«It's yours?»

«It is now. It was my Dad's.»

The short run to their old house entailed several new misses with boys on bicycles, swerving to avoid motor scooters and furious honking at trucks assuming right of way. Shaafia was glad she had opted not to accept Rana's invitation to ride in the front seat.

At the back of «*DarouAl Bahr*», on the Rue de Rome, there was a wide double door made of wood. When Houda screeched to a halt in front of it, she got out and pulled hard on one of the doors until it began to open out. It took some effort to get the other one to move, but finally she managed and it revealed a space inside, big enough to park the car. It was empty except for several cats who scattered as soon as the doors were opened. Houda jumped back into the Porsche and moved it inside.

«We don't want anyone to see us being here.» explained Rana, as Houda dragged the damaged doors back together.

This was a part of the house Shaafia had not seen when she came with Haj Kabir. There was a ramshackle garage with double wooden doors that had rotted to the point of partial collapse, and inside she could see the outline of a vehicle.

Rana smiled ruefully. «That was my one and only car,» she said, «my Coccinelle,» using the French word for a VW beetle.

«It must be worth something as an antique.» joked Houda.

Then Omar came shuffling round a corner.

He shyly greeted both Rana and Houda before he turned to face Shaafia.

«He is sitting in the garden waiting for you.» he said, and gestured to the long front garden.

Shaafia nodded, sensing exactly what he was alluding to.

She smiled at Houda. «He travels faster than your Porsche.»

«Who is it?»

«He is called Malak,» said Rana, «but no-one is sure what his real name is.»

«The one who protects us?» asked Houda.

Shaafia led them round to the garden and there he was.

He was sitting on a low rock wall that had once been the border of what had probably been a long flower garden, but now only hosted a mass of tall and twisted weeds. The orange cat sat at his feet.

«*Sidi.*» said Shaafia as she put her hand to her heart.

He returned the gesture.

Rana approached him and sank to her knees in front of him.

«I have waited a very long time to come back.» she said looking up at him.

He put out his hand and rested it gently on the top of her head.

« I had to wait,» she said, «until I had the power to do so. She has given us this.» she said as she looked over at Shaafia.

«Not so, my child.» he said softly, speaking in Berber. «You have always had the power. She has simply shown you where you had hidden in it, deep inside yourself.»

«Of course.» She lowered her eyes.

Suddenly he looked up at Houda and a ray of light seemed to shoot from his eyes towards her.

«Wake up!» he said, his voice suddenly strong and clear. Now he spoke in Arabic. «Now is the time for you to stop being a child, a miserable small person who only feels sorry for herself. Wake up.»

It was as if he had struck her with his fist. She dropped to the ground beside her Mother and began to weep. It was an explosive outpouring as if he had released a dammed-up stream of stored emotion.

Rana put her arm round her daughter's shoulders, while Shaafia stayed still, knowing that this had to pass on its own. Omar hovered in the background.

As her crying subsided, the Sharif got to his feet.

«You have neglected this place.» he said, once again speaking in Berber. «This place which was once filled with holiness, where the divine sounds of devotion floated constantly in the fragrant air. You have allowed the evil that lay buried deep in your family to hold sway over this place and to leave this poor man, a wretched skeleton, without family or food. Now you will take it back. This girl will show you. Soon my debt to your father will be paid and I will be free. When you both recognise who you are, then you will not need me. You will not need my protection. The protection that she has (gesturing to Shaafia) you will have. Then I will be free.»

Looking down at them for a long moment, he walked out of the garden. Or did he? It seemed that he disappeared.

It was as if they all needed time to ingest what had just taken place. No-one moved. The cat jumped up to where the Sharif had been sitting and arched and rolled backwards and forwards on its back. Birds twittered in the trees and scooter horns intruded over the walls. Another scrawny grey cat found a patch of sun near Shaafia's feet and pulled itself into a neat ball and closed its eyes.

At last Rana got to her feet.

«So now we start.» she said, her voice strong with intent. She looked at Omar standing a little apart, not sure what was required of him.

«We have not treated you well.»

He lowered his eyes and did not want to look at her.

«Show us where you are sleeping.»

He turned and led them to the back of the house where there was a set of small low buildings that were previously used for storage and laundry, workshops and tool sheds. In one of them was a camp bed and some boxes of old clothes.

They stared at it.

«How could I have done this to you?»

He shook his head. «I do not blame you.» He could not look at her, but instead stared down at his battered sandals. «It is as much my own fault. I listened to her. I did what she asked and I have suffered ever since.»

«My sister.» said Rana, and he nodded.

Shaafia turned to Houda. «So now you see what our task is?»

«I have lived my selfish life totally blind to all this.» she said, wiping away her tears. «He said I have to wake up. So I will. I promise I will.»

Rana turned and headed for the main house. Omar meekly followed behind them.

They walked from room to room, mostly in silence, until they arrived in the back room with the faded photo of Haj Hussein and Florence.

Rana gazed up at it.

«Oh my Father,» she said, her voice laced with emotion. «Now we are back and we will reclaim *Darou Al Bahr*. We will take care of your dear brother, my uncle, and we will restore this place to the way it was.»

Looking up at the photo, Shaafia said: «The house has occupants. We must evict them.» Then she looked at Omar. «Then they will not torture you any more.»

«*Ham delilah.*» he murmured.

«We must ask Haj Kabir to begin the cleansing.» said Shaafia. «Nothing can be done until that happens.»

Rana nodded. «I know. What you say is right. I carry such a burden of guilt, I will need my own form of cleansing.»

«And I too. *Inch Allah.*» murmured Omar.

Houda said nothing, but Shaafia sensed that inside she was churning.

«We should go back to the Mosque now.» Shaafia said.

The red Porsche travelled at a more regular and unhurried pace and Houda parked behind the Mosque. It was early and the Mosque was deserted. They washed outside and took their shoes off. Omar went by himself into the men's section and then Rana and Houda followed Shaafia into the women's section.

They sat for a long time, each in her own silence.

As soon as Shaafia closed her eyes, she was swept away into another space. It was familiar to her, a refuge, where benign beings floated, some she recognised, others she did not. She felt at home there, as if she had once lived there. She found herself acknowledging some of the beings, putting her hand to her heart as she saw who they were.

She was gently brought back as the voice of Haj Kabir began the midday prayers. She revelled in them, her heart filled with joyful certainty. She recalled how Malak had said she was protected. The prayers were a melody of deep conviction, and as she performed the physical rituals that accompanied them, with Rana and Houda on either side, her heart swelled with love for them.

«Amour.» she heard, as a descant to the prayers, and her heart was filled even more with her love for Pia, the one who had awakened her, her divine Pia.

Darou Al Bahr, the cleansing

After the prayers had concluded, as Haj Kabir left the Mosque, he saw Rana, Houda and Shaafia waiting for him. Hovering close by was Omar but unwilling to stand with them.

«I have a very strong feeling that I know why you are waiting for me.» he said, smiling. Then he invited them to sit in his courtyard. Once again Omar hung back until Haj Kabir went over to him.

«It is so many years since you have visited us in the Mosque. We are happy to see you come back.»

«You know why I could not come.» murmured Omar, barely more than a whisper.

«In the eyes of the Lord, there is no reason ever not to come to the Mosque. No matter what crime you may have committed, the Mosque is never closed.»

«I am cursed.» Omar said, and his head dropped onto his chest in self-disgust.

«I think you are wrong, my friend.» said Haj Kabir, taking the older man's hand. Then he pulled Omar close to Shaafia. «You see this girl?»

Omar shyly looked up at Shaafia, who studied his face without expression.

«To be in her company, you cannot be cursed, no matter who has tried in the past.»

«Why do you say you are cursed, Uncle?» asked Rana.

«You must know.» he muttered.

«My sister?»

Then suddenly he seemed to draw himself more upright. He was in fact quite a tall man, but he had developed such an ashamed slouch that it was not apparent.

«I brought it upon myself. She made promises. I had felt left out when my brother died and he did not leave me anything to live by. She promised that I would thrive. She said, no matter what happened, she promised that I would live in *Darou Al Bahr*, that it would be mine.»

«But she made a bargain, did she not?» asked Haj Kabir.

Omar nodded. «She gave me things, disgusting things to put in different parts of the house. She told me to repeat certain phrases on certain days.»

«But your wife and your children were not included in the bargain, were they?» asked Shaafia.

He shook his head. «I did not think to ask. I only thought of myself.»

«So up until now the house has been yours.» said Rana.

«I do not want it!» he cried out. «It is like a prison to me. It has eaten me slowly, slowly like a terrible worm in my gut.»

Haj Kabir put his hands on the old man's shoulders.

«Truly, my friend, you made a very poor bargain and you have lived in hell to pay for it. But I tell you. There is some good fortune left in you. This girl has brought it back to life.»

Omar turned his head slowly to gaze at Shaafia. Then he dropped his eyes and began to waver on his feet.

Haj Kabir guided him to a stone bench and sat with him.

«Now is the time to change.» Haj Kabir said softly. «You have nothing to fear from Daad any more. You are protected. But I have to tell you, you must now make up for what you have done in the past. You cannot bring back your wife and your children, but you can support the family you still have. If you do that, then the rest of your life will not be lived in vain.»

«*Sidi,*» whispered Omar. «I hear you. I will do as you say.»

Haj Kabir stood up and faced Rana.

«Tomorrow we will come. I will bring a group of saintly men and we will begin to eradicate the darkness that has shrouded your house. But before we come, you must prepare a space for us.»

«We will.» said Rana. «I will send for our people to come. It will be done.»

Shaafia had watched all this, while at the same time keeping an inner awareness.

Then something new prompted her to speak to Rana.

«Please take me and Omar back to the house.» she said. «There is something that he and I must do. You and Houda go back and collect all your people and bring tools and products to make a clean place for the prayers.»

Haj Kabir nodded.

«She is right,» he said. «Listen to her.»

They were about to leave, when Shaafia turned back to Haj Kabir.

«I have a request for you. Could you please give Omar a new and clean robe to wear.»

He nodded and went into his house, returning a moment later with a simple long white robe.

«Myriam just bought this for me. It is indeed brand new.»

He handed it to Omar, who bowed his head low without a word.

«I will look after it for now.» said Shaafia taking it from Omar.

Rana immediately offered to pay for it, but Haj Kabir smiled. «It is the least I can do.»

As Houda drove back to *Darou Al Bahr*, Rana turned to face Shaafia sitting in the back seat with Omar.

«What is it you have to do?»

Shaafia smiled. «I am not sure yet, but I will know when we go back.»

As the red Porsche took off and turned into the Rue de Rome, heading for the compound, Omar watched it go. Then he turned back to face the small girl standing beside him, the white robe folded over her arm.

«Who are you?» he asked.

It was not a question that required a response.

Then he turned and opened the gate.

Just inside, as they looked up at the stone steps leading into the house, Shaafia began to feel a powerful inner movement. She stood still with her eyes closed.

The old man stood a little way off, not altogether steady on his feet, watching her.

She still had her eyes closed when she said: «You must build a fire. It should be at the end of the garden where it comes to a point. You must collect lots of wood to make it burn hot. Do it now.»

He nodded.

He left her there and went round to the long front garden.

Shaafia stayed still for a long time to be sure that she understood what was being communicated, then she went up the steps and, with some effort, got the front door to move just enough to let her in.

As she did, the scrawny orange cat that had sat near her earlier in the day, appeared and walked in beside her. She looked down at it. It had hazel eyes, and as she looked, it closed one eye and then rubbed itself against her leg. She knelt down and ran her hand along its back. It was all bone.

She walked to the back of the house to the room with the photo of Haj Hussein. She sat on a faded bench opposite, laid the white robe beside her and closed her eyes. Then the cat jumped up and sat beside her.

She sensed them, as if they were descending from the photo in front of her. She could see them, not in sepia as they were on the wall, but becoming animated and coloured as if they had just walked into the sunlight.

No words needed to be spoken, as she accepted their presence and the mantle of warm protection that settled over her.

Finally she felt a movement in the room and opened her eyes. Omar stood watching her from the doorway.

«It is ready.» he said.

She walked with him to the end of the garden and the cat followed.

He had collected a mass of dried wood, old boxes and dead branches, with piles of old newspaper in the centre. Now he knelt in front of it and lit a match.

The paper caught immediately and flames leapt up.

She watched it grow in strength and heat, then she turned to him.

«Now you will collect all those evil things that you have placed all over the house, make sure you do not miss a single one, and put them in the fire.»

He stared at her for a long moment and she met his gaze until he could not hold it. Then he nodded and walked away.

She had no need to see what he brought, so she took herself up to the front of the house facing the garden. She sat on the top step in the warm afternoon sun, lay the robe across her knees and began to repeat her Koranic verse. The cat sat one step below her, watching the fire.

As she looked out into the garden, her vision shifted. She could see dark forms moving in the undergrowth. At first she thought it was other cats, but then she realised they were not concrete forms but ethereal dark presences. When she focussed on any one of them, they would shrink back into the brambles. She sought them out, one after the other, and she found within herself an energy that was forcing them back against the walls of the garden until they began to merge into the exterior wall.

«You have no place here» was her powerful thought as she focussed on each one. «Be gone.»

Oblivious to this, Omar came and went, carrying boxes, jars and lengths of cloth, which he threw onto the fire. Different coloured flames rose and small explosions erupted sending up sparks and dark acrid smoke into the cloudless sky.

When the last of the dark forms melted away into the walls, he came up to her and nodded.

She scanned the long perimeters of both walls to be sure there was no more dark presence, then she got up.

«You will take all the clothes you have, the ones you are wearing and any others that you have, and you will burn them.»

«This is all I have.» he said, gesturing at his shirt and shabby pants.

«There is nothing in your room?»

«A few old things.»

«Bring them.»

She watched him go and then, finding a low tree branch close by, she folded the new robe over the branch.

He came back with a small armload of grey and tattered apparel.

She gestured with her head and he threw it into the fire. It blazed up immediately.

«Now all your clothes.» she said.

He turned to take the robe and she stopped him.

«No. Not yet. You must stand naked before the fire.»

«Naked?» He stared at her.

«Do as I say.» There was no mistaking the power of her command and he shed his miserable garments and his battered sandals and threw them into the fire. Then he stood trembling with his thin gnarled hands over his genitals.

«Stand close to the fire.» she said.

He took a few shuffling steps forward. Then she was beside him and she knelt down at the edge of the fire where there was already mounds of smouldering ash. She plunged her hands into the cooling ash and began smearing handfuls all over his bony frame. She did not seem to feel the heat and he bore it with his eyes closed.

She did not miss any part of this body. Pulling him down so she could reach, she scrubbed the ash into his hair, his eyebrows and his ears. At the other end, she raised his feet, one by one, to cover the soles. She gently lifted his protective hands away to coat his genitals. He whimpered as she touched him.

Although the afternoon was warm and the ash was hot, he shook as if he was shivering.

When he was totally covered, she stood back.

Her Koranic verse surged up inside her and she called it out loudly several times.

The fire flamed up and a wind shook the trees above.

Omar stood there, bowed over and shaking.

She waited until the flames had died down again and then she sent him to the back of the house. She had seen water barrels back there and she told him to wash off all the ash and to come back naked to the fire.

With his eyes barely open, he took himself away.

She watched him go, and as the smoke lazily floated up and away into the late afternoon sky, she felt a deep release. She looked around the garden. There were no more dark forms.

When he returned, with his shameful shuffling naked feet and his hands over his crotch, she felt a wave of love for him. Now she knew he was ready to regain something of who he once was.

She handed him the robe and he put it on.

They were standing side by side, looking down at the last glowing coals of the fire, when Rana and Houda came round from the back of the house.

Rana put her staff to work. The women had come armed with an array of tools and products to attack the years of grime and dust. The men worked more on the outside, scrubbing the steps and the paths and cleaning away debris from the entrance.

The cats took off in fright.

By the time the sun began to set, the two front rooms of the house had been thoroughly cleaned up, new covers had been put on the benches along the walls, and new rugs had been laid. The kitchen had been scrubbed.

As the sky darkened, Rana gathered up her people ready to transport them back to the compound. Shaafia spoke to the security man who Rana had asked to stay for the night.

«During the night, it is possible that you will see the same man that you saw the night before the funeral.»

He looked at her with a frown.

«What do I do about that?»

«Nothing, except be very respectful. He is in charge of security.»

That made him smile. «So I am out of a job?»

«Not at all. You are a team.»

While Rana went back to the compound with the two vans conveying her staff, Houda drove Shaafia home in the red Porsche.

They were nearing the Mosque when Shaafia noticed a shop selling shoes. She asked Houda to wait for her while she went inside. She came back with a pair of men's leather sandals.

«Please give these to your uncle.» she said.

When the Porsche pulled up beside the café on the corner, Shaafia told Houda about her brother Samet and his group of intellectuals, and how Shaafia had challenged them to create their own podcast.

«You know about podcasts?» asked Houda in admiration.

«About as much as I do about legal papers.» smiled Shaafia.

Houda studied her passenger with undisguised awe. «But you get help.»

«I do.»

As they were sitting there, Samet came out and he looked at the car with interest. It was not such a common sight in that part of the city. Then he saw Shaafia sitting in it.

He came over.

«My sister is riding in style these days.» he remarked.

Shaafia introduced Houda and told him she had been studying in Bordeaux.

«What did you study?»

«Mostly the boys in my classes.» she replied, with a challenge in her voice.

«Plenty of boys in Casa, why go all the way to Bordeaux for that?»

«Superior quality.»

He shook his head and walked away.

Shaafia smiled. «I thought you two would get along. He's your kind of guy.»

«You are turning into a matchmaker now?»

Shaafia shook her head. «Not really, but it would be fun to watch.»

Houda spun the Porsche so that the tyres made a screech as she left, and Samet turned to watch it. He waited till Shaafia caught up.

«She's something, that girl.» he said.

«Not your style, I think.» said his sister, matching his steps as they walked.

«She's wealthy, isn't she?»

«Very.»

«That's exactly what I need, a wealthy woman to support me.»

«Too late. She is engaged to marry Ihab and Ayman's boss.»

«Wealth marrying wealth. What a waste of resources.»

Over the evening meal, Shaafia shared how she had spent her day. Her Mother nodded. «It will be wonderful to see Haj Hussein's house brought back to life. Your Father loved to go there. He met many great sufis there.»

Before she went to bed, Shaafia went out and sat under the fig tree with her cell phone and called France. She wanted them to know what was happening to her. It was to these people that she could share how she was discovering that she could do things, she could see things, she could intuit, in a way that she had never done before. In their turn they shared how life was unfolding in the château, where people were continuing to come to pay reverence to the grave of Pia, to sit in the chapel, and to share what had changed in their lives as a result.

For Shaafia to hear all this was an immense comfort, an acknowledgement that she was not alone in what was happening. It was undeniably apparent that each of them, now in different places, was beginning to fulfill the potential that they all had, and what Pia had revealed in them.

When at last she lay down to sleep it was again to be bathed in gratitude.

The following morning, Houda waited for Shaafia at the end of the lane, and they made their way through the morning traffic up the hill to the house.

The back gates were already open and several of the compound vehicles were already there. In the kitchen, Rana's team was making pots of green tea, baking flat bread, and preparing to serve the influx of hungry chanters.

Haj Kabir arrived with his group of older men, all dressed in white. They rolled out a large white cloth in one of the front rooms, now freshly cleaned and neat, and sat round it on all four sides. There was a long prayerful silence, and then Haj Kabir spoke. His voice was strong and clear rising into the high ceiling round the newly de-cobwebbed chandelier.

«On this day,» he said, looking round the group of men seated before him, «We pray to God to restore the peace and harmony that once reigned in this fine house. We pray to God with all our hearts and all our fervour that the wishes of our dear departed Haj Hussein, *Allah y rahmou*, be at last realised. We pray that any negativity that has been laid upon this house be lifted away and permanently exiled. We pray that those who will come to reside here will have the courage and the devotion to make this house a centre of spiritual upliftment for all who pass through its doors. For this we pray. *Inche Allah.*»

«*Inche Allah*» was echoed around the edge of the white cloth and the chanting began. It would continue all day, prayers at prayer times, chanting of the Koran the rest of the time, going on unbroken throughout the day in relays.

Rana and Houda stood with Shaafia in the doorway to witness the opening, and Haj Kabir nodded to them as the chanting began. After a while they turned back and Rana went to the kitchen to oversee the preparations for the refreshments. Houda and Shaafia went outside and sat on the front steps looking out into the garden.

The security man came up to them.

«Was it a quiet night?» asked Shaafia.

He nodded. «The man in charge did a great job.»

«You saw him?» asked Houda.

«He sat over there.» he said, pointing to where they had seen Malak on the first day.

«Did you talk to him?» asked Shaafia.

«To be quite honest with you, now I know who he is, I was too intimidated. But he gave me a wave and I was happy.»

«So now go and get a good rest.»

He laughed gently. «I don't really need it. I have just spent one of the most restful nights of my life.»

When he had gone, Houda said. «I can hardly believe this is happening. I thought my life was finished. I thought I was destined to live like my Mother. I was close to wanting to kill myself.»

«So, do not forget that.» said Shaafia. «It will help you to always make sure that you keep gratitude alive in your heart.»

Houda did not reply. She looked out over the garden that had become a little tidier, where several men from the compound were hacking away at the brambles, and cleaning away the remnants of the fire. As she listened to the powerful renditions of the Koranic verses coming from the front room, she let her tears run down her cheeks.

Darou Al Bahr awakes

There were three days of chanting and prayers.

Each day, as the chanting came to an end with the evening prayers, refreshments were served as the sun set, and the house seemed to resonate with harmony and radiate tranquility.

Over the three days, with the chanting in the background, Rana was intent on restoring every aspect of the house. She had already contracted landscape workers to rebuild the garden, another team to destroy the ramshackle buildings out the back including the one where Omar had subsisted for so long. She had worked on creating a bedroom for him upstairs, and already plumbers had begun to remove the antiquated plumbing, old rusted pipes, one stained and awful toilet and several stagnant water tanks. The house soon had a temporary electric hot water service, a working toilet and running water.

In all this, Omar stood around like a man in a trance. Sometimes he would wander into the room where the verses were being recited and sit hunched against a wall. At other times, he would be found in the garden, just standing there, as still as the old trees that were waiting to be pruned. He spoke to no-one and seemed to be existing inside himself like a crab in a shell.

In the last afternoon of the final day, there was a huge feast offered, both to honour those who had chanted and prayed for three days, and also to welcome friends and family. Rana had let it be known that she was reopening the house and all the neighbours had been told. Some of them had been neighbours when her parents occupied the house, and one or two had been there long enough to remember the French Admiral, her grandfather.

Rana had one of her pavilions erected in the garden with tables laden with pastries and sweets, piles of freshly baked bread, fruit bowls with dates and figs, and jugs of fruit juice and pots of tea.

There were many joyful conversations as the guests shared memories and anecdotes, stories of the house.

One old man recalled that he had seen Winston Churchill arrive for a meeting with the Admiral at the beginning of the Second World War.

«I was just a kid at the time,» he said, «but my Father took me out to see the big Bentley arrive with police escorts. He told me it was a war meeting and that the whole world was going to start fighting each other. He was a wise man, my Father.»

Others spoke of the great sufi gatherings that Haj Hussein had held on festive days. Not all the neighbors were enthusiastic about the sufis, but those who were quietly told Rana that they hoped she would invite them back.

One elderly lady told Rana that she had felt an evil presence hovering over this house ever since they had left. She whispered to Rana that over the years she had seen dark figures floating above the walls.

«It was a very scary place. I would always cross the road to the other side when I went past.» she said, and she fervently hoped that Rana would employ beneficial means to bring back harmony.

«The whole neighborhood needs this.» she said. «Back then, in your father's time, our neighbourhood felt like paradise. Then it was all lost.»

Rana assured her that it had already started to come back. The old lady nodded and whispered: «I don't see them now.» She had been present for all three days of the chanting.

In the middle of the feast, Shaafia looked up and saw Walid walk in by himself. He greeted Rana with a kiss on both cheeks and then did the same to Houda, who dutifully returned the gesture.

After greeting several people that he knew, he came over to Shaafia.

«I have to talk to you.» he said.

She smiled. «More translation?»

«In a way, but not English.»

She led the way to one of the stone benches in the garden away from the pavilion.

As soon as he sat, he turned on the bench to look quite piercingly at her.

«Are you doing something mystical to disturb my dreams?»

Her eyes widened in astonishment, then she smiled shyly, «Not consciously, no.» Then she added «There are nightmares?»

«No,» he said, «not really, just very mysterious. I do not understand them.»

«Can you tell me what you saw?»

He sat quietly for a moment, nodding to himself, trying to get clear about what to say.

«Sometimes,» he said, «you were like you are now and you would tell me things, quite useful things, I have to say. You talked about the Essaouira project and I liked your ideas. And then, this is quite strange, you seemed to think I should get involved in Hamza's business.»

She smiled. «Did you like that advice?»

«It seemed to make sense in the dream, but in reality I imagine the brother will run it now.»

«Quite possibly,» she said, «But you never know. You said there were other dreams?»

«Yes. At other times you were kind of like a ghost, kind of see-through, and you would be very stern with me. You seemed to know about some of the things that I have done that I am not so proud of.»

She nodded as he spoke, not wanting to break the flow.

«When I woke, I wondered: how much do you know?»

Again she smiled, but said nothing.

«And then sometimes,» he went on, leaning forward, «I would see you with a small girl in a wheelchair, all bent over with saliva running out of her mouth.»

Then she really smiled and he stopped.

«You know a girl like that?»

And then Shaafia knew it was time to tell Walid her story.

As she did, she monitored what effect it was having. He listened carefully to how it all began, and she could tell he was not doubting what she was telling him.

When she got to the moment when she and Pia connected, he said: «The girl with the saliva?», and she explained why Pia was like that.

As she began to describe how Pia knew things that no-one could possibly have told her and how these things were communicated telepathically through Shaafia, he said: «So you really are a translator in more ways than one.»

She went on to describe the effect Pia had on the nuns, on Théophile, Kate, and so many others. He listened to it all, nodding now and then. She could see that what she was telling him, he was carefully absorbing and he seemed to be accepting.

Suddenly his phone went and he looked down to see if there was a message.

«Damn,» he said, «I have a meeting. I have to go. I am running it. I am already a bit late. But I have to hear more about this.»

He put his hand to his chest. «I will call you.» he said, and took off through the garden.

She sat quietly by herself for a while. So now Walid was coming into Pia's sphere of influence. She was wondering if she should tell Houda, when Houda herself came over to her.

«Wow, you and Walid really get on.» she said. «I saw you talking together very seriously.»

«Are you feeling jealous?» smiled Shaafia.

«Not at all.» Houda chuckled and gave her hug. «You might make a very cute couple.»

Shaafia smiled.

Then she decided to share one part of their conversation.

«He told me something pretty interesting.» she said. «I came to him in a dream.

«He's dreaming about you?»

«It's not what you think. In this dream I told him he should be involved with your Father's business.»

«Are you serious?»

«That's what he said.»

«Did you do that? I mean did you somehow send that dream?»

Shaafia laughed. «No. At least, not that I am aware of.»

«What does it mean?»

«It means that the energy for that to take place is in the air. When your Mother asks him he will be amazed.»

«No wonder he calls you Mystic Girl.» Then Houda frowned. «Maybe it is time to ask him.»

«Maybe not.»

«OK.» nodded Houda. She had more and more respect for Shaafia's insights.

«How is Rana doing with the lawyer?» asked Shaafia.

«I don't really know. We have been so busy with all this work on the house we haven't talked about it.»

Shaafia sat quietly and checked inside herself. It was quiet. Now was not the time to tell Rana.

As night fell, Haj Kabir said his goodbyes and took his team home. Rana had showered them with gifts in gratitude and they went, not only well fed, but with their arms full.

Shaafia began to feel deeply tired, as if she had done a lot of heavy work, and she knew she had to rest. She found a moment to tell Rana that she needed to go home. Rana enfolded her in her arms and hugged her long and close.

«Thank God for you.» she said, «So much is happening. Truly God sent you.»

Shaafia pulled back a little and said: «And your Father.»

Rana called Houda and asked her to drive Shaafia home. Before she left, however, Shaafia said: «Tomorrow we must talk together. I think it will be time for us to take more action.»

« I can feel it, too. Arrange for Houda to come and get you.»

At home, Shaafia felt the weight of the last three days had become heavier and heavier, as if she had somehow held a certain responsibility for the re-establishment of *Darou Al Bahr.* While her Mother and younger sisters begged her to tell them what had been happening, as soon as she could, she slipped away into the girls' sleeping area and lay on her sleeping mat with a shawl over her head.

She closed her eyes and began repeating her Koranic verse.

She had a lot to absorb.

Renovations

While she waited for Houda at the corner of the lane, Shaafia went into the café. Samet had told her that their new podcast was ready and they wanted to show her.

She ordered and paid for coffee for all the boys and then went over to their table. They were the only clients in the café.

As the owner brought over the tray with coffee and pastries, Shaafia asked about their previous podcast, what kind of feedback they had received. They had to admit it was mixed.

Nabil admitted that although some people congratulated them, most of those were family members.

«At least I am doing something productive, they said.»

Dari said that others had mocked them for self-indulgence suggesting that they should all get a proper job.

Yusuf added that there were a few others who had constructive things to say.

The group laughed when he said that because someone had offered to buy the original of his drawing from the first podcast. He was the only one who seemed to have benefitted.

Finally, Samet said that he had come across some responses from people who felt they were like them, and some who even wanted to contribute.

They showed Shaafia the new one, and she saw immediately that they were running the danger of dropping into a predictable pattern.

«This is OK,» she said, «but it lacks one important thing.»

«Like what?» asked Samet.

«It is as if you are only half there. It lacks life. You are hiding yourselves. We need to see you, you need to talk to the people directly. You have to shoot this like a video. You have to look people in the eye. Let them see you. Let them hear you. Show them the café.»

They stared at her in silence. This was a scary idea.

She heard the Porsche and got up.

«Think about it.» she said.

She could imagine the kind of conversation that was taking place behind her.

Work was continuing at *Darou Al Bahr* and they found Rana talking to several men about the interior renovation that she wanted done. Everything should be implimented as soon as possible. She was planning to create four bedrooms with proper bathrooms upstairs, and a full tearing down and replacement of the kitchen.

She was fired up with energy and had her own staff running all over the house bringing it more and more back to the way it used to be. Painters had begun to strip away the old layers of paint ready for new rendering, plastering where needed, and selecting new colours. She had brought a vanload of the things she had secretly kept of her father's, and was planning where to put everything.

«Your Mother seems like a new person» Shaafia said quietly as they watched her.

In his own way something had also begun to change for Omar. Rana had brought him a suitcase full of her husband's clothes, many of them French designer wear. Omar was now dressed in fashionable slacks and a collared shirt, with black leather loafers.

Houda whispered that he didn't believe in socks.

Although he did not join in planning the renovations or even help with the endless cleaning, he now seemed to have assumed the rôle of overseer, walking from one place to another and sometimes making shy suggestions about what needed to be done.

He was taller, straighter, and more alert.

When he saw Shaafia he gave her a little bow with his hand over his heart.

At the end of the morning, which Shaafia and Houda had spent mostly making strategic decisions, closely monitoring the work and directing a constant flow of deliveries, Rana invited them to a local restaurant for lunch.

«Years ago we used to go there very often.» she said. «I have not been back for such a long time. Hamza never liked anything in this neighbourhood.»

The restaurant was hidden behind a high wall, not far from the Royal Palace, with a security guard at the gate. There was a valet to park the Porsche and as they walked in, Rana said: « I have booked us a private room so we can talk.»

Even though she had not been there for many years, still she was greeted with great respect. Anyone who had the means to book a private room was someone to be cultivated. The *maitre d'*, in his immaculate pseudo-military uniform, did quite some bowing as he ushered them through the main dining area and up a short flight of marble stairs. Various people looked up as they passed, and Rana nodded to several who she evidently knew.

Once they had settled and the waiter had brought menus, Rana said: «This is my small way of saying thank you for everything you have done for us, for me and for Houda.»

Shaafia shook her head. «I have to say there is no need to thank me. I have felt I was simply a messenger, as I have been all along. What we have all received comes to us from that magnificent place of God's grace. And for that we can all be endlessly grateful. *Ham delilah.*«

There was no disagreement from her two companions.

As they enjoyed the four different kinds of pastillas, each wrapped in thin crusty pastry, one of chicken, one of fish, one of lamb and the other a vegetarian, Rana told Shaafia about her progress with the lawyer. It was now clear according to him that she had control, and that she could also name a legal representative. The lawyer had prepared all the paperwork to do that and he was absolutely sure that Taj could not prevent it. Rana asked Shaafia if it was time to approach Walid.

Before Shaafia could answer, her phone went. At first she thought to ignore it, but something prompted her to at least see who it was.

She laughed.

It was Walid.

Her two lunch companions smiled as she answered the call.

«So Walid, you knew that we are speaking of you, so you had to join in?»

Then she added: «No, no, we were not saying anything that would embarrass you. Unless you are embarrassed by compliments of course.»

She told him where she was and he passed on his best wishes to Rana and Houda. What he wanted to tell her was that Alex would be returning in a few days, and he had asked if Shaafia would be available to translate.

She told him she was, and then she went on to say that Rana would like to have a meeting with him.When would he be available? She did not say what the meeting was for, but that it should be soon.

He spoke for a while, and she nodded now and then.

«I will ask her.» she said at last. Then she told Rana that Walid was willing to meet her at the end of the day.

«Yes, that will do very well.» said Rana. «We can have an evening meal together at the compound.»

Once Shaafia had conveyed the message, she added: «Yes of course, I will be there.»

The lunch went on for a leisurely couple of hours, finishing with delicate tiny coloured pastry squares and mint tea in crystal glasses, before they returned to *Darou Al Bahr*. As they left, Rana promised the *maitre d'* that it would not be so long before her next visit.

Rana sent some of her staff back to the compound to prepare the evening meal and then toured the house, inspected the various projects all happening at once. Omar walked with them commenting here and there. It was clear he was becoming a new person.

«You know,» said Rana, «I cannot wait to be living here again. I have decided to put the compound up for sale. Now that Hamza has gone, I have no interest in living there any more.»

Walid arrived at the Bin Salah compound, flying up the drive in a long low bright yellow Italian coupé that growled.

As always, he greeted both Rana and Houda with double cheek kisses, but to Shaafia he simply put his hand up to his chest and she did the same. She understood and appreciated his gesture as one of respect.

Behind the house, in the gazebo, tables had been laid for the evening meal. Rana poured fruit juices and handed round plates of nuts and figs. They made small talk for a while, the progress of renovations to *Darou Al Bahr,* the decision to sell the compound, before Rana decided to broach the reason for inviting Walid.

She outlined the situation with her brother-in-law, the legal opinions about her controlling interest and the pressure coming from him to give it to him.

«So, as it is now clear that I do hold the controlling interest in Bin Salah Transportation I intend to keep it.»

Walid nodded. «But that means you will have to step in and actively demonstrate that you can control what happens.»

«Not necessarily,» smiled Rana. «Shaafia has suggested something else.»

Walid looked over at Shaafia, who kept her face neutral. His eyes narrowed. Then he chuckled. «She has already told me about it.»

Rana looked shocked. Houda,who knew what he was alluding to, hid her smile.

Rana turned to Shaafia. «Is that true?»

Shaafia smiled. «Walid will have to explain what he means.»

Walid told her of the dream, and Rana had to smile. «She is an amazing girl.»

«In this I totally agree.» he said. Then he looked at Shaafia. «So tell me, mystic girl, how is this going to work?»

Without thinking, Shaafia began to speak. «I think it will be like this. Rana's lawyer will call a meeting with Taj and his lawyer to discuss the ownership and control of Bin Salah Transport. You will be there.»

«And hopefully so will you.» he said.

«Of course Shaafia must be there.» added Rana.

«And at this meeting what do you see as happening?» asked Walid.

«Rana will insist in maintaining her controlling share of the company. Taj will repeat that she has no expertise so in his opinion will ruin the company. Then she will nominate you as her representative with executive power. He will dispute the legality of that, but Rana's lawyer will already have the legal papers to show how it would work. Taj's lawyer will see that it is true.»

«How come you know all this?» he asked.

She smiled. «I see what I see.»

«And what if he refuses to accept Rana's decision?»

«She will offer to buy him out.»

Walid looked at Rana. «You have that kind of capital?»

Rana looked confused, but Shaafia said: «She doesn't need it. She has you. You and your Father have the resources and he will know that.»

«Not just a pretty face.» he said.

Houda had been watching all this. Now she leaned forward. «Walid. Do not mock my friend.»

His eyebrows shot up.

«What? I wasn't mocking her.»

«You are making a sexist remark. It is not respectful.»

«I thought it was a compliment.»

All three women looked at him and he knew he was in trouble.

«OK,» he said. «I am sorry if what I said was not appropriate.»

«Thank you,» said Rana. «I think you and I both have a lot to learn about how modern young women see the world.»

He nodded. Then he said: «In all seriousness I am very impressed with what you are suggesting. And I have an admission to make. When our Fathers began to discuss the marriage, I was not happy about it, and I am sure you weren't either. You are, as your Mother says, a modern woman, you have been to France, you know about things. My Father was very insistent, and to prove his point he had research done, quietly, on Bin Salah Transport. He wanted to show me that I would be inheriting, by marriage, as the only male in Hamza's family, a very successful business with vast potential. We Razaks are business people. Marriages, in my Father's eyes, are business transactions and this was going to be a good one. So I know a lot about your company, and I like the way your husband and his brother have broadened it and made it a lucrative enterprise.»

«So you would be willing to be the executive director of my company?»

«I think it would be a very good move. In a way, it simply brings forward what your husband had in mind in the first place.»

Then Houda sat forward. «You would have control of the company even before the marriage.»

«No,» said Shaafia, «Rana has that.»

«Oh,» said Houda, and sank back in her chair.

Walid turned to face Houda. «I know what you were thinking. If I had control of the company, then you would not have to marry me.»

Houda went scarlet with embarrassment.

«I just, I wanted to....»

«You are correct.» said Shaafia to Walid. «As you just said, Houda doesn't want to marry you. Of course you could see that for yourself. She was being forced to, by her Father, as you put it, as a business transaction.»

There was a powerful silence in the gazebo.

Finally it was Rana who broke it.

«It seems to me that I should ask you to be my executive director, as a business transaction, for me. Marriage has nothing to do with it. Forget about that question. I married to fulfill the wishes of my Father. I married someone I did not love. I respected him and I honoured him as my husband. I want my daughter, now I am her only parent, to marry whoever she wishes whenever she wishes.»

Houda lunged across and melted into her Mother's arms.

Walid looked at Shaafia and nodded. «You knew this was coming.»

She smiled. «I see what I see.»

Then Houda pulled back with a tear-stained face. «She told me, she promised me, I would not have to marry you.»

«And she was right,» he said, «and I am as relieved as you are.»

Houda wiped her face and looked at him searchingly. «You really didn't want to marry me?»

He met her look. «It is not that I don't like you, but I would prefer to marry someone that I choose. I am as modern as you in that way.»

Rana pressed her device and two girls came out of the house to take away the remnants of the meal.

When they had gone, Rana said: «So do we have a deal? No marriage but a directorship instead?»

«In principle,» said Walid, «I believe we do. However, there are many details that we will have to think about. You will have to lay out my rôle very precisely so that it is legally solid, we will have to work with your lawyer to be ready to meet Taj. I will expect a decent remuneration for my efforts, and I will need to know exactly how you will define the word 'Executive'.»

«I am not a businesswoman,» said Rana, «but I have a brilliant advisor.» She turned to put her hand on Shaafia's knee. «And I believe we will come to the perfect arrangement for all this.»

He nodded. «I believe you and I have the same advisor which will ensure harmony.»

«And I am a free woman,» shrieked Houda, and she jumped up and danced round the edge of the gazebo loudly making the sound of celebration that women in the Arabic world make at celebrations.

Shaafia smiled.

«So we have begun.» she said.

When Shaafia accepted Walid's offer to drive her home, Rana frowned. «Houda could drive you.»

Shaafia smiled. «Walid and I have much to talk about. You can think of this journey as a business meeting.»

«But still a young woman alone with an unmarried man. I am sure your Mother would not be happy.»

Walid said: «Rana, I will be an absolute gentleman in transporting your business advisor.»

«And anyway,» added Houda mischieviously, «Shaafia can take care of herself. If he tried anything she would simply turn him to ashes.»

He nodded. «That too.»

He courteously opened the door for her and she had to get low down to fit into the car. The seats were strangely uncomfortable, like she was half-lying on a bed with lumps.

«What do you think of my new wheels?» he asked, «I just got it imported.»

«You want the truth?» She tried to face him as she spoke, and even that was difficult.

«Of course,» he said, as he gunned the engine. «I will always expect that from you.»

«OK,» she said, «It is a horrible monster of a thing. It is a symbol of decadence, too loud, too low, too impractical.»

«That's what I thought you might say, but it was fun to ask.»

She stayed silent for a moment as he whipped the car through the narrow streets.

«You said we had things to talk about,» he said over the engine. «And I have a lot of questions for you. I think we only covered the beginning of what you were telling me the other day.»

«I thought we could talk in the car, but it is too noisy.»

So by the time they got to the corner of the alley they had not said much to each other.

The evening was setting in and people were out in the street, many of them staring at the yellow monster purring as it sat outside the café.

Once again it was Samet who looked out to see what was making that noise, and yet again he saw his sister sitting in a fancy car. He came over to lean against her window. Walid asked who the boy was and when she told him it was one of her brothers, he worked the electric window.

Samet leaned in. «Each day my sister comes home in a different set of luxury wheels.»

Shaafia introduced Walid as Ayman and Ihab's employer.

«You're going to marry the girl with the red Porsche?» Samet said.

Walid smiled. «Red and yellow go well together, don't you think?»

«It seems to me that there are much better ways to spend the money.»

«Such as?»

«If you bought a basic Renault, you could use the difference to fund a school in a poor neighbourhood for years.»

«You must be a socialist.»

«Not me,» said Samet, enjoying the play. «Socialists pretend to take care of everyone but they are no better than the rest. They only take care of their own.»

«So if you are not a socialist, what are you?»

«Why does everyone have to have a label?»

«OK. So let me put it another way. Let's say I give you one million dirhams. What would you do with it?»

«I would start a school for brilliant children from poor suburbs, and I would develop a curriculum where each child would discover their particular talent, and then I would have teachers trained to develop those talents.»

«You are a teacher?»

«No, just a victim of bad teaching.»

Walid smiled. «I can see you and your sister are rather like each other.»

Shaafia had been watching this interplay with pleasure. Samet and Walid were a good match for each other.

«Well, boys,» she said at last, « this could be a very long discussion and I need to go to bed.»

Walid nodded and got out of the car to come round and open her door, then he shook hands with Samet.

«You know,» he said, «if I thought you were serious, I'd back you.»

«I'm always serious.» retorted Samet.

Shaafia managed to scramble out of the low seat, and she stood next to her brother.

«He's too serious if you ask me.» she said.

Walid put his right hand to his chest which seemed to have become his habitual way to greet and farewell Shaafia. «I will call you tomorrow.» he said. «We have a lot to talk about.»

«We do.» she said, and waved as the yellow monster roared away.

As they walked home up the alley, Samet said: «Do you think he meant that?»

«Probably,» she said. «But you would have to prove to him that you could do what you said, that you have a workable plan, a budget, a team of teachers. He's a businessman and he knows what works and what doesn't.»

«Wow.» He stopped in the middle of the alley. «Imagine if we could really do that. I mean that would be something really worth doing. I hate the education system we have.»

«So start work.»

«Wow.» He bit his lower lip, and he looked his sister. «You certainly know how to shake things up.»

She laughed. «Ha. I didn't do anything. I just sat in his ridiculously uncomfortable car and you two had a chat.»

«You can't fool me.» he retorted without anger. «I am beginning to see that you have an incredible influence on people.»

When they arrived home, Habib jumped in front of Shaafia with excitement.

«He's going to Bordeaux!» he shouted. «They are getting married.»

She gave him a big hug, and said: «Yasser and Rachi you mean?»

«Who else? Rachi just came looking for you. We are all invited to the wedding.»

«When?»

«Next Friday.»

Shaafia smiled as she held her little brother in her arms.

«We will all have to be there.»

A lunch

It was early in the morning when Walid called Shaafia. Her sisters were preparing to go to school, and Habib was being slow at getting ready, so she took the phone outside and sat under the fig tree.

«I am hoping that you do not have a lunch engagement today.» said Walid.

«I will have to check with my social secretary.» she said, smiling to herself. Then she added: «I believe I could cancel my appointments, if it was necessary.»

«That is very kind of you. My father wishes to invite you to lunch with us.»

«Then I am very happy to accept.» she said.

«Ayman will pick you up.»

After the call, she continued to sit under the tree, resting her back against its old gnarled trunk. How many comings and goings had this tree been a witness to? What secret information did it have? She let her head drop back against the bark and felt the energy of the tree flow into her, and she closed her eyes.

She could feel the free flow of the tree's energy not only into her, but at the same time going out from her to the tree, as if they were in conversation. The spirit of her nanny Dada with whom she had sat so often under this tree came to her. It felt as if Dada was in fact part of the tree herself, and that they could converse. Shaafia felt that Dada knew what Shaafia had experienced, Dada was pleased with her, having said often she was sure that one day Shaafia would succeed. And more than anything else, she felt Dada's love, freely flowing and warm. Dear Dada.

She came back from her inner focus to see her brother Samet standing looking at her.

«Stay there much longer,» he said, «and you'll turn into a tree yourself.»

She smiled. He wasn't so wrong about that.

As she got up, he said: «I keep thinking about the conversation I had with your friend.»

«Walid?»

«Yeah. Would he really do that? I mean fund a school like I described?»

«Like I said, you would have to show him that it wasn't just an interesting idea. You would have to have a concrete plan. He doesn't invest in fantasies.»

«If I did make a plan, a thorough plan with a budget and all that, would he listen?»

«He might.»

«Would you ask him?»

«I could, but you would have to show me your plan first. Where would it be? Who would be the teachers? Who would manage it? How would you set it up? How would you find the students and persuade their parents that you were offering something worthwhile? You would have to change a fantasy into a feasible reality.»

He stood there nodding.

«I will ask our group. These guys are all bright, clever, and have nothing else to do. We will do it together.»

She nodded and put her arm round his waist. «Maybe this is the start of something very good,» she said.

He kissed her on her forehead. «I have spent a lot of my life making fun of you.» he said, «Boy, was I wrong.»

«That's the most intelligent thing I have heard you say in a long time,» she said, «and it is a very good sign. You are learning how to recognise other's abilities. It will serve you well.»

When he left her, he was almost running down the alley to tell the café boys.

Shaafia went back inside and spent the rest of the morning helping her Mother with domestic chores. It was pleasing to do something so simple and useful. She and her Mother worked mostly in companionable silence, talking now and then and pausing mid-morning for tea. Her Mother was easy, warm company. Now, as her children had all grown more or less independent, she could relax a little. Since Shaafia's return she had seen how all of her children, with the obvious exception of Nayla, were doing well, and all seemed to be happier than they had ever been. For her, in a subtle way, Shaafia had become something of a replacement for her husband, Jalil. They seemed so similar.

When Ayman arrived, she was dressed and ready to go. She kissed her Mother and told her that spending the morning with her had been such a pleasure.

As they drove out to the Razak compound, Ayman wanted to know everything that had been happening. At first she talked freely about what she had been doing with Rana and Houda, until suddenly Shaafia began to feel uneasy. There was something behind his questioning and she found herself being careful about what she told him. At first she could not see what was making her uneasy until he said something about Nayla, and she instantly understood that somehow, Ayman had come under Nayla's influence and was working for her in some way. As soon as this thought came to her, it was followed by a strong inner confirmation.

She was going to be careful.

Walid came out to greet her when they arrived, putting his hand up to his chest in greeting. He told Ayman to take the car away, before escorting her inside.

Rami was waiting for her in the dining area, and she bent to shake his hand.

«I am glad to see you Mr Razak.»

«My dear, the pleasure is mine, and please you must call me Rami.»

She dipped her head in acceptance.

«I am very happy you could accept my invitation.» he said, «I feel that it is important that I get to know you.»

A table had been set for three at a height that allowed him to wheel his chair into it. Walid helped his Father to settle and then held a chair for Shaafia, before taking his own.

«So now,» Rami said, «I want to hear how you see the events of the last few days.»

«How much has Walid told you?»

«His version. I want to hear yours.»

Monitoring herself inside, she had a good feeling of being able to trust this old man. He was a businessman, but she sensed that he was also open to other things. She shared with him not only the obvious events of the past few days, but also something of how she trusted her own intuition and how she would be given knowledge of things that were useful and timely, but of which she had no previous knowledge. She used the strategy for Walid to become Rana's representative as a good example.

«I have no experience of business,» she said, «but I could see exactly and clearly what had to take place.»

«You are very astute.» he said, «I believe we are very fortunate to have met you and to have been the beneficiaries of your ability.»

She smiled in acceptance. He had a courtly way of speaking that she appreciated.

The first course of the meal was served, and once the servers had withdrawn, he wished her «*bon appetit*», and then told her that the soup was his personal favourite. He owned a country property deep in one of the valleys of the Atlas Mountains, and the ingredients of this soup had all come from there. He spoke proudly of the breeding goats that he had introduced from Turkey, and that his orchards that were all organic. He asked Walid to find some photos to show her his extensive vegetable gardens that had been laid out by an expert from France.

The soup was superb and Shaafia complimented him.

He put down his soup spoon and nodded. «I am very happy you like it. I wanted to share my favourite with you.»

Following the soup, the next course was a wide flat dish of tiny red fish. The girl who brought it in served each person, laying the little fish out in a semi circle on each plate.

Once she had withdrawn, Rami said: «Now I must ask you about something. You knew all along that Walid would not be marrying Houda. Is that true?»

She nodded.

«But you let it run its course. You did nothing to prevent the marriage.»

«It was not for me to do. I could see that there was not going to be a marriage, that it would not happen, but not exactly how.»

«You were never tempted to tell Walid?»

She shook her head. «Why should I do that? He behaved very well when Hamza was killed. In part, he did that because he felt he was part of the family.»

Walid smiled. «You think I might not have done that if I knew I would not be marrying Houda?»

She turned to face him so he could see that she was serious. «No. I could see that there was a natural progression of events, steps if you like, that had to be taken. I could see what they were and I knew that it was not the time for you to know.»

«And the dream that he had, when you told him to get involved in the Bin Salah business. You did not deliberately do that?» asked Rami.

She laughed. «I do not control other people's dreams.»

«Maybe not, but it is very strange.»

«Are you disappointed that Walid is not going to marry Houda?»

His head moved from side to side as he considered his response. «Perhaps not. I thought it was a very good match, as Hamza had a very good business. I thought it would be a great union where Walid would end up in a very powerful position, and both families would benefit. But now I am not sure what I think. He tells me Houda's Mother prefers her to choose her own future husband, so it is no longer an agreement between parents.»

«And,» said Walid, putting his hand on his Father's arm, «now I too can choose who I would like to marry.»

His Father smiled. «I hope you will consult with me before you do. Sometimes parents can be wise people.»

The next course was brought in. A tall, beautifully decorated tajine was placed in the centre of the table, and Walid did the honours of lifting the lid. The aromas that floated out were exquisite, spices mingling in the air.

The taste matched the aromas and it was enjoyed in silent appreciation before Rami put down his fork.

«Now about Essaouira.» he said. «Walid tells me you can see it already. What do you see?»

So Shaafia outlined what she had perceived, especially the traditional village with the locals living there and constructively serving the resort.

«The woman who seems to be the natural leader of this group is a wonderful woman. I believe she is a healing woman. She will be an extraordinary asset to the success of this project.»

«Next week, you will have the opportunity to work with Alex and see if we can design what you can see,» said Walid.

«You will,» smiled Shaafia, «I have seen it.»

«But you still refuse to come and work for us full-time?» asked Rami.

Shaafia smiled. «I would prefer to think of it like this: I am happy to work with you when it seems like the right thing to do. What the future will bring, that I do not see yet.»

The serving girls took the tajine away.

An elegant silver teapot, with tiny gold rimmed glasses and pastries were brought in its place.

As the tea was poured, Walid said: «I think you should tell my Father what you told me about the girl in the wheelchair. And I think you have more to tell me too, because I had to run off in the middle. There was more, wasn't there?»

She nodded. She breathed in, checking to see if this was a good time to be talking to Rami about Pia. It was.

They sat very still as she told them of the many different interactions that had taken place with the support of Pia. The incident with the boy not wearing a safety hard hat made them smile. When she got to the point where Pia in Lourdes rose out of her chair, her unsighted eye coming into focus at last, and then her frail body crashing to the ground in a pool of blood, they both stared at her.

Finally Walid said: «And that was the end?»

«Not at all.» said Shaafia, and she went on to tell them about the continuing posthumous communication. As she told them, she saw no resistance in either of them. They were obviously not religious, so they had no formal objections to such things, but most people like them had little belief in the supernatural. Perhaps it was the power of her own belief that they were experiencing, because they seemed to be totally there with her as she spoke.

«She does not speak to you now?»

«Not since I came back to Morocco. Now there are other voices. One of them is Haj Hussein.»

«The Father of Rana?»

«Yes. It was he who told me, back in the Bordeaux Airport, to take care of Houda. It was he who told me that they should reclaim their house.»

«Did you know that Hamza would die?» asked Rami.

She shook her head. «I was warned that something was about to happen and that I should be with Rana and Houda.»

The two men sat back with their tea, both seeming to need a pause to take in what she had said.

Finally Rami said: «I must tell you that my Father, who started the first hotel of our chain, had a spiritual advisor who was a bit like you. He was a strange man who would appear now and then at our house. He was a sufi, and he would whisper things to my Father and then he would disappear. My Father had total faith in him.»

Shaafia nodded. «There are many like that in the world, but only certain people are able to appreciate what they are and what they know. They are well-wishers.»

Then Rami leaned forward, as best he could, and with his good hand, he reached for Shaafia's hand. She leaned over so he could reach her.

«I feel very privileged to know you, my child.»

She smiled in acceptance of his compliment.

«And I will trust what you say. I believe you are gifted.»

A great bolt of energy shot through her body, emanating from the touch of his hand and she jolted in her seat.

He felt it and stared at her.

«What is it?»

She closed her eyes for a moment and they waited.

When she opened them again, they were both looking at her with expectation. She faced Rami with tears in her eyes.

«You sit in a wheelchair because you feel guilty.» she said.

He stared at her with his mouth open and his face went pale. His breathing suddenly seemed to be shallow and laboured.

Walid leaned in. «He has had a stroke.» he said gently. »He cannot walk.»

«The stroke is self-punishment. You cannot forgive yourself because of Wassama.»

Rami closed his eyes and tears ran down his cheeks. His son leaned in and gently wiped them away.

«Wassama was my Mother.» said Walid. «She died when I was a teenager.»

«He broke her heart.» said Shaafia, gently massaging the hand of Rami that still rested in hers.

«The doctors said she died of heart failure.» said Walid.

«It is as you say.» murmured Rami with his head down. «It was my fault.»

«She loved you.» said Shaafia softly. «She was devoted to you. You betrayed her.»

«I did.» He had his head down.

«She wishes you to know that she forgives you. She wants you to walk again. She wants you to make amends for what you did. She wants you to take care of people the way she would have done.»

«She is.....?» He lifted his eyes at last to look at Shaafia. «She is talking to you?»

She nodded.

«*Ham delilah,*» he said. «How often have I begged her for forgiveness. How often have I talked to her in my thoughts.»

«She has heard you, every time.»

«*Ham delilah.*»

A long silence followed. Walid's face was creased in pain, close to tears himself.

He looked at his Father, sitting bowed over, breathing shallowly, and he leaned in to rub his Father's back. At the same time, he looked up at Shaafia who sat still and indrawn. He had no words.

The silence was broken by the serving girls who came in to take away the tea things. Walid waved them away and they retreated looking worried.

At last, out of the silence, Rami asked: «She wants me to walk?»

«She has plans for you. You get up from that chair which is your seat of shame. You learn to walk again. You learn to believe that you are a good person and that you have been fortunate enough to have the means to do great things in this world, for people, for this country. The last thing is that you come to understand that she has been with you all along. She has been waiting for you to wake up.»

He nodded at all this.

Still holding his hand, she added: «And she wants you to use your whole face again. You will learn to smile with your whole face.»

«Please tell her I am so sorry.» he whispered.

«No!» Shaafia's voice was harsh and strong, not really her voice at all. «The time for sorry is gone. You have to do something active to be able to move forward. Just saying sorry is just empty, weak words. Stop it.»

He nodded.

He gripped Shaafia's hand more strongly. «So what should I do?»

«Learn to smile and learn to walk.» she said. Then she let go of his hand and stood up. She came round to his chair and said: «Stand up.»

Walid stood up to help but Shaafia put up her hand. «He has to do this by himself.»

Rami leaned forward to put weight on his legs and then with the help of the arms of the wheelchair he hoisted himself upright. Shaafia stood beside him but without touching him.

«Now,» she said, her voice clear and strong. «Take one step.»

It was clear that his right leg was active and he used that to take a short sliding step. Then he dragged the left leg to join it, and he stood there wavering.

«She wants you to walk.» said Shaafia staying close, but making no physical contact.

He wavered on his feet then slid his good leg out and put his weight on it. Then he slowly pulled the left leg along to join it.

«One step is a good start.» said Shaafia, then moved the wheelchair so he could sit again.

He dropped back into the support of the chair and looked up at her, gradually getting his breathing back.

«I will do it.» he said, «I make this promise to her.»

Walid sat back down and breathed out in relief.

«We can get a physiotherapist to work with you.» he said. «I always thought it was permanent so I never considered rehab.»

«It would not have worked, even if you did.» said Shaafia. Then she looked down at Rami. «You were not ready. Now you are.»

He nodded, then he reached for her hand again and she leaned in to help.

«I cannot tell you what this is doing to me.»

«I can see it.» she said softly. «You have a lot to do.»

«Let's walk.» he said, smiling, with half of his face, at his own little joke.

Walid came round and took charge of the wheelchair as they went out to the front of the house.

«If you have time, said Rami, «I would like to show you my garden.»

Shaafia smiled. «As I told Walid, I have cancelled all my appointments for the day, just to have lunch with you.»

Shaafia sensed that this was Rami's way of saying thank you as he showed her the beds of exotic flowering plants that he had imported from South America, his lilly ponds with lotuses from India, and his Japanese garden with Koi fish.

«You are obviously a man who loves beauty,» she said, after a while. «But I think Wassama is expecting you to begin a new way of living your life.»

He nodded. «You are telling me that all this money that I spent on these wonderful gardens nobody sees, except my honoured guests, is really a terrible indulgence.»

Shaafia laughed. «It is not me telling you this. You are telling yourself.»

«So if I didn't spend all my energies on all this, what would I do?»

«It will come to you.»

«Do you see it?»

«Sometimes what I see is not to be shared.»

Finally Rami began to tire and he admitted that he really needed to take a nap.

«This has been one of the most remarkable days of my life, at least in the recent past.» he said. «Please come and see me again soon.»

«When I come next time, I will expect that you will smile as you walk to greet me.»

«*Inche Allah,*» he said.

When they reached the house, the older man, who often wheeled Rami in the chair, was waiting patiently. Shaafia bent and kissed Rami on both cheeks and he held her hand for a long moment.

«May God protect you.» he said, his voice laced with emotion.

She watched him being wheeled away and then she turned to Walid.

«You are going to see a side of your Father that you have never seen.»

He nodded.

«I know you don't like being thanked,» he said, «but what you have done in one short day, over one simple meal, is miraculous.»

She dipped her head, and then said: «It is just the beginning.»

Ayman had brought round the black Renault ready to drive his sister home.

When she saw it, she turned to Walid. «Would it be too much to ask you to drive me? We can talk on the way.»

«Of course.» he said, and went over to Ayman. When he told Ayman that he would be the driver, Ayman got out, frowning, but did not say anything. He shot a look at his sister and walked away to the back of the house.

The Renault was much quieter than the growling yellow Italian monster, and they could talk.

«Did you know, before you came, that we would be talking to my Father like this?»

She shook her head. «I think you will have to give up trying to work out what I know and what I see.»

«OK.» He manoeuvred round a slow moving truck laden with carrots, then he said: «I get that. I will try to let it come as it comes. I am grateful that I have heard as much as I have. My Father's life will never be the same again. You have lit a fuse under him. And my life, too. As his son, as a no-longer-to-be-married man, as a new business partner for Bin Salah, and all the rest of it.»

«You left out the most important thing.»

He took his eyes off the road for a moment to look at her, then had to quickly dodge a man on a bike.

«What did I miss?»

«When you begin to understand who you are, on the inside, your life will be like starting all over again.»

He nodded.

«I want to say a few things about my brothers.» she said.

«Ayman and Ihab?»

«Ayman. I would like to ask you to do something for me about him.»

«You name it.»

«I am a little ashamed to have to say this about my own brother, but it is necessary. I sense that he has become dangerous.»

«What do you mean?»

«My sister Nayla is unfortunately determined to destroy my family.»

«Why?»

«It is something old that lurks inside her and drives her to practise black magic against us.»

«Oh.»

«You know about Rana's sister?»

He nodded. «Same thing?»

«My sister has learnt much from her. They work together.»

«So where does Ayman fit in?»

«She has turned him.»

«So you want me to get rid of him?»

«No. I think we can save him from himself, but he needs to go some-where. I am asking if you could employ him as a security person in Essaouira. I sense that he could be useful to you while being away from the influence of his sister. Something good could happen for him there.»

Walid braked suddenly to avoid a motor scooter that crossed his path. The young helmet-less rider shook his fist and was gone.

«That boy won't live to enjoy his grand-children.» he muttered. Then he glanced sideways at Shaafia. «Ayman goes to Essaouira. I don't have a problem with that. I am going to need some people down there anyway. I can tell him I am promoting him, find him an apartment, lift his salary a bit. He can be in charge of security. The man I have now isn't one of ours.»

«That would be good. Thank you.»

«That was easy. But you said brothers, plural.»

«Yes. The other one is Samet, who you met yesterday. He is fired up with the idea of starting a kind of school for gifted but poor children.»

«You want me to back him?»

«Not yet. He has to earn your trust. If I tell him that we spoke and that you might be interested, if he can prove himself, then and only then you might support him.»

He laughed. «I am going to ask you that question again. Do you see him succeeding? Is it realistic?»

«You are asking if I can see it and my answer is no. However, I do believe he has the potential and it is up to him to find it.»

«So I will leave it to you,» he said. «If you think he can do it, I open my wallet.»

Then she frowned as she had a new impulse. «Maybe it is not you.» she said.

He nodded. «You think it might be my Father?»

She smiled. «You are becoming intuitive.»

He pulled up the Renault at the corner of the alley.

He let the engine idle as he turned to her.

«One last thing.» he said. «You said that my Father betrayed my Mother. Do you know what my Father did?»

She nodded. «I sensed what it was, but you know what he did.»

«Yes. Her name was Aliya. She was Greek. She was a dancer and very beautiful. He built her a house in the grounds.»

«She was a second wife?»

«No. She was not Muslim.»

«And your Mother had to live there too and live in shame.»

«And I did nothing about that.»

«You were young.»

«I was, but I knew and I saw what was happening to her. I stayed silent.»

«The house is still there?»

«The cook lives in it now.»

«Aliya left?»

«She took off. She also took many things with her. I suppose she found someone new to attach herself to. My Father had his stroke soon after.»

Shaafia nodded. «So the only thing I have to say about that is that you must make sure that there is no guilt left inside you.»

He thought about that, then he shook his head. «I am OK,» he said at last. « It was his own fault, I could maybe have done something, but he was my Father. In my family the Father is the boss. You don't question it. He did what he did.»

«It is different now.» said Shaafia. «The rôles are reversed. Now you look after him. You do it very well. And he is very proud of you.»

He sighed. «*Ham delilah.*»

She opened the door and turned to face him.

«Thank you for driving me.»

He smiled. «It was my pleasure. And I really mean that. I am learning a lot from you.»

«I think we are just beginning.» she said, as she closed the door.

He wound down the window. «I will call you when Alex arrives and we can get on with business.»

No-one took any notice of the black Renault as it drove away.

Family Business

The next day Shaafia went to Rachi's house to see how the arrangements for the wedding were progressing.

Even though it was still quite early, the house was a hive of activity. When Rachi saw Shaafia, she ran and gave her a long and strong hug.

«It's all happening!» she laughed in Shaafia's ear, «I am going to get married and we are going to Bordeaux!«

«Yasser is happy?»

Rachi pulled back from the hug and smiled. «Yes he is.»

«So what is the plan?»

«We will have the formal wedding on Friday. Haj Kabir will marry us. On Thursday we will do the henna, so you must be here for that. I feel that if you are there then everything will go perfectly.»

Shaafia smiled. «I will be there, I promise.»

When Rachi's Mother saw Shaafia she too gave her a warm hug, and once again thanked her for the rôle she played in changing Rachi's mind.

Shaafia shook her head. «I didn't get her to change her mind. She had a change of heart. I was just a witness.»

«Nevertheless,» said Rachi's Mother, «without you she would not have changed anything.»

The coming days were indeed being carefully planned. Although neither of the families were wealthy, the wedding was a big occasion. Caterers were being tested. The »*Negafas*», the ladies who traditionally serve the bride, were being appointed. One of them was Rachi's aunt who had assigned herself to be in charge of everything to do with the bride. She was already there with several other ladies.

Rachi's house would become the centre of focus every day for the next week.

Shaafia asked if she could help with anything, but Rachi's Mother was very insistent. «You have done more than we could have wished,» she said. «You will be our honoured guest. And of course all your family must come.»

At last Rachi found a quiet moment to go up onto the roof with Shaafia. They sat in the warm morning sun looking out over the rooftops of Casablanca to the minaret of the Mosque.

«So when do you go to Bordeaux?»

«They say it will be in a few weeks. We have to get our passports done, and mine will have to be in my married name so we can't apply for them until next week. But it won't be long. Yasser really wants to go soon.»

«Habib will miss him.»

«Habib is so sweet. He told me he will come for the wedding for sure.»

At midday Shaafia went to the Mosque for the noon prayers. When they had concluded, she sat quietly bathing in gratitude for the unending goodness that was floating around her.

When she finally emerged, she saw Haj Kabir heading home for lunch. They spoke about the progress being made to reanimate *Darou al Bahr*.

«Haj Hussein is happy.» said Haj Kabir. «He appeared several nights ago in my dream.»

Shaafia smiled and added another element to her list of gratitude.

When she arrived home, her Mother was making lunch. It was a school day and she and Shaafia were home alone. They sat quietly together while Shaafia recounted the activities in Rachi's house.

«You do not think of getting married?» asked her Mother.

Shaafia smiled at the perennial question and shook her head.

«If I am supposed to do that then it will happen. I don't feel any urgency.»

Her Mother nodded. «If it were like in the old days, like for your Father and me, our parents found the right person and we made it work. In those days that was the way it worked.»

«I think I might be a difficult person to find a husband for.» said Shaafia.

«No.» said her Mother. «You have so many gifts, you would be a prize for any man.»

As they were clearing away the lunch things, Samet came in.

«Ah!» he said, «I was hoping I would run into you. We are working on our school proposal. The guys are really keen about it.»

«When you think it is ready, let me see it.»

«Maybe by the end of this week.» he said. «We are thinking of nothing else right now.»

«Have you researched the legal issues?»

He looked puzzled. «Like what?»

«Is it legal to just suddenly open a school somewhere? None of you have teaching qualifications.»

«Who cares about teaching qualifications? That's the trouble with the current system.»

«Maybe so, but if you did open a school without the right legal requirements what would happen?

«Who cares?»

«Walid would.»

«Oh.»

She patted him on the shoulder. «Better do some homework.» she said.

In the warmth of the afternoon, she sat under the fig tree and called the château in Bordeaux. Théophile answered and she shared what had been happening for her since they last spoke.

In his turn he told her how many people kept coming to the château and reporting all sorts of positive changes in their lives. They were keeping a book of what people had been telling them. Maybe it could be a second book about Pia.

Zena came and spoke about how she and Michael were doing well and that Berenice was fluent in French now.

Thérèse was out shopping with Claire who had become brave enough to drive the Mercedes van on the other side of the road from how she learnt in Australia. Guests were continually coming to stay in the château, many of them people who had met Pia or had strong experiences of her and very often they were taking personal retreats. Michael was beginning to lead sessions in which they would share what they were experiencing.

After the call, Shaafia sat in the shade of her beloved fig tree and let the waves of gratitude course through her.

She sat with her eyes closed, leaning back against the tree when her phone went. It was Rana.

«Can you please come to the house?» she asked, sounding agitated. «Daad is here.»

Shaafia jumped to her feet.

«Yes, of course.»

«Houda will come for you.»

Shaafia went inside and told her Mother she was going to visit Rana, but not why, and then walked to the end of the alley to be ready for when Houda came.

As she walked, she wondered why she had not felt anything, no warning, no message from Haj Hussein. What did this mean? As she pondered it, she found her mind simply going back to her gratitude list as if the question about Daad was not important. After a few minutes of this, as she neared the end of the alley, she let it go.

She glanced into the café and saw the boys at the back gathered around their table, but she didn't draw attention to herself and they did not notice her.

Houda came fast in the Porsche, and as soon as Shaafia got in, she took off just as fast.

«What's happening?» asked Shaafia as she struggled with her seatbelt.

«She is just sitting there. In the garden. She won't talk. She just sits there.»

«Is she by herself?»

«I think so. We were out shopping, getting some new furniture, and when we came back, Omar was standing out on the street, shaking. He told us she had come earlier and had gone through the house and then out to the garden.»

Once again Shaafia checked inside but it was calm. And then she began to feel a gentle surge of energy which was nurturing and supportive. It was as if she were being shown that whatever needed to be done she could do. She was in no need of help.

Rana came out as they arrived, while Omar hovered in the background.

«She is still there.» she said, pointing to the front garden.

Shaafia stood still just inside the gate, taking a moment to feel the air. It was still, calm, no sense of any threat.

«I will go and meet her.» she said.

«Shall we come?» asked Houda, having parked the Porsche.

«No. It would be better not to.»

«Please be careful.» said Rana.

As she walked slowly round the house and into the long front garden, Shaafia felt at ease. There was an immense sense of inner support, not coming from any particular entity, but as a general inner state.

Daad was dressed in black, including a black head scarf. She was sitting exactly in the same place as Malak.

As Shaafia approached her, she looked up. Her face was lined and ashen. Her dark eyes radiated pain more than menace.

«You took them away.» she said. Her voice was low and harsh. She lifted her right arm and gestured round the garden. «All of them.»

Shaafia came and stood in front of her, waiting.

«It should be mine.» snarled Daad.

Shaafia shook her head.

«Your Father could see it was not for you.»

«My Father.» she spat.

«He loved you as much as he loved Rana, but he could read your heart.»

«All the power he could have shared with me, he kept away from me. If he had loved me he would have taught me. You know he had that?»

«We all have that. The dark and light in equal measure. You chose it for yourself anyway.»

«If he had only.....» and her voice cracked and she groaned in pain.

«You could come back.» said Shaafia taking a step closer and looking intently into the other woman's eyes.

Then Daad dropped her head onto her chest.

«Too late now. No strength left. I don't know who sent you.»

«Your Father.»

«So he goes on punishing me.»

«No. He never, ever punished you. You have decided that. You are wrong. Your Father does it out of love.»

Slowly Daad lifted her eyes. Her face was twisted in anguish.

«There is no love.» she growled, and hauled herself to her feet.

«At least,» said Shaafia gently, «leave your sister and her daughter in peace.»

«Peace?» she sneered.

«And let there be peace in my family, too. Let my sister go, show her how to find peace.»

«She suffers like I do.»

«Go away, Daad,» said Shaafia. «If you want to stop this suffering you will have to go back to the source of darkness and get it out.»

«I cannot,» she muttered. «He will not let me.»

In an instant she saw him. He hovered over the form of Daad. He was tall and very dark skinned. He wore the decorated robes of the men of the Sahel and had long earrings. Shaafia recognised a wave of fear inside herself, but suddenly Malak was there hovering in the same way.

She backed away a little and saw that Daad could see them too.

The two forms swirled and twisted, rising higher above the garden. She was watching an aerial battle, two equally powerful forms circling and thrusting at each other

A strong wind blew up as if created by the swirl around the two figures. Neither had a weapon, nor did they attempt to touch each other, but instead it was as if they were pitting their forces against the other. As they did they rose into the air and the wind grew stronger. .

Then, just as suddenly, they soared up, high above the garden and the wind dropped to a gentle breeze, and they were gone. There was no sense of one having triumphed over the other. It was more like a kind of dance between opposing forces.

Daad had rocked on her feet as she watched, but now she dropped back onto the rock bench and collapsed. She seemed to have trouble breathing.

«If you wish it,» said Shaafia very quietly. «If you truly wish it, you can save yourself.»

Suddenly Daad was back on her feet lunging at Shaafia, her eyes now glowing coals.

«What do you know of saving yourself? What do you know? It is too late. Too late.»

Shaafia stood still and breathed out. It was as if she had created a protective shield that the other woman could not penetrate. Daad's own breath came in short agitated pulses as she stared at her small adversary. She took a step towards her with her eyes ablaze. Then she rushed away across the garden, up and out of the gate.

Omar had been watching fearfully from the steps, and as she rushed out she lunged at him, screaming incoherently. He threw himself back against the house to avoid her and lay on the ground, curled up.

Shaafia stood still breathing in the air of the garden. There was a subtle fragrance in the air, perhaps jasmine?

Then she turned and looked up at *Darou Al Bahr.*

The white walls of the house glowed in the afternoon sun. A gentle breeze caressed the leaves in some of the taller trees, and somewhere a small bird sang a short melody.

She walked across to Omar and squatted down next to him.

«She has gone. You will not see her again.» she said.

Rana and Houda had obviously been watching from inside the house, and now came out.

«Is he hurt?» asked Rana, and Shaafia shook her head.

They helped Omar to his feet and took him inside.

One of Rana's girls was in the kitchen, and she asked her to make tea. While they waited, they sat in the back room with the photo of Haj Hussein and his wife.

«She has no power over anything in this house.» said Shaafia, as they looked up at the photo. «In fact it looks like she has been so deeply wounded that she has very little power left at all.»

«Are you sure?» asked Rana.

Shaafia nodded. «She is diminished.»

«Can you help her?» asked Houda.

Shaafia thought about that for a moment before she said: «She does not want to be helped.»

The girl brought in the tea.

Once the drama of the garden had begun to fade, they spoke of the progress with the house. Rana had found an international agent who would put her big compound on the market. They had assured her that such a property would find a wealthy buyer in no time.

At the same time contractors were already working on all the different projects for returning *Daru Al Bahr* to its former state. Rana hoped that within a few months they might be able to move in. The ramshackle buildings at the back had already been demolished, and a builder was preparing plans to build a row of small self-contained apartments for Rana's staff.

«We will renovate the garage for the cars,» said Rana. «We will keep the Mercedes and the Porsche.»

«We have to keep the Porsche!» smiled Houda.

«The other cars we will sell,» said Rana.

Then Shaafia had a thought. «What about your old Coccinelle?»

Rana smiled sadly. «She is beyond repair I think.»

Shaafia voiced her thought. «My brother Toufik is training to be a mechanic. Maybe he could fix it.»

«He is very welcome to try.»

After the tea, Rana took Shaafia through the house to show her what was being planned. More and more Rana was bringing her staff to work on the house, endlessly cleaning, getting rid of old stuff, and preparing a house to live in. As Rana showed what was happening, Shaafia could see that Rana was so happy within herself. She could feel how happy Haj Hussein was as he saw his old house come back to life, and his daughter become a free woman.

Towards the end of the afternoon, as Houda was about to drive Shaafia home, Rana told her that the meeting to determine the future of Bin Salah Transport was scheduled for next week. She had already contacted Walid who assured her he would be there. Shaafia smiled, and said that of course she would be there too.

«I would not think of having this meeting without you.» Rana said, and gave her a warm goodbye hug.

«And thank you for whatever you did to make Daad go away.» she added.

Shaafia shrugged. «I really think I did nothing. She did it all to herself without my help.»

«I am sure you are right, but until you came back, she was always a danger.»

«But you had Malak.»

«I know, but I was always worried that maybe she would get more power and do terrible things. I don't feel that any more.»

Houda dropped Shaafia off at the Mosque so she could attend the evening prayers.

At the last minute Shaafia said: «Come in with me and pray.»

Houda hesitated, but then decided to accept the invitation. It took her a while to find a spot to park the car, but when she did they were just in time.

The mellifluous voice of Haj Kabir floated through the evening air as they walked into the women's section of the Mosque.

As the prayers continued, and the women followed the sequence of movements that went with them, Shaafia felt little surges of joy come up. The events of her day replayed themselves as she moved, as if they were marching past her in a parade, and as each one passed, she felt a little more joy, a little more gratitude.

As they left the Mosque they saw Haj Kabir and told him what had happened that afternoon with Daad.

When Shaafia shared what she had seen in the garden, floating in the air, the two forms battling in the air, Malak and the dark skinned man, Haj Kabir nodded.

«He is the Master who taught Daad. He is from Mali and very powerful. He and Malak would make a fine battle.»

«But it looks like he can't support her. She is a broken woman.» said Shaafia.

«Which, sad to say, is the destiny of those who become entrapped in that world.»

Shaafia nodded. «I have a bad feeling about my sister. She will end up the same way.»

«It is very likely.» said the Imam. «To come back from there is very difficult.»

«There is nothing we can do?»

«We can offer our prayers, but until someone like that wants to be rescued, there is no hope.»

Saying goodbye to Houda, Shaafia walked the few blocks home. At the corner of the alley, she glanced into the café, but the boys had dispersed for the day.

As she passed Brahim's house, she saw him through the window and gave him a wave. In response he came out.

She thanked him again for taking Toufik to his new school, and he told her he had heard from his brother that Toufik was doing really well.

As they were talking, Toufik came up the alley with his brother, Loqman.

«We were just talking about you,» said Brahim. «You like the new school?»

Toufik shuffled his feet, a bit embarrassed.

«Yeah. It's good.»

«How about you, Loqman?» asked Shaafia.

He glanced at Brahim, one of the teachers at his school.

Brahim patted him on the shoulder. «Tell her the truth,» he said.

«I don't know why I'm there,» he said, «I don't see the point.»

Shaafia nodded. « When you find something that you really like to do, then you will see the point.»

He shrugged. «I don't know what that would be. It looks like everyone else seems to know what they are supposed to be doing except me.»

Again Brahim patted him on the shoulder. «Sometimes it takes a while to find out.»

As they walked home together, Shaafia told Toufik about the old Volkswagen in Rana's garage.

He nodded. «An old Coccinelle? Yeah. I can take a look at it, although I prefer bikes. At school we have been working on diesel engines. Can't be too hard.»

She smiled at his confidence.

When they arrived home, their Mother was already preparing a set of big pots for couscous.

She sent the boys off to clean up, and then she turned to Shaafia.

«So how is Rana doing?»

While there was no-one else in the kitchen Shaafia quickly told her Mother about the confrontation with Daad. Then she added that she had shared this with Haj Kabir.

Her Mother nodded.

«It is tragic that people like that get trapped in the darkness. I fear that your sister will end up the same way.»

And Shaafia shared what Haj Kabir had said: «We can only pray.»

Her Mother sighed. «I do that every day.»

Their conversation was interrupted when Sadik came in. Shaafia asked how the shop was doing, and he grinned.

«You must come and visit, we are making big changes. It is going to be a much better shop soon. Did you know that the shop next door is going to be empty soon?»

That shop had been a small textile shop for as long as Shaafia could remember.

«She is not going to sell cloth any more?»

«She is too sick. She has cancer and none of her children want to do it.»

«That's a shame.» said their Mother. «Her childen should support her.»

«But the good thing is,» said Sadik, «We are thinking that we might take over the shop. She needs the money, and Uncle Samad is offering to buy it from her.»

Shaafia smiled. «It was your idea, wasn't it?»

He nodded shyly. «I like cloth. We could sell it as part of our shop, it will bring new customers.»

She was so pleased to see how he seemed to be flourishing.

«Being a shopkeeper suits you.»

He nodded.

Samet came in a little later, and came over when he saw Shaafia.

«You have made our job a lot more complicated.» he said.

«You can do it.» she replied.

«To tell you the truth, when I told the guys about what you said, they agreed. It has to be done. And we will do it.»

One after the other, the other family members appeared. The two youngest sisters immediately began to help their Mother prepare the meal while they chatted about their school day. They both loved school, and both aspired to follow in Shaafia's steps to study in France.

Habib came in very sweaty from soccer practice, but very excited. For the next game he was actually going to be in the eleven. Despite his sweatiness he got hugs from his sisters before he was sent off by his Mother to clean up.

They had just begun to eat when Ayman came in. Normally he and Ihab only came on Fridays.

He went over to Shaafia and kissed her on her cheek.

«You returned my favour.» he said. Then he faced the room. «Thanks to my dear sister Shaafia, I have been promoted. I am now head of security in the new Razak project in Essaouria. He has even found me an apartment, so I will be going to live there.»

Samet said: «How come you are thanking Shaafia?»

«Walid, he's my boss, is very impressed with our sister, so when she suggested me for the position, he agreed.»

Samet grinned. «You are turning into a power broker, little sister.»

Their Mother gestured to Ayman. «My son, I am very happy to hear your news, and I ask you to sit and join your family to share in your good fortune.»

He dipped his head in acceptance and dropped down to sit next to Shaafia, giving her a sideways hug as he did so.

As he helped himself from the big central serving dish of couscous, he said: «I hear we will be seeing you in Essaouira soon, when the English come back.»

She nodded, then she asked: «When will you go?»

«Tomorrow. He's going to show me what he wants me to do, then I am on my own.» Then he whispered: «He gave me a raise of salary, as well as not having to pay rent on the apartment.»

She smiled. «He must trust you.»

At the end of the meal, as he was about to leave, Ayman approached his Mother with an envelope.

She kissed him on both cheeks, and told him how proud she was.

In the cool of the late evening as the two school girls worked on their homework, Shaafia watched them. They were enthusiasts and vied with each other. Like Shaafia they both loved languages and could talk to each other fluently in French and in English. It was Hawa's final year and she was beginning to research the possibilities for study in France. Shaafia promised to help all she could. The best person to help would be Madame Clae.

Finally going to bed at the end of a day full of activity, once again Shaafia reconnected with her sense of gratitude. So much had happened in one single day. As she recounted for herself all the different events and how each person was affected by them, she saw how it was like a pilgrimage toward a benevolent place. Each of them was journeying at their own pace. For some it was easy and direct, but not for others. And yet, maybe even for Daad and for Nayla, perhaps there might be a beneficial outcome.

As she dropped off to sleep, her Koranic verse resonating steadily inside, she felt cradled, taken care of, and at the same time supremely confident in the future.

Marriage

The day before the wedding, the bride and all her female attendants, family members and friends all go to the *hamam* together. It is a steam bath party with lots of singing and stories while everyone gets bathed, scrubbed, massaged if the funds permit, and perfumed. Then there is the ceremony of the henna where they all get their hands and feet decorated with intricate sepia-coloured designs. The bride has the most ornate, and often the name of the groom is woven into the temporary tattoos.

Shaafia, her Mother and the two younger sisters all went for Rachi's *hamam* party, and by the end of the afternoon they all had their hands decorated.

For Shaafia it was a day without thought, without challenge. She allowed herself to be carried along in the joyful events with all the celebrating women. Every now and then some woman or another would engage her in conversation, and she found herself telling more or less the same shortened and selective stories depending on who they were. Most often it seemed that the question of her getting married occupied a central place in the women's conversation. She bore with it.

In the evening, there was a big all-women's feast with music and song. Rachi's aunt had not only taken on the rôle of chief « *Negafa* », but also mistress of ceremonies. She obviously loved to sing and had a powerful voice.

On the morning of the wedding itself, as the guests filled Rachi's house to bursting point, Haj Kabir arrived to conduct the formal wedding. Rachi's aunt tried to organise the assembled guests to make a corridor for him to enter with several other sufi men who would be chanting as part of the wedding.

Once he was settled in the focus of the main front room, Rachi was brought downstairs beautifully arrayed in traditional Morrocan dress, a *takchita,* a full white caftan with gold and green threads. Her headdress was of matching colours and she wore many different gold ornaments.

At the bottom of the stairs she was placed in the *"amaria"*, a decorated platform with a canopy. She was carried on the shoulders of several men to the middle of the room and set down in front of Haj Kabir. Amid lots of joyful cheering as she came, she kept her head down, but there was no disguising her smile.

Then everyone turned to face the door to await the groom.

He came wearing a *djellaba*, a full robe with ornately embroidered edges. As he came in, he looked distinctly nervous, and did not dare to make eye contact with Rachi. Beside him walked his proud parents smiling and nodding to people they knew, and behind him his younger brothers, all washed and combed to look their best. His Mother carried a traditional Berber *handira* blanket which she laid across Rachi's legs. Then she very carefully kissed Rachi on both cheeks, not to disturb the ornate bridal make-up

Then Yasser took his seat beside his bride and Haj Kabir began. He welcomed everyone to bless these two young people in marriage, then he read some verses from the Koran about marriage before the sufi men chanted. Once they began, the whole crowd swayed along with them.

Finally it was time to sign the marriage certificates and Rachi's Father came forward with the documents, pens, and a low wooden desk was brought forward for the signatures. Everyone leaned in to watch, and there was a sea of cell phones flashing, trying to catch the action.

Shaafia let herself be carried along with all the activity, but in a certain part of herself she was detached. She stood close to Rachi with Habib and her Mother, pressed in by the crowd of well-wishers. It felt very much like she had arrived at an end point where Rachi and Yasser would lead their own lives. She would have perhaps no further active rôle to play. Like everyone else she sent her blessings. As she did, she felt the presence in the room of other beings, unseen by the wedding guests but as happy as everyone else to be there. As she gazed up at them, she made eye contact with Haj Kabir. He smiled and lifted his hand. He could see them, too.

Once the wedding was concluded and shouts of blessings were hurled from all over the house, the wedding couple were led to the courtyard outside where two thrones, decorated with fresh flowers, had been set up for them. They walked together now holding hands and smiling at people. Once the certificates were all signed, they could relax a little. At one moment Habib could not restrain himself any longer, and he jumped forward to give his football idol a hug. Yasser was nearly knocked off his feet, but turned to return the gesture. At another moment Rachi made eye contact with Shaafia and such a smile came over Rachi's face. She let go of Yasser's hand and lunged to hold her friend in a fierce and long embrace.

Then somehow they all got untangled and the couple was installed on their thrones. Specially decorated plates were brought for the couple and laid out on a table in front of their thrones. Now everyone watched as Rachi took a little from the first plate and fed her husband. In return, he did the same for her. Then there was wild cheering and everyone else helped themselves to the copious plates awaiting them, while in one corner a small group of musicians began to play.

The celebration went on late into the night before the couple was escorted to their wedding room where a new bed and bed clothes had been installed. These were all gifts from Yasser's family. It was temporary, as hopefully within a few weeks they would be leaving for Bordeaux.

There was lots of shouting and catcalls as the couple went in, and even after the door was closed there were songs sung about love and wedding couples for quite some time outside.

Shaafia, her Mother, two younger sisters and Habib all walked home together through the quiet streets of the late night.

It was as they approached the house that they saw the figure half hidden in the shadows behind the old fig tree.

Instantly Shaafia knew who it was.

«Wait.» she said quietly.

«What is it?» asked Habib, who was nearly asleep on his feet.

«Nayla.» hissed Hawa.

«Be careful.» whispered their Mother.

Shaafia took several steps towards the shadowed figure then paused, taking in a long breath. She remembered vividly her instructions from when Nayla had attacked her before.

However, now she sensed that there was no threat. Instead she saw that her sister was bent over and seemed to be in pain.

When Shaafia approached, Nayla lifted her head.

«You go off and have a joyful time at Rachi's wedding,» she snarled. «but you don't know anything.»

«You are in pain.» said Shaafia softly, moving closer.

«What do you care?»

«She can't help you now.»

«I don't know how you did that. I don't know what kind of power you've got, but I hate you for it.»

«I think you hated me long before that.»

«Always so smart, always so innocent, our Father doted on you.»

«I have been given no more than you, but you used what gifts you had for a purpose that will destroy you.»

«So that makes you happy?»

«No. But I have learned how to take care of myself and those I love.»

«You can't save me.»

«Then why are you here, in the middle of night, hiding behind a tree?»

Suddenly Nayla leaped out from behind the fig tree and lunged at Shaafia, screaming.

«You destroyed her, now I have nothing.»

Shaafia stood her ground and breathed out. Her breath was like a powerful cloud, she could see it, it expanded out in front of her and enveloped her sister as she lunged. As if Nayla had been dowsed by a water canon, she dropped to the ground.

Shaafia stood over her.

«Even if you were able to get your powers back, I would still love you as my sister. If you ever manage to understand this, you may be able to save yourself. If not, you will never know a moment of peace.»

Nayla's red eyes glared up at her small but dominant younger sister.

«How I hate you.» she snarled through her teeth. Then she scrambled to her feet and screamed at her Mother, younger sisters and Habib standing together horrified.

«I hate you all.»

Then she took off down the lane, stumbling and screaming at the shuttered houses. «I hate you all. I hate you all.»

Shaafia breathed in and sent a silent prayer of thanks to the beings who she knew were surrounding her.

She looked at the stricken members of her family.

«She cannot hurt us any more.» she said.

« Why did she come?» asked Yamina.

«Desperation probably.» said Shaafia as they walked the last few metres to the house.»

«What did she mean when she said you destroyed someone? » asked Hawa «She said «her».«

«Nayla has been a follower of Daad, Rana's sister. Daad was taught by a black magician from Mali.»

«We always said she was a witch.» said Yamina.

«But she said you destroyed her. Is that what she said?» asked Hawa.

«That's what she thinks.»

«Did you?»

Shaafia shook her head. «I didn't do anything, but I am lucky to have learned how to ask for help from forces more powerful than hers.»

Her two sisters stared at her.

«Will you teach us?» asked Hawa.

Their Mother said: « You must all go to bed. Habib is playing football tomorrow.»

And so they did.

As the three girls laid out their sleeping mats, Hawa said: «Promise us that you will show us how to do what you do.»

«I will,» said Shaafia. «*Inche Allah.*»

Step by step

The following days were quiet, and Shaafia spent most of her time with the family.

She went with Hawa and Yamina to watch Habib play, and although the game was a scrappy affair and his school team did not win, or even manage to score a goal, he was very happy. On the way home, he kept reminding them of the one good pass he did, and they had to assure him they saw it and how good it was.

She visited the shop and saw that Sadik and his uncle had already begun to tear down the wall between their existing shop and the now vacant one next door. Sadik was full of enthusiasm for the new emporium, and had already been with his uncle to the wholesale cloth market to purchase their first stock.

Uncle Samad seemed a bit breathless with all this innovation, but he adored his nephew's enthusiasm.

Toufik took several of his alley friends off to *Darou Al Bahr* to tinker with the old VW and two days later drove it back, chugging and coughing but definitely working. Shaafia went out when she heard the noise. It turned out that Toufik did not have a driver's licence and should not have been driving, but she was so impressed with his achievement that she let it pass. She did insist that he not drive the car again until he got a licence. He shrugged and said he would but there was no hiding his pride, especially as Rana had told him if he could get the old car going he could have it.

One morning when she dropped into the café on the corner to see how the boys were doing, they were, as always, huddled round the table. When she approached Samet looked up.

«You have great timing. We are ready to send out our new podcast and it is just as you suggested.»

They found a chair for Shaafia, and Dari turned his computer so she could see it.

They had indeed improved. Now the podcast had music to introduce it, and then there was Samet looking very casual inviting their viewers to join them in the café.

The camera work was a little wobbly, and a nasty motorbike roared by in the background, but it had an authentic feel to it. Even the café owner had his moment shyly saying: «Welcome» to the camera.

There was a segment where Yusuf created a colourful cartoon of the café group where the camera was speeded up showing the whole process in a matter of sixty seconds.

One of the other boys was a reasonably good flute player who played a short melody before Nabil recited his new poem, sitting on the low rock wall near the café. Passing traffic again added authenticity.

All the others had live appearances, some more at ease than others, before Samet returned and invited their viewers to send in their comments, and if they wanted to contribute their own pieces they could contact them.

Shaafia sat back and smiled as she saw how intent they were on seeing her reaction.

«So what do you think?» asked Samet.

«A good step forward.» she said.

«Oh, come on. It's brilliant.» said Samet, not altogether serious.

«You know what is missing?» she asked in response.

«A bigger audience?»

«Probably, but that's not what I was thinking. It is so male-oriented. It's all about a group of boys.»

«That's what we are.» said Nabil.

«True. But what would it be like if you found some female perspectives?»

They looked a little stricken. They were a tight friendship group, and to be challenged to open it to members of the opposite sex was not far short of terrifying.

«If you are serious about this school idea,» said Shaafia, «you will need girls, women to be a part of it. You had better start now. Anyway, think about it.»

Waving to the café owner as she went out, she took herself off to the Mosque. She had to smile to herself as she could imagine the agitated conversation she had left behind.

She found herself thinking about Nayla as she waited for the prayers to begin. There had been no further sightings of Nayla, and Shaafia wondered if she was a danger to herself. She knew very little about Nayla's adult life, other than she worked for a bank and had her own apartment somewhere. As the voice of the Imam began, she offered her prayers to her sister, wondering if there was any way she could help to redeem her.

She felt no sign of it.

In the afternoon she walked to *Darou Al Bahr*. She found Rana supervising several sweaty men delivering new beds and other furniture. Rana proudly took her upstairs to show how the new bedrooms were developing each with its ensuite bathroom. Then she took her up onto the roof to show the first structures being prepared for the solar panels. She had decided against having a wind turbine up there as the neighbours were very likely to object.

As they made their way downstairs, Rana told Shaafia that the meeting with her brother-in-law had been scheduled, and that Walid had agreed to be there. Rana wanted to be sure that Shaafia would be there, too.

«I will be there, of course,» Shaafia said, «and Houda should be there, too. I suggest that you do not mention that they are not planning to get married now.»

Rana nodded. «We have not told anyone about that.»

Rana ordered tea to be served in the garden. As one of her girls brought out the tray with the *Cornes de Gazelle* pastries, Rana talked about renovating the garden. She definitely wanted to have a gazebo which was one of the few features of the compound that she wanted to include in her new residence.

As they sat there, the orange cat came and sat at Shaafia's feet. She bent to stroke it, and as she did she had an insight.

«The spirit of this cat has waited for you to come back.» she said. «It tried to take on as much of the negative energy as it could. That is why it is so thin. Now you should take care of it and feed it well. In its turn it will take care of you.»

Rana nodded, and she too bent to stroke the cat. She offered it a piece of the pastry. It looked at it for a moment, then leaned in to take it, before it went to sit a little way off to enjoy it.

«It makes me wonder,» said Rana, «why I am here.»

«In this house?»

«In this house, in this garden, in this life.»

Shaafia nodded, and they sat in silence with the question hovering in the air.

Finally Shaafia said: «It is the same for all of us, one way or another. Why were we born, when we were, where we were? What did our souls want to achieve with this life that they chose?»

«Some people just think it is all just an accident. Life has no purpose,» said Rana, «but even in my most negative moments I still had to believe there was a purpose, because my Father believed that.»

«For me I have learned from Pia that it is all about love. It is almost as if love is the real secret of life, and that our purpose is to solve that mystery and to share it with those who don't know about it.»

«So is that the reason I am in this house?»

«Even in this garden,» smiled Shaafia, and she shared the Koranic verse that she recited every day. «They who have faith and work in righteousness, they are companions of the garden. They will abide there forever.»

Above them a pair of small birds squabbled together in the branches, and a single leaf gently spiralled down to land at their feet.

When Walid phoned, it was not only to let Shaafia know that Alex had arrived and was keen to start work, but Walid also wanted Shaafia to know that his Father had engaged a physical therapist to work with him every day, and he was now able to walk around the house slowly but without a walker. He was using a stick, but he no longer needed his wheelchair. Once again Walid wanted to tell Shaafia how grateful his Father was.

«And the other aspect of his progress?» asked Shaafia.

«Nothing yet. He thinks about it a lot. Do you have a suggestion?»

«No. He must find it for himself.»

«He asks when he can invite you to lunch again. He is very fond of you.»

«I will come when he has some news about how he plans to take care of people.»

«That will spur him on. I will tell him.»

Shaafia told him that she would be coming to the meeting with Taj, and that Houda would be there too. She asked him if he had told anyone that his marriage would not be happening.

«Only my Father knows,» he said, and then added: «and Khalil, my brother, but I doubt he has told anyone.»

Shaafia agreed to meet with Alex the next day, and Walid volunteered to pick her up.

«You are becoming such a central part of our lives, Mystic Girl.» he said.

She sat for a moment after his call, letting the new information settle inside her. In part of her consciousness all the different elements of meetings and people seemed to work like machines in a factory. It was as if together they were all manufacturing something, but she could not tell what it was. At the same time, in another part of herself, there was a deep stillness. She could move from one to the other with ease, like walking from one room of a house to another.

As she walked down the alley to wait for Walid the following morning, Samet dropped into step with her.

She told him where she was going and he nodded.

«Soon we will have a plan for him to see. The boys are really keen about the idea.»

«And the girls?»

«Um, we haven't quite got to that yet.»

«Too scared?»

He stopped. «Maybe.» he said, and then walked on.

«You'll get over it.» she said, and caught him up.

«So you have researched the legal requirements?» she asked, matching his steps.

«Dari is working on it. He likes that sort of thing. He could be a bureaucrat if he wanted to.»

«So you can't have a plan till you know what is legal and what is not.»

«Kind of sad, isn't it.» muttered Samet. «We could do this. We could create an environment in which the most brilliant kids of the next generation could thrive, without any nasty government officials looking over our shoulders.»

«You could, but they would shut you down and maybe send you to prison as imposters.»

As they reached the door of the café, he stopped and nodded. «You are probably right.» he said. «You usually are these days.»

The black Renault was already there and Walid came over. He shook hands with Samet.

«Looking forward to seeing what you come up with.» he said.

«So are we.» nodded Samet. «We are working on it. It's not as easy as we thought.»

«Starting a business never is.» agreed Walid as he opened the door for Shaafia.

As the Renault edged its way into the heavy incoming morning traffic, Walid asked: «He's serious about this project?»

She nodded. «He is. He is driven by a deep sense of unfairness, inequality. Suddenly he has found a way to do something about it. He's on fire with it and so is his group.»

«Do you think he has the capacity to do it?»

«On his own? No. But if he is smart enough to find the right people then he will.»

«Knowing you, can you see it working?»

She laughed. «You want a guarantee for your investment?»

«In a way.» he grinned. «I am getting to have more and more trust in your ability to «see» things.»

«So, quite honestly, it might work, if he does the right thing, or it won't if he doesn't. It's up to him and the others.»

He let it go.

The meeting was to be held in the Razak headquarters in central Casablanca. Although Walid had offered to host Alex at the family compound, Alex, while graciously thanking his host, had insisted on staying in a hotel close to the Razak office.

It was Shaafia's first visit to the office.

Walid drove the car into the underground parking lot where the security camera recognised the car and the solid metal grille was raised.

As they went up in the lift, Walid explained that most of the building was used for the administration of the chain of Razak Hotels, telling her what was on each floor as the lift went up. The top floor held the offices of the three Razaks, Rami, Walid and his brother Khalil and an office of private secretaries. One section was reserved for the development of new projects. Walid had given Alex his own office on that floor and they would meet there.

Alex was delighted to see Shaafia again and he embraced her in a very un-English and un-Moroccan hug. He was quite tall and smelt of some kind of male perfume, perhaps cinnamon. She gently pulled herself back and smiled.

«You are very affectionate for an Englishman.»

«Sorry,» he said, «was I a bit too effusive?»

«It was a little unexpected.»

In an adjacent meeting room, Alex had set up a big screen so he could project from his computer.

He showed a sequence of drawings and photos that outlined the way he saw the design of the resort in Essaouira. There was the landplan of the whole site with the orientation of the buildings and outside facilites, pools, a nine-hole golf course, tennis courts and gardens. Then there was a sequence of the proposed buildings with some floor plans, as well as sketches. He had developed a whole subterranean plan for water, drawing from deep bores to create the gardens, the golf course and the fountains. Off to one side he had set up a circle of small buildings which he had labelled as the village.

Neither Walid nor Shaafia commented while he talked, Shaafia translating as he went.

Once the sequence had concluded, Walid nodded. «You've been busy.»

Then he turned to Shaafia: «Did he get it right?»

She knew what he meant, but she said: «He's the planner.»

When she translated this for Alex, he laughed. «He wants to know if I have reproduced accurately what you saw when we were there. So did I.»

She nodded. «Mostly.»

«What did he miss?» asked Walid.

«The village.» she said.

He back-tracked to the drawing. «Here.» he said

She shook her head «You can't plan that.»

Alex looked puzzled. «Why not?»

« They will.»

«The people?» Walid was incredulous. «They're just fishermen and their families.»

«No.» she said. «They are traditional people who have a long history and their own culture. They have a relationship with the sea, with the land, the wind. They will know where it should go, where it should face. There will be those who can tell you exactly how it should be.»

«I'd be interested to get that. I do see your point.» said Alex.

«Only if you do that, will it be an authentic village.» said Shaafia. «And if it is authentic then it will make your resort unique. It will become famous.»

Walid sat back in his chair and looked at Shaafia with his eyes narrowed. «And you will find the people who can do this?»

She nodded.

«OK. You are going to need a title soon.» he said. « You are playing such a rôle on this project.»

«At least a sizeable consultant's fee!» laughed Alex.

By the end of the morning, they had covered a wide range of subjects: planning permits, cost estimates, proposals for work schedules, details for subcontracts and so on until Shaafia began to tire. The hardest aspect of translation was always the numbers.

At last Walid said: «We have done enough for one day. I feel that we have made an excellent start.»

«So far so good.» said Alex, closing his computer.

« I like the way you work, Alex.» said Walid «I would like to take you both to lunch. Unless you are too tired.» He looked at Shaafia.

«No,» she said, «but I am ready to stop for today.»

«Great. And then tomorrow, if it suits you, we can go down to the site. Maybe there you will find the village planners.»

«I love that,» said Alex. «I have to say this is the most interesting project I have ever had.»

«Are you available tomorrow?» asked Walid.

Shaafia nodded. Then she smiled. «But you have to let me choose the restaurant.»

Alex laughed. «Absolutely!»

Walid walked them just a few blocks from his office. He was taking them to a very European restaurant where the menu was almost entirely French. As they walked in they were greeted warmly at the door, and it was clear Walid was a regular and valued client. They were ushered to a table with a reserved sign.

Walid invited Alex to choose a wine and he opted for a Moroccan one. When the sommelier brought it, Walid insisted that Alex be the tester. Alex held up his glass to the light, swilled it round, sniffed it, then took a little sip for tasting. He held the wine in his mouth for moment, before he swallowed and then he smiled up at the sommelier who was studying Alex's face carefully.

«Very mellow,» he said. «This is my very first local wine. I like it.»

The sommelier gave him a courteous little bow, refilled his glass and poured for Walid. Then he turned to Shaafia who put her hand over her glass.

«Madam?» said the sommelier. «Can I get you something?»

She smiled. «A juice?»

He ran through a long list of juices with just the slightest hint of distaste as if juice was really below him. She opted for a fruit cocktail and he left.

While they looked at the extensive menu, Walid asked Alex what he would like to do in his spare time.

«I want to explore the city,» he said. «When we were here last time, I had the strangest sensation that I had been here before.»

Something indistinct flashed through Shaafia's mind, too fast for her to grasp it, but she sensed that there was something behind what he had just said and she would know more if she was attentive.

«When we were in Essaouira last time it, I felt like I should have known where I was. Like if I had a home here in Morocco but I had forgotten where it was. Is that weird?»

«Maybe in a past life you did.» said Shaafia.

He looked at her nodding subtly. «Maybe. I don't really believe in past lives much but I guess you do.»

«I do.» she said. «When I worked in France, I was with a group of people who not only believed it, but knew who they had been.»

«How could they be sure?» he asked.

A look passed between Walid and Shaafia. Having heard about Pia, he knew what she was referring to.

«Sometimes it is hard to prove, but there were times when it was confirmed from more than one source.»

«How do you mean?»

«There are people who can see things, clairvoyants.»

«Is that what you are?» he said, leaning forward.

She thought about her response. «Perhaps.»

«I call her Mystic Girl.» said Walid. «I think she can see a lot more than we can.»

The waiter came for their orders, and the conversation drifted onto other things.

When the meal finally came to an end with the men drinking *digestifs,* and Shaafia drinking coffee, Walid told them that he had meetings all afternoon in his office. He asked Shaafia if he could call her a taxi to take her home, but she shook her head.

« Alex wants to explore Casa, so maybe this afternoon I can be his guide.»

«I would like that very much.» said Alex.

They parted ways outside the restaurant.

«So,» said Alex, «What do you want to show me?»

«I have an idea,» she said, and pulled out her phone. She called Rana and asked if she could bring a guest of Walid's to see *Darou Al Bahr.*

When she closed the phone, Shaafia waved to a passing taxi which turned around instantly nearly wiping out an elderly man with a large lady passenger sitting precariously sideways on the back of a tiny Vespa. There were shouts of recrimination, but the taxi finally pulled up at the restaurant.

When they got in, Shaafia told the driver to go to Boulevard de Londres. As it took off, she told Alex she would show him a famous house that had historical English connections.

As the taxi tooted and swerved its way through the melee of traffic, she pointed out various landmarks, Mosques, market places, and then the Royal Palace behind its massively high walls, just before they arrived.

When the taxi pulled up at the house, Rana came out to meet them, and Shaafia introduced her. Rana had some English, enough to welcome Alex very warmly.

They were about to go in, when Shaafia took Alex by the arm.

«Listen carefully to whatever comes up in your mind.» she said.

He frowned. «What do you mean?»

«This is no ordinary house. Listen inside yourself.»

«You mean because it has an English connection?»

«Just listen.»

«OK.» he said, rather liking the touch of her hand on his arm.

Rana led them inside and as she did, Shaafia said to her in Arabic: «Take him to the room where the Prime Minister of his country sat during the war.»

Walking up the front stairs, Alex looked up at the fine stone building.

«It's a great house. It was English?»

«No,» said Shaafia, «It was build by Rana's grandfather who was a French Admiral.»

Once inside, Rana turned to the right and led them into one of the large meeting rooms with the circular bay window at the end.

Alex gazed around the room with its high chandeliered ceiling and the lush red tapistery covered benches that lined the walls.

«Sit here.» said Shaafia, pointing to the bench under the bay window.

He sat back and looked around him, and then suddenly he shivered.

Shaafia smiled. «You are listening?»

«I have been here before haven't I?»

«January 1943.» she said, then she quietly explained to Rana what was happening.

Rana nodded. By now she was used to what Shaafia could see.

When Shaafia turned back to Alex, he had his eyes closed.

Rana and Shaafia sat across from him quietly waiting until finally he opened his eyes.

«Who was I?» he asked, his voice hoarse with suppressed emotion. He looked at Shaafia. «You saw this?»

«It came to me at lunch. All I saw was that you and this house knew each other.»

«I wasn't Winston Churchill, was I?»

She shook her head. «No, but he was here. You were young. You wore a uniform. Do you know the word «Adjutant»?»

«Yes, a kind of military assistant or something.»

«That's who you were. Winston Churchill sat exactly where you are sitting. You sat over there, taking notes.»

«Incredible.» he said. «I can feel it. Sitting here, it felt, I don't know, so familiar.»

«So now perhaps you can believe in past lives.»

«Either that or you are one incredible magician.»

She smiled. «I leave it to you.»

Then Rana invited him to visit the rest of the house, which he politely did, but Shaafia could see he was deeply occupied. At the end of the tour, Rana had tea and pastries served outside where the garden was undergoing major renovation, and was becoming a little neater and more ordered. The wooden structure had been replaced with new beams arching along the central pathway, and new climbing plants had been arranged in pots beside the uprights so that in time it would be covered in jasmine vines and flowering creepers.

Houda arrived while they were having their tea.

Shaafia introduced her as Rana's daughter, but did not mention any relationship to Walid.

However, Alex said: «Houda?» he asked. «Are you the Houda that Walid is going to marry?»

Houda smiled very sweetly. «He told you about that?»

«Last time we were here,» he said. «We were fascinated by how marriage is like a business arrangement here.»

«You don't do that in England?»

«Not at all. Oh I suppose maybe they did back in Victorian times, but not now.»

«You are married?» asked Rana.

«Not me,» he said. «Haven't met the right person yet.»

«We could find you a nice Moroccan girl.» said Rana.

«Well,» he smiled, «judging by present company, Moroccan girls are very attractive.»

Houda laughed. «The English are so «*galant*»!» using the French pronunciation.

When Shaafia mentioned that she was being a tourist guide for Alex, Houda offered to take him to Murdoch Park.

Shaafia nodded. «I think maybe you have been there before.»

«Really?» he said.

« I think the British Prime Minister and the American President Roosevelt walked together there as they planned how to attack the German forces.»

Houda looked surprised, so Shaafia filled her in, speaking Arabic, about Alex's experience in the front room.

Still speaking Arabic, Houda said: «Did you know that about him?»

«I knew there was something about him and this house.»

Houda reverted to English. «So this is not your first visit?»

«So it seems.» he said.

«Do you ride horses?»

«I do.» he said.

«So then you must see Murdoch Park.» she said.

It was a short walk to the Park, just one block along the Boulevard de Londres. As they went, Houda told him something of its history. Murdoch was an English merchant who created the park to exercise his horses. These days, the government owns it and it's called Isesco Park. It is a favourite place for walking.

«People say this is one of the lungs of Casablanca.» said Houda.

There were people everywhere, families walking with kids on little bikes, ladies in head scarves walking small dogs, and serious joggers in lycra, both male and female.

As they walked along, Alex looked around, and then he nodded. «It does feel familiar.»

«Maybe you have been here many times, maybe you rode horses here.»

«I am beginning to think almost anything is possible.» he said.

As the afternoon waned, both Alex and Shaafia began to tire. Houda volunteered to drop them home, taking Alex to his hotel first. On the way Alex, sitting in the front seat, made a great effort to be sociable and talked enthusiastically about the resort project in Essaouira. He stressed the crucial rôle that Shaafia had played in it.

Houda laughed. «Maybe you should call it Villa Shaafia.»

Alex loved that. «I am going to tell your husband about that one.» he said.

Houda glanced at Shaafia in the rear vision mirror and a little smile crossed her face. She wasn't going to tell him just yet.

Once they had dropped Alex off, Shaafia now sitting in the front seat, Houda started laughing. «It is such fun having you as my new friend.» she said, «You have such an interesting way of making things happen.»

Return to Essaouira

Walid picked Shaafia up from the corner before going downtown to Alex's hotel. As they drove, Shaafia told Walid where they had spent the afternoon and what Alex had experienced.

«You knew about that? I mean you could see it?» he asked.

«Not exactly.» she said. «Sometimes there is just a hint about something, but if I get it then I follow it. I sensed there was some relationship between Alex and *Darou Al Bahr.*»

Walid nodded. «I wonder what he made of it?»

«I am sure he will tell us.» Then Shaafia added: «He met Houda, but he still thinks that you are getting married.»

«She didn't say anything?»

«She let it go.»

«He doesn't need to know about that.»

Alex was waiting outside his hotel, talking to the doorman. He carried a small backpack which he threw into the back of the car, and jumped into the back seat.

«Good morning!» he said with great enthusiasm.

«Did you sleep well?» asked Shaafia.

«That depends on what you mean by well. I had the wildest dreams. What you showed me yesterday has turned my whole sense of who I am upside down.»

«So what was in your dream?» she asked.

«I was in that house and I saw myself in a mirror. You were right, I was a young man and in uniform. I recognised myself but I didn't look like I do now. I had a little moustache and I looked very dapper. I have to say it was very strange. I saw Winston Churchill and I saw Roosevelt. I was right there. I carried a big briefcase and I could feel the weight of it. I felt nervous and on edge. This was historic and I had a big responsibility. I wasn't feeling confident. And then everything changed. I was riding horses in that park, but it was not with Churchill. I think it was at another time. Maybe earlier. Maybe I was some kind of horse trainer or something. I have loved horses all my life and maybe that's why. I tell you, after all that, I think I am convinced that you are right. I have been here in another life, maybe more than once.»

Walid and Shaafia exchanged smiles.

Halfway to Essaouira, they stopped in the coastal town of Asfi for coffee.

In one corner of the coffee shop, a group of old men sat like statues, fixed on an episode of the Simpsons, flickering on a big old black and white television, translated into shouty Arabic.

In the quietest corner they could find, Walid gave Alex a short history of the town which was an old Portuguese *Fortaleza* in the 16th century, now famous for its potttery. In the Second World War the Allied forces used Asfi as a base when they attacked the Vichy French.

«Maybe I was here, too.» said Alex.

«Do you feel it?» asked Shaafia.

He sat still for a minute, then he said: «I don't think so.»

«Good.» she said. «If you learn to listen you, will know many things.»

When they arrived at the resort site, outside Essaouira, Ayman was there to greet them. He wore a kind of uniform, and he obviously had dressed to impress his boss that he was doing a good job.

He opened the gates for the car to go in, then came over and kissed his sister. He shook hands with Alex. In his best English he said: «Welcome to Essaouira.»

Not much had changed since their previous visit, except there were no protesters outside.

Alex pulled out his backpack and opened his computer. The first exercise for the day would be to walk the site, following the planned developments, and make sure that he accurately plotted them with his architectural software applications.

He had followed Shaafia's vision of the entrance roadway, and the locations and orientations of the buildings were very much as she had seen them. With the aid of his software he could now show it. Where the village was to go, however, he had taken it off the plan. It was now just a blank, ready to be filled.

When they arrived at the point where the village would be, closest to the sea, Shaafia sat on a rock.

«Tired?» asked Alex.

She shook her head. «No, I must send a message.»

Instead of opening her phone however, she closed her eyes. The men paused. By now their respect for Shaafia was such that whatever she wanted to do they would wait.

At last she opened her eyes.

«She will come this afternoon.» she said and stood up.

Walid asked: «The woman of the village?», and she nodded.

Alex chuckled. «You don't need a phone.»

Ayman had watched this from a distance, walking like an escort. Shaafia said to him: «This afternoon an old man will come with a woman from the village. You will let them come in.»

«OK,» he said, frowning a little that his sister was now giving him orders.

Then it was time for lunch and as promised Shaafia got to choose which restaurant. As they drove back into Essouira, she laughed. «It has to be the same as last time. I think it is the best one in town.»

«But it only serves one dish.» complained Walid.

«But a really good one.» said Alex. «Anyway, we agreed she gets to choose.»

As soon as they arrived at the open area where most cars were parked the same young boy appeared.

«I remember you.» he said. «I will take special care of this car.»

Walid smiled and gave the boy a coin.

Shaafia led them back to the small narrow alley where the rather battered sign that read «*Hout*», Arabic for fish, had tipped a little sideways.

Just as they reached it Asad the big bellied, moustachioed owner came out.

«Oh,» he said, «It's you. English.»

«You were expecting us?» asked Walid.

«Sometimes I get the feeling someone important is coming. I got that just now so I came out to see who it was.»

Walid laughed. «Another mystic!»

Shaafia translated all this for Alex who loved it. «What's the dish today?» he asked.

«Asfi Sardines.»

«Sardines?»

Shaafia reminded Alex that Asfi was where they had stopped for coffee.

«Asfi is famous for the best sardines in Africa,» said Asad, «and my wife's secret recipe makes them heavenly.» putting his finger tips to his mouth making the universal gesture of deliciousness.

Inside, he showed them to a table in a corner, passing tables crowded with the locals, mostly men. The smell of spices hung in the air, and the happy loud conversations created a vibrant atmosphere.

As he sat and looked around, Alex said: «I could get very used to this.»

When their plates were brought, he had to admit he had never in his life tasted sardines that good.

When they returned to the car, the boy had found a bucket and had given the car a wash, not that it really needed one.

However, Walid clapped the boy on the shoulder and gave him some more money.

«See you next time.» said Walid.

As they drove away, Shaafia glanced back and saw the boy standing in the road looking after them.

«That boy will be working for you one day.» she said.

Walid chuckled. «He is already.»

Then he looked up in the rear vision to look at Shaafia in the back seat.

«Or did you mean something else?»

«Who knows?» she smiled enigmatically.

At the resort site, the older woman in the white headscarf was there with a very old man who walked carefully using a stick. Ayman had let them in, as instructed, and they sat outside the small security shed on boxes.

When she saw Shaafia, the woman got up and came over. She kissed Shaafia on both cheeks. Then in her ear she whispered: «Surely God has sent you to us.»

Then she took Shaafia's hand and led her to the old man sitting on the box.

«This is my Uncle Rassem. He remembers how our village used to look long ago, many years before it was sold and destroyed.»

He gazed up at Shaafia with milky eyes, and she could see that he was close to being blind.

Ayman found boxes for everyone to sit.

Alex pulled out his computer and showed the lady the place where the village would go. She talked to the old man for a moment, and then he began to speak. Shaafia did the translation.

He was speaking Berber.

«Long ago our village was called Rifat and there were many fishing boats. The village faced the sea and in the centre, one of the buildings was three storeys high. All the other houses were one or two storeys, some were made of stone and wood. The stones were whitewashed and the wood, especially the shutters, were painted blue.»

Alex asked: «How many houses were there?»

The old man thought about that. At last he said: «Maybe ten or twelve bigger houses and then some smaller ones. In the middle, the big house had several shops on the ground floor.»

«And how close to the water?»

«When the tide was highest, there was just enough room for the boats to be pulled out of the water. Our boats were small, just for one to two fishermen only. All the boats were always painted blue.»

Alex worked with his computer for a few moments and then he showed the man what he had done. The old man peered at the computer, bringing his eyes very close.

«The houses were in a curve with more space in the middle. Women used to sit there and mend the nets.»

Alex made some changes, and again the old man brought his face very close.

«On the top floor of the biggest house there was a terrace.»

And so it went on for quite some time until the old man sat back. «Yes.» he said «That is how Rifat used to look.»

Then there was some spirited discussion with the woman in the headscarf about who could live there, and Shaafia explained about the idea to invite the previous villagers to live there, to work for the resort. She explained that they would be able to control their own village as they had done in the old days, but the village would be owned by the resort. Everyone who lived there would not be asked to pay rent, but would be guaranteed residency Not only that, they would be employed by the resort.

The woman nodded at all this.

«We are like a large family,» she said. «Most of us are related to almost everyone else. What you are offering us is truly a great gift from God. If what you say comes to be, then you can be certain we will honour our commitments. If this girl says it will be so, then I will trust it.»

Once Shaafia had translated all this into Arabic and English, Walid said: «If this girl tells me that you will honour your commitment then I will promise to keep my commitment.»

There was more talk about how many residents, how to determine who would live there, how many families were involved, how many people would live in the biggest house. The woman was very clear, she knew the names and the relationship of everyone. She suggested roles for many of them. Every now and then she would check with her Uncle, who mostly nodded in agreement.

As all this was taking place Walid had his own computer out and was making notes.

Finally the old man was obviously tiring, so they decided they had enough information to work with.

Walid told the woman that he would appoint a local person to represent him as they developed the idea of the village and turned it into a reality.

«She cannot do it?» she asked, putting an affectionate arm round Shaafia.

«You can be sure she will be very involved.» he said. «I make this promise to you. Nothing will be decided until she agrees. Is that suitable for you?»

«She is the one we trust.» she said.

At the end of the afternoon, they said goodbye to the villagers with a great sense of wellbeing. The woman promised that she would hold a series of meetings with her people, and they would form a committee to work with Walid's representative.

Walid repeated his promise that Shaafia would be intimately involved in every step, and the woman embraced her with a lot of love.

As they were about to leave Ayman, who had watched all this from a distance, came over to Shaafia.

«You have become a very important person.» he said, with just a hint of jealousy. «He listens to you.»

She reached up and kissed her brother on both cheeks.

«It works for you being here?» she asked.

He nodded. «Yes, I am happy. He pays me well and he trusts me. This is the best job I ever had. Thanks to you.»

«I am happy to see that you like it. I think it suits you very well here. There was something about Casa that was not good for you. And I think maybe your life will be in Essaouira from now on.»

«You think so?»

She smiled. «You might find yourself getting married to a good local girl and becoming the head of security in a very successful resort.»

He stared at her. «That would be a miracle.»

«Miracles are not impossible.» she said, and kissed him again on both cheeks.

Then he handed her an envelope. «This is for our Mother.» he said.

On the road back to Casablanca, Walid was effusive in his enthusiasm. He had felt a great upswell of joy as they had worked with the villagers, and now he was almost euphoric. He kept telling Shaafia how incredible she was, until finally she had to laugh. «Wait till you see my fee for all this work!» she said. «You might have to ask the bank for help!»

«You are worth every dirham.»

Then Alex remembered what Houda has said.

«Your future wife had a great idea. She said that the resort should be called Villa Shaafia.»

This made Walid chuckle. «She's a smart girl.» he said, not wanting to allude to the change in the relationship with Houda.

However, Shaafia said: «We should use the original name. It belongs to that place.»

«What was it again?»

«Rifat.»

«What does it mean?»

«Rifat means a noble place. I think it is a name that carries good fortune.»

They left Alex at his hotel, and Walid drove Shaafia home.

«You have become so much of my life,» he said. «Why do you think that is?»

She did not answer right away. She looked out the window at the passing shop fronts and apartments of the city. She felt no immediate response to his question.

«Perhaps,» she said at last, «you have a destiny of some kind and I can help you to realise it.»

«What would that be?»

«Who knows. Something you brought with you, something your soul wants for you to do. What that is, well, that is for you to discover.»

When he stopped at the café on the corner, he turned to her.

«I have known lots of girls, women, in my life, but I never met anyone like you.»

She nodded. «Maybe you only saw girls in a certain way.»

«Maybe so.»

She gave him a sweet smile as she closed the door.

A meeting with lawyers

The next time Shaafia saw Walid was in the office of Rana's lawyer. Walid had already met with the lawyer and had discussed how the meeting would go. Walid had studied the documents that the lawyer held, and had developed a sense of the strategy.

Houda picked up Shaafia in the Porsche. As they drove, Houda told Shaafia that her uncle had been calling Rana almost every day and was not being friendly at all. She feared the meeting was going to be difficult.

Rana and Walid had arrived together, and when Shaafia walked in, she was introduced to the lawyer as Rana's advisor.

«You have a business background?» he asked.

She smiled. «Not in a conventional sense, no. I work mostly as a translator.»

The lawyer looked a little puzzled, but noticed that what Shaafia had said made everyone else smile.

He led them to a large meeting room where one of his assistants had prepared tea.

When Taj walked in with his lawyer, Shaafia immediately saw the dark cloud he was carrying.

Introductions were made and tea was served. Walid was introduced as Houda's future husband, and Shaafia as an advisor. Both Taj and his lawyer glanced at Shaafia, but she was content to see that neither of them thought she was significant.

Rana's lawyer opened the meeting. At the end of the long table another of his assistants sat with a computer to take notes and record the meeting.

«The purpose of the meeting is to formalise the ownership of Bin Salah Transport in the light of the death of Hamza Bin Salah. We have been discussing this for some time, and hopefully by the conclusion of this meeting we will have arrived at a point where everyone is in agreement.

«It is obvious,» interrrupted Taj, «there is only one way that Bin Salah Transport can continue as a viable company. I have tried and tried to demonstrate to my dear sister-in-law that the only way is for me to take control.»

«Which I do not accept.» said Rana.

Her lawyer tried to regain control. «Legally, as we have established,» nodding at Taj's lawyer, «that Madam Bin Salah is now legally the majority stakeholder in the company. You agree?»

The other lawyer nodded. «However,» he said, «my client is willing to make more than a fair offer to buy her share outright.»

«Which I reject.» said Rana. «My stake is not for sale.»

«You know nothing about the company.» retorted Taj. «You know nothing about business. How can you even think of being in control?».

Rana smiled. «I know more than you realise. One thing I am sure of is that I can judge the character of people very well. In my new rôle as director of this company I will ensure that I have the best advisors I can.»

Taj sneered. «Like who?»

Rana took his angry look and did not flinch. «I am sure you are aware of the Razak company and their business sense. My intention is to appoint Walid as my chief operations officer.»

«Hotels are not the same as transportation and petroleum.»

Walid leaned forward: «Business is business. Mine and yours are not all that different.»

«So if I agree to this,» said Taj, scowling, «he has the last word in our decisions?»

«No,» said Rana, «I will.»

Taj stared at her. «My brother married a monster.» he muttered.

«Now,» smiled Rana, glancing at Shaafia, «if you are not happy with this arrangement then I would like to propose an alternative.»

He glared at her, with his jaw tight.

She held his look. «I am making you an offer for your minority share of the company. I will buy you out.»

This shocked him and he looked at his lawyer.

«She can't do that, can she?»

«If you accept her offer, then she can.»

Taj sharpened his glare at his sister-in-law. «Where would you get that kind of capital?»

Rana turned slightly in her chair and gestured at Walid. «I have powerful support.»

His eyes narrowed as he assessed Walid, knowing that what she said was probably true. Then he turned back. «Anyway, I am not selling.»

Rana's lawyer nodded subtly in the direction of Taj's lawyer. «Then it does seem like there is only one solution.»

The other lawyer agreed.

And then Shaafia came to life. She had been sitting quietly next to Houda, feeling the room, and sensing that she was being given information. Now she knew what it was and how to use it.

«Can I ask something?» she said, sitting forward.

The whole room seemed to be stunned at her intervention.

«Of course,» said Rana's lawyer.

«You have documents that show the assets of the company, do you not?»

Rana's lawyer nodded. «I do.»

«They show everything that is owned by the company?»

«Everything.»

«And you do as well?» she asked, looking at Taj's lawyer.

«I believe so.» he said.

«Can we see them?» she asked.

Taj's lawyer turned to his client, who shrugged. His lawyer turned on his computer. Rana's lawyer nodded to his assistant.

«So now,» said Shaafia, «we will see if they match.»

Taj jumped in his seat, as if it was on fire.

«That's an insult. Are you suggesting that there is something wrong?»

Walid looked at Shaafia. «What do you mean?» he asked, knowing that she had sensed something.

«Can we put the two sets of documents side by side?».

While Taj fumed in his seat, they pulled the two computers together, and although the layouts were different, the basic categories were easy enough to follow.

«Look at natural gas.» said Shaafia.

The entire room stared at her in puzzlement, except for Taj who slammed his fist on the table.

«What is this?» he shouted, «Who is this girl? Why are we listening to her?»

Rana yelled back: «Shut up, Taj.»

Meanwhile, Walid had leaned forward and was studying the two screens going from one to the other.

Shaafia said: «You will find that there is a discrepancy when you get to the natural gas terminals, the leasing of natural gas powered trucks and the equipment that transfers natural gas.»

Taj leapt to his feet. «It's not true. It is still being negotiated.»

Walid found the section, and sure enough in the document held by Rana's lawyer the natural gas assets were all listed. In Taj's lawyer's documents they were not there.

«Tell them,» shouted Taj, standing over his lawyer.

The lawyer had gone white in the face and was having trouble swallowing.

«I know it does not look good,» he said.

«Negotiating.» said Taj, threatening to strike his lawyer.

Shaafia looked at the lawyer and there was something powerful in her eyes that struck him much more than the potential strike of his client.

The lawyer looked at the faces staring at him, and ran his hand across his now sweaty forehead.

«I .... well to be honest, these assets have been sold.» he said.

«But the money from the sale did not go back to the company, did it?» asked Walid, now looking furious and ready to start a physical fight with Taj.

«They did not.» replied the lawyer.

«It was just temporary,» yelled Taj. «You know how it is in business.» He was looking at Walid. «Sometimes you have to move things around, do a bit of balancing. You need funds to underwrite a project, then you put them back afterwards. Temporary.»

«It is theft.» said Rana. «If I understand what has happened, you have sold one of the major assets of my company and kept the money for yourself.»

Then she turned to her lawyer. «Is that how it is?»

He nodded. «As far as I can tell, it looks that way.»

«What are the legal measures I can take to get back what belongs to me?»

«There is no need.» said Shaafia with a strong voice that cut across the tension in the room.

Everyone in the room seemed to be held in suspense. Shaafia looked from one to another, finally facing Rana.

«Mr Bin Salah will pay you exactly what he received for the sale.»

«And why would I do that?» he demanded.

She turned to face him. «You will do that, because if you do not, your lawyer, who is not willing to work for you any more, will reveal to Rana the other secret deals that you have made.»

His face told her how stunned he was.

His lawyer sat with his head down, looking at the table in front of him. He dared not look at Shaafia.

Shaafia was not finished.

« If you do not pay within a week, he will also reveal the details of your Cayman Islands bank accounts, both of them, and how you have evaded paying personal tax for a very long time. »

The room seemed to be a frozen tableau of shock.

The lawyer sat bent over in his chair, but eventually he lifted his head to stare at this small and quietly spoken girl who seemed to have total power over him.

Taj had dropped back into his chair and seemed to have trouble breathing.

Rana, Houda and Walid waited, barely able to contain their delight and amazement.

There was a long silence.

At last Rana's lawyer felt he should try to regain control. «Perhaps,» he said, trying to keep his voice steady, «we could draw up some articles of agreement between the two parties based on what this girl has just suggested. What do you think?»

The other lawyer seemed so shaken he couldn't respond.

«OK, OK, OK,» muttered Taj.

Then he looked across at Shaafia. «I don't know who you are or what you do, but you'd better watch your back, girl.»

She looked right back at him.

«My back is safe, I can assure you. But yours is not.»

His eyes narrowed. Was she threatening him?

With a quiet voice, Shaafia said: «Only when you have done the right thing will you be rid of the devil who sits on your shoulder. Only then will you be able to sleep at night.»

He stared at her across the table, unnerved by her lack of fear.

She met his look steadily. « You always hated the thought that Hamza was the real driver of this company. You believed that he thought of you as second class.»

His look darkened but it was no longer threatening. She had touched a nerve.

«But this is what you did not know. Your brother knew exactly what you were doing.»

Rana's lawyer nodded. «He did say something to me about that.»

Shaafia held Taj's look, which was shifting to horror.

«When your brother died,» continued Shaafia, «you were not unhappy. You expected that you would naturally have total control.»

« I lost a brother.» he muttered.

«But you thought you had gained the enterprise.»

«Of course. Who else?» he growled. «We ran it together.»

«But he had control. Once he was out of the way, you thought you would have it.»

«Obviously.»

« You don't have control of the company, Rana has that. But more than that, Mr Bin Salah, you don't have control over the torment that goes on inside your soul.»

He continued to stare at her and then something inside him collapsed. His head dropped onto his chest and a kind of sob came out of him.

Rana stood up and nodded to Houda who joined her Mother.

«It is agreed then?» said Rana.

Taj's lawyer had shrunk back into himself, but he looked at Rana with lowered eyelids and nodded.

«He will pay in full?»

Again he nodded.

She looked at her own lawyer.

«We will draw up the necessary documents,» he said, «and as I understand it, you wish to nominate Walid Razak as your Chief Operations Officer.»

«That is my wish.» Rana said, looking at Walid.

«You agree?» asked Rana's lawyer.

Walid said: «I do.»

Rana's lawyer looked at Taj's lawyer. «Will you be willing to work with me on these documents?»

The lawyer looked at his client bent over with his head on the table.

«It will be the last thing I do. After that I will no longer represent him.»

Rana looked at Walid and Shaafia. «We are satisfied.» she said. «When you have the documents ready, please call us and we will return, Walid and I, and we will sign them.»

Walid and Shaafia stood up.

«I will expect the payment to be made within the week.» said Rana, and turned to lead her team from the room. However just as she reached the door, Shaafia stopped and turned back. She looked down at Taj's lawyer who looked like he was going into shock.

«Sometimes the decision you make feels painful, but if deep in your heart you know you have done the right thing, your heart will be pleased. God will be pleased. *Ham delilah.*»

He gazed up at her and she saw a small tear run down his cheek. Then she went over to him and gave him one of her business cards.

«You have done the right thing.» she said, and turned to follow the others.

As they entered the lift to go down to the carpark under the building, the minute the doors closed, Houda grabbed Shaafia in the tightest of hugs.

«Amazing, miraculous! How do you do that? How did you know?»

Rana joined in the hug, rubbing Shaafia's back and laughing. «Truly, you are the most extraordinary advisor a person could ever have.»

They had to pull back when the doors opened at a lower floor and a man in a suit stepped in. He nodded at them and stood with his back to them until the lift arrived at the ground floor, and he left. Then they continued down to the carpark below.

Only as they stepped out of the lift, did Walid say anything.

«I think,» he said looking at Shaafia, «that you are by far the scariest person I have ever met.»

Houda hooted, laughing. «She's not scary. She's incredible.»

«I don't disagree with that,» he said, «but what we saw upstairs shows me that there is nothing in my past, all my actions, all my thoughts that can be hidden from wherever she gets her information. That is scary.»

Rana smiled. «That would only be scary if you had something to hide.»

Houda grinned «So you'd better come clean.»

Shaafia had let all this flow around her, but now she looked at them seriously. «We should be grateful for what happened today. The universe saw fit to support us in what was right. I am just a translator. I was happy to translate what needed to be conveyed.»

Then she smiled at Walid. «So don't be too scared. If you need to make some changes in your life, maybe it would be good to do that before the universe decides to give you a hard time.»

He nodded. «I have a bit of work to do then. You will let me know if I miss anything.»

«You won't need me. You will know what to do.»

He smiled at her and put his hand up to his heart.

«*Inche Allah.*» he said.

Time to Rest

Shaafia had turned her phone off at the end of the day so it was only the following morning, after a quiet breakfast with her Mother, that she discovered she had multiple messages.

She took the phone outside and sat under the fig tree to check her messages. Suddenly everyone wanted to talk to her.

Alex was keen for another business meeting, and also wanted to go back to *Darou Al Bahr*.

Walid was calling on behalf of his father who wanted Shaafia to come to lunch again.

Rana's lawyer was asking if she would be interested in working for him from time to time as a translator. Could she come right away?

Théophile had left a message asking how she was doing, and airing the idea of coming to Morocco for a visit.

Rachi had exciting news and wanted to see Shaafia to share it.

And then there was the message from Taj. He was abject in his apology. His voice was low and harsh as he spoke. He had been in torment since the meeting, he said. He believed she was haunting him. Could she please meet with him?

At the end of all the messages, she closed her eyes, resting her head back against the friendly solidity of the old tree. A familiar quietness flowed into her mind and gently ushered away any lingering thoughts.

At one point there was a rustling overhead and she opened her eyes to see a crow on a branch just above. It seemed to be watching her.

The image of the sharif who had first given her the quest to search for the bird with crooked wings when she was a child, came to her mind. As she gazed up at the big black bird, it bent its neck to preen under one wing, opening the wing out wide. Then it folded the wing and did the same to the other wing. Then it let out a harsh cry and flew off.

When she closed her eyes again Shaafia recognised the bird's preening as a symbol. She too had to take care of herself before she could fly on.

It was unclear whose voice she heard inside, but the message was clear. «You have done so much. You have sown so many seeds, helped so many pilgrims to find the path forward, now you need to rest.»

She turned the phone off.

Rest.

She held that idea in her awareness and felt that indeed she was tired. Her body felt strained, almost as if she had bruises in her muscles.

Rest.

She wondered how she should do that. At this moment the tree was of great comfort, but it was also exposed being on the path to and from the house. The house itself was not exactly a restful place, with her brothers and sisters constantly coming and going. She thought of *Darou Al Bahr*. That would be a place of refuge in the future, but not yet. It was in the midst of renovation.

As the best immediate option she decided to go to the Mosque.

As it was mid-morning there was no-one about. She passed Haj Kabir's house but did not go in. She left her shoes at the door and went into the women's section. A lady was mopping the floor and she gestured to Shaafia that she was nearly finished. Shaafia stood back against a wall as the lady worked to dry the floor. Shaafia smiled to herself. Even the Mosque has to take care of itself like everything else.

When the lady left, nodding to Shaafia as she went, Shaafia settled into a corner where an oblique ray of morning sun picked out the dappled stone wall. She sat with her back to the warmth of the wall and closed her eyes.

At first there was just reassuring dark stillness calming her mind and allowing her to be deeply still.

Then images began to flow, ethereal forms, angel-like, some winged others merely hovering in space. They felt familiar as they floated and turned this way and that. They were aware of her, seeming to invite her into that weightless flow. She allowed herself to be drawn towards it, feeling free and light.

Her inner state lasted only until the voice of Haj Kabir, calling the midday prayers began, and she rose to perform the rituals that went with them.

With each movement, she felt that whatever tension was left in her body was being massaged away. When the prayers concluded, she returned to her warm spot by the wall, having been the only participant in the prayers in the women's section.

At last she opened her eyes and saw Myriam, Haj Kabir's wife, looking down at her.

«I am sorry to be breaking into your serene state,» she said, «but my husband asks that you join us for lunch.»

Shaafia smiled and slowly got to her feet.

«With pleasure.» she said.

Haj Kabir was already seated at a low round table with his little son on his lap. They had obviously decided, or at least the child had, that lunch could not wait for their guest and he was stuffing his mouth with pieces of flat bread which he dipped, messily, from time to time in a big bowl of vegetable soup.

«I am happy that you could join us,» said Haj Kabir, when he saw Shaafia. « because I have a message for you.»

As Shaafia took her seat, Myriam dished her up a big bowl of the soup.

«In prayers today,» said Haj Kabir, «while I was reciting them, I had a vision of a sharif. He told me that you have done much work for his people, but that you must now go into retreat because your energy is getting low.»

She nodded. «I too have received a message like that, although not from a sharif.»

«There is a little bit more to the message.» Haj Kabir had to quickly rescue the big soup bowl when his little son leaned too far and grabbed at the bowl. Shaafia gratefully drank her wonderfully spiced soup while she waited for the rest of the message.

«I am to take you to El Chakour. There are wise people there who will help you.»

«Where is it?»

«In the Atlas. It is a small village quite high up and difficult to get to. I have been there many times. It is a place where your spirit can regain its strength.»

Shaafia felt a great wave of gratitude pass through her, and she smiled.

«It is almost as if I am there already.» she said.

«So after lunch and when this glutton on my lap is satisfied, we will go.»

Feeling elated that she was being constantly guided, Shaafia returned home after lunch to pack her new small suitcase. She took very little. Haj Kabir had warned her that it was cold up in the mountains. She dug out the warm false fur coat that Sister Geneviève had helped her to buy in the secondhand shop back in Bordeaux and the cosy Alpaca wool beanie. She kept the red mittens that Sister Agnés had knitted for her. She had nearly decided to leave it all behind. Why would she need such a warm coat and mittens in Morocco? Now she knew why.

As she left the house, she told her Mother that Haj Kabir was taking her for a retreat, just for a few days, and her Mother kissed her on both cheeks.

«Surely Allah himself is taking care of you.» she said.

As she passed the fig tree, she had a strong impulse. Remembering all the messages that she had received on her phone that morning, she stopped, pulled out her phone and quickly sent messages to all those who had tried to contact her. She let them know she was going on retreat and promised to get back to them when she returned. Then she closed her phone off and went back inside the house. She asked her Mother to look after her phone for her, and that as it was turned off, it would not ring. Her Mother put it in a drawer and kissed her daughter again.

Haj Kabir was waiting for her at the end of the alley in his dusty old Dacia. She put her suitcase on the back seat and they headed off into the afternoon traffic. He was something of a fatalist as a driver, tending to plunge ahead where there was no realistic opening. Somehow he managed not to hit anyone, although there were some near misses, especially with scooters. Shaafia quietly repeated her Koranic Verse as they charged ahead, and it was not until they left the outlying towns that she began to breathe a little more freely.

As the Dacia trundled through the rocky countryside with occasional olive groves and goat herds here and there, she asked Haj Kabir about the village they were going to.

«Ah,» he said, «you will see. It is deceptively simple. It looks like a very ordinary, just a poor collection of small old stone houses, one little shop, a simple stone Mosque, not much else. But, as you will no doubt discover, there is a spirit in El Chakour, a vortex of the most beneficial energy. Very few people know it is there, almost as if it protects itself from unwanted attention. To be invited there is a gift. I am not at all surprised that I find myself bringing you into its warm embrace.»

«Who lives there?»

«Well that is a bit of mystery. Of course there are people who do live there permanently, not so many. Some elderly couples, some older ladies whose families have gone to the city. However, there are those who come and go, sharifs, wise people, some from the desert. Whenever I have been there, I have seen such people. Some of them are quite strange. Some do not talk, some only laugh, while others appear to be like normal simple men, like shepherds, but do not be fooled. Many of them are great souls, close to God, full of deep knowledge.»

The car rattled on through the afternoon as Haj Kabir told her stories of men and a few women who he had met in El Chakour over the years.

Finally the old Dacia began to climb. The road was narrow and potholed. Now and then a truck or a bus would come barrelling down towards them, so Haj Kabir would have to take evasive action, sometimes teetering perilously close to the edge of the road, overhanging precipitous drops to a dry river far below.

None of the continuing minor emergencies seemed to bother him and he kept on with his storytelling, grinding through the gears to encourage the Dacia to keep going, and shouting over the noise.

It was almost evening when a thin mist began to form, and as the car wound its way higher and higher, the mist condensed into fog until it was so thick it was almost impossible to see the road.

«Allah is our guide!» shouted Haj Kabir over the roar of his engine.

Suddenly he swung the car off to one side where it bounced and rattled along a rocky steep track, until it flattened out in front of a low stone building with a rickety verandah in front.

«Welcome to El Chakour,» said Haj Kabir. «Our pilgrimage has been a success.»

The Dacia rattled a few times after he turned it off, and they sat for a moment in the deep foggy silence. Nothing moved.

The door of the house opened and a tiny woman, supporting herself with a walking frame, peered out. She obviously did not recognise the car, but as soon as Haj Kabir got out, she let out a delighted shriek.

He went over to her and kissed her on both cheeks. Shaafia followed and stood back until he turned to introduce her.

«This is Haja Manar.» he said. «She is the queen of El Chakour.»

The old lady cackled delightedly and gently smacked Haj Kabir on his cheeks.

«Such a naughty boy.» she said. Then she looked searchingly at Shaafia.

«You have guardians.» she said. «You have brought them with you. You will not need them here.»

Shaafia put her hands up to her heart with respect. She could see what a joyful state this lady was in. She had the feeling that she was meeting one of the beings that she normally encountered with her eyes closed.

«*A salam aleikum.*» she said softly.

The woman returned the greeting then swung her walker around to go into the house, saying: «Come in, come in» over her hunched shoulders.

The air was crisp and cold as Haj Kabir and Shaafia went back to the car. He had brought a small bag for himself, and with their two bags they followed their hostess inside.

The house was wonderfully warm after the clammy cold of the foggy evening. Candles burned in various niches along the entrance corridor. The corridor opened to a larger room where an open fire burned in a stone chimney. Around the room were rows of low benches with many dark red cushions. On one of the benches lay a tiny thin man in a long white robe.

As she came into the room Haja Manar went over to the man and said: «The girl you wanted to meet has come.»

The old man sat up with surprising agility and dropped his feet down from the bench. He studied Shaafia from across the room. Then he beamed a wide toothless smile at her.

«Aha,» he said, «so there you are. They told me you were coming.»

She smiled at him. He seemed so familiar to her as if she had met him long ago.

«They told me it was time to take a retreat.» she said, knowing that they were both talking about the same voices.

«Of course you should. *Maryam Al Adhra* has a lot of work for you to do. You have to build up your strength and your power.»

Shaafia smiled. He was using the Arabic name for the Virgin Mary.

The old man gave Haj Kabir a friendly wave. «So here you are again, bringing another pilgrim.»

Haj Kabir went over to the old man and kissed his hands.

«It is my duty.» he said.

He turned to Shaafia. «This is Haj Saif.»

She approached the old man and bent to kiss his hands.

«She is the daughter of Jamil Jilani.» said Haj Kabir.

«Ah.» the old man nodded.

«You knew my Father?»

He nodded.

«He was a pure soul.» he said.

«Ibrahim!» called Haja Mana with a surprisingly loud voice, then she said to Haj Kabir: «He has made a mountain soup.»

A very tall, wide-shouldered, dark-skinned man, in a long white robe appeared, carrying a heavy pot in both hands.

He bowed to Haj Kabir and Shaafia, before placing the pot on a low table. Then he went over to a dresser and pulled out a porcelain scoop and five bowls. Then he kneeled at the table to begin serving the soup.

The five bowls sat steaming on the table and the aroma was intoxicating. As if by some invisible signal Haj Kabir, Haja Mana and Haj Saif simultaneously started to sing a prayer. The large dark-skinned man put his hand to his chest, and Shaafia did the same. It was not a prayer she recognised.

When the prayer concluded with a rousing: «*Allah Akbar!*» Ibrahim passed round the filled bowls.

«In honour of our guest, this soup was made with the last of the sheep we slaughtered for Eid Al Adha.» said Haja Mana.

«It is wonderful.» said Shaafia, after her first sip. Then she looked at Ibrahim. «Thank you for making this.»

He nodded and put his hand up to his chest.

«He does not speak.» said Haja Mana.

The soup was enjoyed in respectful silence. Ibrahim gestured to Shaafia when she emptied her bowl, and she smiled and handed him her bowl which he refilled. As he did so their eyes met, and she knew that he had no need to speak. She could hear him clearly inside.

To conclude the meal there was sweet flat bread, small round almond cookies and mint tea. As this was being consumed, the old couple asked Haj Kabir for news from his Mosque.

As he spoke of different people and what was happening, Shaafia found herself feeling deeply tired, as if the soup had a soporific effect.

Haja Mana noticed and gestured to Ibrahim. He stood up, took Shaafia's small suitcase, and beckoned to follow him.

Shaafia stood for a moment in the doorway.

«My heart feels so full.» she said. »It is a blessing to be here.»

«It is a blessing to welcome you, my child.» said Haja Mana.

Shaafia followed her tall guide out to the back of the house and then plunged into the fog. The cold was sharp and chilled her face as she walked. She was grateful she had brought the coat, the beanie and the mittens.

There was a stony path leading away from the house up a short rise to a small stone hut. Ibrahim pushed open the door and stood back, inviting her to enter.

It was a very simple interior, just one room. In one corner were sleeping mats and a pile of blankets. In another corner was a water butt. High on one wall was a sconce with three tall candles already burning.

Ibrahim put down her suitcase and turned to face her. His eyes shone and she felt so much love coming from them. They stood facing each other with hands on their hearts, before he turned and went to the door, then giving her a little wave, he closed it behind him.

Although there appeared to be no source of heating the room felt warm. Shaafia opened her suitcase and prepared to go to sleep. The desire for sleep was powerful. She washed her hands and face from the water butt, laid out a sleeping mat and several blankets and snuggled under them. Instantly she dived into the deepest of sleep, even before she could begin to recite her Koranic verse.

In the silence of the early morning, she came awake to the sound of the Muezzin calling the first prayer of the day. She jumped out of bed. The candles were still burning, seeming not to have diminished even though they had burned all night.

She felt drawn to find the Mosque. Using the water butt in the corner she sluiced her face in the cool water. She put on her coat, beanie and mittens, and plunged out into the fog. She could still hear the voice of the Muezzin over a crackly loud speaker. She was about to walk in the direction of the sound, when Ibrahim appeared out of the fog.

He gave her a little wave, and then beckoning for her to follow him, he loped off along a rocky little track.

Feeling snug in her winter clothes, Shaafia hurried to keep up with her long-legged guide. She noticed that he had no shoes and his naked feet were not troubled by the stones on the path.

The Mosque was similar to the house of Haja Mana, built of stone but with the addition of four large, somewhat rusty loudspeakers on the roof facing in the four directions. There was no minaret.

Ibrahim washed his feet and hands from a tap at the side of the building, and invited Shaafia to enter. She washed up and then left her shoes by the door before following him inside.

Several shadowy figures were already there in the one single space, without any obvious male and female section. Shaafia went into a corner to watch what was happening so she could follow, however it seemed that each prayer and ritual appeared to be individual. Some were further into the ritual movements than others, while several appeared to be doing actions that Shaafia did not recognise at all. She saw that Ibrahim had begun his own set of rituals so she simply followed her own at her own pace.

As she went through the motions of the morning ritual she began to sense that there were many more beings in the Mosque than at first appeared. Some were definitely real while others were more ethereal, some floating above the floor. In several instances she began to see how some of the physical attendees were actually in communion with some of the less physical. While she completed her own ritual she was fascinated to glimpse what was going on around her.

Soon a deep desire to become still overcame her, and she backed up against the wall and closed her eyes.

At first there were the echos of her prayers eddying at the edges of her consciousness before she found herself diving deep. She rested in a warm cavelike environment in which gentle waves of wellbeing caressed her spirit.

How long she stayed like that she could not tell, but when she eventually ascended back towards physical consciousness she felt as if she had been bathing in some warm nurturing pool and was deeply refreshed.

When she opened her eyes the Mosque was empty, and the first hints of daylight touched several small square windows high up on the Mosque walls.

When she stepped out of the Mosque the fog was still very thick. Ibrahim was squatting calmly on a rock slightly up the hill. He could have been a statue, he was so still. When he sensed her he opened his eyes and rose up on the rock. He opened his arms wide so that the folds of his white robe dropped out on either side. Then he took a big jump from the rock and seemed to float in the air before he landed near her. He flashed her a smile of dazzlingly white teeth and, expecting her to follow, he set off down the path towards the house of Haja Mana.

The house was warm and Shaafia hastened to take off her coat, hat and mittens as soon as she entered.

Haja Mana appeared from what was obviously a kitchen.

«You came well prepared.» she said, seeing Shaafia's outer garments. She fingered the fine Alpaca wool of the beanie. «So soft.» she said.

It looked like Haj Saif had not moved, still lying on the same bench as the previous evening.

«You saw some of our neighbors in the Mosque.» he said.

She smiled knowing what he meant.

«You will meet more of them.» he added.

Haj Kabir appeared and they enjoyed a cheerful breakfast of freshly baked flatbread, served with olive oil and mint tea.

Haj Kabir had to return to Casablanca later in the morning. He told Shaafia that when she was ready there would be transport to bring her back.

«You will know when is the right time to return.» he said.

With Haja Mana, Shaafia stood outside the house and waved him off, then they both went inside.

Haj Saif had finally come off his bench. He had shuffled himself to another bench and was running prayer beads over his fingers and muttering to himself with his eyes closed.

Haja Mana motioned for Shaafia to join her in the kitchen. She was unhurried in her movements, placing the walking frame out in front of her, then a right and then a left step to catch up, then repeating the process. She seemed infinitely patient with it.

There were wooden chairs round a small square table in the kitchen and she parked herself on one of them, and then invited Shaafia to join her.

«Haj Kabir has told me something of what you have done,» she said, «but I would like to hear it in your own words.»

So Shaafia told her story, and to this listener she spared no detail, knowing that she would understand everything. Haja Mana nodded now and then, laughed often, and shook her head in wonderment. Shaafia not only told her of her early childhood, the sharif and the search for the bird with crooked wings and her journey to Bordeaux, but she also included Théophile, Kate and Claire.

Part way through her narration Ibrahim came in and Haja Mana waved him to a chair to listen.

When she reached the moment when Pia left her body and ascended to be with the Virgin Mary, they both put their hands up to their hearts in salutation.

Then finally she got to describe her return and the guidance she had been given ever since. It seemed so easy to tell them what she had done and said and where her instructions seemed to come from. They knew what it was.

«And so they told me I should take a retreat to get my energy back. And here I am.»

«We will take very good care of you,» said Haja Mana. «You have a lot to do. It is good that you are young and strong. You will find there are those who will support you, like our friend Haj Kabir, but there will be others who will oppose you. The darkness does not like the light and fights to extinguish it.»

«I have seen it.» said Shaafia. «Even one of my own sisters.»

Ibrahim got up and made more mint tea and brought it to the table. He smiled at Shaafia and gestured to a window. The fog was lifting.

«He wants to take you to meet someone.» said Haja Mana.

Wrapped again in her warm clothes, she followed him out into the thinning fog.

The palest of morning suns was peering at them through the mist as Ibrahim climbed away from the house, up beyond her own little hut and on up into the craggy overhangs above it.

He strode along and she had trouble keeping up. By a large outcrop of rock he paused to wait for her. When she reached him she was breathing heavily. He gave her a friendly smile and gestured with his hands that he would go more slowly.

When she had rested for a moment she nodded, and they continued up the incline.

Finally they reached a high cliff that had no way to climb further. She looked up at the vertical rock face, wondering where he was taking her. Instead of climbing, however, he bent down and crawled into a low opening that she had not noticed. Hoping he was not going to leave her behind, she followed him into the hollow. It was only low for a short way and then opened out into what was clearly a cave.

At the far end candles were burning on natural rock shelves, several rugs were scattered on the stone floor, and on one of them sat a boy, cross-legged, draped in a white shawl.

As they entered the space he opened his eyes.

«Good morning.» he said in English with a decidedly Oxbridge educated accent.

«Good morning.» she responded, without thinking that it was strange that they were exchanging greetings in English.

Then in perfect Arabic, he said: «Ibrahim told me you were here.»

She looked at Ibrahim with surprise, and he smiled back.

«Not verbally.» said the boy, reverting to English. Then he gestured at the rug on front of him. «Please, take a seat.»

As she sat, Ibrahim went to the back of the cave where a small rivulet of water ran from high up on the wall, gathered in a small rock pool, then ran off through a crack in the floor. He held an earthenware pitcher under the rivulet and filled it. Then he brought it back with three small silver cups.

The boy thanked Ibrahim in Arabic as Ibrahim filled the cups and passed them round.

«This water is unlike any on God's earth.» said the boy. «Try it.»

Shaafia sipped the water. The effect was instant. It was as if a wave of electric energy passed through her body, it was intoxicating, somehow perfumed and soft.

He smiled as she responded to it.

«Have you ever tasted champagne?»

When she shook her head, he said: «This is champagne times ten.»

«It is wonderful.» she said, taking another sip.

«They tell me you are doing interesting things in Casablanca.» he said. «I would like to hear your story. And I suspect you are wondering about mine.»

The water was coursing through her veins and she felt lightheaded.

«It is very powerful.» she said.

«You will get used to it. How about I tell you who I am and why I am here while you let the water do its work.»

She nodded.

«As you can tell by my accent, I am English. My English name was Andrew Chauncey, but here they call me Bani. I was at Cambridge studying Classics in 1967, when something rather remarkable happened. I had a friend who was experimenting with LSD. You know what that is?»

«It is a drug?

«Hallucinogenic.»

She nodded, hoping that she understood what the word meant

«So he persuaded me to try it. I found myself tripping off. I was travelling out of my body and into some other universe. It was scary as hell, but at the same time it was fabulous. I saw universes and galaxies and all sorts of wild things. Then in the middle of it I saw this man. He was tall with white wisps of hair on his head, wearing a simple white robe, what I now know is a *djellaba*. He put his hand on my head and I smelled jasmine. He said to me, in English, because that's all I spoke back then, he said: «Do you want to live forever?» I didn't hesitate. I said «You bet I do.» Then he opened his hand and he showed me a place that I had never seen. It was here. It was El Chakour. I could see the cliffs, the fog, the remoteness of it. I wanted to go there. «Drink the water of *Ain Baraka,* in Morocco, » he said, «and you will live forever.»

He paused, making sure she was following.

She nodded, then she smiled. «You said 1967, didn't you?»

«I did.»

«You were maybe eighteen or something like that?»

«I was.» Then he grinned. «I still am.»

«So the water works.»

«It does.»

Shaafia finished the cup of water and sat there letting its effect swell through her. «Now I have drunk this water will I live forever?»

«Ah,» he said putting down his own cup. «That is something else. Destiny. We, each of us, are given maps to follow, tasks to complete. You know all about this by now. You have already met some who have followed their maps. Whether, ultimately, this is your time to live forever, that is not yet apparent. You have work to do in the world. For whatever reason, I do not. It has been shown to me that I have a different task to perform here. The catch is I may not leave here. If I did, I would revert to my actual age.»

«You have stayed here ever since?»

«Ever since.»

«Can I ask you: do you know what your task is?»

«Certainly. I support you, and others like you. By being here and following my destiny, I ensure that you, all of you, succeed.»

Shaafia felt a shift in her heart as if he had touched her there. She smiled.

«Did you know that you had that task when you came here?»

«Not at first. At the beginning I had no idea about anything. All I knew was that I wanted what he had offered. I was so intent on keeping the feeling of that encounter that I rushed out of the university, leaving everything. I told no-one where I was going. I got a cheap flight, not really knowing where I was flying to, except that it was somewhere in Morocco. That's all I knew. I landed in Marrakesh. I walked out of the airport and just kept walking. I held in my mind what that man in the *djellaba* had told me. And then there he was. Or maybe it wasn't him, maybe it was another being like him. There are lots of them, as you probably know. I spoke no Arabic back then, but whoever he was, he put me on a bus and he told the driver where I was going. It took several buses and was guided by other men in *djellabas*, until I got here. You have met Haj Saif?»

She nodded.

«He wasn't a haji back then, but he was in much the same state as you see him now. He can see things that few others can see. He was standing there when the little rattly old bus that still comes up here stopped outside the shop. Remember I had no Arabic so he couldn't talk to me. He just grabbed my rucksack and held my hand and brought me up here. I have been here ever since.».

»You never go outside?»

«I can but I don't like it much. The air here is very pure because we are in the mountains, but even here, there are currents of unpleasantness that float on the wind. I am very sensitive to them.»

Shaafia took a moment to let what he had said sink in. Then she frowned. «Why did you greet me and speak to me in English? I am Moroccan.»

«The one who awakened you spoke English.»

She smiled to think of Pia as the one who awakened her, and yet it was true. Until she met Pia she had no idea who she was or what she was capable of.

«That's true I suppose, except she didn't really speak at all, not much.»

«Some people don't need it. Do you, Ibrahim?»

Ibrahim had listened to the conversation from a far wall where he sipped his cup from time to time and rocked gently back and forth.

Now he held his hand up in benediction, and distinctly in her head Shaafia heard him, in the Berber of the south, her first language. «You are a translator. Blessings to you.»

She smiled and put her hands up to her heart.

Then she turned back to Bani.

«Can I ask you something?»

«If you think it is something you don't already know.» he said with a wry smile.

«Maybe I know the answer to this, you are right, but still you could tell me what you think. Why was I sent back to Morocco?»

«*Darou Al Bahr.*»

She nodded. «Haj Hussein, Houda and Rana.»

«Yes, them too, but mostly the very house itself. It's like a ship sailing through the choppy waters of the city. It has a destiny and you will bring it out. The daughter of Haj Hussein has nearly completed her work, but the granddaughter has not. She still sleeps.»

«Malak told her that. He yelled at her to wake up.»

«Yes. He told me about it. He told me all about you, too.»

«He comes here?»

«In a way. Then again he is a bit, what you might call, omnipresent. He tends to pop up when he is needed.»

Suddenly Shaafia laughed. «I just thought about how strange it is that you were a student in a very fancy English University, and then suddenly you are an ageless knower of things that the English would never believe in.»

He laughed with her. «Yes indeed, if only some of my chums could see me now.»

«You don't ever feel homesick?»

«Why? What an illusion I lived in, back then. No, no, I count my blessings.»

Ibrahim had returned to the small rivulet of water and had filled a large bottle. He brought it over to Shaafia.

«This is what you came for.» said Bani. «You will take this back. Malak and you together have begun to rid the house of its dark shadows, but the work is not done. There will be attempts made to draw it back into the darkness. The house can be protected. You will always have our support for that. Take this water and scatter a little in each corner of the house, in each room, in the garden, but keep plenty for later. Every drop has the power to protect you. *Darou Al Bahr* will become like El Chakour, but right in the middle of Casablanca. It will be a great support for many, many people.»

Then he closed his eyes.

Shaafia waited expecting that he would resume their conversation, but he was gone. Ibrahim gestured that they should go.

She stood facing this extraordinary «young» man. Inside herself she thanked him, and she sensed his response. «We will meet again.»

Then she dropped to her knees and kissed his feet.

He did not move.

As they descended the hill, with Ibrahim carrying the precious water, she spoke to him in Berber.

«Thank you for being my guide.»

She heard him on the inside. «It is my honour.»

When they reached the house of Haja Mana, she found several other people had arrived. They were all women of much the same age. As she walked into the house, ushered in by Ibrahim, she heard them laughing.

Haj Saif was sitting up and telling some kind of story.

«There she is,» he said. «Come in my child, I have just been telling our neighbors what you have been up to.»

As she looked around the group, what struck her was their eyes. They were older women, faces lined with the experience of long life, but their eyes were clear and full of light. Instantly she knew that each of them was special.

She smiled and felt a lightness in her own heart. How grateful she felt to be in such company.

«So you have been to see Bani.» said Haj Saif. «You are fortunate. He sees very few people. He is very sensitive to impurity.»

«I have never seen him,» said one of the women, «and I have lived here all my life.»

«These ladies invite you to join them for lunch. They were waiting for you.» said Haj Saif.

«Come.» said one of them, and got up.

Ibrahim gestured that he would put the precious bottle in her little house, then Shaafia followed the ladies.

As they walked, they chattered away, telling her about their village. It was not that they were describing something strange or supernatural, but in the telling Shaafia could sense that there was deep knowledge in these women.

As they passed each house they would say who lived there. At one point one of them pointed high up above the village to rocky outcrops like the one Shaafia had climbed to visit Bani.

«Up there,» said the woman, «there are others like our Englishman. Some have been there, so they say, for hundreds of years.»

«If you look at our Mosque,» said one of the others, «see how we have the big loudspeakers? That is so that all of us, even those who have not left their caves for centuries, can hear the muezzin.»

«We take care of them», said another of the women, «and they take care of us.»

They entered a house very similar to Haja Mana's house.

The low table around which they sat had multiple small tajines, each with a different ingredient. Each lady had brought her own speciality.

«Our village is remote.» said one of them as the meal progressed. «We are protected from many things. The fog that descends almost every day is no ordinary fog. It is a shield. There are forces that attempt to destroy us, constantly. Every one of us, even if we look like simple country peasants, each of us is engaged in that battle.»

Another of the women added: «We are also a haven for those who engage in that battle out in the world. You are one of those. Haj Saif has told us about what you are doing. We salute you, we wish you well, and we support you.»

They in their turn asked her about her own jouney, her awakening. What amazed them was that Pia was Australian, and the nuns who totally accepted her were religious Christians. These women had all grown up in the sufi tradition and from their perspective the mystic aspects of their lives was rooted in that tradition. That this kind of mystical work took place in other religions fascinated them. They adored her stories, laughing and clapping as she told them so many anecdotes. They all said that they would offer their prayers for the good work that was being done by those who had been awakened by Pia. They loved the idea of the château in France, as being a little like El Chakour.

Shaafia felt close to tears as she looked at this group of women. There was a time when she knew nothing except the command of one mysterious sharif who gave her the quest. Now here she was in the company of many who knew who she was, knew what she was being asked to do, and were able to help her. It moved her deeply.

In the late afternoon, walking back to her small chalet on the hill, feeling nourished on every level, she felt the need to close her eyes.

She went inside and saw the bottle of *Ain Baraka*. She laid out a sleeping mat and sat with her back against the wall. She uncorked the bottle and took a small sip, knowing that the water was precious and should be kept for the future.

As the cool liquid ran down her throat her focus dived inside. A great swirl of light coursed around her, and she felt as if every cell of her body was being recharged with that light. Then she dived even deeper and descended into a vast dark cave of superb serenity, and she rested there.

When she came back it was evening and the fog had shrouded the hills above the village. She heard the muezzin call the last prayers of the day, but could not summon the will to get up and go to the Mosque.

Then she noticed the covered pot just inside the door. The aroma of soup became apparent. Ibrahim had been and gone, silent as ever.

The soup was delicious, its warmth seeming to reach the far extremities of her body. She placed the empty pot outside the door and went back to her sleeping mat. Within minutes she was asleep and did not wake until she heard the morning prayers being called.

She dressed in all her warmest clothes and headed through the fog to the Mosque. Ibrahim was not to be seen.

Inside the Mosque were shadowy people, hard to recognise in the dim light of only a few candles.

She completed her own set of rituals and sat for a while.

When she went back to her little chalet, by the door, was another pot. It was hot, and inside she found a kind of barley broth sweetened with honey.

Once again, as soon as she had finished the pot, its warmth powering through her veins, she was drawn back inside herself.

When at last she opened her eyes, he was sitting there.

«Good morning, Ibrahim.» she said in Berber and he smiled, gesturing out through the one small window. It was dark outside. She had been gone all day.

He showed her the warm pot he had brought.

Then with his hand over his heart he was gone.

The next two days followed the same pattern. She would wake to the sound of the *Muezzin*, go to the Mosque for the morning prayers, come back to find the breakfast pot hot and ready to be enjoyed, and then she would sit in long and deep meditation. She could feel the recharge happening inside herself. There was a strength building in her, a power that she knew was her own, long dormant, but now being unleashed.

And then on the last day as she awoke to the *muezzin's* call, she knew she was ready. She felt a great surge of energy, full of love. She ran to the Mosque, and with great delight offered her prayers to Allah.

She was ready.

She prayed that she would be able to serve in whatever way God wanted her to serve. She sat in the Mosque deeply absorbed for the rest of the morning. A fleeting thought made her wonder about a hot pot for breakfast, but that thought was soon gone.

At last she came back to consciousness and opened her eyes. The Mosque was empty.

She bowed deeply, her heart filled with gratitude.

When she walked back from the Mosque towards the house of Haja Mana, the the red Porsche was parked out front.

Houda was sitting with Haja Mana, who raised her hand in greeting as Shaafia walked in.

«I have just met the granddaughter of Haj Hussein.» she said.

Houda rushed across the room to hug her friend.

«We have missed you so much.» she said.

After a lunch of hot soup, retrieving her bottle of *Ain Baraka* and her suitcase, Shaafia said goodbye to Ibrahim, Haja Mana and Haj Saif. She hugged them all with tears in her eyes.

«There will be times in the future, my child, when you will need to come back. We will be here for you.» said Haja Saif.

Before she closed the door of the Porsche, Shaafia looked up the hill. She could not see the cliffs above the village in the fog, but she knew where Bani's cave was. She put her hand up to her heart.

Inside herself she said: «I know you are with me.»

As Houda carefully negotiated the rocky track that served as the only road into and out of El Chakour, nursing her precious Porsche, Houda told Shaafia how she came there.

«Yesterday Haj Kabir called me. He said it was time to bring you back. He gave me some very basic instructions about where El Chakour was, but he said there were no sign posts once I got into the mountains. He said I should listen to my heart and I would know where to go. It was so weird. Once I had no more directions I just kept driving. I turned here and there, without thinking about it too much, and when I got onto this goat track I began to wonder if I might end up going off a cliff, but I had faith in Haj Kabir. The fog was so thick I could barely see anything, and then suddenly I got to that house and the car stopped. I swear I did not turn it off. It just stopped.»

«El Chakour is that kind of place.» said Shaafia. Then she did her best to describe the power of El Chakour, the people who lived there, and what her experience had been over the three days.

Houda said little as she heard all this. There were moments when she wanted to ask questions but she held her tongue to let Shaafia go on.

Finally as Shaafia arrived at how she spent long periods in deep silence, and how she felt rested and ready to do what God wanted her to do, Houda said: «It is amazing to me that I had such a grandfather who knew all these powerful people, and yet I had no sense of it. My Mother more or less hid that from me as I grew up. I suppose she wanted me to be a good daughter to my Father who I am certain did not believe in any of this. And now I have to wake up. That's what Malak said to me. It is what you tell me the Englishman said to you. But what does it mean?»

Shaafia sat with the question as the Porsche now purred along a regular freeway.

«I think for each of us it is different. I think that to wake up is to be aware of what is going on around us and to be aware of how best to be helpful. I was lucky because Pia guided me so clearly. Then there were other guides, other voices. Haj Hussein, your grandfather, told me that you have a destiny. Now you have to work out what it is.»

«And I have you to help me.» said Houda.

«And I will have help.» returned Shaafia. «You have seen Malak. You sense what Haj Kabir knows. There are others. Soon you will be able to hear them and they will guide you. We are not alone.»

They drove in silence for a while, and then Houda decided it was time to tell Shaafia what had taken place while she was gone.

«Everybody missed you.» she said. «I got so many calls asking where you had gone and how to contact you.»

«That's why I left my phone with my Mother, and turned it off.»

«Well my Mother was so worried about you. She thought maybe her sister had done something.»

Shaafia smiled. «Where I was, Daad could not touch me.»

«And then there was my Uncle Taj. The effect you had on him the day we did the meeting, was incredible. He would call my Mother, many times, and he was crying on the phone. He was begging her to forgive him, and he was desperate for you to help him. He said he can't sleep because his mind keeps going crazy. He can't organise anything. His life is in ruins, he says.»

«He left me a message.» said Shaafia.

«Will you help him?»

«The question is whether he can help himself. We will see.»

There were others, Houda reported, several people hoping Shaafia would work for them as translator, especially Rana's lawyer. Walid had asked several times if they had heard anything, and Alex was keen to meet her again.

Shaafia nodded.

«Soon enough,» she said, «I will be busy again.»

Entering the chaotic traffic of the city was something of a shock. As Houda braked and tooted her way round trucks and taxis, avoiding scooters and the occasional donkey, Shaafia felt like her eyes and her ears were being assaulted, her heart was being battered, her mind was being impregnated. She had sat with the bottle of *Ain Baraka* in her lap and now she took a small sip.

«Thirsty?» asked Houda.

Shaafia nodded. She had not mentioned what kind of water was in the bottle that rested on her lap. This was not the moment. She slipped the bottle back into her bag.

However the effect of the sip was immediate and soothing. It was as if a muffler had surrounded her to soften the impact. The chaotic streets seemed remote and benign, like watching bees at a flower. There was a certain beauty to it.

Her heart eased and her mind was at rest.

She asked Houda to drop her at the Mosque so she could attend the early evening prayers. She promised to call Houda the next day and they would get together soon.

She sat in the quiet of the Mosque, so familar to her, and yet since her retreat there was a new energy there. She knew that energy was in her, not the Mosque.

When the prayers were over, she took her suitcase and the bottle of precious water and began the short walk home. The sky had pale wisps of cloud now roseate with the setting sun. Crows sat observant on roof tops, black silhouettes against the sky.

She felt at peace with herself and the world. Her retreat had been just what she needed, and she felt ready to face whatever was to come next.

Whatever came next

It came fast.

As she approached the house, she heard shouting. When she ran in, she saw Nayla standing over her younger sister Hawa, screaming at her and hitting her with her fists. The other younger sister, Yamina, was trying to pull her off. Their Mother lay against a far wall crying.

Dropping her suitcase and her handbag, Shaafia screamed at the top of her voice.

«Allah!»

It had the effect of freezing the entire scene.

Still holding the bottle of water, she walked purposefully up to Nayla, who had turned at the sound of her voice, and Shaafia blew forcefully directly into her face. The power of her breath pushed the girl back against the wall and she crashed to the floor. Yamina crouched to help Hawa to her feet and their Mother pulled herself up from the floor. Shaafia could see that her face was bruised and her nose was bleeding.

Shaafia stood over Nayla.

«You think because I am not here that you can terrorise the family? You have no power here. Even if I am not here you will have no power. Not until you have purged all the darkness out of your veins can you come back into this house. This house is forbidden to you.»

Nayla tried to speak, but somehow she seemed to be choking instead. She gasped for air, backed up against the wall. Shaafia stood over her watching. Then she lifted the bottle of *Ain Baraka,* took a mouthful and then she stood over Nayla and spat it over her head.

Nayla screamed and writhed as if she were being burnt, then she struggled to her feet and ran.

Hawa and Yamina had watched all this, but now turned to help their Mother who was sobbing uncontrollably. Shaafia joined them. She took another small sip from the bottle and put her fingers in her mouth. Then she passed her wet fingers over her Mother's face.

It had the effect of an anaesthetic. Their Mother quietened and let herself be held by her daughters.

Samet rushed into the house yelling. «Nayla is out there. She's mad.»

Shaafia turned to face him. «She won't be back. Let her go.»

«She tried to hit me.» he yelled. He was close to hysteria.

Shaafia spoke sharply. «Samet, stop. She has gone.»

He took a breath and then noticed the state of his Mother's face.

«What did she do?»

«She is possessed. She cannot help herself.» said Shaafia calmly. «But she will not come back. May God take care of her.»

«*Inche Allah,*» murmured their Mother.

The girls helped their Mother to bathe her face and the bleeding of her nose stopped. Hawa had a big bruise reddening on her own face.

When things became quieter, Shaafia took her suitcase into the girl's sleeping area.

When she came out Hawa explained that they had been preparing the evening meal when Nayla had burst into the house and had tipped some kind of powder into the food. When her Mother had tried to stop her, she started hitting their Mother, and then the two girls tried to fight her off.

«Then you came.» said Hawa, gazing at her sister. Shaafia was by far the smallest of all the Jilani children, but very quickly they were coming to recognise that she was the most powerful.

«She cannot fight you!» said Hawa in awe.

«It is not me.» said Shaafia, gently touching her sister's bruised face. «I have help. Powerful help.»

Yamina joined them.

«You said she will not come back.» she said. «Are you sure? What if you are not here?»

«I will protect this house.» said Shaafia. «She will not be able even to walk up the alley.»

«After what you did to her, she won't want to,» said Hawa.

«Oh she wants to.» said Shaafia. «She is driven now. She is desperate. The one who taught her is also desperarate. They are fighting to survive because the forces against them are strong. They will try and they will fail.»

Samet growled. «We should kill them, slit their throats.»

Shaafia smiled at her brother. «No,» she said, «too messy. We should send them our love. That will kill them in a different way.»

«It is the way.» said their Mother. «This is what your Father would have said. He knew what she was but he never hated her.»

Then Hawa frowned. «You spat liquid on her. What was it?»

Shaafia decided to tell them.

«First,» she said, «we must empty all the pots that she touched and clean them thoroughly. Then we should make some simple soup and then I will tell you where I have been.»

They bent to the task, and as they did, the other boys came home, Habib, Toufik, Loqman and Sadek.

While they eliminated all the contaminated food and scrubbed the pots, the boys were told what had happened.

«Do you need anything?» asked Sadek, «I can go back to the shop.»

Their Mother stroked his cheek and assured him she had plenty.

They worked at making a soup, and as they did, Shaafia told them where she had been. None of them had ever heard of El Chakour.

«However, some of the residents of El Chakour knew our Father.» she said. «It is a village that shelters many great beings, some of them have been there for a very long time. It is a protected and sacred place.»

«So why did you go?» asked Loqman.

«I have work to do.» she said. «I know for some of you it is hard to believe, but I have to tell you that I am being directed. I am to help many people.»

«You have certainly helped us.» said Samet.

«Of course. You are my family. I will protect you all. I will protect this house. But I have much more to do than that, and so I had to make sure I was strong enough.»

«You are very strong, my daughter.» said her Mother as she stirred the pot.

Hawa asked: «Can you teach us to be as strong as you?»

Shaafia paused before she answered, wanting to be sure of her response. «It will be up to you, each one of you.»

Once the soup was served, they sat round the large low table as Shaafia described what the village was like and some of the people she had met. As she spoke Shaafia began to sense how each of her siblings was taking in what she was telling them. She could feel that all of them seemed to have arrived at a place inside themselves that recognised what Shaafia could do and were not threatened by it. However, she could also see that there were differences in each of her siblings. Some were more open than others.

«Soon,» she said, «I will move to *Darou Al Bahr*.»

They protested that they wanted her to stay with them, but she was clear. She told them it was the reason she had come back. It would be the place where her work would bear the most fruit. They would all benefit from it she promised them. And she also assured them that she had the power to protect them and their home. Nayla could not come anywhere near it.

«And even more than that,» she said, «If she ever approaches you, somewhere else, if you have no fear of her, and you should not, then you simply say my name. She will not be able to do anything to you. The protection I have, you have.»

They gazed at her. Not so long ago she was just one of them, the best student in the family perhaps, and the first to travel out of the country, but otherwise just like one of them. But not now. As she returned their looks, one after the other, she felt a great love for them, beyond just the bonds of family. There was a great power of love hovering in the air and she knew they could feel it. Some more than others, but none of them could deny that they saw their littlest sister as someone to be reckoned with.

By the time they prepared to go to bed there was a very warm feeling in the household, as if Nayla did not exist.

In the drama of the previous night, Shaafia had not thought to retrieve her phone. In the early morning she remembered.

She took it out to the fig tree. Her message bank was full. She scrolled through them deciding who had priority.

She called Walid.

«So,» he said, delighted to hear from her at last, «You ran away. There must be a story to this.»

«There is,» she responded, «But I will not tell you until you and your Father are in the same place.»

«That sounds like you are inviting yourself to lunch. Are you free today?»

«I could be.»

«Don't tell me you have competing requests.»

«My phone is full of them, but maybe your Father could be on top of my list seeing he is the oldest and the elderly deserve our respect.»

«I will pick you up myself,» he said, «and my father will walk you to the table.»

After that call, Shaafia knew she had some time before her chauffeur would reach the end of the alley.

She returned the call of Taj Bin Salah.

The phone rang for some time, and she was beginning to think he would not pick up when he finally did.

His voice was strangled and blurry.

«Why are you calling me?»

«I am answering your call.» she replied, her voice calm and quiet.

«That was days ago.»

«I have been away and I did not take my phone with me. I have just returned. However, if you do not want to talk to me then I am sorry I have disturbed you.»

«Disturbed me? Listen girl, I don't know who you are or how you did what you did, but you have ruined my life.»

«Is that what you think? If you recall, which I am sure you do, I did nothing to you at all. I simply let everyone at that meeting know the truth.»

«Why did you do that?»

«Truth forces itself to be known. When it is hidden, truth is not happy.»

«But what did you get out of that? Are they paying you?»

She let that hang in the air, until he thought she had gone.

«Are you still there?»

«Oh yes,» she said. «I was trying to think of what to say to you. I see that you live in a world where money, however it is gained, is the most important thing. I don't live in that world.»

«OK,» he said, «Look I am sorry about what I just said, but you have to understand that my life is hell now. I can't sleep. Everything in the business is going crazy. I have debts that I can't service. I have to pay Rana or I will be in huge trouble. My lawyer refuses to do anything for me any more. I blame you for that. He knows a lot about what I have done. And it seems you do, too. How you know all that I can't work out. Now I am asking you, no I am begging you, can you please turn this off, this nightmare?»

«Ah, now I can hear you very clearly.» she said.

«Can you help me? Please.»

«I can,» she said, «but only if you are willing to help yourself.»

«I don't know what that means.»

«It means you will have to do many things that will be painful. There will be things that will make people despise you.»

«I have those already.»

«Do you know the Mosque where Haj Kabir is the Imam?»

«I do.»

«You should go there for all five of the daily prayers tomorrow. You should fast all day and you should offer *sadaka* of ten thousand dirhams to Haj Kabir at the end of the day. Then on the day following I will meet you there after the morning prayers.»

«I will do as you say.» His voice was flat, there was desperation and resignation in it.

«Tonight,» she said, «before you go to bed, pray to your brother for his forgiveness. Pray with deep sincerity. Then you will be able to sleep.»

«I will.»

«May God give you the strength.» she said, and closed her phone.

She sat there for a moment, her back against the fig tree.

The conversation had drained something from her and she took a moment to regain her inner strength. She saw El Chakour in her mind, the fog swirling around the four rusted loudspeakers of the little Mosque, and she smiled to herself.

«I hear you.» she said to them, in her mind.

Then she called Rachi.

Rachi screeched in excitement when she picked up the phone.

«Where did you go?» she yelled, «We wanted to tell you our news. We have our passports, we have our visas, we have our tickets. We are going to Bordeaux!»

Shaafia told her she was so glad to hear that. She told Rachi she was going to be busy but she would come and see her soon.

The last call was to France. As it rang, she felt the deep love for the people at the other end. They were part of her awakening. They knew what she knew. When Marie-Louise picked up, the sound of her voice brought a lump to Shaafia's throat. Her beloved Marie Louise, her protector. For her part Marie-Louise was ecstatic to hear who had called, and she yelled to whoever was close that it was Shaafia. Suddenly there was Berenice shouting in her now very fluent French, demanding when Shaafia was coming back. Shaafia promised it would not be too long, and then the phone went back to Marie-Louise. Berenice had obviously run to tell her parents who was on the phone, and soon Shaafia was talking to Zena and then to Michael. Théophile and Claire had gone into the city. Shaafia shared some of her news and learned that life in the château was going well. Many people were visiting, some came to stay overnight and even longer. Hélène was doing well, and now had some work tutoring some local children.

When she closed her phone Shaafia bathed in the afterglow of the contact. Talking to them was a tonic, no matter what was said.

She said goodbye to her Mother, whose face was healing, and walked towards the corner of the alley. The morning sun warmed her face and she felt at peace with herself. The recharge of her retreat was pulsing inside her and as she walked she was conscious that with each step she was aware, alert and confident. It was perhaps as if she was feeling, for the first time, that she was an adult now.

Long gone was the shy, nervous young girl, so unsure of herself.

Respecting her dislike of the noise, Walid had left his Italian monster at home and had come in the more sedate Renault. When she saw the car she went over, but he wasn't there.

She glanced into the café and saw that he had joined the boys at their accustomed table.

She went in and gave the owner a sweet wave.

«Can I make you a coffee?» he called. «On the house.»

She smiled and nodded, and went to join the boys.

They all jumped up when they saw her.

«Gentlemen, please be seated,» she said in English, and they laughed and did as they were told.

Walid said: «I wanted to hear how the school project is coming along.»

Samet shook his head. «We have to admit that it is not as easy as we thought.»

Shaafia took a spare chair next to Nabil. She looked around the table. The boys were looking at her with serious faces. She felt a wave of love for them. They were good boys, well-intentioned but lost. Inwardly she prayed that they find their way, each of them.

«Why is it so difficult?» she asked.

«Regulations,» said Dari, as ever wearing his suit. «You can't just open a school. It's illegal.»

She nodded. «So what is the solution?»

«That's what we can't agree on.» said Samet. «None of us has any qualifications, no teacher training.»

Yusuf added: «To be a teacher you would have to go to a teacher training college or university. That would take years. Even then, to start a school, you would have to apply, show all kinds of evidence that you had the right credentials. It's a nightmare.»

«So you are giving it up?» asked Walid.

They all shook their heads.

Samet said: «We love the idea of helping gifted kids who get stuck in the dull ditches of education, the way it is now. We just can't think of how to do it.»

«So maybe,» said Shaafia, «it is because you are thinking about it the wrong way.»

The entire table fixed its eyes on her.

She smiled and looked up. Her coffee was being brought to the table. She thanked the owner and took a sip.

Then she said: «What is the the core of this project, this idea?»

«Like I just said,» Samet growled, «to give kids the opportunity to make the most of their gifts.»

«So why does that have to be a school?»

The boys frowned. «How else?» asked Yusuf.

Shaafia looked across at her brother. «You rail against the education system, but the only way you can think about your project is in the context of the education system you criticise.»

His eyes narrowed at her critique, but he nodded.

Walid asked: «You have something in mind?»

«Maybe,» she smiled, «but you have to work it out. Go back to your original impulse. And then think about all the ways it could be achieved, eliminating what is not possible. Find what is possible.»

«Why don't you tell us what to do?» asked Nabil.

«Because it has to be your project. When you find the right way, it will be yours and you will succeed, not because you did what I told you to do.»

Then she drained her coffee and stood up.

«You will find it.» she said, and nodded to Walid who got to his feet.

«You should take that as a blessing.» he said to the boys. «Let me know when you have something.»

At the door Shaafia turned back.

«Next time I don't want to be the only girl in the room.»

He opened the door for her, and then as they drove away he laughed.

«You certainly know how to get them going.»

She smiled. «They are great boys, very smart. They will find something.»

«Can you «see» what it is?» he asked, accentuating the «see».

«It doesn't matter whether I can or not. If they find it, and they work at it, they will succeed. It is up to them.»

«You are not going to tell me?»

«No.»

«OK. I am not offended.»

She turned to look at him and he glanced sideways, although the traffic demanded his constant attention.

«You believe me?»

«Not entirely.»

«I should be more careful what I say.» he grinned.

They drove in silence for a moment, then he asked her where she went for her retreat. She said a little about El Chakour, but wanted to wait till his Father was with them.

Then she asked about what he had been doing while she was away.

«Oh, I thought you would know all about that already.»

«How could I?»

«Because you have that Mystic Girl power to know a lot of pretty strange things.»

«I think you misunderstand me.» she said. «Sometimes I am given something, some information, because it serves a good purpose. What you did while I was away doesn't seem to qualify.»

«Oh-oh, I could be offended again.» he said with a smile. Then he told her that he had been to Bin Salah Transport with Rana, and had begun to work out how they would proceed.

«Have you met with Mr Bin Salah?»

«He seems to have gone missing. No-one has seen him and he doesn't answer Rana's calls.»

«He will.»

«He is probably terrified of you.»

«I think he is terrified of himself.»

He nodded.

When they reached the Razak Compound, there was Rami sitting in a wicker chair under the front portico. There was no sign of his wheelchair, just a walking stick leaning by his chair. As the Renault pulled up, he came to his feet, took up his walking stick and approached the car.

He took several slow but steady steps then leaned forward to open the door for Shaafia.

«My dear girl.» he said as his face lit up with a gentle smile. «You cannot believe how happy and grateful I am that you have graced our home again.»

He kissed her on both cheeks, and she kissed his hands in return.

«You are walking,» she said. «and you look so healthy.»

«I am, I am.»

She took his arm as he slowly but confidently walked her into the house while Walid parked the car.

When they reached the first sitting room, there was a table arranged with all sorts of fruit juices in carafes and bowls of fresh fruit and dried fruit.

«All this for you. You are our guest of honour.»

When Walid joined them, they sat while a serving girl came in to pour whatever they ordered. When she had gone, Rami said: «I have much to tell you. And I also have so many questions. First, I really want to know where you ran away to.»

Shaafia laughed gently. «Everyone seems to think I ran away, like a fugitive. It was not like that. By now, you both know that I get instructions.»

They nodded, sipping their fruit cocktails.

«I was getting tired, maybe drained by so many things happening, and each needing my energy, so I was called to go to a place where I could recharge my batteries.»

«It looks like you did. You look very beautiful.» said Rami.

Walid added: «My Father is braver than me. I had that thought but I was not courageous enough to voice it.»

«So where did you go?» asked Rami.

Shaafia gave them a detailed description of where she went, what it was like, who lived there, and what kind of atmosphere it had. They listened intently, only now and then asking questions. The fact that Bani had not only not aged, but was also English, fascinated them.

«We should take Alex up there and then he could work for Razaks forever.» laughed Walid. Then he quickly added: «I mean that as a joke.»

She smiled. «If it is in his destiny, why not. He might outlive Razaks.»

«You don't think Razaks will last forever?»

«Nothing worldly lasts forever, only what is eternal.»

After a while Rami invited them into the adjacent room where the low round table was already laid out with many dishes. Now Rami was able to sit the way he had done all his life before his stroke.

Again, the serving girl appeared to dish out what each person chose. It was a sumptuous feast, more than enough for a dozen people.

When it felt like the right moment, Shaafia asked Rami: «So you took part of my suggestion to heart and you are walking again. Can you tell me about what else you have done?

«I have not been idle.» he said.

«I can see that. Whatever it was, the change that I see in you is not just because you have rediscovered your legs.»

«We have done something that I would never have dreamed of.» said Rami, looking at his son.

«After our meeting with Taj Bin Salah I told my Father what you had done. How you knew about his double dealing and hidden assets.»

«It made us think about ourselves.» said Rami. «We are business people, as successful as anyone and, like so many business people, not everything we have done was, what shall we say, completely honest, legal, or even fair.»

«We imagined having a meeting with you.» said Walid.

Shaafia nodded.

«We listed everything we could think of, that was not right in the eyes of Allah, or as we imagined, in your eyes.»

«Your mystical eyes.» added Walid.

Shaafia said quietly: «And you have made efforts to undo the damage.»

Rami reached over and patted her hand.

«Exactly.» he said.

Walid added: «Some of it was not possible to undo. There are people who we did not treat well, who have passed on. It is too late. In some cases we could help their families, but not all.»

«You cannot imagine what a relief it was to do all this. It has been my full time occupation ever since Walid talked about it.»

«I can see it.» she said.

«So, in one way, I have taken your words to heart about taking care of people, but I am sure you meant more than that.»

«There is always more,» she said, «and it is closer than you think, if you look carefully enough.»

«What do you mean?»

«I will give you an example. How well do you know the girl who served our beautiful lunch?»

Rami frowned. «She is good at what she does. Very polite. I like her.»

Walid was looking at Shaafia seriously. «What do we not know?»

«She walks with a slight limp. Did you notice that?»

Rami said: «Now you mention it, you are right.»

«But you don't know why.»

Rami shook his head.

«But you do.» said Walid.

«Both her parents are partially paralysed. She carries them from their beds, she bathes them, she gets them their meals, and then she comes to work. Her salary is the only money the family has. She has not married because they need her. She limps because her back has suffered from carrrying them.»

«You can see this?» asked Rami.

«Ask her.»

Walid got up and went to the kitchen.

When he came back the girl followed.

«Is something wrong, sir?» she asked, her voice a little shaky.

«No, not at all. You have done a wonderful job.»

She smiled nervously and dropped her head in acknowledgement.

«I want to ask you something. First, please, take a seat.»

He gestured to a cushion next to him and she shyly perched on it, not really looking at ease.

When Rami asked her about her parents, her eyes widened. She admitted, with some prompting that, yes, they were both unable to take care of themselves. Yes, her salary was the main family source of income. No, she was not married.

The girl was clearly shaking with nervousness having to answer all these questions. Was she about to be fired?

«You have done very good work in this house.» said Rami.

The girl smiled nervously.

«Even though you have a big challenge in your life. So this is what I would like to do. I have a good friend who is considered perhaps the best surgeon in Casablanca. I will arrange for him to see your parents. My people will drive them to appointments as we make them. I will pay for all treatments that are required. I will engage and pay for a full-time person to take care of your parents.»

She stared at him in disbelief.

«But sir, I ... we....,» and then she began to cry.

Shaafia got up and went round to the girl and put her arms around her.

«Listen carefully.» she said. «You have given your life to your parents as a good daughter should. Now God has seen a way to repay you for your love and care.

You must learn how to accept what God gives.»

The girl wiped away her tears so she could look intently at Shaafia.

«You sing, don't you?» asked Shaafia.

The girl's eyes widened with amazement. She nodded.

«But you are not trained.» said Shaafia softly, «You have no time.»

«What do you sing?» asked Walid.

The girl looked up shyly. «My grandmother taught me how to sing to God. She told me she could hear her voice in my voice.»

«Then we must do something about that, too.» said Rami. «Tomorrow you will come to see me and we will discuss how to take care of you, your parents, and your voice.»

«One day,» said Shaafia, «Your voice will reach many. It will be the way that you repay God.»

The girl stood up.

«I don't know what to say. My heart is too full.» Then she turned and ran back into the kitchen.

Rami sat there staring after her.

«I had no idea.» he said.

«There are so many like her.» said Shaafia. «More and more you will recognise them. And as you help each one you will become lighter and lighter.»

When finally it came time for Shaafia to leave, Rami escorted her to the front while Walid brought the Renault.

«I am beginning to believe that I must have done some good things along the way to have you come into my life.»

She smiled. «You have done many good things. And you will do many more. Your life will become more and more interesting as you go along.»

«Such wisdom from one so young.» he said, and kissed her on both cheeks. She in turn kissed his hands.

«You will come back soon.» he said. «You must.»

On the homeward journey Walid was quiet.

At last he turned to her and he said: «I have to stop asking you how you know things. I would never have guessed that the girl could sing. How could I know that?»

«If you need to know something it comes to you. If something comes to you it is because you need to know about it.»

«That's all too much philosophy for me.»

«Well now you know she sings because now you need to know about it. She will be so grateful to you and your Father. What you will do for her will bring joy to many people.»

«The truth is,» he said, «I really know almost nothing about any of our people. We just hire them to do a job.»

«So you have some work to do.»

«That's funny», he said with a grin, «I first hired you to work for me, now I work for you.»

She smiled. «No you don't. You work for yourself. You work for your best self.»

«OK. I can't really argue with that.»

He dropped her off at the corner.

«Alex would like to meet.» he said. «Can you come tomorrow?»

«He tried to call me before I left.» she said. «I can meet him tomorrow.»

«I have early meetings at the office so I will get Ihab to come and get you.»

Then he handed her an envelope. «This is for the previous meeting and something extra. I know we have not discussed a fee, but if you think it should be more let me know.»

She smiled. «I am sure it is more than adequate.»

«OK. Tomorrow.» and he put his hand up to his heart.

As she watched the Renault drive off into the late afternoon trafic, a warm wave of gratitude flowed through her. She loved how the ripples of beneficence radiated out from the guidance she received, passing from one person to another, waves of benevolence..

As she turned to walk up the alley she saw Rana's old Coccinelle drive up with Toufik at the wheel and one of his friends beside him.

«I did what you said,» he yelled out of the window. «I got my licence and the car goes like a dream,» and he revved the engine to demonstrate.

Another wave of gratitude passed through her.

Before she went into the house she opened Walid's envelope. The cheque was so much more than she expected.

She sat for a moment with her back against the trunk and closed her eyes. She allowed the sensations to radiate through her body. She felt a deep harmony.

When she opened her eyes her brother Loqman was watching her.

She smiled when she saw him and beckoned for him to come and sit with her.

«Do you remember Dada?» she asked.

He nodded. «She died, didn't she.» he said.

«Yes. It was very sad. She used to look after me.» explained Shaafia, «In some ways, when I was little, she was my best friend.»

He nodded. «Were you thinking about her?»

«She used to say that one day I would do very important things. She always believed in me.»

«She was right.»

«She was. Do you know, when I was about nine years old, I went with her one Friday to the market to buy *Ras el Hanout.* I used to do that every Friday.»

He nodded.

«We met a holy man, a Sharif. He put his hand on my head and he told me to find the Bird with Crooked Wings. And I did, and everything that has happened to me since has come because of that.»

«The crippled girl in France?»

«No, she wasn't crippled. She was a mystic, a kind of sharif herself, even though she could not speak or do anything for herself.»

«But you could hear her voice.»

Like everyone else in the family he had heard the story already.

«Yes. And then somehow she seems to have transferred to me what she could do.»

«I wish I could meet someone like that. I feel sort of useless.» he said.

«You have to wait. Soon enough you will find out what you are supposed to do.»

«You really believe that?»

«I can see it.»

«Why don't you tell me what it is?»

«Because you are not ready yet.»

They sat together for a moment.

Finally he leaned over and gave her a hug and they got up and went into the house.

Moving in

The following morning when she checked her phone, Shaafia saw that there was a message from Rana urging her to call as soon as she could.

Again, once the house had emptied, she sought refuge under the fig tree to call.

Rana was full of enthusiasm when she answered. She told Shaafia that Malak, the sharif who had protected her for years, had appeared in the garden of *Darou Al Bahr*. He had informed her that his work in the world was coming to an end. At first she had felt terrified, she said, fearing that she was losing that protection until he told her that he was not needed any more. As soon as the new sharif arrived in *Darou Al Bahr,* he could leave.

«The new sharif?» asked Shaafia.

«Yes. He said that as soon as she moves in he will be free.»

The words landed deep inside Shaafia's heart. She knew what it meant. The long silence that it took for her to be able to speak again made Rana think she had lost connection.

«Shaafia?»

«I am here.»

«You know what he is referring to?»

«I have already told my family that I will be moving to *Darou Al Bahr* soon.»

«When?»

«I am ready now.»

«Oh dear Shaafia, it is you. You have become a sharif.» said Rana. «What an honour for our house to have such a person living there.»

«You will move in as well?»

«We will. We will start today. When can you come?»

«I will come today.»

There was an audible sigh at the other end.

«*Ham delilah*,» said Rana, her voice resonant with emotion.

Houda would come to collect Shaafia in the afternoon.

She sat under the tree for a long while with her back against its comforting solidity.

«What does it mean to be a sharif?» she wondered to herself. And then she found herself gently laughing. «It doesn't really mean anything. It is just a label.» And yet to hear it spoken by another sharif was deeply affirmative. She let herself drop into what was becoming habitual, the deep well of gratitude.

Time disappeared and she only returned when she heard her name.

Ihab stood in front of her.

«Did you forget your appointment?» he asked.

She smiled up at him. «I think I did.»

As they drove through the morning traffic, she told Ihab about her visit to El Chakour. He seemed to be open to hearing about that, and the mystical aspects did not seem too strange for him.

«You have changed a lot.» he said. «I used to resent how our father seemed to think you were something special. Now I can see what he meant. Our family was in such bad shape when he died and I think somehow you have saved it.»

She put her hand on his elbow as he drove, and she said: «I am glad you can see that. I think that our father was a great person, but in his life he could not do for his family what he hoped. Now he can.»

He dropped her at the Razak office.

«You don't need to pick me up afterwards,» she said, «I have things to do in the city.»

Alex jumped up when he saw Shaafia and gave her a spontaneous hug, lifting her off the ground.

Then he gently put her down.

«Sorry,» he said, «I know that is not a very traditional way to greet a young lady in Morocco but I couldn't help myself.»

«I don't think you did any damage.» she smiled.

«Thank goodness. That would be a black mark against my name and I wouldn't want that.»

They walked to Walid's office and found him on the phone. He waved them to chairs while he concluded his conversation.

When he finished, he spoke into an intercom and ordered refreshments to be brought, then he looked up.

«Well,» he said, speaking in Arabic, «Things are looking very interesting at Bin Salah Transport.»

«When you say «interesting», I hope you mean good things.» said Shaafia.

«Very good. Taj is behaving a lot more honourably. He reappeared yesterday and he was polite, even apologetic, and what's more he has made some good offers.»

«*Ham delilah.*»

The refreshments were brought in and laid out on a table.

«So Alex leaves us tomorrow,» said Walid in his best English.

«But not for too long.» agreed Alex.

While they enjoyed their choice of mint tea, English tea or coffee with little pastries, Alex laid out his latest plans using his tablet.

«Walid has seen these already, but we wanted you to see them. It seems like you are the final approval for this project.»

She looked at the different designs and let herself become empty and clear in her mind. She studied the landscaping, the resort buildings, and then the village. There was no inner signal or interference, and finally she looked up and nodded.

«It is good.» she said «It is a great first step.»

The two men smiled at each other.

«We didn't miss anything?» asked Alex.

«Not yet.»

«We hoped you would like it.» said Walid.

«When will you begin the work?»

Walid said: «It has already begun with some earth moving. All these waterworks that Alex has planned will take some preparing. Hopefully within six months we will have basic construction finished. We will take you to see it whenever you would like.»

They spent more time going over details, and Shaafia wanted to be sure that the connection with the local people was being handled well. Walid promised her that she would be involved whenever there was anything to do with the villagers.

«There is one more thing.» he said, «We want you to become a member of our team in one formal way.»

She studied him carefully and he caught the look.

«I know you have said you will not work for us full time and we respect that. However, we feel that your contribution is so important that we want to give you a retainer, a regular payment, whether you meet with us regularly or not. Will you accept that?»

She breathed in and let it sit. There was inner silence.

«OK,» she said, «If it makes you feel good to do that.»

«It does. And it will make my Father feel very happy if you accept.»

When this was translated for Alex he leaned forward and looked into Shaafia's eyes. «This is very good,» he said, «because you are the heart of this project.»

Then Walid went back to his desk and pulled out an envelope.

«We knew you would accept, so we have prepared the first payment.»

She smiled. «You are becoming something of a mystic yourself.»

Without opening it, she slipped it into her handbag.

«It goes to support my family.» she said.

When they had finished with the plans, Walid took them back to his favourite restaurant for lunch.

While they waited to be served, Alex said: «When I come back I want to go back to that house.»

Shaafia smiled. «I will be happy to welcome you,» she said, «because I will be living there.»

Walid was surprised.

«You are moving there?»

«This afternoon.»

«There is a story to tell?»

«There is.»

But she would say no more.

After she left them, she walked the few blocks to the Attijariwafa Bank. While she waited for the young woman who had been assigned to her, she opened the new envelope. Her family would be very well supported.

She banked her two cheques, and withdrew a large amount of dirhams for her Mother.

Holding her bag close to her, she took the bus home.

As the bus filled, stopping often, she began to sense the people around her. They each had a life, some were content, others not, some had uplifting destinies that she could sense, while others would face hardships. As she read what was being carried within all these people she realised that she had to protect herself from too much input. She deliberately closed down so that her mind could stay quiet. She smiled to herself when she thought of how so many younger people did that by using headphones to shut out the world around them. She repeated her Koranic verse and enjoyed the rest of the journey in solitude, even as the bus became more and more packed.

She stopped at the Mosque before walking the last few blocks. It was well after prayer time so there would normally be no-one there. She took off her shoes and peeped into the men's section.

Taj was slumped against a wall.

She stood there for a moment sending him her silent blessings, then slipped away to the women's side.

With her back to the wall she allowed the images of the last few days to flow through her.

She lost the sense of her physical body and felt she was floating in the air of the empty Mosque, but to her the Mosque was not empty. She saw her Father, an ethereal presence floating near her and radiating such love. She put her hand up to her heart and he did the same.

Then she heard his voice: «You bring great honour to the family.»

«Thank you, Ba.» she whispered.

At last she found herself back in her physical body. She bowed in the direction of Mecca as she would at the end of prayers.

That her Father was pleased with her was the best thing she could imagine.

She walked contentedly home.

Her Mother was just rising from an afternoon nap. She gave her Mother the dirhams and told her that she would be moving into *Darou Al Bahr*.

Her Mother gave her a long hug.

«Such a blessing you have become.» she murmured.

Both her parents were pleased.

Her Mother helped her to put all her things in the two red suitcases. The bottle of *ain baraka* water went into Shaafia's handbag.

Before she left the house, she sprinkled a few drops in each room and in the courtyard.

They walked together to the end of the alley towing the two big suitcases, rattling against the cobblestones.

Houda's Porsche was already there.

«Is there more to bring?» she asked.

When Shaafia shook her head, Houda said: «That's all you have in the world?»

«It's all I need.»

She gave her Mother a long hug and promised that she would come often.

«Now you have a phone you can call me whenever you like.»

Her Mother stood and waved as the Porsche shot off into the afternoon rush.

Darou Al Bahr was alive with activity.

Obviously it was all a bit last minute as Rana was organising where some of her staff would be housed in the newly completed buildings at the back. Omar hovered in the background, unsure what he could contribute. Vans were unloading at the rear by the garage, and men were carrying furniture and boxes. Rana stood in the middle of it all giving orders and yelling at misunderstood instructions.

When she saw Shaafia with her two red suitcases, she rushed over to give her a welcome hug.

She whispered as she held her. «You can't believe how happy this makes me. Now you are here. My Father must be so pleased.»

«When our Fathers are pleased then all is well in the world.» smiled Shaafia.

Rana and Houda proudly took Shaafia upstairs to her new room. It overlooked the garden and had its own ensuite bathroom.

«Do you like it?» asked Houda.

Shaafia had walked over to the window and looked out over the garden. Instead of replying, she let out a small squeal of delight and ran out of the room.

Houda came over to the window and saw why Shaafia had fled. She could see Malak sitting in his usual place. As Houda watched she saw Shaafia run to him and drop at his feet to kiss his hands. He laid his hands on her head then leaned forward and kissed her on her forehead.

Rana stood next to her daughter at the window looking down at their newly rejuvenated garden.

«Two sharifs.» murmured Rana.

And then, as if they had heard her, Malak and Shaafia both looked up to the window and raised their hands.

Houda turned to her Mother and saw tears streaming down her face.

She enfolded her Mother in her arms and held her.

When Rana and Houda arrived in the garden, Malak had gone.

«We missed him.» said Rana, still with some tears in her eyes.

Shaafia stood up and came over to her.

«He is free now.»

«He won't come back?»

Shaafia shook her head.

Rana smiled sadly. «I wanted to tell him how grateful I was for everything that he has done. How he has protected us all these years.»

«He knows.»

«We won't see him again?» asked Houda.

Shaafia turned to face Houda. «You will.» she said.

There was something powerful in the way Shaafia had spoken. Houda found her heart pounding.

«What do you mean?»

«He says you must go back to El Chakour. You will stay there for quite some time. You have to remove the layers of ignorance that have stopped you from waking up. You will take nothing with you but some simple clothes. You will not take your car or your phone. You will immerse yourself in the energy of El Chakour and the people there will help you to wake up.»

«Do I have to?»

«No.»

Houda bit her lip, knowing there was more.

«What will happen to me if I don't go?»

«Nothing.»

«Nothing?»

«Nothing. You will be like you are now. Asleep.»

Rana had watched in silence.

Now her daughter turned to her. «What do you think?»

Her Mother wiped her face with the back of her hand. «You must decide for yourself. But you will recall that when Shaafia first helped you, even in the plane, she was told that you have a destiny. You can finish what my Father could not.»

Houda looked at her Mother and something powerful opened inside her.

«I will.» she said. « Yes. I will!»

Shaafia nodded.

«Tomorrow, Haj Kabir will take you.»

«You will ask him?»

Shaafia smiled. «He already knows.»

That evening, when many of Rana's staff had returned to the compound and only two had moved into the buildings at the back of *Darou Al Bahr* Rana, Houda and Shaafia sat in the garden in the cool air. Omar busied himself watering some newly potted plants.

Birds played in the leaves above their heads, the roar of traffic was muffled by the high walls, and the far off resonance of the last prayer of the day floated in from the nearest Mosque.

After a long silence Rana said: «It feels like we have completed something.»

Shaafia nodded.

«It is true. For me it feels like I have fulfilled at least the first part of why I was asked to come back.»

«And we have regained the house.» said Houda.

«And you have found your purpose, my daughter.» said Rana.

Houda laughed, «And there I was scared to death that I would have to marry Walid.»

Rana put a hand on her daughter's knee. «Now we know him better, I have to say, he would have made a very good husband.»

«Oh, he will,» agreed Houda, «for some lucky girl. But that's not me.»

When it came time to retire and Shaafia went up to her new room, she indulged in the luxury of her own private bathroom, and then sat on her big soft bed for her evening prayers.

As she sank deep inside herself she heard their voices: «Welcome to the Sharif of *Darou Al Bahr*. We have waited patiently for you to come. Now our work will go very well.»

The Sharif of Darou Al Bahr

She woke to the sounds of the birds in the garden long before the sun rose. She lay still, her Koranic verse eddying in and out, shallow waves at the edge of the deep ocean. There was such inner contentment, while at the same time she felt the ripples of energy coming with each wave of the verse. She felt herself standing at the edge of this vast ocean knowing that she could sail out without fear.

She came back from her inner journey to the sound of a gentle knock on her door. Rana apologised for disturbing her, but wanted her to know that Haj Kabir was downstairs having breakfast with Houda and was keen to leave for El Chakour.

Shaafia found them in the kitchen. As she walked in, Haj Kabir jumped to his feet.

«What a blessing that this house has now come back into its glory. This very morning in morning prayers Haj Hussein let us know how he felt about having an awakened soul once again in *Darou Al Bahr.*»

He came over and kissed Shaafia on her forehead, and she in turn bent to kiss his hands.

«And now she begins her own blessed journey as her Grandfather had predicted.» he said, gesturing at Houda.

Houda gave Shaafia a warm hug, whispering in her ear. «Now I am ready.»

As they drank their tea, Haj Kabir told them that the previous day his Mosque had received a very beautiful large *sadaqa* from a very humble man. He offered it in the name of his brother, who had died.

Shaafia nodded. «Then surely he will be blessed for his offering.»

«No doubt.» agreed Haj Kabir.

Rana and Shafia stood and waved as the old Dacia chugged off down the Boulevard de Londres leaving a light blue trail of smoke curling lazily in its wake.

Rana sighed as the Dacia turned the corner and was gone.

«So she goes to her destiny.»

Shaafia nodded. «When you see her next time you will barely recognise her.»

As they walked back inside Shaafia told Rana that the donor of the *sadaqa* was Taj Bin Salah.

Rana stood still when she heard this.

«He gave a *sadaqa*.» she said, «and yesterday he contacted Walid to work out the payments that he promised. Perhaps this is the beginning of a new life for him.»

«If he wishes it.» said Shaafia. «This morning I will meet with him.»

«Do you think that is wise? He must be very angry with you.»

«No, he is full of remorse. He has been living in torment, and he tried to call me. When I called back, he begged me to help him. He is no danger at all except perhaps to himself.»

«Maybe you are right.»

«And even that might be changing. There is always hope that someone like him can become a good person.»

«I don't think of him as a bad person. He did what so many businessmen do.»

«I think maybe that will change. I am going to meet him this morning at the Mosque.»

«This morning? Then I will call the driver to take you.»

When Shaafia protested that she could take the bus, Rana frowned.

«You have to understand that as far as I am concerned you are now part of this family. You will use the resources that this family is blessed with. I must insist.»

He was waiting for her as the white Mercedes pulled up.

He was sitting on the step outside the Mosque, dressed in modest clothes as if he were just one of the local men after prayers.

When he saw her, he stood up.

She told the driver that she would make her own way home, and he left.

She smiled at Taj.

«Did you sleep well?» she asked.

He nodded, fearing his voice would betray his emotion.

«We can talk in Haj Kabir's garden.» she said, pointing to the gate beyond the Mosque.

As they walked in, Myriam, Haj Kabir's wife, came out.

«This is Mr Bin Salah, the brother-in-law of Rana.»

«Aah,» said Myriam, knowingly. «I will bring you some tea.»

Shaafia gestured to a bench and Taj sat with his hands in his lap, his head down.

Once Myriam had laid out the teapot and glasses on a small table and retreated inside, Shaafia leaned forward to pour the tea. She passed him a glass and took her own and sat on a bench facing him.

Above them a small sparrow twittered in the branches of an olive tree and another sparrow came to join it.

Shaafia watched them and sipped her tea.

At last she put down her glass.

«Mr Bin Salah,» she said softly, and he lifted his head and looked at her bleakly. «at this moment you may feel that your life has no value. You may think of yourself as an unworthy person. You may be full of regret for the way you have treated those who trusted you and who believed in you.»

He nodded and sipped his tea.

«How you think of yourself is important.»

Again he nodded, unwilling to say anything.

«Yesterday,» said Shaafia, «a good man performed all observances in the Mosque. He offered *sadaqa*. He began to make amends for his past actions. Last night he slept deeply. You are that man.»

His face trembled and his hand shook. He put down his glass.

«That good man can be who you wish to be.» she said softly.

«What do I have to do?» His voice was husky.

«You will know.» she said. «You will undo whatever prevents you from being that man. You will look at your life and what you have done, and you will discover what to do in order to become that man.

«That man.» he whispered.

«That good man.»

He shook his head.

Shaafia read his self-doubt. «You may not succeed all the time, but if it is your deepest wish to become that man, then you will succeed.»

«Do you think Rana will ever forgive me?»

«There is no need. Rana is a woman of great compassion. If she sees you become that good man, then she will respect what you have become. You can be certain of that.»

«My family do not know about any of this. I have hidden it. My wife and my children think I am a successful businessman.»

«They know more than you think. They can see you are in pain, but they don't know why. They will surely notice if you are able to become a different person. They will perhaps begin to see you, not just as a successful businessman, which you can still be, but perhaps as a more dutiful husband and loving father. They will be very happy about that.»

«I have not been a very good husband or father.»

«Until now.»

«Until now.»

He drained his glass and put it down.

Then he leaned forward and seemed to have a new energy.

«Do you really think I can change?»

«*Inche Allah*. Anything is possible.»

«You really believe that?»

«What is important is whether you believe it. If you believe you can change, then you will. It is up to you. If you are willing, you will have help. Help is always there.»

«Will you help me?»

«I can help you to help yourself.»

He stood up.

«I have not been very polite to you and yet you have been most generous to me.»

She stood up.

«I wish to thank you.» he said, «I don't really understand what you are and how you seem to know what you know. But maybe you were sent to make me see what I have to do.»

«*Ham delilah.*»

«May I call you from time to time?»

«If you wish.»

As if she sensed the meeting was concluded, Myriam appeared.

«Thank you for the tea.» he said.

Then he bowed to Shaafia and walked out of the courtyard.

Myriam gathered up the teapot and glasses.

«Every day another small miracle happens.» she chuckled, and Shaafia smiled.

Being so close, Shaafia decided to walk round to Rachi's house.

She found the house in a chaotic state.

Rachi grabbed Shaafia when she saw her and showed her the new suitcases she had just bought.

They would be flying to Bordeaux the following day. Yasser had been invited to attend a training camp that started sooner than expected, and so they were going as soon as possible.

Yasser seemed to be overwhelmed by the activities as his Mother and Rachi's Mother took charge of packing, choosing clothes to take and what to leave behind. He stood in the middle of it all like a soccer player who can't read the play and has lost sight of the ball.

Shaafia gave him a hug and told him she believed he would do really well in France.

«Are you nervous?» she asked.

He nodded. «I'll feel better when I get to play,» he said.

Rachi dived into her handbag and dug out the documents that she had received back from the University in Bordeaux, informing her that she could enrol in the language courses that she had chosen.

«I am so excited. We are really going!» she screamed at the top of her voice.

As Shaafia took in all the activity, the happiness of the occasion, the nervous timidity of Yasser and Rachi's anticipation, she breathed in.

Yes, they would do well, she felt.

As she stood there, she reached inside herself to a place where the voices of support came from.

«Please take care of these two young, innocent people. May they find success, and may they become good examples for others.»

«We will be with them.» she heard, and she breathed out in deep contentment.

Then she said to Rachi: «Do you have room for some gifts?»

«Of course.»

«I must send something to Madame Clae and to my friends in the château.»

«Better be quick. We fly tomorrow.»

Giving Rachi and Yasser one more hug each, Shaafia headed for her Uncle and brother's shop.

When Sadik saw her, he was delighted.

«We are opening our new shop next week.» he said, and he took her to show what they had prepared.

It had been a very small shop filled with rolls of cloth, but now they had knocked down some of the internal walls in the back to what had been storage rooms. The larger space was now lined with new shelves and displayed different kinds of cloth.

«We will have cotton in one section and wool in another section, and even some silk,» said Sadik, obviously immensely proud.

Their Uncle Samad joined them.

«What do you think?» he asked.

«I am very impressed.»

«This brother of yours is very ambitious. I would never have dreamed of doing something like this. I wouldn't have dared to take the risk.»

As she gazed around at the new premises Shaafia could sense something very clearly.

She put her hand on her brother's shoulder.

«This is just the beginning.» she said. «Soon there will be more.»

Uncle Samad was a little shocked. «Even more?»

«Oh yes. You will sell many things and your shop will be well known. In a little while you will have other shops.»

«I think I might be a bit too old for this.» he said.

«It won't matter,» Shaafia told him. «This little brother of mine is a natural shopkeeper and he needs to expand. He has inherited the shopkeeper genes of our family. You will be able to watch everything grow and you will be amazed.»

«*Inche Allah!*» said the older man.

When Shaafia told Sadik why she had come, he took her back to the other shop.

«Please take whatever you would like with the compliments of Jilani Enterprises.» he said, opening his hand in a welcoming gesture.

She chose some boxes of green tea to send to Madame Clae and some Moroccan sweets for all the others in Château Des Messanges to share.

Sadik wrapped her gifts in pretty paper and steadfastly refused to accept any payment. His Uncle totally agreed.

«You have earned it.» he said.

The chaos had died down a little when she got back to Rachi's house. Rachi took the gifts and promised to call Madame Clae as soon as they were settled.

Shaafia was about to go, when Yasser handed her a wrapped package.

«This is for Habib.» he said.

«He will miss you.» said Shaafia. «He is your number one fan.»

She gave them one last hug each and walked back to see her Mother.

Her Mother made lunch and they sat together outside in the shade of the fig tree.

«We miss you already.» her Mother smiled.

Shaafia patted her Mother's hand. «There is a part of me that is always here.»

As they were finishing, Habib came home and Shaafia gave him his present from Yasser. It was another of Yasser's football jerseys from his club. Habib was thrilled and he instantly put it on over his clothes. It was big on him but he strutted round the courtyard as if he had just scored a magnificent goal.

Shaafia stayed for the rest of the afternoon and was still there when Toufik came.

«You moved out,» he said, «but you're back again.»

«Just for a visit. I am about to go back now.»

«Are they picking you up?»

«No, I will take the bus.»

«No you won't,» he said, «I have an excellent Coccinelle that will take you there.»

She smiled and accepted his invitation.

He proudly showed her how he had begun to clean up the interior of the old car which already boasted new seats. He told her that his teacher at school had offered them to him out of an old BMW. His next project was to repaint.

«Bright blue.» he proudly told her

He was an excellent driver and she complimented him on his ease behind the wheel.

«I just love cars.» he said.

«When you find something you love then life is good, eh?»

When he dropped her off, she told him to wait while she went to find Rana. When Rana saw what Toufik had done to her old car she was very pleased.

«She went to a good home.» she said.

They had a quiet evening meal together as Rana laid out her plans for completing the renovations, shared her impressions of Walid's skill in handling of the company, and her deep pleasure in knowing that Houda had found a sense of direction.

«It seems like everything is coming together so well.»

Shaafia nodded.

«Just such a short time ago,» said Rana, «Hamza did everything and I sleep-walked obediently behind him. How things have changed.»

Shaafia nodded. «Sometimes it takes us a long time to wake up.»

Rhythms

In the weeks that followed, life in *Darou Al Bahr* established its own natural rhythms.

For Shaafia it meant rising with the first call of the Muezzins, several of which she could hear echoing like bird calls from her upstairs room. Her ensuite bathroom was a daily luxury she never quite got used to, but she loved it. As soon as she had enough money, she promised herself, she would instal modern plumbing with hot water in her Mother's house.

She and Rana would breakfast together. When it was not too hot they would sit on the terrace facing the garden. Rana had taken only four staff from her previous house. The rest would stay until the compound was sold.

Their days were spent with Rana continuing with her renovations, preparing the compound for sale, and going to the offices of Bin Salah Transport. She had taken over her husband's office and installed Walid in an office next door. Taj kept a low profile, but had accepted that Walid now oversaw the day-to-day operations. When Hamza had been in charge, Taj had been responsible for his own departments within the company, and Walid insisted that he continue while reporting to Walid.

Taj was a changed man and Walid began to see that he was actually very skilled at many things. From time to time, Shaafia would accompany Rana and they would meet with Walid and Taj.

Both men now watched Shaafia carefully in their meetings, both very aware of what she could do. It brought an honesty and clarity to their meetings which ensured that there was harmony. Both men deferred to Rana for the final decision on important issues as they knew Rana would check with Shaafia.

Several times Walid invited Shaafia to accompany him to Essaouira to look at the progess being made, and most importantly for Shaafia to meet with the fishing village folk to inform them about what was happening. Shaafia had suggested that some of the younger men be employed on the work site which was dutifully put in place. At another of Shaafia's suggestions, at the end of the month of Ramadan, each of the women in the group was given a small retainer as a goodwill gesture to ensure their continued acceptance of what was being planned. Shaafia was present for that, and they were deeply moved.

Whenever they met, Shaafia would sense how central to the village was the woman she had first met. Now they were very warm with each other as each recognised that the other had qualities that were admirable.

«We feel this is our project now.» said the woman. «We will bring our best goodwill and it will be successful.»

Shaafia asked the woman to tell her about the villagers, and as she did, Shaafia could sense who was going to be the most connected to the project and who might be problematic. The woman's insights carried an authenticity that Shaafia knew was the truth.

On each visit to Essaouira, Walid made it a routine that the same young boy would take care of the car. It was on one of those visits that Shaafia asked the boy if he was still going to school. He shook his head. His father had been a fisherman but had been injured in an accident. The family was very poor and the money the boy made from looking after cars was important for the family survival.

As Walid listened to the boy describing his life in a very simple and unashamed way, Walid glanced at Shaafia. He knew what she was thinking. He paid the boy as usual, and as they walked away Walid said: «You think we should support him?»

«Is that what you think?» she returned.

«It would cost me so little, but it would change that family's life.» he said.

When they returned to the same restaurant, warmly greeted by Asad, they quickly found out that it did not matter which day they went, the dish of the day was always superb.

Now they were treated as honoured guests and several of the regular customers would greet them like old friends. In that restaurant there was no sense of social standing or class. Everyone was there for the fish.

When they returned to the car after lunch, the car was shining.

Walid smiled. «Such a clean car.»

The boy ran his wash cloth over the door handle for a last polish.

«For you, sir, it is my pleasure.»

«What is your name?» asked Walid.

«I am Chams.» said the boy.

«Well, Chams, we have been thinking about you. We think that you should be going to school.»

The boy smiled. «I would love to go back to school. I liked it. I was good at school.»

«Maybe this will help.»Walid said, and gave the boy probably more dirhams than he would see in a week. The boy was astonished.

«Now,» said Walid, «We wish to speak with your father.»

Chams looked puzzled. «My father?»

«Yes. I wish to tell your father that I think his son is a good boy and that he should go to school.»

The boy smiled. «My Father, he knows that. He says that to me every morning.»

Shaafia put her hand on the boy's shoulder. He was the same height as her.

«This man is Mr Razak and he wishes that you have enough money to go to school. He wishes to help you.»

He stared at her and then up at Walid.

«So?» said Walid, with his eyebrows raised.

«Come!» said Chams and took off through some of the narrowest back lanes of the old city.

They arrived at a place where several motorbike workshops cluttered a cul-de- sac with bike parts and bike bodies, pools of grease and the stench of exhaust. The boy saluted several of the young men, most of them covered in grease, as he went past. Shaafia smiled as she followed the boy, stepping carefully to avoid puddles of filthy water and thinking of her brother Toufik.

Beside one of the workshops was a narrow stairway that led to a small open flat roof. At the far one end was a wooden structure in need of paint and repair. On a box in front of it sat a man in a worn traditional long robe.

«Ba!» yelled the boy, as he ran up the stairs.

When Walid and Shaafia got to the top, they saw the boy breathlessly talking to his Father. The Father held the dirhams that Walid had given to Chams.

The man struggled to his feet as they approached.

«Your son has looked after my car very well.» said Walid.

The man nodded.

«He tells me that he cannot go to school because you are injured.»

«He tells the truth.» replied the man. His voice was quiet and he did not like to make eye contact with Walid. Instead he glanced at Shaafia.

She smiled at him.

«Your son brings honour to your family.» she said.

The man put his hand to his heart, unwilling to speak.

Walid brought out his wallet. «I wish to sponsor Chams so that he can get an education.»

He took several hundred dirhams out. He handed them to the man.

«It would be my honour to support such a good boy.»

The man put his hand round his son's shoulder.

«May God bless you, sir.» he said, his voice thick with emotion.

Walid then told Chams how to find Ayman, his security person. It would be Ayman who would give the boy a regular payment.

As they walked back through the narrow streets, Walid said: «There must be a thousand boys like that.»

«There are,» said Shaafia, «but this one boy will reward you in a way that will astonish you.»

«You can see that?»

She smiled.

When they went back to the resort site, Walid explained to Ayman what had just happened, telling him that he would be responsible for looking after the regular payments.

«This boy is a special project for me so I want you to look after him.»

From then on, on each trip to Essouira, Walid would ask Ayman to arrange to make sure that Chams was there. Walid would ask about school, and the boy was always effusive. He loved going back to school.

At the same time Walid instructed Ayman to find an apartment at ground level so that the Father would be more able to move around. As soon as it was located, Walid paid for a year's rent up front.

Every time Walid went to Essaouria, Chams insisted on washing the car.

On one of the trips, Ayman shyly asked Shaafia if she would be willing to visit a family whose daughter he had been introduced to. He admitted that he really liked the girl and he thought that maybe she liked him. As his Father was no longer alive he felt Shaafia would be the best person to represent his family.

Shaafia sensed immediately that there was a very good energy in this, and she accepted. Walid smiled when she asked him to accompany her.

«You need an escort?»

«You are his employer.» she said, «It will impress the family and you can put in a good word for him.»

Walid willingly went along, more than anything to see what Shaafia would do.

The family owned and ran a shop that sold herbs in the middle of the old centre of Essaouira and lived in the apartment above the shop.

Ayman had told them his sister would be coming, and most of the family was there to meet her.

The girl, whose name was Rabia because she was the fourth daughter, was a very energetic young woman who seemed to be quietly self-confident. She immediately embraced Shaafia with kisses on both cheeks as if she had known her all along. Shaafia kissed her back, and then greeted the rest of the family.

Ayman introduced them. Although he was a little intimidated by all this, he held himself well. Rabia's Father and Mother were there with two younger brothers. Her three older sisters, all already married and living away from Essaouira, were not present.

The Father of the family made a little welcome speech to Shaafia and to Walid who Shaafia had introduced as Ayman's employer. The family was already well aware of the resort project because of Ayman, but when they met the boss of the whole enterprise they were very impressed.

The family had prepared a table of refreshments and all sat round it, with Rabia sitting unashamedly next to Ayman.

«As your father has passed away,» said Rabia's Father, «I am happy to greet you as the representative of your family. It is also an honour to welcome Mr Razak, which I take to be a sign that Ayman is well regarded.»

Shaafia responded. «My brother is a good man and I am sure he will make an honourable husband. As you say, he has the confidence of Mr Razak. I am sure that I speak on behalf of my family when I say that it looks to me like Rabia would be a very suitable wife for my brother. «

She smiled at Rabia who blushed, and seemed to shift her weight ever so slightly closer to Ayman.

«I am sure my family would welcome a relationship with yours.» added Shaafia. «We are both shopkeeper families. My Father ran a shop which my younger brother now runs with his Uncle.»

Over the refreshments, there were many questions asked, mostly from Rabia's family. Shaafia described her family and then had to tell her very carefully edited personal story, which impressed them all. None of them had ever left Morocco and most had not finished high school. The two younger brothers were being pressed to get there.

When Shaafia asked Rabia to describe herself, the girl was a little surprised, but there was something in the way Shaafia asked her that gave her confidence.

Rabia spoke of herself in terms of her family and where they lived and worked and how she contributed to that life, and then she paused. There was something else. She felt that she had something inside herself that she wanted to discover.

Shaafia nodded as the girl spoke, which gave her more confidence.

«I feel that there is something that I can do, something to benefit everyone,» she said, «but I don't know what it is yet.»

«Being married and having children is very beneficial.» said her Mother.

«Of course,» nodded her daughter obediently, «but I think there might be something more.»

Shaafia leaned over and took the girl's right hand. She turned it over and ran her fingers across the palm.

«I believe you are right.» she said «You have healing hands. You will be able to help many people.»

There was a ripple of shock in the room and Walid found himself smiling. There was no end of fascination for him at what Shaafia could do.

Ayman looked at Shaafia with amazement.

«You can see that?»

Shaafia nodded. Then she turned to Rabia's Mother. «I believe the ability to heal was given to her by your Mother, her grandmother.»

Rabia's Mother had wide eyes, but she nodded.

«My Mother died when I was quite young, so none of my children knew her, but as you say, she was a healing woman.»

Rabia still had her hand in Shaafia's and she looked at her with shining eyes.

«My heart tells me you are right,» she said, «but how will I do this?»

«There is a woman from Rifat. She will be living in the new resort when it is finished. Ayman knows who she is. She is a healing woman. She will teach you.»

Ayman nodded. «She is a good woman, I have gotten to know her quite well. As soon as she discovered I was the brother of Shaafia, we became very good friends.»

When it was time to leave, the family embraced Shaafia with great fondness, begging her to come and visit them whenever she was in Essaouira.

They thanked Walid for his presence, as if he were royalty.

As they drove back to Casablanca, Walid marvelled at what was happening around him.

He told Shaafia that he was the happiest he could remember. He felt powerfully creative, while at the same time he was now constantly conscious of the effect of his decisions. He felt he was working in an entirely new way and he really liked it.

«I know I have thanked you very often,» he said, «but there seems no end to the good fortune you have brought to me, to my Father, and to everyone.»

She accepted his thanks silently. He glanced sideways to see what she was thinking.

«What I am lucky enough to give is only because I have received so much,» she said. «There is a flow. And I think those who have benefitted from what I have received will be of great benefit to others. You are one of them.»

«I will do my best.»

She laughed gently and reminded him that what was happening was that his best self was coming out.

«You are a very different man from the one Houda was so horrified about.»

Every so often Rami Razak would insist that Shaafia come to visit, and he too was voluble in his gratitude for what had changed in his life. He now walked with ease, although slowly. His face had softened and he could smile.

He proudly told Shaafia that he had been attentive to the needs of his staff and was amazed at the change in the atmosphere in his house. He shyly admitted that he had come to love his staff and he rather thought it was reciprocated.

Shaafia assured him it was.

«I never had the good fortune to have daughters.» he told her, as she was leaving one day. «I would like to think of you as my daughter. Would you be my daughter?»

She kissed him on both cheeks.

«It would be an honour.» she said.

Several times a week Shaafia would return to her mother's house and there too Shaafia could see a marked change, a sense of harmony amongst the family members that there had never been before. Nayla had not been sighted, and when her Mother asked if Shaafia knew what was happening, Shaafia told her Mother that Nayla was wrestling with her dark tendencies and that, for the moment, she would be no danger to anyone.

«For the moment?» her Mother asked.

«Right now she has no power to cause any harm to anyone except herself, but it is always possible that she could descend again into that dark world and try to recover her power. That darkness is never destroyed. We can be protected, but we will never be totally rid of it.»

The addition of textiles to the Jilani shop had made it very popular, and Sadik seemed to have grown not just taller but also had matured into a confident young businessman. His Uncle was mostly a bemused bystander to the rapidly developing enterprise.

Whenever Shaafia visited, Sadik would tell her of new ideas that he had for expansion. He was on fire with it.

He had begun negotiations with the butcher who had the shop next door on the other side. Sadik had noticed that the butcher seemed to have trouble with his eyes. He wore thick glasses, and very often he would have to take them off and rub his eyes. Sadik had started a conversation asking the butcher how he was doing, and the man had admitted that it was not easy.

When Shaafia dropped in one day, Sadik invited her to come with him next door. Shaafia had known the butcher since her childhood, as he had been her Father's next door neighbour in business since they were both young men.

He greeted her warmly and told her he had heard all about her travels and her new work, and he told her how impressed he was. She smiled at all this, and then she gently asked him about his eyes.

«I cannot be a good butcher without good eyesight.» he said, «I am in danger of losing my fingers every day.»

She nodded. «So maybe it is time to use your eyes for something different.»

«Something different?» he frowned, «This is the only trade I know.»

She came close to him and she reached up and took his glasses away.

Very softly she said: «If you start to look at life in a different way, you will discover something about yourself that you never knew. Your time as a butcher is coming to an end. Something else is coming to take its place. You will see it when you close your eyes.»

His glassless eyes began to gently weep.

He apologised, and wiped his eyes with the hem of his robe.

«It touches me deeply what you say.» he said.

Sadik had watched all this with quiet detachment. By now he was very aware of the power that his sister wielded.

He put his hand on the old man's shoulders.

«We will talk.» he said.

As they left the shop, Sadik turned to his sister. «Do you really think he will start a new job?»

«No.» she said «It has nothing to do with work. He has neglected his soul all these years, killing animals and cutting up their meat. Now he will see that he has to make amends and he will become a carer of animals instead, and he will be very content.»

«You can see this?»

«*Ham delilah.*» she said.

Then she smiled. «Your shop will get even bigger.»

Now and then Shaafia would visit the corner cafe and see how the boys were progressing. Their podcasts were gaining an audience, and they were intensely creative in responding to the feedback. Other young people wanted to contribute and their group was growing. To her satisfaction Shaafia saw that at last they had included several girls.

It was one of those girls who made the suggestion that turned the group in a new direction.

Badria who lived not far from the Mosque, had begun to train as a teacher but, like Samet, she was very disillusioned with the rigidity of the formal education system. She had seen their podcast and agreed with much that she read there.

However, when she had heard about their desire to form a school, she scoffed that it was a hopeless idea. The bureaucracy would never let it happen.

At first this depressed the group, confirming their worst fears. However, although Badria was critical of the school idea, she was very inspired by the idea of working outside the system to benefit gifted children.

She came up with a radical suggestion.

The podcast should become their school, she said. At first they were sceptical but she persisted. She described how it could be a vehicle. They could be offering a free alternative education to any children who wanted it.

The boys took their time to warm to the idea, and there was a lot of spirited debate. However, Badria would not let it go. With the podcast, she said, they could reach children far away not just those who lived in Casablanca. She was forceful, and slowly they began to see the wisdom of it.

The next time Shaafia visited, she sensed a new energy in the air. When Badria explained the idea, Shaafia had nodded.

«And you boys agree?»

They proudly showed her their new podcast about to be posted. Its whole orientation was an invitation to young people: «Come and learn what school will never teach you.»

«What do you think?» asked Samet.

Shaafia nodded. «Now you have seen the wisdom of listening to an intelligent woman, you will do really well.»

Badria smiled.

«You do think this idea will work?» she asked.

«It will depend,» replied Shaafia. «on how well you manage to persuade others to believe in it. If you believe in it, so will they.»

Samet nodded. «If this works, then we won't need your boyfriend's millions after all.»

She ignored the innuendo and said: «You never did.»

In the midst of all this, Shaafia began to receive more calls asking her to be a translator.

The first of these had been Rana's lawyer. He had called her to say that he had an important client from Belgium, who wanted French to Arabic translation. Shaafia sensed immediately that there was another motive behind the request, and she accepted.

She was now very confident in asking a high fee which was agreed without question.

Her Mother's plumbing would be updated very quickly.

Her instincts proved accurate when she attended the first meeting.

The client was French-speaking, but the lawyer spoke perfectly good French and could have done the transaction by himself. What the lawyer wanted, however, was something different. He asked Shaafia to tell him if the client was truthful or not, and for that he was willing to pay.

She dutifully did the translation, and after the client had left, she told the lawyer that in fact the client was only telling him half the story. It was not that he was lying, but that he did not trust the lawyer. She explained that was why the client had asked for a translator. Shaafia told him if he was openly honest with the client, then their relationship would be healthy and prosperous.

Several days later, the lawyer called her with great excitement, and told her that he had followed her advice and the client had been very forthcoming. They now had agreed on a long term relationship. She told him if he was able to work like that, open and honest with all his clients, he would be incredibly successful.

Soon after this, there were other calls for her services. With each one she would feel the intent behind the request, and for some she would accept, and for others she would tell them she was not available.

Her income was growing fast.

Her visits to the Attijariwafa Bank became a weekly event, and the girl who was assigned to her was very attentive.

At first, their brief conversations were business-like and focussed, but slowly the girl began to talk more. She was interested in what Shaafia did.

Shaafia shared about her translation work but little else. The girl had been to France, studied finance at the University in Grenoble, and even hinted at having had a French boyfriend.

As they talked more, Shaafia became aware of the girl's inner state. There was deep unhappiness there.

After several visits, Shaafia decided to help.

«You were hoping to be promoted?» she asked.

The girl frowned, then she nodded. «How did you know that?»

«Sometimes I see things.» Shaafia replied, watching to see how the girl reacted. «The promotion that you expected has been blocked.»

The girl nodded. «I am disappointed.»

«The woman is jealous of you.»

The girl's eyes narrowed. «Why?»

«You are young, you have education, you are very good at what you do. You are threatening to her.»

«That's not my fault.» said the girl, with some tension in her voice.

«No, it is not, but you can change it.»

«Change her?»

«Perhaps.»

«What would I have to do?»

«She feels she has to be in competition with you because she fears you will take her place. If you were friendly to her, praised her for her good qualities, she would feel less threatened.»

«That would be a big challenge. She is not a nice person.»

«She is a disappointed person. She has unhappy relations with her children who accuse her of ruining her marriage. Her husband does not live with her any more. Her life is empty, and all she has is her work. And just like you, she was not promoted when she hoped to be. She has been stuck at the same level in the Bank for a very long time. And she has no real friends at all.»

The girl shook her head.

«That is sad. I never knew that. Are you sure?»

«If you can be just a little friendly, you will see.»
«I will. After all it won't hurt to try.»

Each week Rachi would call from Bordeaux, having discovered the new way to call for free on the internet, and they would have long talks.

Yasser was in training and attending different football clinics. He was helping with young players and also getting to play in a local league. Rachi had begun her studies at the University and she was in heaven.

It had taken several weeks for her to be settled enough to find time to visit Château des Mésanges, but when she did she loved it. Madame Clae had enfolded her in her arms and they had both cried. Rachi took Yasser and they met all the other members of the château community who all wanted to hear about Shaafia.

At the same time Shaafia would call the château once a week so she got to hear the story from the other point of view.

It made her feel very happy.

The rhythm of life in and around *Darou Al Bahr* had a sweetness to it that touched Shaafia deeply. She felt that she had landed in the place of her destiny which, on one level, protected her, while on another level she felt that she was responsible for the safety of the house. Every evening she would visit the garden to sprinkle a few drops of the *Ain Baraka* water before going upstairs for her evening prayers.

As she closed her eyes at the end of every day, her Koranic prayer would resonate inside, now so ingrained that it ran itself and she would drop into the deepest of peaceful sleeps.

Security

Several months went by and life in *Darou Al Bahr* continued in a gentle pattern. More and more, Shaafia found herself being guided, both when to act or speak, and when to hold back.

Word spread, as people came to know who she was and what she could do. As more people came to see her, she began to feel the need to be protected, not from danger, but rather from over-exposure. Every encounter took a certain amount of energy, and after several meetings in one morning she would feel drained.

Rana saw this happening and she decided to step in.

Her first idea was to offer to employ a secretary for Shaafia, someone who would field the different requests. Shaafia shook her head. She didn't feel it would be appropriate because each person was worthy of being considered but not just by some anonymous secretary.

So Rana offered to be that person herself.

At first Shaafia was reluctant, not wanting to bother Rana, especially as she was now effectively the CEO of a large transport company.

However, as time went by, it became clear that something had to be done.

Rana would not give up and finally Shaafia relented. During the day Rana would hold Shaafia's cell phone. She would take Shaafia's calls and then pass the phone to Shaafia if it was private but otherwise she would gather the information about each person and why they wanted to see Shaafia. Then she would show Shaafia. To some Shaafia would shake her head, to others she would accept, then Rana would make an appointment.

One of the large downstairs reception rooms became the area where Shaafia would meet people, while the smaller reception room at the back would be a kind of waiting room.

However, not all people paid the courtesy of calling first and people began to turn up at the house looking for Shaafia and not all of them were well behaved. Some even became demanding.

This was how Ihab became head of security for the house. Rana had spoken to Walid about what she was seeing, and it was his suggestion that Ihab could do the job.

When Rana approached Shaafia about that, Shaafia nodded.

«I knew that one day Ihab would come here.» she said. «It will be his way to pay his debt.»

«He has financial debts?»

Shaafia shook her head. «He will be able to right some wrongs from his past. It will free him.»

Ihab was surprised when he was asked, but when Walid described his rôle as «Head of Security», just like Ayman in Essaouria, he smiled and he accepted. He moved into one of the small newly-renovated rooms behind the house, and with the help of Walid's head of security, a thorough system to safeguard the house and its inhabitants was installed.

Although Shaafia gently protested that the house had its own protection, nonetheless the house soon boasted closed-circuit cameras and electrified entrances. The Admiral who built the house would have been amazed.

When Ayman and Rabia's wedding date was set, the Jilani family were ecstatic. Shaafia had described Rabia to her Mother and she nodded. «She sounds perfect.»

By now her Mother had total faith in Shaafia's judgement and if Shaafia approved, then that was good enough.

Toufik had proudly driven his Mother to meet Rabia's family and she came back very pleased. At last one of her sons would marry.

A joyful period of planning elsued until the date was set.

Walid offered several of his vehicles so that the whole Jilani family could all travel to Essaouira for the wedding celebrations.

One member of the family was conspicuously absent. When it came time to organise the family, including the older sisters and their children, Shaafia's Mother agonised over Nayla. Shouldn't she be invited, too?

«She is family,» pleaded her Mother.

Shaafia shrugged. «Do you really think she would accept?»

«At least we should ask.»

Zarifa, the oldest of all the sisters, knew where Nayla worked and she, somewhat reluctantly, accepted the rôle of inviter.

She called back later the same day to say that Nayla was no longer working at the bank and that they did not know where she had gone. She hinted that maybe Nayla had been fired.

When she heard this, Shaafia felt a shiver run through her body, and she closed her eyes to be aware.

«Be careful.» she heard. «She is preparing to come back. She is desperate. She feels she has nothing to lose now. She has regained some of her strength. Be ready.»

She said nothing to her Mother who was resigned to not having Nayla present.

Shaafia took her Mother shopping to buy wedding gifts. At first, her Mother was reluctant to spend too much money, but at the same time Ayman was the first of her sons to be married. It was significant.

Shaafia gently scolded her and insisted that she should buy everything that she would like.

«*Mui*,» she said gently, «You have to change they way you think.»

Her Mother nodded and so, as they shopped, her Mother kept reminding herself that their family fortunes had changed. Not wanting to dampen her Mother's new enthusiasm, Shaafia smiled and tolerated the repetitions.

They chose many of the gifts at Sadik's expanding shop, but he insisted that he wanted them to be his own gifts to his brother.

His Mother put up token resistance, but he and Shaafia could see that she was secretly very proud of him.

By now he had completed the acquisition of the old butcher's shop which had been completely emptied and renovated. Furniture, pottery and other household goods were arranged on stands and shelves illuminated by large spotlights in the ceiling. What was once a single shopfront was now tripled in size.

The butcher himself had come to visit several times marvelling at the changes. Meanwhile, as Shaafia had predicted, he had retired, using the proceeds of the sale of his shop to buy a small cottage in a village outside Casablanca.

He shyly told Shaafia that he had been thinking a lot about his life.

She nodded, knowing that he would discover things about himself that would change his life even more.

«I have goats now.» he said proudly.

On the day of the wedding, Walid's cars were lined up at the corner of the lane, and all the family piled in. Ihab would have the honour of driving his Mother. Toufik was very reluctant to leave his Coccinelle behind, but his Mother insisted that they all travel together.

Rami Razak had been invited, and he was very happy to meet Shaafia's family for the first time. He told her Mother how much he appreciated what Shaafia had done for him and his family, and her Mother smiled with pride.

Walid had also been generous in helping to fund the event. A large tent had been erected, at his expense, on the beach front where the resort was rapidly beginning to take shape. The first bores had been sunk and there was now water available to service the wedding.

The wedding itself was a joyously social affair where many of the villagers from Rifat were paid to assist the caterers. By this time, Rabia had begun her training with the healing woman, and she was there as Rabia's special guest. Chams and his family were invited by Ayman who had become good friends with them.

It was towards the end of the day, when the wedding ceremonies with the local Imam had been concluded, and the big feast was in full swing, that Shaafia became aware that Nayla was close.

«Do nothing.» she heard inside herself, «There is no need. Watch. Let them deal with her. They can do it.»

She smiled to herself as she got up without telling anyone, and stood off to one side. In her handbag she had a small vial of *Ain Baraka*, the water from El Chakour, and her hand rested on it gently as she watched to see what would happen.

Nayla was dressed in a black hooded robe with thick black mascara round her eyes. With her came a large, muscular, dark-skinned man. He had a warrior's stance, fierce eyes, and was very obviously her bodyguard. He stood close to her and looked around constantly.

She strode into the middle of the tent and glared at Ayman who was sitting at the bridal table with his new wife.

«So Ayman, my brother!» she shouted. «I take care of you and this is how you repay me?»

The wedding party froze and a hundred pairs of eyes turned to see who this was.

She looked around the room with a sneer. «This pathetic brother of mine, who I could have made into something, turns his back on me.»

Ayman jumped to his feet.

«I don't owe you anything, Nayla. Now I have seen what you are, you cannot touch any of us. »

«Oh you think your little sister can save you?».

Walid, although he did not know who she was, decided to take action. He got up from his chair and stood directly in front of Nayla.

Shaafia watched and waited. She drew the *Ain Baraka* from her bag.

Walid took several steps towards Nayla, and Ihab jumped up to stand beside him. The black man advanced menacingly towards them.

«This is a wedding.» said Walid with a quiet but strong voice. «Why would you want to disrupt it?»

«Because it is pathetic.» sneered Nayla. « This miserable family thinks they can ignore me but they can't. I can destroy this whole stupid spectacle.»

«No you can't!» yelled Hawa, jumping up. «We have Shaafia.»

« We have Shaafia!» yelled her sister Yamina.

«Shaafia!» It was Samet.

«Shaafia!»

Toufik, Loqman, Sadik and the rest of the family were on their feet and yelling.

As if she were on a battlefield and her enemy had launched missiles at her, Nayla stood there, trying to hold her fierce stance while the chant of Shaafia's name got stronger and stronger. Almost all of the other wedding guests knew Shaafia and they all seemed to be pulled into joining the assault on the intruder. Rabia's family, the healing woman from the village, young Chams and his family and others were all chanting her name. Even Rami was on his feet chanting with force. No-one looked at Shaafia herself, seemingly invisible, but the intent was to use her name as their weapon. They closed in around the intruders.

The black bodyguard began to sway and grabbed at Nayla for support, his weight throwing her off her feet. She fell to the floor as the wedding guests crowded in on them, standing over them, chanting the name of Shaafia in unison. Then Ihab jumped in and grabbed Nayla, pulling her roughly to her feet, Ayman and Walid did the same to the bodyguard. The chanting crowd parted, and the men propelled the intruders towards the entrance.

Suddenly blocking their path was Shaafia's Mother. She put up her hands to stop the ejection, and the crowd went silent.

«My daughter,» said her Mother coming up very close, her voice shaking but clear. «We have known the trouble you carry for a long time. We always prayed and hoped that God would help you to find a way back. It was no use. You are lost to us now. You see how we are protected. You cannot do anything to us any more. My heart aches to see you like this, but I know what I must say. You are no longer my daughter. I disown you. Do not come near any of us ever again. «

Then she took a step forward and with surprising force she leaned in, reached up and smacked her daughter's face.

«Take her away.» she said and turned her back on her daughter.

The blow seemed to rob Nayla of the last of her strength and she wilted. Ihab dragged her out of the tent, while Walid and Ayman did the same to the bodyguard.

And then an explosion of joy hit the wedding. As if they had all just succeeded in a great victory, they were laughing and clapping each other on the back. The Jilani girls surrounded their Mother and hugged her and kissed her. Ayman went back to his bride and embraced her. Her family gathered around him talking animatedly.

Shaafia quietly returned the vial of water back to her bag, recognising that she had been repeating her Koranic verse the whole time. She marvelled at her own detachment. She saw Rana looking at her across the tent and they smiled at each other.

Walid noticed her standing there, still and remote. He took a few steps towards her, but then stopped and put his hand up to his heart in salutation. She did the same in response.

Meanwhile, as if there had been no intrusion at all, the wedding feast went on. A local group of Berber musicians, hired for the event, now struck up their instruments which prompted dancing and joining in the well-known songs.

The celebration went on late into the night.

Work

The wedding seemed to be a turning point in Shaafia's relationship with those around her, certainly her family, but also those people she had met or worked with. Now there was a sense of awe, and perhaps even a little fear and trepidation.

This heightened, as more and more people who had come into contact with her began to experience changes in their lives. At the same time her name was shared by many who had benefitted from knowing her, and the calls that Rana fielded became more and more frequent.

Now almost every day she held a kind of salon for several hours when she would see people, scheduled by Rana who had now become an excellent secretary, hostess and guardian of Shaafia's personal space. With each person, Shaafia would assess the person, the minute they walked in, but she would listen to what they wanted to tell her and she would wait to see if there was a response. There almost always was, even if it was very simple, often telling a person not to worry, that there would be a solution coming very soon and they should be patient. Now and then she could see that what the person had wanted to talk about was irrelevant, and Shaafia would have an insight into something completely different.

Rana became used to seeing people stagger out of the salon in a state of shock. Many wanted to express their gratitude, and gifts were offered and, very often, money. When people would ask Rana what was the fee she would say that there was no fee. Nonetheless, many people felt compelled to offer something. The money went to the Mosque of Haj Kabir.

However, there were times when Shaafia had to slip away to be by herself. Sometimes she would ask Ihab to go with her and he was always ready. His love and admiration for his little sister was heartfelt.

Sometimes she would walk in Murdoch Park, just a block away, and her footsteps would keep time with the repetition of her verse. Ihab would walk a pace behind her, looking around him to make sure no-one would disturb his sister. On one of these walks, she shared with him how as she walked she was repeating her verse and she taught him how to do that for himself. Very quickly she sensed how repeating the verse was helping him to be even more alert, more conscious in a new way. He was becoming more than just a bodyguard.

More and more he was able to anticipate what she needed. She would smile at him, acknowledging his new ability.

Whenever Shaafia went to the bank, the girl assigned to her would breathlessly share what was happening in her life. She had taken Shaafia's suggestions. She and her supervisor had even gone out for several meals together, and there was a tangible change in their relationship.

While there had been no result from the request for a promotion Shaafia told her to be patient.

«When the time is right,» she said, «it will come, totally naturally. You will see.»

When the change did come, the girl had flowers sent to Shaafia.

She told Shaafia that her supervisor had become such a better person that the Attijariwafa Bank had recognised the change and had promoted her to be a personnel manager at another branch of the Bank. The girl was offered the vacant position. The day the supervisor left, she had kissed the girl and thanked her for her friendship.

When all the renovations were nearing completion in *Darou Al Bahr*, Shaafia approached the man who had been in charge of all the plumbing renewals. She asked him to visit her Mother's house and estimate what it would cost to modernise all the plumbing, including hot water and solar panels.

She was a bit shocked when he showed her his estimate of what it would cost. The house was old and in bad shape. A lot of work would be needed. It would consume nearly all that she had earned since her return. She shared the news with Rana, who immediately offered to help.

Shaafia shook her head.

«No, it has to come from me.» she said. «I feel it is something that I owe to my family.» Then she added: «If I need help then I am sure it will come.»

Rana frowned. «I am your help. Please accept it. There is no way I can ever repay you for what you have done for me and for Houda. Please.»

Shaafia gave her a warm hug. «Let me think about it.» she said.

It did not take very long.

That evening as she sat on her bed repeating her Koranic verse, Haj Hussein floated into her awareness.

«Our families are like one family.» he said. «We help each other. It is God's will.»

The next morning Shaafia called the plumber and accepted his quote.

It was the same morning when Rana received the news that a buyer had been found for her compound. A minor prince from one of the Gulf Emirates had decided to buy it, without even visiting. He had seen the agent's drone video and wanted it. He would pay cash.

Rana turned to Shaafia after she had received the call. «You see how God works.» she said. «I offer to help to pay for your Mother's house and I get to sell my house, all on the same day.»

There was a sense of stability in Bin Salah Transport too.

Taj very quickly came to accept and respect Walid's leadership. Taj was a changed man, and both Walid and Rana found themselves respecting his abilities and welcoming his new humility. Whenever he saw Shaafia he would put his hand up to his heart and salute her with deep feeling.

He told her that his relationship with his family had begun to mend. He told her that he and his wife were meeting each other, as if for the first time, and that he and his children had a new and loving connection.

At least once a week Ihab would take Shaafia to the Mosque for the midday prayers and leave her there while she had lunch afterwards with Haj Kabir and Myriam.

With Haj Kabir she could share what was happening in her life in a way that she could not really share with anyone else.

He would nod as she told him about people's experiences.

« This is the work God wishes for you, and you have answered his call. There are so many beings who are aware of what you do and they support you, they shelter you, and they praise your courage. »

« *Ham delilah,* » she said, « Thanks be to God. »

Two Dreams

«He is your husband. Now is the time for him to protect you.»

The voices came in her sleep, and when she woke, she lay still trying to catch exactly what they were referring to. Whatever they were trying to convey was not yet clear to her. She let it rest, got up and had a shower.

As she went downstairs, Rana was closing Shaafia's cell phone.

«Walid just called and he said he had something urgent to ask you.»

Then Shaafia knew.

She walked out onto the terrace to call him back.

«I am sorry to be calling you so early in the morning,» he said, «but I had to.»

«You had a dream.» she said.

«You know about that?» he asked. «Did you send it?»

«No.»

«So what do you think?»

She laughed. «I don't think. This is not about thoughts.»

«OK, but still. Tell me what this is all about.»

«I also had a dream, and I am now quite certain that we received the same message.»

«But the point is, what I am trying to say is, is this real? I mean, I don't know how to respond.»

Shaafia gazed out into the garden and let herself breathe. She had let the dream rest inside her, confident that its message would become clear when it was ready. Now she knew what it was, she had to sense how she herself felt about it.

As she sat there, the orange cat approached her and rubbed itself against her legs. The contact sent a little shiver through her body and she felt a confirmation arising.

«Are you still there?» he asked, spooked by her silence.

«Yes. I just had to be silent for a moment.»

«Can I come to see you?» he asked. «I think we have to talk face to face.»

«You are right.» she said.

«Good. I am coming right now.» and he hung up.

How did she feel about it?

She was not sure. She had received the message, quite clearly, and now understood it unequivocally, but how did she feel? She was not sure. Up to this point, with all the messages that came to her, she acted on them with faith, but this one was close and personal.

Shaafia said nothing to Rana other than Walid was coming to talk to her. Rana nodded. By now she was very respectful of whatever Shaafia wanted to do.

It would take Walid a good half hour to reach *Darou Al Bahr* so she went upstairs, had a shower and sat on her bed to repeat her verse for a while.

She sank deeply inside to a place where her verse resonated all by itself in its own echoing inner chamber. The verse deepened and diversified itself and became the voices. They were chanting her verse back to her. Then she began to see them, dozens of them. Some she recognised. To her joy there was her Father, strong and upright as she remembered him from when she was a child. Haj Hussein was with him and Malak was there. And then as she gazed at this wonderful assembly she saw, hovering above them, the silvery form that she knew was Pia, and beside her the Lady in Blue and White.

They all looked at her with such love, and as they chanted, they put their hands together in salutation.

The gentlest of knocks on her door brought her back.

«Walid is here.» said Rana as she gently opened the door.

Shaafia slowly opened her eyes. Her room seemed to glow with a warm light different from the sun's morning rays.

«Thank you Rana.» she said softly.

Rana stood looking down at Shaafia, as she sat cross-legged on her bed. «You look very beautiful.» she said. «Has something happened?»

Shaafia dropped her head in a subtle nod and smiled.

He was waiting for her, pacing up and down in the garden.

As she approached, he put his hands up to his heart in his now habitual salutation. He dropped his head, but as he raised it again, he looked into her eyes.

«So?»

She returned his hands-on-heart gesture and she pointed to the bench. He sat next to her but with distance between them.

«Tell me about your dream.» she said.

«It was very vivid.» he said. «You were standing with this silvery sort of person, kind of like a ghost I suppose. Then she spoke to me. It was female I am sure. She said now is the time for you to take her as your bride.»

«You knew who it was?»

«Not really.»

«And you understaood what she meant.»

«It was very clear.»

«You knew who it was referring to?»

He nodded, then he smiled. «It wasn't Houda.»

«Are you sure?» She was smiling back.

«I knew what she meant.»

«Did you agree?»

He frowned. «I don't know. I think I was too surprised.»

«Dreams can be illusions.»

«Not this one. I know what it was.»

«So you accept it was a command?»

«I woke up in a sweat. Did I accept it? I don't know.»

They sat in silence for moment, then he said. «What about you? You said you had a dream, and if I understand you properly, you think we had the same kind of dream.»

She described her dream.

«I would be happy, I would be honoured to be your protector.» he said, turning to face her. «You know that I feel I am already, in a way, but this is different.»

«Very different.»

«Are you willing?»

She let the question hang in the air.

«It's what they would like.» she said at last.

«But what about you? Is this what you want?»

She shrugged. «I am not sure it really matters what I want.»

«But how do you feel?» he asked, with an edge creeping into his voice.

«I feel.....» She let herself pause to be sure about what she wanted to say. «I feel such confidence in the guidance that comes. I have no doubt it is what should happen.»

«OK.» he said. Then, all in a rush, turning to face her, he said: «Do you want to marry me?»

She smiled at him. «Why not?»

«Aaagh!» he said, now quite agitated, «Why are you being so evasive?

She turned to face him, full on. Then she leaned in and stroked his face. It was the first time she had ever touched him.

«This is not like an ordinary «man marries woman» kind of situation. But if it is my time to marry then I will marry you. It is as simple as that.»

He took a breath and then reached for her hand.

«So you will marry me?»

«If you are willing.»

He gazed at her in silence.

«I have never, ever met anyone like you.» he said at last, his voice now thick with emotion. « You are not the kind of girl I would imagine myself marrying and yet, oh yes I want to be married to you.»

She nodded.

«Your Father will be pleased.»

His face relaxed into a smile. «Oh sure. He already thinks of you as his daughter.»

They were sitting in silence looking into each other's eyes when Rana appeared with a tray.

«I thought you might like some tea.»

She joined them and poured the tea, then she looked at them both.

«So what is it?» she asked, looking from one to the other.

Walid looked at Shaafia, and she nodded.

«Shaafia and I will be getting married.» he explained.

Rana stared at him in disbelief, then she put down her cup and came to Shaafia to enfold her in her arms.

«How perfect.» she said.

Later that morning he drove Shaafia to see her Mother.

In the car on the way, she called. It took her Mother a long time to answer, apologising because the girls had already left for school.

Shaafia told her Mother that she had some news and that she would be there in a few minutes.

He left the Renault at the end of the lane and they walked up together. It was the first time he had set foot inside the house.

«This is where you were born?»

She nodded.

When she heard the news, her Mother screamed with excitement and grabbed her daughter in a tight hug. Then she turned to Walid.

«I give you all my blessings!» she said and impulsively kissed him on both cheeks.

Then she added: «You have told your family?»

«That comes next. We would like you to come with us and meet my Father.»

«Oh, I am not dressed well enough. I must change.»

While they waited for her, Shaafia took Walid outside to the fig tree and she told him the many important things that had happened under that tree. She told him about Dada, and how the tree represented a treasured place of peace and comfort for her.

He ran his hands over the rough bark and fingered the leaves.

«This is a tree of wisdom.» he said.

Rami's reaction was measured.

«What took you so long, my son?»

Consecration

August the fifteenth is a day of significance.

It was the day Pia completed her short life, the day the Virgin Mary is said to have ascended to heaven.

For the wedding of Shaafia to Walid, it seemed to be the perfect date.

At first, Shaafia felt that all they needed was a legal marriage and the religious marriage and nothing else, but around her the pressure built for a big occasion. The family of course were insistent. Rana was too. On Walid's side, Rami could not help himself but feel as if he needed to do something big. This was the first of his sons to marry and to marry a girl that Rami already regarded as his daughter.

Shaafia resisted all this pressure until, even in her meditations, suggestions were being made and she accepted the inevitable.

«It is not just a wedding,» she heard. «It will be a gathering of love. Many people will benefit. It will be a consecration.»

At first Rami Razak expected that the wedding celebrations should be in the grounds of his compound, the home of the groom, but Shaafia knew it had to be in *Darou Al Bahr*. In this she was adamant. Rami found her impossible to resist and so he switched to engage himself in the preparations with Rana. They became a joyful team. The garden underwent major transitions as they made space for a massive pavilion.

In the meantime, invitations were sent and acceptances received.

Claire and Théophile would come, and they would bring Marie-Louise who had never travelled outside France in her life. There was talk of the whole group from Château des Mésanges coming, but it was impractical as the summer had been a time when pilgrims were descending on the shrine of Pia in great numbers. Berenice put up a big fuss to be included, but she did not win them over.

The acceptance that came from the furthest away was from Brad and his new wife, Indira. He had published the book and, as Shaafia had predicted, married the editor. He would bring the first copies of the book to Shaafia's wedding with his bride. The trip would double as their honeymoon.

Rachi and Yasser would come back to Casablanca, if only for a few days. Yasser had been named in the starting squad for Les Girondins and he could not leave for long, but Rachi insisted that they be there.

Haj Kabir seemed to know from the very first moment what was taking place, and he had arrived at *Darou Al Bahr* the day after Shaafia and Walid's first conversation.

He bustled into the house quite early in the morning, having come straight from morning prayers.

«I heard the news in prayer this morning,» he said, coming across Shaafia and Rana at breakfast. «As soon as you decide the day, I will organise the chanters. And» he added with a broad smile, «there are beings who will come to bless this event.»

Shaafia said. «They have already begun.»

He smiled broadly and helped himself to some flatbread. «Thank you for the invitation that came to me this morning.»

Rana broached the subject of Houda. What should they do about that?

Haj Kabir had the answer. «She will be there. I myself will go to El Chakour the day before. She is ready now. She will come back and she will begin to realise her destiny. »

The rest of Shaafia's family went into a flurry of preparations. Their first reactions were a mixture of shock and excitement. None of them had seen it coming.

Her Mother had made the best use of her telephone since she had received it, calling cousins and uncles all over the country. Rana generously engaged Shaafia's Mother in the preparations, checking to see if she approved of the plans. Shaafia's Mother felt a bit overwhelmed in the company of so much wealth and happily acceded to everything.

The only family member not involved in any of it was Nayla. No-one had seen her since Ayman's wedding, but Ihab quietly asked Shaafia if she thought Nayla might appear.

She breathed in as he put the question and she felt nothing but a sense of peace.

She shook her head. «At this wedding there will be much too much power for her to dare to come close. She will not be there.»

«We know what to do if she does.» he grinned.

In the days leading up to the wedding, Shaafia let herself be handled as bride-to be, with her Mother and sisters as well as Rana organising all the traditional female-only rituals and gatherings. She let herself be carried along, floating through the big *hammam* party with the women, where Rana had booked and paid for one of the most expensive and exclusive *hammams* in Casablanca, then the henna party dominated by Shaafia's four sisters, excluding Nayla.

It was almost as if Shaafia was watching some other girl getting ready to be married. Seeing herself in the mirror, as she tried on different wedding outfits in a salon in the centre of Casablanca, she was so detached that Rana worried that maybe she was not so keen to get married after all.

When Rana gently asked, Shaafia smiled.

«All this activity,» she said, «it seems to be happening a long way from where I am.»

«But you are still happy to be married?»

«Oh yes.»

The detachment bemused Rana, but she let it go.

The exception to this detachment, for Shaafia, was during morning meditations where she would plunge inside herself, and find that there too preparations were being offered, but of a very different kind. Many of the beings she saw on the day she became aware of her impending marriage, were constantly present and they were busy. They would chant over her, they would bring gifts of light that would flow into her subtle body, the body of her dreams, the body she existed in as she meditated.

Often the words of her Koranic verse would provide the melodies and the rhythms of these encounters, and after each one, she would emerge and have to sit still for a long time before she could regain the awareness of her physical body again. Her mind would be utterly still, and she was aware of how free from any emotion she was. She simply was there, still and quiet, receptive and at peace.

At the deepest level Shaafia knew that they were initiating her into the next level of what she was becoming.

Théophile and Claire arrived with Marie-Louise two days before the wedding. In Rana's white Mercedes, Shaafia went out to the airport to greet them. As soon as Marie-Louise saw her, she ran towards Shaafia and lifted her off the ground in her big-bodied hug. Claire and Théophile stood back until finally Shaafia managed to disentangle herself. She hugged them both, with her heart overflowing with love for all of them.

As they drove back to *Darou Al Bahr,* they wanted to know about everything that had happened. Although she had talked to them often enough on the phone now they were there in person, they needed to hear it all again. She had to trace the trajectory of her relationship with Walid, what had happened to Houda, how she dealt with Nayla, the wonders of El Chakour and all the miraculous interventions that had emanated from the benevolent beings who had gathered to serve Shaafia in her work.

In their turn, they were able to speak of how people had been changed by their visits to the château, to the chapel, and to the gravesite of Pia. They also had the same sense that behind what was happening for people, there were benevolent beings.

They had just returned from Chennai in India for the wedding of Brad and Indira. It had been a sumptuous wedding. Indira came from a very wealthy family who put on a three day festival of celebration. Brad's parents had come from America and were treated like royalty. Claire showed Shaafia the henna designs on her hands that all the women received.

A day later Brad and Indira flew in, and with them came the first copies of the book of Pia's life «Listen to Love». When she held the copy that they lovingly handed her, Shaafia felt waves of love pass through her, and tears ran down her cheeks. She hugged them both.

Once they had all arrived and had been housed in *Darou Al Bahr*, Rana organised a welcome tea for Shaafia's spiritual family. They gathered in the big front room where Shaafia usually met people who wanted to see her. Théophile hooked up his cell phone so that the other members of the «family», still in Château des Mèsanges, could join.

One after the other, Thérèse, Michael, Zena, Berenice, Jourdan, Angela and Hélène gave their blessings for the wedding. Berenice cried and said she was so sad that she could not be there.

Then Brad read the first chapter of «Listen to Love», and an electricity filled the room, a surge of energy that they all immediately recognised. As he finished the chapter, describing how Pia had first begun to communicate, the air seemed to shimmer.

Marie-Louise began to murmur: «Amour, amour, amour» and the others sweetly joined her.

«She is here.» said Marie-Louise at last, and Shaafia nodded.

The legal aspects of being married in Morocco usually take place before the celebrations begin. With Rami and Shaafia's Mother, Walid and Shaafia went to the registry office and filled in the papers, so within several hours, they were in fact legally married. Then they went to see Haj Kabir who conducted a private ceremony with just the four of them, and they emerged from his house as a religiously married couple.

Their first activity as a married couple was to go to Walid's favourite restaurant for lunch where Rami saw many of his business friends, so could not resist telling them all that Walid was now married. Throughout the lunch there were visitors to their table offering their congratulations. Often Shaafia would catch her Mother's eye as she watched all these very wealthy people around her. This was a totally new phenomenon for her.

As they left the restaurant later in the afternoon, Walid turned to face Shaafia.

«Now, Mystic Girl,» he said with a warm smile. «I am officially, legally and religiously your protector.»

She stood still and looked up into his eyes.

«I have been your protector since the moment we met.» she said.

Accommodation in *Darou Al Bahr* was going to be full, and so many of the guests were now welcomed at the Razak compound where Rami, now walking confidently without even a stick, seemed to relish the rôle of host.

As soon as they heard the news, Alex, Ben and Graham had immediately accepted, booked their flights, and when they reached the compound, they were amazed to see the transformation in Walid's Father. They beamed as they heard the story of what Shaafia had done. They needed no convincing about her abilities.

At Walid's insistence, Ayman chartered a small bus in Essaouira to bring his new wife and her parents, Chams and his parents, and the Healing Woman from Rifat. When they arrived, all of them were in awe at the size and luxury of their compound accommodation.

The evening of the fourteenth saw a huge feast being offered at the Razak compound. If he could not host the actual wedding celebration, Rami was determined to hold a feast to remember.

Big as the pavilion was, it was filled to capacity, and Rami had hired extra staff to handle it all. He himself bristled with energy and enthusiasm.

While many of the guests were staying in the compound, the driveway thronged with cars of the Casablanca residents. Waves of guests assembled so there were endless introductions, many needing translation.

The Englishmen met the locals and everyone got to meet the family from the château in France.

Marie-Louise loved meeting Shaafia's Mother, whose French was only basic. Samet brought his whole cohort, all of them in uncharacteristically good clothes. The podcast was shown to whoever was interested.

Habib never left Yasser's side.

At the ceremonial moment, Walid and Shaafia were each carried in by Shaafia's brothers and Khaled, Walid's brother, on twin decorated ceremonial chairs to great cheers from the guests, and then placed on throne-like seats so that everyone could see them. They sat for a few minutes waving to everyone, but neither of them wanted to sit there too long. Instead they jumped to their feet and mingled with their guests, Shaafia often functioning as the translator.

The Englishmen were very keen to talk to the Healing Woman.

Zarifa's husband, Ahmed, was keen to talk to Théophile and Claire.

Brad proudly showed off the new book, and many people asked when it would be translated both into French and even Arabic.

Late in the evening, the battered Dacia of Haj Kabir rattled up the driveway, and there was Houda.

She came into the big pavilion dressed in very simple traditional clothes and a headscarf, and at first no-one noticed her. She stood still looking around the crowd. Then her Mother saw her and ran across to hug her. When she finally pulled back she gazed at her daughter.

«As Shaafia said I can barely recognise you.» she said softly.

«*Mui*, I am not the same person who went to El Chakour. I have so much to tell you. We, you and I, we have so much work to do. Shaafia will need us both.»

Shaafia had been watching them from across the pavilion and she now came over. Houda scooped the smaller girl into her arms.

«You cannot believe how happy I am. I know what I am supposed to do. I know who I am. And it is you have married Walid. Everything is just perfect.»

When she eventually landed back onto her feet, Shaafia reached up and stroked Houda's face. «You have come a long way from the Business Lounge in Bordeaux airport.»

Then she turned to Haj Kabir who was standing back watching the reunion.

«She is ready now, as you say.»

The feast went on late into the night. There were tables of the most exquisite food, and a small traditional orchestra played at one end. And then Rami revealed a little surprise he had prepared.

The girl who had been on his staff now stepped forward and began to sing.

The crowd was transfixed as her voice, full and powerful rose into the evening air. The song was a traditional love song, full of sweetness. She sang in Berber and although most of the guests did not speak it, the feeling of the words spoke for themselves.

And then, at a certain moment, Shaafia suddenly felt an urgent need to retire. She found Rana and asked if they could go.

Although it took ages to say goodbye to so many guests, they finally made it to the Mercedes, where the driver lay asleep behind the wheel.

Walid walked with them.

«Is something wrong?» he asked.

«No,» Shaafia shook her head, «but there is something I must do before tomorrow.»

«What is it?»

She shook her head. «I don't know yet.»

He nodded.

«I will get used to your mysterious ways, I promise.» he said, and lightly kissed her on both cheeks.

As the car made its way back to *Darou Al Bahr,* Rana let Shaafia sit in silence.

They were about to enter the Boulevard de Londres when Shaafia let out a long sigh.

«What is it?» asked Rana quietly.

«They are waiting for me.» said Shaafia. «There is a gathering. They wish me to attend.»

«Here?»

Shaafia nodded.

In the stillness of night, under a crescent moon, she climbed the stairs to her room and took a moment to look out over the garden. The night was silent and calm, a gentle warm breeze fingered the leaves of the palms. She watched the orange cat walk across the path in front of the big pavilion ready for the next day, and she saw it stop and fix its look at the bench off to one side.

He was sitting there looking up at her.

She ran down the stairs and out to the terrace before she dropped at Malak's feet. The cat rubbed itself against her.

In his habitual Berber, he said: «We are all here.» and opened his right hand in a wide sweeping gesture.

She followed his hand as it moved, and there they were.

They seemed to be part of the garden and yet not connected to it, many ethereal forms and so many of them already known to her.

Her hands came up in salutation as she saw her Father, Haj Hussein, and many others. Some she recognised from her Father's funeral, others she had seen in El Chakour. Above them, floated the two blue swirling forms she knew and loved, interwined, their love towards her in a flow that she could both see and feel.

Pia and the Lady in Blue and White.

How long she stayed there, she could not tell, as she melted into a reverie of bliss and lost all sense of time. It was only when Rana tiptoed towards her with a shawl and laid it around her shoulders that she came back to consciousness.

She opened her eyes and looked up into the sky.

It was nearly dawn.

The morning of the fifteenth of August was devoted to wedding celebration preparations. The celebration would be held in the late afternoon and go on into the night.

The women descended on Shaafia, bathed her, perfumed her and prepared her wedding outfits, three of them. Each dress would be worn at different stages of the celebration.

Claire, Marie-Louise and Indira did their best to help, but mostly they stood back in fascination at the Moroccan traditional preparations. Indira loved the henna designs that adorned Shaafia's hands and arms, remarking that in India they do the same thing for weddings. She still had the henna on her hands from her own wedding. Claire did, too.

Downstairs, Théophile and Brad took their breakfast on the terrace. Ihab came to join them and they shared their different perspectives on how the life of Shaafia had been so important to them. Although Ihab knew Shaafia's story, to hear it again from Brad and Théophile moved him deeply. He had no English so he could not read the book, but he held it in his hand and looked for a long time at the photo of Claire and Pia.

Later in the morning, Ihab took them on a short walk to Murdoch Park and told the stories that he had learned about *Darou Al Bahr*.

Towards the end of the morning, Shaafia emerged, still dressed in her day clothes, and announced that she wanted to go to the Mosque where Haj Kabir would be leading the prayers. Shaafia wanted her spiritual family to see her family Mosque and experience the atmosphere of the midday prayers.

There was a scramble to find enough vehicles for those she wanted to go with her. Houda drove the Porsche that had sat idle in her absence, taking Shaafia, Claire and Marie-Louise. Rana took Shaafia's Mother and Rachi in the big Mercedes, while Ihab drove Théophile, with Brad and Indira. Shaafia had asked Ihab to be the guide for the boys in the men's section of the Mosque.

When they arrived, the non-Muslims were guided in preparation for entering, leaving their shoes and washing their hands and feet. Théophile and Brad laughed that it was just like the temple in the Ashram of Swami Padmananda, but without the big statue of the goddess Durga on a tiger.

With Ihab, Théophile and Brad stood at the back of the men's section while he whispered to them about what they should do.

In the women's section for Claire, Marie-Louise and Indira it was the same.

As the mellifluous voice of Haj Kabir swelled out from the loudspeakers Shaafia dropped deeply inside herself. Beside her, she felt Houda do the same. Then she felt them begin to merge together as if their two souls were ascending out of their bodies and high into the domed ceiling of the Mosque. An image of the ethereal forms of Pia and the Lady in Blue and White folded itself around them.

For quite some time after the prayers had been concluded, Shaafia sat indrawn. Eventually, she opened her eyes and looked lovingly at the girl beside her. Houda's tears were streaming down her face.

As they met outside the Mosque, everyone seemed to have felt the powerful energy that had arisen. There were many hugs.

In the late afternoon, as the sun set on a hot August day, the wedding guests began to arrive. The logistics of getting all the guests from the Rami compound meant that the bus from Essaouira did several trips, as did many of the compound cars.

In the front salon of the house, Haj Kabir laid out the long white rectangular cloth, and with his team of chanters, he began to lead in recitations of the Koran. It would go on for many hours and guests would wander in, sit for while, often swaying with their eyes closed, before going back to the celebration.

At the far end of the garden, where it comes to a point, a temporary wooden stage had been erected where a trio of Berber musicians played traditional flutes and drums. They played without amplification so that each end of the garden hosted different musical atmospheres.

Once again there were the same two thrones for the wedding couple installed close to the apex of the pavilion.

As the guests arrived they were given little baskets of flowers to shower the couple when they came in. As with the night before, the couple would arrive carried in on the ceremonial chairs.

In the first of her wedding outfits, a pure white satin with a high neck and pearls appliqued over the bodice, with flowers woven into her hair, Shaafia came down the stairs followed by the women who had prepared her. At the bottom of the stairs, her brothers held the chair for her to mount and then they carefully stepped down across the terrace, negotiating the steps without losing their precious cargo and entered the pavilion.

On the other side of the pavilion, Walid was now lifted, his chair carried by his brother, Taj Bin Salah, and the delighted Englishmen, all three. The two chairs circled each other as the crowd cheered and threw their flowers. As the chairs drew closer, Walid reached out for her hand and then the two chairs grew closer and closer. He looked into her eyes and she returned the look.

At last the chairs stopped in front of the thrones, and the wedding couple dismounted while their sweaty bearers took the chairs away.

The cheering and flower-throwing went on for quite a while, until eventually Walid stood up and asked for a microphone to be brought.

The crowd of wellwishers fell silent as he looked out.

Then as he turned to face Shaafia, he said: «This is my wife, who I vow to protect with every fibre of my being. My destiny is with her. Since the first day she came into my life Shaafia has given me gift after gift, she has saved me from error after error. There is no way that I can praise her enough.»

Then he bowed to her and the crowd erupted again. Whatever flowers were left were showered upon them.

Shaafia watched the flower petals float around her, and she watched the ethereal beings who floated amongst them.

She brought her hands together in salutation.

«Hum delilah.»

Appendix

Given the number of the characters in this book and the complexity of their interactions, I have taken compassion on you, the reader. Below you will find a list of characters in their groupings.

I hope this helps!

The Château des Mésanges family

Thérèse de Fortelle, the matriarch
Théophile her second son
Claire, his wife, previously the wife of the older son, Hugues de Fortelle.
Pia de Fortelle
Kate Dunlop, Pia's nurse
Marie-Louise, ex-nun, now resident cook
Michael Feeny ex-priest, Zena his wife, Berenice their daughter
Jourdan, pastry cook
Angela, translator from South Africa
Hélène Clae, previously Shaafia's teacher in Casablanca

The family of Jamil Jilani (Shaafia's Father)

Zarifa, married with two girls, her husband is Ahmed
Ayman, the oldest son, who marries Rabia
Afifa, married with one daughter
Samet (and his cafe group of young intellectuals: Nabil, Dari, Yusuf, Badria
and others)
Ihab
Nayla (who works in a bank and has her own apartment)
Adila (deceased)
Shaafia
Toufik
Loqman
Hawa
Yamina
Sadik
Habib

Uncle Samad, who runs the shop

Other Key Casablanca characters

Haj Kabir, Imam of the local Mosque and his wife Myriam
Rachi, Shaafia's school friend, affianced to Yasser
Brahim, friendly neighbor.
Haj Hussein, married Florence the daughter of the french Admiral
Rana Bin Salah, daughter of Haj Hussein, married to Hamza
Daad, older sister of Rana
Omar, brother of Haj Hussein, caretaker of *Darou Al Bahr*
Houda Bin Salah, grand-daughter of Haj Hussein, daughter of
Rana and Hamza
Taj Bin Salah, brother of Hamza
Rami Razak, wealthy business man
Walid, his older son, engaged to marry Houda
Khalil, his younger brother
Wassama, their deceased Mother
Graham, Alex and Ben, English businessmen working on the Essaouira resort

Essaouira and Rifat

Asad (fish restauranteur)
The Healing Woman
Uncle Rassem (elder of Rifat)
Rabia and family (Ayman's future wife)
Chams. (the boy car attendant)

El Chakour

Haja Mana
Haj Saif
Ibrahim
Bani (Andrew Chauncey)